Divas
Las Vegas

Divas Las Vegas

By Rob Rosen

CLEIS
PRESS

Published in the United States.
Cleis Press Inc., P.O. Box 14697, San Francisco, California 94114

Printed in Canada.
Cover design: Scott Idleman
Cover photograph: David Vance and Richard Price/Getty Images
Text design: Frank Wiedemann
Author photo: Ken Blackwell
Cleis logo art: Juana Alicia
First Edition.
10 9 8 7 6 5 4 3 2 1

ISBN 13: 978-1-57344-369-2

Library of Congress Cataloging-in-Publication Data

Rosen, Rob.
Divas Las Vegas / Rob Rosen.
   p. cm.
ISBN 978-1-57344-369-2 (trade paper : alk. paper)
1. Gay men--Fiction. 2. Eccentrics and eccentricities--Fiction. 3. Las Vegas (N.M.)--Fiction. I. Title.

PS3618.O831565D58 2009
813'.6--dc22

                                        2009021011

Acknowledgments

Special thanks to Michael Luongo, the first to believe in my dream. To Felice Newman and Frédérique Delacoste at Cleis Press for turning my dream into a reality. To Mark Rhynsburger for making sure the dream was grammatically correct and properly punctuated. And to my mom, Patti Weir, for raising me to be the dreamer that I am.

For Kenny,
my one and only diva

Contents

Into the Closet

OKAY, I SUPPOSE YOU'RE WONDERING WHAT I'M DOING IN here. I mean, really, it's not every day you find me locked in a closet, crouching behind two boxes of Bibles, three cases of votive candles, and covered by a dozen choir robes. And I suppose you think it strange that all I've got on is a pair of underwear—albeit a snazzy pair of Armani silk briefs. Weirder yet, what am I doing in a church out in the middle of the desert? Not exactly my usual venue, right? Jeez, full of questions and we've only just begun. Why not save your queries until the end; it'll make this a hell of a lot easier on the both of us.

This whole ordeal did start innocently enough, surprisingly, and ended, well, here, for now. Though with Justin and me, ordeals seem par for the course. Oh, and in case you didn't already know it, Justin is my best friend. Just as crude, just as conniving, just as troublesome and full of mischief as when we first met. Naturally, I'm right by his side, come hell or high water. Though I wasn't counting on the water to be as high and as choppy as it is right now. Yet here I am in this closet, and guess who we have to thank? (Well, I'm sort of to blame too, I suppose; though you'll never hear me testify to that in a court of law. My mother didn't raise no stupid son, you know.)

Anyway, I guess now's as good a time as any to try and explain how I got here. There's not really much of anything else I can do. Besides, I'm sure it'll all be hilarious in retrospect, though right now it is a bit daunting. (Well, terrifying is really the word for it, but I don't want to alarm you too much. You don't happen to have a gun on hand, do you?)

Okay, so here we go.

This mess began a few weeks ago. Me and Glenda, my other best friend, who, on a side note, just so happens to be stunningly beautiful and unabashedly bisexual, were managing Buy the Book: your average small-time bookstore/coffeehouse. Justin, at the time, was out gallivanting around an unusually sunny San Francisco, looking for love in all the wrong places and, generally, finding it. And life, for the three of us, was sweet and luxuriously boring. Even I, looking back on it all now, was seemingly content.

Of course, life rarely remains that humdrum for very long. The bottom was about to drop out from under us and there we were, as usual, without our protective bottom-dropping safety apparatuses on. Luckily, there was a silver lining, but again, only in retrospect do I now see how tarnished that silver was. Why, oh why, is hindsight twenty–twenty? Too bad you can't have some kind of LASIK surgery on your foresight. Oh, well, I guess, as they say, that's what makes life interesting. Anyway, here comes that dropping bottom I promised.

Brian, the owner of Buy the Book, made an unexpected and rare appearance at our little store. He was usually more than happy to leave me to manage the business, and we rarely had much contact with him. So when he walked in that morning, I thought something might be up. That and the nervous look he had on his face. Plus, he locked the door behind him and put the Closed sign on. The two small suitcases he had with him were kind of suspicious as well. Okay, I didn't need a ton of bricks to fall on my head; I knew he was bringing us some shitty news.

Glenda emerged from the back office, noticed the impending-doom look on Brian's otherwise adorable face, and walked over to my side. Brian gave us a weak smile and motioned for us to have a seat. Naturally, we both grabbed for a life-sustaining cup of java first.

"Yo, dude, what's up?" I asked.

Brian sat across from us and set the minisuitcases down on the table before he responded. "Um, okay, I have good news and I have bad news," he said, his feet tapping furiously beneath the table. My heart was beating along to his rhythm and I had a lump in my throat the size of a lemon.

My stomach was doing the gastric samba as I proceeded to the next question. "And are these two lovely Guccis the good news or the bad news?"

"*They* would definitely be the good news," he responded, strumming the cases with his fingers.

"Um, Brian, could you stop with the tapping and tell us either one of these two newses? You're wrecking my last gay nerve here." I grabbed his hands to keep them still.

"Ditto," Glenda chimed in. "Out with it."

"You're not going to be too happy with me for the bad news, so wait until the good news before you start screaming."

"No promises," I warned him.

There was a pregnant pause before he continued. Whatever he was about to tell us must've been really awful because Brian was usually cool as a pack of menthols. "Okay, here goes," he began. Glenda reached for my hand and I gratefully squeezed it as we heard the bad news first.

"Well, you guys know that business has been really good lately."

We nodded our assent, though how that would be the bad news I couldn't begin to imagine.

"Actually, our revenues have almost doubled compared to last year," he informed us, but he wasn't smiling as clearly he should've been.

"And this is bad why?" Glenda asked.

"Oh, for us this is great, but for the Edges store down the street…" he trailed off, and we both knew what he was getting at.

"Let me guess," I said. "The competition is none too happy with our success."

"That would be putting it mildly. Though they were nice as they could be about it, they would prefer it if we were no longer in the picture. Damn chain stores."

"So, again, this is bad why?" Glenda asked, yet again.

Brian looked at us with a pitifully sad expression. He reached over, grabbed our free hands, and blurted out, "I sold them our store."

Drop went my heart. Drop went my stomach. And drop went that floor I was telling you about. We had been sold out and I was about to lose a job I dearly loved. And, truth be told, I wasn't exactly qualified to do much else. That degree in English lit wasn't about to open any big doors for me. Visions of restaurant aprons and brief romances with busboys ran through my already addled brain.

"But why?" I moaned. "If business was so good, why did you agree to sell it to them?"

Brian reached into his back pocket and pulled out a copy of a check with the Edges logo neatly printed in the left-hand corner. He handed it to me.

"Holy shit," I gasped, and dropped the paper onto the table.

Glenda picked it up, took one look at the amount, and

echoed my sentiment. "Holy shit."

"That much?" I asked in disbelief.

"That much," he answered. "And I know I should've filled you guys in sooner, but I needed to work this out on my own. I'm really sorry. I know how shocked you both are and I know how unfair this all must seem, but—"

He pushed the suitcases toward us. "The good news."

I had an inkling that Brian was about to assuage his guilt with some cold, hard cash, but neither one of us was ready for what we were about to behold. What lay before our gaping mouths and bulging eyes went way beyond what I had expected. It turned out there were mounds and mounds of cash in those lovely cases.

"Dude, there must be, there must be thousands of dollars in these," I sputtered.

"Thirty thousand each, to be exact," Brian informed us, and allowed himself the slightest grin. "Am I forgiven?"

Glenda and I looked at each other, then looked at him, paused for a few seconds to be cruel—what are friends for?—and then nodded a vigorous and heartfelt yes. We jumped up from our seats and ran around to hug our newfound sugar daddy.

He looked incredibly relieved—which was great for him, but I was rich, and that was even better. Thirty thousand was a lot for a lowly bookstore manager. That was almost what I cleared in a year. And Glenda made a lot less than I did, so I was pretty sure that she was just as excited as I was.

"Oh, my God," she screamed, "I just wet my pants."

Yep, she *was* just as excited.

"Now, one more question," I stopped jumping up and down just long enough to ask. "When is our last day?"

"Next Friday. And they're buying our entire inventory. I made that part of the bargain so that we don't even have to pack up. As simple a transition as we could've hoped for," he replied, though even through his smile I could clearly detect a note of sorrow. Brian had put many years into making the store successful, and what did he get for it? His reward would be to lose it all. Bitter irony. I hoped he would take those lemons and make some lemonade. And with all the money he was getting, I hoped the lemonade would be heavily spiked. Least that's what I was planning to do with mine. (Planning and doing are two totally separate things, mind you.)

Ten minutes later, Glenda and I were once again alone.

But not for long. "What's up? You two look like you just won the lottery." It was Justin, swishing in and looking fabulous as ever. I had hoped that age would take its toll on his almost-perfect being, but alas, he got more and more devastating with each passing year. Was it wrong of me to think such nasty thoughts? Well, probably, but I'm sure Justin's thoughts were even more wretched, so I didn't worry about it too much. Besides, I did love him, jealous as I was and all. Plus, I was temporarily rich and seriously thinking about some nips and tucks to try and keep up with the Joneses.

Justin walked over to our table and took a seat. "Well, Miss Things, what on earth caused this outbreak of jocularity at such an ungodly early hour?" (To Justin, any time before noon was too early. Unless, of course, Mimosas or Bloody Marys, or both, were involved.)

We answered by pushing our suitcases toward him and nodded for him to lift the lids.

"Um, I take it that I should open these up?" he asked, with a tilt of his head and just a touch of curiosity to his voice.

"Open 'em," I said.

"What's in 'em?" he asked.

"Just lift the lids and see," I replied, starting to get testy.

"Big old snakes aren't going to pop out, are they?" He pushed his chair slightly away from us in mock fear.

"Bitch, just open the damn things." Typical Justin to turn the tables on us.

"You know how I hate snakes," he said, grimacing.

"Oh, for God's sake," Glenda shouted, and then jumped up and threw the lids wide up, revealing our joyous loads of wampum.

"Ah, *cash*," he purred, drawing the word out. "Whose?"

"Ours," we told him.

"Nuh-uh," he nuh-uhed.

"Yuh-huh," we yuh-huhed.

"No way."

"Dude, it's ours," I asserted.

"Well, I seriously doubt it, all things considered." Man, he was aggravating.

"Fine, you're right," Glenda replied. "It's just sitting here waiting for its owner to come pick it up. There, happy now?" Glenda's minute-ago good humor was now replaced by hostility, which Justin simply adored.

"Okay, okay, no need to get huffy. Man, you guys should really lay off those double mochas. Te-ense."

"You are one big fucking fuck fucker, you know that?" I spat, and slammed the lids down in front of him.

I locked the suitcases and started to leave him there while I went to my office for some much-needed peace and quiet, but as usual I was stymied.

"Know what you're gonna *do* with all that cash?" he asked. I stood there motionless. Glenda stopped her getaway as well to turn around and stare at him. His Cheshire cat grin was disturbing if not completely intoxicating. Too bad for us.

"We just now got the damn things," I answered. "How on *earth* could we know how we're gonna use it?" Which was true, but Justin wasn't from this earth. "Do *you* know?"

I asked, though I should have known better.

"Maybe, but tell me how you got it first," he commanded.

So we told him. It was a short story, and by the end he had that look that I had grown to both adore and be utterly terrified of. And rightly so, I might add.

"Well?" I asked, with just a bit of trepidation.

"I'll tell you at the party on Thursday. Let me work it over in my head a bit."

Oh, Lord, we were in some deep shit now that Justin was involved. I know it, you surely know it, and Glenda knew it; but we also knew better than to tell Justin to just forget about it. Never tell a child no; it's better to let him make his own mistakes and learn from them. Of course, Justin was no child and none of us ever really learned from our mistakes, so we just tried to enjoy what good fortune we had until the police, the ambulance, the press, or the preacher showed up.

"What party?" Glenda thought to ask, but Justin's mind was already far, far away.

Needless to say, by the end of that fateful day, I was depressed as hell over losing my job and just wanted to go home and slip into something comfortable—like a bowl of chocolate-chip ice cream covered in hot fudge and Kahlúa. So when seven-thirty rolled around, I locked up, said my goodnights to Glenda, and lumbered on home.

I made it just in time to catch my all-time favorite program: *Antiques Roadshow*. I love watching those inbred hicks bring in an heirloom that they normally keep on the back shelf of a cupboard because they think it's so hideous. Then they find out that it's worth a small fortune, and claim that they don't care how valuable it is because they would never part with a piece of their family's history.

Yeah, right. As if. You know as well as I do that they

turn around and hock that piece of crap the very next day.

Anyway, the show usually keeps me riveted for the full hour. But even though they had some nifty things to display on that particular episode—a thirty-thousand-dollar Tiffany lamp, bought at a yard sale for twenty-five dollars; a dresser purchased at Barbra Streisand's home auction (I know, I had goose bumps just looking at it); and a signed, original Rembrandt that had been hanging in a child's bathroom (are people really that stupid?)—I just couldn't get it out of my head that I was about to lose the only real job I ever had and one that I truly and deeply loved.

And then, boy howdy, fate stepped its big, fat, stinky foot in, and I nearly fell off my chair. For there, on the screen before me, was my dear departed grandmother's favorite vase. It had sat in her home for as long as I could remember, and she constantly warned us not to go near it and never, ever to touch it. When she passed away, it was left to my mother.

Now, normally, my mother would've cherished anything her mother gave her, but this vase was the bane of her youth. Up until the time she married my father and moved away from home, she was told to stay clear of it. Even as a child, I had noticed that she completely avoided the side of the room that the vase was on. Hell, I couldn't even look at the damn thing without getting nervous myself.

So, when it came into my mom's possession, it was no great surprise that she sold it at a garage sale and was glad to finally be rid of it. Or at least she thought she'd be glad. The very same night she sold it, the guilt started to creep in. By morning my mom was a big old miserable mess. She felt horrible that she'd sold something her mother valued so dearly. Plus, she had sold it for a mere two dollars and fifty cents. Grandma must've been rolling over in her grave. (Well, except for the fact that we cremated her, but you get the gist.)

To try and get it back she posted reward signs all over the neighborhood. There was no response; she felt worse and worse with each passing day. She even took out classified ads in all our hometown papers to try and locate the damn thing. Again nothing. All these years later, my mother still rues the day she let that vase out of her sight. And now, large as life, that very object was staring at me right through my television screen.

That particular episode was being televised from the Las Vegas Convention Center. Mary, the lovely older woman chatting away about Grandma's vase, was explaining how she had found the item at a garage sale and knew it must be worth a great deal more than what it was being sold for. The television appraiser was nodding her head and said that Mary was right in her quick assessment. (Well, duh, she bought it for less than three dollars.) She went on to ask what Mary thought the vase might actually be worth. I leaned in to within a foot of the television screen, holding my breath, anxiously waiting for her response.

"Um, maybe a hundred dollars," came the timid reply.

What an idiot. They never put you in front of the camera unless you have something truly valuable.

"Well, Mary, I'd say it was worth a considerable amount more than that. Your vase"—my grandma's vase!—"is a good two hundred years old. Possibly made by one of this country's earliest china makers and extremely rare to find in such pristine condition. The original owners must have taken impeccable care of it. It looks almost new." (That's because no one was allowed to touch it for fifty years.) "Would you like to know what I think your vase is actually worth, Mary?" she asked, and my heart started racing. I was also getting awfully pissed at hearing the appraiser repeat "your vase" when it was clearly not her vase, but my family's vase, accidentally lost in a moment of temporary insanity.

"Yes, please," Mary chirped, clearly eager to hear what her two-dollar-plus bargain was actually worth.

"Well, Mary, conservatively, I'd say that your garage sale vase would sell today, in a well-advertised auction, for about twenty-five thousand dollars."

When I saw the photo of the vase flash across the screen with the appraised value printed beneath it, I knew then and there what I had to do—besides fix myself a strong cocktail and take a pretty blue pill to relax my extremely frazzled nerves. (Yes, I'm aware that you shouldn't mix booze and pills, but there are exceptions to every rule. Naturally, I've memorized all of them.)

The next day, I decided to do some research. First thing I had to do was find Mary. Shouldn't have been too difficult, right? How many Marys could there be in the greater Las Vegas area? So I locked myself in my office with my morning coffee and set out to search. And really, I had only one place to look. Yep, that was to the good people at *Antiques Roadshow*. Naturally, they were much less enthusiastic to talk to me than I was to talk to them.

"*Antiques Roadshow*," said the voice over the phone.

"Um, hello, my name is Bill Miller and I'd like to speak to one of your producers, please," I asked, ever so politely.

"And the nature of this call?" replied the voice.

"Oh, er, well, you see, I'd like to find one of the people you had on the show this week. She had that two-hundred-year-old vase and it used to belong to my grandmother and I'd like to try and buy it back from her," I tried to explain.

"I'm sorry, sir, we can't give that kind of information out. It's confidential. Thank you for calling *Antiques Roadshow*, and have a nice day." Click.

Click. My heart shattered.

Click. There went my good intentions.

Click. Now what?

11

Click came the sound of the doorknob turning to reveal the answer to my prayers—though the good Lord sure has strange ways of answering you sometimes.

"Dude, how's it hangin'?" asked the one man I knew who could help.

"Dude, like, the fickle finger of fate has rammed itself up my ass and I need some help lubing it up," I answered, somewhat metaphorically.

"*That's* a visual. And am I supposed to supply the lube or actually do the lubing?"

"Never mind. Just help."

"Gladly, old friend. Does it involve anything illegal, immoral, decadent, depraved, wicked, or corrupt?" He was beaming in anticipation.

"Oh, poor Justin, you must be bored."

"Totally, so lay it on me, sis."

And I did. I told him the whole story of the vase, all the way up to the previous three minutes. His face went from jaded to jaw-dropping in a flash.

"Man, that fickle finger has just been joined by a thumb up your ass. You ain't gonna believe this, but this totally jibes with what I had planned for you to do with your moolah," he practically shouted at me.

"Tell me, tell me," I shouted back.

"Wait, can you remember if Mary said she lived in Vegas or not?" he asked me.

"Yes, definitely. She said she had retired there because that's where her daughter lived. I remember it very clearly because I thought I actually liked her. Thought she reminded me of my own grandma. That is, until I found out how much that damn vase was worth. Why?"

"We're going to Vegas, Em!"

Most people call me Em, as in Auntie, in keeping with the whole Oz theme Glenda and I have going on. Sometimes I refer to Justin as the Tin Man, as he clearly is in need of a heart. "We are?" I thought to ask.

"Boy howdy, yes! It's what I was planning anyway. Now fate has stepped in and showed us the way."

That fickle finger was starting to feel good up there. (I prayed it wasn't into fisting.)

When the jubilation died down a bit, I asked, "But how do we find Mary?"

"Hard, but not impossible. Did you happen to tape that episode last night?"

"Of course I did. It is my favorite show, you know," I proudly answered.

"Man, you need a boyfriend, Em. That is *really* sad. But on this occasion it bodes well for us," he said, squashing my already diminished pride.

"How so?"

"Because now we can get some pictures made of our dear friend Mary to take with us to Vegas. Duh. Make that a boyfriend *and* some common sense."

"Hey, can we throw in a new best friend, too?" One small point for moi.

"Fucker."

"Fuck fucker."

"Love me?"

"Of course. Now get out of here and go get that picture made for us. The tape is in the VCR."

Before I knew it, Thursday night had rolled around. A chapter in our lives was ending and a new one was about to begin. To be certain, I was going to miss my morning cup of coffee with Glenda, miss hanging out in the café with Justin, miss all my regular customers, the arrival of the newly printed and fresh-smelling books, and everything that my life as a bookstore manager entailed; but I was still relatively young and I had a major adventure ahead of me. More important, I had a suitcase with thirty thousand dollars in it. So when it came time to close up shop and start the farewell party, I was, more or less, ready.

Justin organized the whole shebang. Brian, Glenda, and I had nothing to do but show up and invite a few people. Was this a wise idea? In truth, handing over responsibility to Justin was never a smart thing to do. But what were a few fines and shattered brain cells in the grand scheme of things, just so long as everyone had fun?

The first surprise was the arrival of an entire minicasino, complete with dreamy card dealers and ravishingly handsome bartenders. All of whom, apparently, knew Justin in some way or another. My guess, if history is any indication, was that he had slept with a good number of them. My best friend was an easy lay. Sometimes this worked in my favor. Just you wait and see how.

The second surprise was the guests. More specifically, the increasingly large number of them. With each passing minute after we closed, the shop became more and more congested, every other man looking more stunning than the next. I felt awed and completely out of place. Luckily, the bar was well stocked with high-quality booze, and, several gin and tonics later, I felt like the belle of the ball.

And so, newly relaxed and recently out of work, I mingled. Well, at least I tried to mingle. Besides the couple of customers I invited, plus my few other friends, I really didn't know anybody there. Though I did of course recognize nearly all of them, what with San Francisco being a teeny, tiny town and all. Then, after a full half hour of small talk with nobody in particular, I found myself at a Blackjack table in the rear of the store. And, to my extreme good fortune, the bar was situated to my side.

With my right hand I received a hundred dollars' worth of chips. Everyone received that upon entering the party, and the person with the most chips at the end of the night received a weekend at Beck's Motor Lodge. If you know San

Francisco, you know that this is no great reward; not that winning the grand prize was a goal of mine, really. Anyway, with my left hand I reached for the real desired treasure: a nice, tall, frosty glass of gin with just a splash of tonic and a twist of lime. Heaven on earth.

Now that my hands were full, I looked up for the first time at the waiting Blackjack dealer. Heaven, it seemed, was missing an angel. I set my drink down, I set the chips down, and my stomach sank down to my feet. Yu-fucking-ummy. Chris (it said it on his name badge) was five-seven, blond hair, deep, dark eyes, and, be still my heart, he had a light tuft of chest hair peeking out over his collar. He was thin and tight and oh so stunning. And he was smiling right at me with his dazzling pearly whites. At first I thought he was cruising me, but, of course, he was just waiting for me to place my bet.

Okay, I was no seasoned card player, but I knew how to play Twenty-one pretty well. And there wasn't anyone else playing, what with all the schmoozing and drinking going on, so I plopped down a five chip, smiled nicely up at Chris, and waited for my cards. Chris drew an eight and a six. I drew a seven and a jack. I indicated that I wanted to stand. Chris did the same.

"Um, aren't you supposed to hit?" I inquired.

"Says who?" he responded, with a sly and glorious smirk.

"Oh, well, them—the people who say, er, who say you're supposed to." I was eloquent.

"Nah, the rule is that the dealer can stand if the guy sitting across from him is a hottie."

I pointed at myself inquisitively and turned around to make sure that he wasn't talking to anybody behind me. Glenda was behind me, actually, grinning, so I assumed that he must've been talking to me. But just to make sure, I pointed to myself again and tilted my head, as a dog does

15

when it's confused. He nodded in the affirmative that he indeed was referring to me. (Me! Holy cow, me!)

Bravo for me. I received a pretty yellow chip. And a pretty, glimmering smile from the handsome dealer. Then I got another gin and tonic. And so did the dealer. "Just keeping up," he explained, which was fine by me. I figured my chances were better the drunker we both got. Though I had no use for a weekend at a so-so motel, I certainly didn't mind sitting there all night flirting (and drinking).

"I'm Bill," I said, by way of introduction, and shook his hand. "But my friends call me Em."

"Chris," he said, pointing to his badge. Man, I just wanted to sit there and listen to him and stare at him and never, ever let go of his big, strong, and somewhat hairy hand.

But I did have to let go. And, lo and behold, a good bit later, I was awash in chips. Piles of yellow and blue and red chips lay strewn before me, and before I knew it, the party was drawing to a close. This made me sad for two very important reasons. First, I hated the night to end because it meant the closing of my beloved shop. And second, for a much more selfish and shallow reason, I didn't want my night with Chris to end either.

At precisely midnight, when we no longer owned our bookstore, Brian made a short but sweet speech. He thanked everyone for coming and for their years of support. Though, looking at the crowd, I seriously doubted that there were a whole lot of heavy readers among them. (*Inches* and *Honcho* excluded.) Then, just before we all piled out, Justin walked through the crowd and counted up everyone's chips. "We have a clear winner, folks," he shouted. "And it just so happens to be the manager of this very store. Come on up here, Em."

Oh, my God, I won. I won! I had never won anything in my life. And I was embarrassed as hell. The person who throws the party is never supposed to win the prize. But the crowd was cheering for me and pushing me up toward Justin to claim my prize, so I humbly accepted. Why not? I mean, after all, I *had* just lost my job. I did deserve something good. (Besides the thirty thousand dollars.)

Now, I know you probably saw this coming way back at the beginning of all this, but I didn't realize it until Justin handed me my certificate for the motel and I just happened to glance up and see Chris grinning at me that—"You planned this whole thing," I whispered in Justin's ear.

He winked at me and kissed me on the forehead. "Nice gift, huh?" he whispered back.

I looked over my shoulder at Chris, then back to Justin, then down at my weekend pass, and I nodded a yes; indeed it was a good gift. Even if it was sort of cheating. But you haven't seen my dealer man. Sometimes the ends do indeed justify the means. And Chris had one mean end.

So I kissed my friend on the cheek, ran through the crowd, grabbed my gift's hand, and headed on out the door for the very last time. Holding on to Chris, I walked as fast as I could away from it all—feeling, well, I don't really know. Sort of a mix between terrified, elated, and super horny. A fairly nice feeling, I must say.

Chris and I walked in silence for a while. Being alone with him made me nervous. Mind you, I've slept with my fair share of cute guys before—well, someone's share anyway—but there was something about Chris that gave me those fluttery stomach butterflies.

"Um..." I tried.

"Um..." he echoed.

And we kept walking. And my tummy was doing flips. And my pants were starting to get some heavy lumpage in them. So I stopped walking and pulled Chris to a stop as well. And there on the sidewalk, just in front of a lovely flower shop, I turned to him, put my hands around his thin waist, looked him deep in the eyes, and softly, gently, delicately kissed him on his beautiful, full lips. They tasted sweet, with just a hint of gin and lime. And with the smell of roses and lilacs wafting over us, we stood there in a comfortable embrace and made out, mere yards away from the motel.

His dick pressed up hard against my leg. "Um, can I see it?" I asked, emboldened by all the gin. Not so much by the tonic, though.

"The motel is just over there," he said, with a sly grin, pointing up ahead, yet already sliding down his zipper.

"Yeah, but, well, just checking out the merchandise."

"Okay, but once the package is opened, there's no taking it back."

As if there was a chance in hell of that happening. In any case, I gave him a nod and then stared down, the moon now bathing him in a soft, silver glow. His prick sprang out, thick, the wide mushroomed head already slick with translucent precum. I ran my hand across it, then sucked the salty-sweet jizz off my fingers. "Yep, that's a keeper, all right," I told him.

He swayed it from side to side, slapping the underside. "Anything else you want to check out before, um…" Again he pointed to the motel.

"Nope. I'm good," I replied, leaning in for another kiss, harder this time, more urgent.

There were, of course, some questions that still needed answering. I asked them a few minutes later, while leaning on the metal railing of the motel, before we walked into thc room.

"So, obviously you know Justin somehow?" I asked, rhetorically.

"Somehow, yes," he answered, cryptically.

"Sexually?" Another rhetorical question.

"Is that how *you* know him?" Another cryptic reply.

"Hmm, hard to answer. Yes and no. At first, sort of, but nothing ever really happened. We became friends instead. Best friends. Thankfully. His sexual friends don't hang around as long. Which class do you fall into?" I tried again.

He leaned in and slid his long, wet tongue in my mouth, and then down my neck and around my earlobe. "Both," he whispered. "But we're just friends now."

"Did he pay you to be here?" Last question. Not that it would've scared me off if he had said yes. I simply wanted to know.

"He paid me to work the party and to let you win. I'm here because I want to be here and because I like you. Okay?"

Well, that was just fine and dandy by me. "Okay," I responded, and unlocked the door to the motel room. I'll let you use your vivid imagination to fill in the rest of the details. (Fine—the backside was just as nice as the frontside. Happy now?)

He spent the next two nights with me there. We ventured out only to get our meals at nearby Castro restaurants. (And some lube and some rubbers.) It was nice. Actually, it was more than nice, but I knew he was going to leave on that third day to go back home, someplace not in San Francisco; and I also knew better than to get attached. Too bad my heart wasn't as smart as my head. I could have seriously fallen for the guy. Oh, well. Anyway, I had a big adventure ahead of me, so I enjoyed our time together and, when it was time to leave, I told him how great he was and that I would miss him.

"Thanks, I'm sure we'll cross paths again." That was it. Less than what I would have liked, but he was off before I could get any more out of him. Two nights and days of fabulous sex was more than I usually got, which means I wasn't about to complain.

So, with a smile on my face and a gleeful spring to my step, I left the motel and headed over to Justin's. It was weird not having a job to go to. And by weird, I mean terrifying. But I had money to live on for a while, or at least until I got that vase back. And though I love Justin, I prefer not to rely on him too much for his money, of which he has gobs. His friendship was way more than enough. (Way, way more.) And I was sure I'd find a job once I returned. It was just, well, I wasn't too sure what I wanted to do with the rest of my life. Also, I'm just naturally the kind of person who needlessly worries. Which probably goes a long way to figuring out why Justin and I are such good friends in the first place: he worries about absolutely nothing and I worry enough for the both of us.

"Oh, honey, you look positively fucked out." He greeted me at the door, martini in hand, and then led me to his comfy leather sofa. "Spill."

"Please, you've been there and done that already. Why do you need the nasty details? Must you live vicariously through me?" I giggled into my martini.

"As if. And, for your information, Chris and I have never done *it* before. He's not my type."

"Huh? He breathes. He walks. He talks. Fits your criteria exactly. And, knowing you as I do, the talking thing isn't all that mandatory anyway. So what's the real reason?"

"Yes, dumbass, he meets all that and then some, but he has that one fatal flaw I simply can't tolerate."

I knew the answer. "Ah, he's relationship-oriented. Am I right?" I knew I was. It was the one and only thing that frightened little Miss Fuckit away.

"Bingo. But we did fool around some, just not all the way—which, by that frightful glow you're emitting, I take it you achieved."

"Well, I didn't want to see that lovely motel room go to waste, now, did I?" I was playing coy. Justin knew I was not one to kiss and tell, so he gave up.

"Fine, fuck if I care. So, I take it he left for home already?" he asked, pouring us both a second round of drinks.

"This morning," I replied, rather glumly. "Where is home anyway?"

"He didn't say?" Justin snickered.

"We had other, more pressing topics to discuss."

"Ooh, like which flavored lube to use or who was gonna get spanked first?"

"No, just nothing that personal."

Honestly, it never came up. I'm sure you've been in that kind of situation before: where you spend a whole weekend with someone and don't bother to get their last name, or family background, or career highlights, but you end up finding out who their favorite Backstreet Boy was. Well, Chris and I had one of those kind of short-term things. Blissfully ignorant, I like to call it.

"Whatever, Mary. Never mind." And he made the universal "whatever" sign: three fingers waving in the air. Actually, they were waved in my face. But so was my martini, so I ignored his rudeness.

"Speaking of Mary," I said, now speaking of Mary.

"Ah, our new raison d'être. I just have to pack and then we can skedaddle. Oh, by the way, I bought us our plane tickets," he announced.

"You really didn't have to do that. I have money now, you know," I offered.

"*First-class* tickets," he added.

"Okay, rightee-o, then. First class: drinkees in crystal glasses, warm nuts served on white linen, and hot towels..."

"These are a few of my favorite things," Justin sing-songed. I agreed, though. There's nothing like first class, and I never would have paid for two tickets at whatever price he had paid, so I gratefully accepted the offer.

"And when do we leave on our hunt for the great, white Mary, Tarzan?"

"We swing from big tree vine when sun comes over mountain, little queerboy, Jane."

"Yikes, that early?" I asked, surprised, as Justin rarely if ever woke before sun was over mountain.

"The early bird catches—" he began.

"The Mary," I finished.

"Nope, the breakfast buffet at Caesar's. So let's get packing and get the hell out of this one tree vine town. I so need this vacation."

He had to be joking. The man didn't work, had no stress in his life, and this trip was certainly not going to be a vacation. Finding my vase was going to be work. Or at least I thought it would be. But I let it go. He was paying for the tickets and was going to help me on my journey. Why burst his gin-soaked bubble?

"Okay, then, I'll go home and I'll be over to your place as soon as I finish packing. I'll spend the night and we can get up early and start our adventure."

I was starting to get sort of excited about the whole thing. The whole, I don't know, well, *unknown* of it all. Where would we find Mary? Would we find Mary? Would she sell us back my grandma's vase? I was full of questions and my body was a bundle of nerves all of a sudden. And it was obvious, too.

"Will you take this pill and calm your ass down?" he asked, and magically handed me a nice yellow pill.

"If it will make you happy, fine, I will." And I swiped it from his hand. I did need to calm down a bit, I justified.

"Now go home, pack, and hurry on back over," he commanded. "I'll have dinner ready when you get here. Now scoot."

And scoot I did; though twenty minutes later the pill had kicked in and my scoot became more of a crawl. I arrived home, moving a bit slowly, and packed. Also, I made a few farewell phone calls to some friends. I wanted them to know where we were in case we needed bailing out. I was nervous about going to Sin City with the man who practically invented it—sin, that is.

And then, three suitcases later, I was out the door and on my way. The taxi I had called arrived in less than five minutes. Now that I had some money, I gladly squandered it on such extravagances. Me and my bags were at Justin's a few minutes later.

I lumbered slowly up the stairs with my luggage. Of course, being medicated, I didn't care. I rapped on the door and, lo and behold, was greeted by Justin in full Las Vegas showgirl attire. (A definite plus about living in San Francisco. I doubt you would or could find someone dressed like that in, say, Des Moines.)

"Oh, were we supposed to be *dressed* for dinner? I left my outfit at the cleaners. Damn," I said, and dragged my belongings into his apartment.

"Sweetie, now, you know it's always cheaper to buy these things in *pairs*." Dear God. He pulled a nearly matching outfit from behind his back and handed it to me.

"Before dinner?" I gulped. It looked beautiful floating there. All shimmering in blue and gold sequins. In my present state, I simply didn't know if I had it in me to slip my ever-widening ass into it, though.

"Before, during, and after. Yes. Here," he commanded, and handed me my outfit.

Why not? I figured. I was fast getting beyond my prime to do such things and still look good at the same time. So I gracefully took the ensemble, laid it on his couch, and proceeded to undress.

"Wait!" he shouted, and ran to the kitchen. "Dinner is served." He handed me a martini in a frosted glass and then curtsied. Or at least tried to. The dress looked painfully tight on him.

"Ah, a liquid dinner. How dietetic of you."

As I stood there almost naked in his living room, drink in hand, pill in stomach, dress spread out before me, I had a strange premonition that a bizarre adventure lay ahead of us. Thankfully, I was never one to believe in such nonsense or I might have put my clothes back on and hightailed it out of there. On second thought, maybe not so thankfully. (You might recall I *am* sitting in this closet and I *am* still wearing practically nothing. Even worse, I have no martini in hand. Ah, there's that nasty hindsight dilemma again.)

I set my drink down and lifted my dress up. It weighed a ton. The gown itself started at the neck in vivid blue sequins and, as it worked down to the bustline, turned several shades of paler blue. Beneath what would soon be my fake bosoms, the material came to a sudden stop, creating a large and very revealing circle over the tummy region. There was some sequin-covered Lycra on the left side and around the soon-to-be-padded ass. This was done up in several shades of yellowish gold. The colors for the remainder of the dress, the part that cinched in the thighs and legs, grew progressively darker blue again. It was lovely, actually, though certainly not on *my* body.

"Holy hockey pucks, Batman, this is a doozy of a dress dilemma. Are you sure I can fit into this thing?"

"One size fits all," he told me, reassuringly. "Just step on in, suck in that gut, and pull hard."

"Oh, when you put it that way..." I grimaced, slid my feet through the narrow opening at the middle of the dress, stepped in, sucked in, and pulled with all my might. The heavily weighted gown bunched clumsily around my body, so I had to yank it up in bits and stretches until it encased me. Then I slid my arms through the holes near the top. Justin zipped up the side until the tiny white zipper was at my neck. Voilà—instant diva. Almost.

Again he shouted, "Wait!," and ran out of the room.

"Oh, please, another drink!" I shouted after him. "For dessert!"

He returned, drink in hand. In one hand, that is. The other hand held a stunning and oh-so-high pair of sequined pumps. My heart was racing. It had been quite some time since I last donned heels. In all honesty, I loved that towering feeling. I gracefully slid them on and ventured to stand up. Between the pills, booze, and sheer height of the shoes, it certainly was a challenge. I tottered for a few seconds, but retained my balance. (Drag queens wobble, but they don't fall down.)

Standing there like that, I felt, er, *regal*. Justin slid his heels on as well and stood face to face with me. Other than the colors of his gown, which were red and gold, we had on identical outfits. He looked stunning. I knew better than to imagine that I did.

"Wait!" he shouted, yet again. I gulped as he sauntered out of the room, though he was not as fast in the heels as the previous two times. What next? I thought.

Next came the headdresses. And, goodness gracious me, they were enormous once fully assembled and fanned out. Each one matched our specific dress and was equipped with two dozen extra-long feathers surrounding a high crown covered in shimmering rhinestones and sequins. Glamour, glamour, glamour. Though glamour had a price. Each head-piece had to weigh a good five pounds, and we had to be securely strapped into them so they wouldn't slide off, so we helped each other get them on. The effect was mesmerizing. (Then again, that might have been more from the pills and booze than anything else.)

"How do I look?" he asked.

"Fashion Girl Barbie on steroids," I answered, somewhat awestruck. In fact, he did look stunning.

"And me?" I asked, rather pathetically. I never could pull off the whole drag thing. It must've been some kind of genetic predisposition of mine to look tragic in female attire.

"Come see for yourself." He pulled me into his bedroom and placed us in front of his double-wide, full-length mirror. (Vanity, thy name is Justin.)

"Wait! Don't look!" Again with the wait. I obeyed and shut my eyes tight. Seconds later, I felt the familiar feeling of lipstick being applied. When I was allowed to open my eyes again, I beheld a vision of, if not loveliness, then at least not downright ugliness. The outfit had such a strong presence to it that I think most everyone would have looked somewhat glorious in it.

Justin stood next to me and we both, simultaneously, crouched an inch and flung our hands up in the air as if to say, *Ta-da!* We did indeed look dazzling.

"The return of Marilyn and Tabitha!" he proclaimed. Though officially we were known as Miss Em and Miss T. The EmT Twins. (Pronounced "empty." Though I usually called Justin Humpty and he called me Dumpty. Sad, if not befitting.)

"I missed them. It's been too long." And I was telling the truth. Our alter egos were so much fun. Certainly more glamorous than our usual day-to-day personas. Well, mine anyway.

"Me too," Justin agreed as we stood there and admired ourselves.

"Where did you get all of this?" I asked, when the magic started to wane.

"Good question," came the response.

"And is there a good answer?" I knew better, but tried nonetheless.

"Wait. Just wait."

Well, that word seemed to be working for me so far, so I did. And now, so will you.

One-Armed Bandits & Two Hot Men

THE NEXT MORNING, WITH MEGALUGGAGE IN TOW, WE found ourselves at beautiful San Francisco International airport—ready, willing, able, and fully medicated. I really don't like to fly, even though we were flying first class. Something about being suspended thousands of feet in the air, with nothing holding me up but some incomprehensible technology, makes me highly nervous. Thankfully, my best friend always has something to make me forget my worries.

"Yellow, blue, or white?" he asked, reaching out his hand to me and producing a variety of pills to choose from.

"What's the difference?"

"Ah yes. The yellow reduces stress. The blue reduces anxiety. And the white, er, oh—well, I forgot what those are for, but I think they reduce tension."

"Uh-huh. Okay, so really they all do pretty much the same thing?"

"Basically. Either way, you won't be bothered by the whole flying thing. So take one and shut up." Doctor's orders. I took a blue one. My favorite color. It went down smooth and I felt instantly better. Pretty sick, huh? But I mean, really, anything that helps you get through life a little bit easier can't be all bad, right? What's a little addiction problem in the grand scheme of things, anyway?

Thirty minutes later, they were boarding our plane and my pill had fully kicked in. I smiled and hummed a happy tune as we took our seats. Truly, one of the best things about flying first class is being able to board first. This has two distinct advantages.

One, the obvious perk: you get to board ahead of all those icky poor people. And getting on the plane first also means plenty of room for your overhead luggage. Though on this trip we had way too much stuff with us, and it was all resting comfortably in the cargo hold. Since we had no idea how long we'd be in Vegas, we packed for a very, very long trip. Basically, clotheswise, we were ready for everything: from blizzard to searing heat and everything in between.

And two, and not as obvious unless you're as trashy as Justin and me, you get to cruise all the other people while they board the plane. Plus, they get to see you while you're sitting in first class, sipping your wine and snacking on cashews. No bigger aphrodisiac than gazing at rich, good-looking people. (Yes, shallow, I know. But my pool started draining years ago.)

Unfortunately, this trip looked less than promising: old women on Vegas junkets, families on their way to Circus Circus and Excalibur, straight businessmen traveling to seminars and conventions, etc. Not what I would call good cruising material. And then, as chance would have it, some major hotness stepped on board.

Luckily for me, Justin was absorbed in his *Out* magazine and hadn't noticed. His eyes rarely traveled farther than the drink in front of him when he flew. I don't think he liked to concentrate on more than one or two things at a time.

He couldn't operate on that many levels. (But put him at Macy's during a one-day sale and just watch him go.)

Anyway, I was glad he hadn't noticed the beau-hunk as he walked by and nodded at me. He would have pounced and left me in the dust for sure. This way, I had a clear advantage. His ignorance was my bliss. I decided that I'd make my move when the plane was in the air and Justin's booze and pills had fully kicked in. (Though with the tolerance he'd built up, that could be well into the next decade.)

A short while later, I excused myself to go to the bathroom. Quickly scanning the plane, I saw my quarry seated only two rows from the lavatory; and there was a vacant seat next to him. Oh, lucky day. I nonchalantly strolled down the aisle, past the nasty straight people and their pestering broods, and all the businessmen with their plastic cups and minibottles set before them, and headed for my man. He looked up as I approached. He smiled. My heart sped. I panicked and kept walking straight on to the bathroom. Damn.

So I peed, waited a few moments for good measure, got my heart rate down to almost normal, and then decided to make my move once again. Coming from behind, I wouldn't have to look directly at him. That would make it a bit easier on me. I unlatched the door, squeezed past the several people waiting to use the facilities, walked two feet down the aisle, and immediately noticed a head in the seat that was once vacant. Double damn.

I walked a couple more feet and stopped right to their side. The flight attendant had her cart parked ahead of me and I had to wait as she made her way down. So of course I looked over to take a gander at who had stolen my seat. Can you guess who it was? He looked up when he realized that someone was standing there.

"Oh, Em, there you are. I was getting worried and came looking for you. You know, with your *bowel problem* and all." He gave me a wink and a smirk and then introduced me to the stranger to his left.

"Marvin, this is Em. Em, meet Marvin."

Marvin reached over to shake my hand and I reached down to shake his.

"Nice to meet you, Em. Sorry about your *problem*."

Ugh. I turned red in the face. "Ignore him, I don't have a problem," I informed him, grimacing at Justin.

"Now, now. The doctor told you that denying it won't make it go away." Justin was having way too much fun. He turned to Marvin and added, "Denial is step number two."

"You'll have to excuse my friend, Marvin, he has a strange sense of humor. Honestly, the only pain I have in my ass is him," I explained in earnest, and punched Justin in the arm to keep him from continuing.

"Anger is step number three," Justin informed Marvin.

"Okay, enough talk about my ass. Step four is going to be throwing your nelly self off this plane. Next topic, please." They both looked up at me and nodded. Great way to make friends and influence people: anger. I quickly lightened up so as not to completely scare the man off.

"Is your final destination Las Vegas, Marvin?" I asked, chipper as could possibly be.

"Actually, Em, that brings up an interesting topic as well." Justin practically beamed when he looked back up at me. "Marvin is on his way to Vegas for a convention. Isn't that right, Marvin?"

"Yes, unfortunately this is a business trip for me." Marvin frowned and took a sip of his drink. "Damn KQED." KQED is the PBS affiliate in San Francisco, by the way. And yes, PBS is the station that airs *Antiques Roadshow*.

"What? Did you say PBS?" I practically shouted at him. The people in front of us and to our right looked over to see what the commotion was about. Marvin looked up at me like I was crazy. And Justin, well, he was gleefully giggling away.

"Sorry," I whispered to Marvin and to the people nearby.

"It's the medication," Justin leaned over and explained to him. I punched him again. Poor Marvin. He must've thought I was insane.

"Um, Justin, would you mind coming back with me to our seats now? I need some help with my *colostomy bag*." I whispered the last two words between gritted teeth. "It was a pleasure meeting you, Marvin," I added, and yanked Justin out of his seat.

"Catch you later," Justin shouted back to Marvin as I dragged him to our seats. "Nice try," he added as soon as we were safely back in first class.

"Huh?" I downed my by then watery drink.

"As if I wouldn't have noticed such a cutie amidst all this rubbish. Puh-lease. How long have you known me?"

"I guess too long. Anyway, he did nod at *me* when he walked by," I calmly explained.

"Oh, really? From where I was sitting, it looked like he was nodding at *me*," Justin countered.

"Well, then, it looks like one of us is rather delusional, but let's move on to the more pressing topic at hand," I deflected.

"Ah, the PBS angle. I have to admit, that was a pleasant fluke. Pretty *and* useful. A rare combination." Justin finished his drink and raised his hand at our attendant for two more.

"Did you happen to mention to our new friend Marvin that we had a certain recent involvement with the nice folks at PBS?" I asked.

"Nope, didn't think that it was the right time or place. I thought it best to work up to that. Maybe after he rolls over in the morning to give me a kiss."

"Uh-huh. I see. So that was what the 'Catch you later' was all about? A little espionage work?"

"Now you're catching on, Em. Hey, I'm only doing this for you, you know."

"How nice. A regular Mother fucking Theresa you are these days. And if you happen to get lucky as well—"

"Icing on the proverbial cake," he finished my sentence.

"More like icing on your proverbial shaved chest. Just forget it, dude. I'm going with you."

"Em, I didn't know you were into three-ways. This trip is going to be so enlightening."

"Fuck off. He wants me, not you. I'm just going with you to wherever it is you're meeting him. Now shut up and finish your drink. The plane is landing in fifteen minutes."

"And you call me delusional. Right."

"Trays up and seat belts fastened, gentlemen. We'll be landing in Las Vegas in just a bit," ordered our lovely flight attendant as she took our empty glasses.

"Las Vegas, here we come," Justin announced, and raised his hand up to nothing in particular.

"Let's hope they paid their insurance premiums," I muttered. I made sure to pay mine before we left.

In case you've never been to Vegas, consider me your lovely tour guide. First, there's the airport itself. Very nice. Basically it's one big advertising zone for the casinos. Each hotel has its own store or kiosk, and there are billboards everywhere advertising the latest shows and cheapest buffets. And, of course, there are slot machines at every concourse. But I warn you, these are notorious for *not* paying off—so wait until you get downtown before you start losing all your hard-earned cash.

"Em, look at that," Justin groaned, soon after we had deplaned and were walking through the airport. He pointed somewhere in the distance.

I spotted a massive poster just above where our baggage was coming out. "Oh, my God, you can see every pore on Wayne Newton's face. Totally gross. Isn't he, like, a hundred or something?" I responded, staring at Wayne's overly bronzed visage. (Old entertainers never die, they just wind up at the yuckiest casinos.)

"No, dumbass, not that. That over there." He pointed again in earnest.

"Ah, oh yes, I see now. The other poster. Wow, a ten-dollar, all-you-can-eat buffet at the Stratosphere. Man, look at those lobster tails. Damn, I'm hungry. Okay, we can stop by there, but I'm not going on that roller coaster at the top. Talk about your stupid ideas." (At the time all these shenanigans took place, it got stuck, repeatedly. But hey, it's been replaced by three even more harrowing and equally ridiculous rides.)

"God, are you blind? THERE!" He grabbed my face and used his arm as an arrow to point at what he was raving about.

"The digital temperature reading?" It sat between the two posters I'd been looking at.

"Yes, my dear, nearsighted Em. The temperature reading outside. Finally. Look what it says."

"A hundred and one point three degrees?"

"Yes, a hundred and one point three degrees! Don't queer boys melt at anything over a hundred?" Justin cowered at the thought. "Isn't that why we live in San Francisco in the first place?"

"Better not tell that to our brethren in Key West, Palm Springs, and Atlanta. I think they might take offense," I explained.

"Freaks. Every last one of them. Freaks. Why would anyone choose to live like that? All that sweating can't be good for your complexion," he opined, shaking his head in disbelief.

"Hmm, well, get ready, because we're about to experience it firsthand." The thought was less than appealing to me also, being used to the nearly year-round chilliness of San Francisco. The last time my body temperature was anywhere near a hundred degrees, I had a cold and a fever.

"Well, luckily I came prepared. You wait right here. I'll be back," he barked at me, and then hurriedly ran into the nearest men's room. I dreaded whatever it was he had planned.

I dragged my newly regained baggage to a slot machine and whipped out a roll of quarters I had brought with me in case of an emergency. Since Justin had hauled all his stuff with him into the restroom, I knew it would be a while before he reemerged.

Anyway, on with the tour. Las Vegas. No place quite like it. It's utterly fabulous. And truly, it is the city that never sleeps. But, and this is a big old *but*, unlike San Francisco, you see very few queers. For sure, we pop up here and there, but for the most part, Vegas is very straight, very white, and very middle America. In other words: uptight, overweight, undereducated, and drab. Which, naturally, provokes the über-fruit in Justin. The straighter his surroundings, the queenier my friend gets. Now, after a few drinks and in the darkness of a bar, this can be somewhat amusing; but in the full-strength Nevada sun, and in the middle of the afternoon, well, it could be a tad overwhelming. Thank goodness drinks are free or at least dirt cheap in the casinos, I thought to myself.

And, sure enough, a full ten minutes later, my dear friend reappeared looking queer as the day is long. Gone were the long slacks he was traveling in. A frightfully short pair of Daisy Dukes had replaced them, replete with colored flower iron-ons, like the ones you frequently find on the bottom of bathtubs. The warm button-down was gone, and in its place was a hot pink muscle tee. Oh, yes, it was way too tight. He wore them no other way. I guess if I looked like Justin, I'd dress like that as well. (Or maybe not.) The Bruno Maglis were off his feet, and a very comfortable-looking pair of high-tops were running circles around me. They too were pink, to match the shirt. And, the pièce de résistance, atop his head he wore a very large, and very white, old-lady sunbonnet. The Queen of Las Vegas had apparently arrived.

"Voilà!" he shouted, modeling his ensemble. "Now I'm ready. Slathered in sunblock thirty-five and properly attired."

"Honey, for Fire Island you're properly attired, but I seriously doubt that Treasure Island is ready for the likes of you. You're not really considering walking into a casino dressed like that, are you?"

"Just watch me." And he and his luggage were up and walking, er, sashaying away.

I ran to catch up, and asked, "So you don't think that you look just a tad, um...nelly?"

"Honey, I am not nelly," he insisted, waving his limp wrist at me. (Obviously, I had my doubts.)

"What would you call it, then?" I persisted, as we headed for the airport exit.

"I'd say I'm...*animated*."

"Animated, huh? What's the difference?"

"I can turn off the nelly whenever I like and be just as butch as the next guy."

"Ah, I see. Did you say bitch or butch?"

"Butch, dear. I said butch."

"Okay, then. I see your point," I said, dropping it. But in all the time I'd known Justin he pretty much stayed *animated*. He must have saved the butch side for his tricks. Nevertheless, I let him believe what he wanted to believe. Besides, what's that saying about casting the first stone? Personally, I don't have a butch bone in my body and am not interested in acquiring one. It doesn't seem to be doing straight people any good.

And then, just a minute after stepping outside into the searing heat, we were happily planted in the backseat of a well air-conditioned cab and on our way to the hotel. I knew that we were there to *work*, but I couldn't help feeling excited and eager to do some gamblin' and carousin'. Mary wasn't going anywhere, I figured. Though, for all we knew, she wasn't there at all. In either case, I was bound and determined to have a good time. Having Justin as a traveling companion ensured at least that much.

"So where are we headed?" asked our cigarette-puffing cabbie.

Justin looked at me. I looked at Justin.

"Well?" we both asked, simultaneously.

"What?" we both shouted, simultaneously again.

"You're kidding me." I could tell he wasn't kidding, though. And the look of horror on my face told him the same thing.

"Well?" asked the cabbie, unwrapping a fresh pack.

"I thought you made all the plans," I whispered to Justin.

"No, just the plane tickets, dude. I thought *you* booked the hotel," he whispered back.

"Meter's running," shouted the cabbie, and then took a deep drag on his cigarette. At that moment I felt like shoving it down his throat. Damn, I was pissed. In all the confusion of losing my job and becoming semirich, I hadn't even thought about the hotel. I guess I assumed, incorrectly, that Justin was taking care of everything.

"Um, we thought we'd find something when we got here," announced Justin, off the top of his head. The cabbie gave us a laugh that sounded like one lung down, one to go.

"You guys must be kidding," he rasped. He sounded very much like a young Harvey Fierstein. (Which sounded just about the same as an old one, mind you.)

"Um, no. Is that a problem, driver?" I asked, sensing it was.

"You guys ever heard of COMDEX?"

I had, and I knew what this meant. "No rooms anywhere in Vegas?" I guessed. (By the by, COMDEX was one of the largest trade shows in the world at that time, which should tell you what kind of shit we were now in.)

"Got that right," the driver croaked, and took another long draw.

I turned to look at Justin. He was sitting there thinking. I shrugged at him and mouthed a "now what?" And, in typical Justin fashion, he had the answer. He reached behind him and pulled out his Prada wallet. I could see the driver staring at us in his rearview mirror, and when he saw my friend pull out two one-hundred-dollar bills, he tossed the putrid cigarette out the window and put the pedal to the metal.

Justin leaned in and whispered in my ear. "Gets 'em every time."

Mere minutes later, we were pulling up to our hotel. I use the term loosely. I looked out the window of our cab and read the neon sign that hung precariously over the doorway: The Atlantis. From stem to stern, our humble getaway was painted completely in blue and had happy fish and coral drawn on it. I got seasick just looking at it.

"This it?" I timidly asked the driver.

"This and this alone. The only reason I know about it at all is because my brother manages the place. He always leaves a room or two open for emergencies. Like this one here. Just let me go in and get you guys fixed up."

He jumped out, a brand-new cigarette already dangling from his lips, and trotted on in to our hotel/aquarium.

"Did you bring the lube and some rubbers?" I asked Justin.

"Of course. Why?"

"Because we're about to get royally screwed."

"Ah. Most certainly. Chin up, Em. At least we found *something*. And we can't be more than a mile from the strip. Besides, we'll never even be here except to sleep. And with me at Marvin's, you'll have the whole room to yourself." He grinned and lightly punched me on my arm.

"Fucker," I replied, also with a grin on my face. He was right, it could have been a lot worse. Of course, I hadn't seen our accommodations yet.

Our faithful cabbie emerged a few minutes later, with a wide smile on his face that showed dark, yellowed teeth. He held two thumbs up as he neared us. We got out of the cab to hear what he had to say. By that time, we smelled liked the Veteran's Hall on bingo night.

"No sweat," he informed us. "My brother has one room left, and you can have it."

"How much?" Justin asked.

He paused before answering. I braced for the worst.

"A hundred-fifty a night," he coughed out.

"Well, that's not too ba—"

"Each," he interrupted.

Ouch. That certainly was the worst—especially since we had no idea how long we were going to be there. But we took it. I mean, really, what choice did we have? And this *was* Vegas. Maybe we'd win enough to pay for it all. My luck had been pretty good up to that point. I did win that night with Chris, after all. (Yes, I know that was rigged, but I was thinking only happy thoughts at that point.)

We got our luggage out of the trunk and thanked our stinky savior for his help. "Sure, no problemo. We girls have to stick together," he said, and gave us a sly wink and a hacking cough. Then he handed Justin his private card and told us to call him if we needed anything. I looked down before I pocketed it. His name was Earl.

"Thanks, Earl," I said, and paid him his fare plus a hefty tip. "We'll do that." Then he jumped in his cab and sped off.

"Well, well, this journey is just full of surprises," Justin commented as we entered the Atlantis.

"And it's only just begun," I added, looking around at our new surroundings.

We walked into the thankfully well air-conditioned lobby and set our heavy and numerous bags down. Surprisingly, there was a fairly nice-sized casino just beyond the reception desk, and the place was hopping. Granted, the clientele was somewhat on the shabby side, but at least there was life.

The lobby and casino were all done in the same motif: underwater. The place was a mess of coral, clams, plastic seaweed, and brightly painted fish. The dealers and waitresses were all dressed like scantily clad mermaids and mermen. And everywhere you looked, blue on top of blue. It was ultratacky, but somewhat homey at the same time. Besides, I told myself, gambling was gambling, whether I was there or at the Bellagio.

And then...

"Boys, boys, welcome to the Atlantis." He pronounced it like Ricardo Montalban welcoming us to Fantasy Island. He was dressed in an all-white gabardine suit livened up with a very loud, and very wide, fish-festooned ascot. I half expected a pint-sized sidekick to appear from behind him, blue margaritas in hand. (No such luck.)

And man, let me tell you, this guy was queer, queer, queer. Right down to the lisp and swaying hips. He was also surprisingly cute.

"You're Earl's brother?" Justin asked, shocked. Except for the fact that they were both gay, the two were nothing alike. No similarities whatsoever.

"Ah, yes, I can see where that's a bit of a shocker. My

mother's first husband, Earl's father, was a truck driver. Suppose he still is, actually. But only Earl would know for sure. Now, my papa, my mother's third husband, was and still is an accountant. In between came our sister's father. He's a construction worker and she's, well she, bless her heart, is a bit long in the tooth. The first marriage was for love, the second was for sex, and the third was for security. Hell, Mom's pushing sixty now, guess she figured she needed something to fall back on in her old age. Anyway, that explains why Earl and I seem so *different*," he explained, rather long-windedly. Luckily, between breaths, he waved his rather limp wrist for a cocktail waitress, and moments later, we were sucking down a tasty glass of Malibu rum and pineapple juice. Nice and tropical.

"Uh-huh," responded Justin, not really knowing how to reply to all that.

"Well, anyway, welcome, and make yourselves at home. Sorry for the room, in advance, it's the last one we have. Quite possibly the last one in Vegas. My name is Jacques, and if you need anything, anything at all, just let me know." He was looking right at Justin, all come-hithery-like.

"Thanks, Jacques, we'll do that," Justin replied, shaking his hand. They lingered like that for a second too long (I know, gross, right?) and then we went and checked in.

"What was that all about?" I asked, accepting our room keys from the friendly mermaid.

"What was what all about?" Justin asked, signing the credit card receipt and knowing full well what I was talking about.

"That. That back there. Not your type at all. You could make juice out of all that fruit."

We headed on up to our room. "Please, Em, it was nothing. Remember: never bite the hand that gives you the only room in Vegas. Besides, he was kinda, well, sorta... cute."

I let it go. To each his own. Besides, in two minutes it would be someone else, and then someone else after that, etc., etc. Then we were in our room and I knew why Jacques had apologized in advance. First, it was at the end of the hall, with the windows facing the outdoor pool. The smell of chlorine permeated the tiny room, and so did the noise of the screaming kids outside as they splashed each other. The room itself was done in the same style as the rest of the hotel, but being such a small space, it had a claustrophobic effect. I was beginning to understand what a goldfish felt like.

"Welcome to our bowl away from home," I said, grandly, and plopped down on the bed. The journey had depleted my energies.

"Em, it's not so bad," he shouted, while peeing in the bathroom. "Hey, they got soap shaped like seashells."

"Oh, okay. I feel much better, then, thanks," I hollered back, dripping with sarcasm.

"Now, sweetie, chipper up. We're here, we're queer, there's money to be won, vases to be found, and men to lay. Plus, there's a bar in every corner of every casino in this town. So let's Coppertone ourselves up and go have some fun," he proclaimed, and smacked my ass for good measure.

I thought about it for a split second, realized he was absolutely right, and jumped off my squeaky bed.

"Let's go gamble!" I shouted.

"Sounds like a plan!" he shouted back at me as we raced out of the pool-stinking room and into the still scorching Las Vegas air.

"Where to?" I asked, getting into another cigarette-infused cab.

"Well, nowhere with an underwater theme, that's for sure," Justin said. I readily agreed to that.

He told the driver that we were headed for Paris. Vegas is

a small town and we were there in minutes, which was good because I can only hold my breath for so long. And Paris is a gorgeous hotel and casino. The outside architecture is magnificent. There's a diminutive version of the Arche de Triomphe, and, of course, a replica of the Eiffel Tower that also penetrates the casino, offering a splendid view of the Strip at the very top. But for us, the best part was the scrumptious frozen drinks we bought and promptly began to drink. They were in blue, plastic miniature Eiffel Towers. How very creative.

With drinks in hand, we decided to do some gambling. The Paris casino is somewhat different from the others. It's very self-contained, which makes for a unique din when you're inside. Like the other first-class casinos, all the machines are jacketed in identical frames, and in Paris they're silver. Combined with the trelliswork over the card tables, the gazebo bar, the live entertainment, and the legs of the tower in the middle of the place, you couldn't ask for a more beautiful setting to lose your money in.

Speaking of losing money, I don't know what it is, but squandering my hard-earned cash while gambling doesn't bother me in the slightest, whereas, at home, I only buy Target-priced clothes, I never eat out, unless it's at Mickey D's or the like, and, more or less, I put away every nickel and dime that comes my way. In other words, I'm a tightwad. (Doesn't that word convey a totally different picture from what it actually means?) But when I'm sitting at a slot machine, well, I just drop money, drop money, drop money. One quarter or nickel after another. (And now Vegas is awash in penny slots!) And, provided there's a free drink sitting somewhere in front of me, which there *always* is, I couldn't care less that I'm rapidly depleting my meager funds. Just so long as every so often I win one nice-sized pot, I'm a happy little camper.

And, since Justin is practically made of money, he feels

the same way. Only more so. And he plays the dollar slots. Yikes! That I simply cannot do. Nickels and quarters are one thing, and trust me, even that adds up to big bucks in a short amount of time, but dollars are a whole other kettle of fish. That's major gambling in my book. I do, however, enjoy watching other people toss those large coins into the slots. And the sound of a dollar machine paying off is so much louder and clunkier than its smaller-denomination counterparts. Though, sadly, most of the casinos pay off in paper receipts nowadays; the noise of your winnings is nothing but a recorded tape. Anyway, when a nickel machine pays off big, say, hundreds of coins, you really haven't won that much money. But when a dollar machine pays off, now that's some heavy-duty cash. My friend simply lives for that large payoff. I, on the other hand, am just hunky-dory playing my penny-ante games.

So, with me at my quarter slots and Justin sitting on a stool behind me playing the dollars, the two of us sat and drank and gambled happily for over an hour—shifting stools every so often if a machine wasn't paying off, or, if a machine paid off big, as the true gambler will tell you, moving on to another one, as the odds are against a machine paying off two times in a row. In the short amount of time we sat there, I was down about forty dollars. I have no idea how much Justin had lost, but judging by the scowl on his face I'd say it was a considerable amount.

"I'm done for now, Em," he announced, plopping down on a stool next to mine and finishing my gin and tonic. "Let's go sit in the lounge and listen to some music. I'm getting carpal tunnel at these machines and my index finger is simply throbbing."

"Sounds good to me. I've lost enough for now, too."

We left the money-sucking devices and walked a short way to the casino lounge. A lovely woman, bedecked in a shimmering emerald evening gown, was belting out the classics and chattering blithely to the beleaguered gamblers sitting before her. We sat down and ordered a couple of drinks, but I could hear the noise of the slots behind me, drawing me back, begging me for my quarters. It was all I could do to not run to them.

If gambling is a disease, I was riddled with it. I ached to dump my quarters into the slots. I burned to pull the "arms" of the twinkling machines. I sweated in anticipation of my next big win. I throbbed… I throbbed… Well, I throbbed because I had turned around in hopes of running back into the casino, when who should I spot but our new friend from the plane, Marvin, standing in the distance and looking absolutely adorable.

"Well, well. Isn't this a pleasant surprise?" I said, pulling on Justin's shirt until he turned around to see Marvin as well.

"Oh, yes, this is a pleasant surprise," he concurred.

"It's not a surprise at all, though, is it?"

"What? Are you implying something?"

"No, not implying anything. Clearly stating, yes. I know you too well, sweetie. This is no coincidence. Vegas is small, but not that small."

He paused, looked down at his drink, then conceded, "Well, he might have mentioned that he'd be here right about now. But you know how groggy I get when I fly. I could be mistaken."

"You get groggy because you dope yourself up and drink yourself down. And you're never mistaken when it comes to men. Now let's go chat with him before someone else snatches him up." Though that was highly unlikely considering the crowd at Paris. Single gay men were about as rare in the nicer casinos as, say, in a Utah church—male tabernacle choirs excepted.

"Howdy, Marvin," I beamed. "Great seeing you again so soon."

"Whoa," he said. "It's like being at the Rose Bowl parade. You wait around long enough and a prize float is bound to come by." Damn, he was fine. My heart was fluttering and I nearly spilled my drink in all the excitement. (Nearly.)

"What are you doing here?" I asked him.

"I told your friend Justin that I'd meet you guys in the casino tonight, and here I am."

"My friend Justin, huh?" I huhed, and gave Justin a quick jab in the arm. "No, my *friend* forgot to mention it. It must have slipped what's left of his mind."

"Well, what with all the confusion when we got here and all, I must have forgotten to tell you," Justin tried. (Lied is more like it.)

"What confusion is that?" Marvin asked.

"Long story," I answered.

"Let's just forget about it," Justin interjected. "We're all here together now, and this place is utterly too straight and too boring. What say we move this gathering to a more respectable location."

We nodded our heads in agreement. Marvin took the lead and headed to the casino exit. We gladly followed. Luckily, for us anyway, he looked just as yummy from the back as from the front. Certainly a good trait in a man.

"You fucker," I whispered in Justin's ear.

"It was going to be a surprise," he whispered back to me, and then mouthed "Surprise!"

I shoved him forward and outside the casino. No harm, no foul, I figured, and let it go. Besides, I was happy that Marvin was with us. Maybe the evening was finally becoming profitable.

"Where to?" Marvin asked.

"Well, I've lost enough money for one night, so let's avoid the casinos. How about a disco?" I suggested.

"A disco it is, then," Marvin announced, and started hailing passing taxis.

I dreaded another stinking cab, but cigarettes and Vegas go hand in hand. There are people smoking everywhere you go. There are ashtrays over practically every urinal in every bathroom in every casino, guaranteeing that you never have to put out your cigarette if you don't want to. It's a wonder that Philip Morris doesn't have its own hotel/casino. They could call it Marlboro Country, and could hook up individual lung machines to the slots. Their mascot could be the Kool Camel. They could have the Benson & Hedges dancing smoke machines. The possibilities are endless.

I think Justin had had enough of stinking cabs as well, because he suggested the disco at the Aladdin, which was close by. Right next door, actually. So Marvin stopped hailing and we jaunted on over to the hotel.

The Aladdin was easily my favorite hotel on the strip. I say *was* because now it's Planet Hollywood, but not way back when all these events occurred. Planet Hollywood is nice, but much more sterile than its predecessor. In any case, the disco was amazing. We walked in and I felt like Barbara Eden on acid. They had the genie motif down pat. A mesmerizing light show practically drenched the dance floor with rotating beams of gold and red and blue and glorious orange lights. It was so bright in there that all I could make out was the hands of the dozens of dancers as they swayed overhead to the rhythmic techno beat. Surrounding this beautiful sight were overstuffed, circular, pink and baby-blue couches. Young, chicly dressed men and women were lounging comfortably on these while drinking from overly tall hurricane glasses. And everywhere, I mean everywhere, there were sheets of multicolored chiffon draped down from overhead. It was plush and exotic and sinfully decadent-looking—just the way we like it.

Naturally, we headed straight for the bar. (Straight being

the optimal word for it. We were obviously the only gay boys there.) A handsome, dark, and ever so young bartender, dressed in nothing but a purple and gold vest and gold satin pants, glided down to us, right past the waiting hordes of revelers, and asked for our drink orders. *That* could mean only one thing.

"What can I get you gentlemen?" he asked, oozing charm in a deep, rich, foreign accent. We were riveted.

Marvin ordered first. "I'll have a Thousand and One Nights," he said, after perusing the thematic drink menu.

"Ooh, what's in that?" I asked, excited at the prospect.

"Everything and lots of juice. Might as well go all the way, right?" Marvin answered, winking flirtatiously at me. I couldn't have agreed more and ordered the same.

"And you, sir?" the bartender asked Justin, with a playful grin stretched across his splendid face.

"Please, don't call me sir," he said, seductively, leaning in close. "Master will do just fine."

"Yes, Master, what can I get for you?"

"Ah, now, that's better. I'll have the Three Wishes."

"Wise choice, Master. Your wish is my command." He crossed his arms and bowed. Then he was off to fix our cocktails, which couldn't have come too quickly for me. The close proximity to Marvin was making my mouth as dry as a riverbed in the Sahara. (No, not the casino, the desert. P.S., stay away from the Sahara casino unless you like your gambling in a geriatric fashion.)

Moving on, maybe I should describe Marvin to you so you'll have a clearer understanding of my wanton lust for him. First off, his full name is Marvin Tanenbaum. And yes, as you might have guessed, he's Jewish. Jewish men, by and large, are, in my opinion, hot. Not to mention exotic. Granted, growing up in Kansas, the closest I ever came to exotic was a kiwi fruit I once ate at a wedding; so I think you can appreciate my eagerness.

That and the fact that he was my type really sent me over the edge. (Where I teeter on the brink at all times.) He was about five-eight. Shorter than me, but not by much. I liked that because it would make it easy to drape my arm around him and bend down slightly to kiss him on his full lips. (Yes, I was madly planning ahead, but why not?) He had shockingly blue eyes that narrowly sat alongside a large, somewhat humped nose. His face was slender and dark and beautifully stubbled with a perfect little pointed goatee on his dimpled chin. Atop his lovely head sat a full mane of deep, dark, shoulder-length hair. He certainly stood out in a crowd, that's for sure.

And his body, well, from what I could make out beneath his comfortable Gap clothes, looked lean and tight and hairy. I guessed that he was hairy from his arms, which were covered in a thick matting of curly black hairs. (Are you salivating yet? The man was fi-ine.) If it wasn't love at first sight, I'd say it was at least a deep case of puppy lust. Which, for a man pushing thirty, was largely pathetic. Still, it felt queasily nice.

Okay, back to the bar.

Our drinks arrived. Tall, frothy, richly colored, and completely stoked with alcohol. In other words, perfect. I grabbed mine and Marvin's, and we scooted away from the bar to make room for our fellow imbibers. Justin stayed and flirted. The object of his desire seemed more than happy to neglect his work, and flirted right on back. I was delighted to have Marvin to myself for however long I could—which, unfortunately, was only a scant few minutes. The bar was getting packed with thirsty dancers, and Justin had to make way.

He came back over to us, leaned in to me, and whispered, "His name's Ahmed, he gets off work in a half hour, and then he's going to join our little party. So looks like Marvin is all yours for the evening."

"He was mine to begin with, but thank you for your generosity, *Master*."

He was about to argue, thought better of it, knowing he would get Ahmed as an alternative, and then dropped it to start working on his drink instead. I gave him a kiss on the cheek, patted his butt in a congratulatory manner, and turned my attentions back to Marvin. When confronted with opposition, Justin always takes the path of least resistance. In other words, a good drink was significantly better than a good fight. (Amen to that.)

"How's it going, Marvin?" I asked.

"The drink, the music, and *the company* are all wonderful. How about yourself?"

Well, I couldn't have agreed more, but rather than tell him, I showed him. I leaned in and down a tad and grabbed his goatee. I pulled him toward me. Then, staring adoringly into his eyes, I planted a deep, soulful kiss on his sweet-tasting lips. A little presumptuous of me, yes, but I hate missed opportunities. Thank goodness he responded in kind. His lovely tongue found its way to mine. There's nothing like kissing a beautiful man while he's drinking a tropical drink. Talk about having your cake and eating it too.

"Nice," he moaned, our lips still centimeters apart.

"Mm-hm. Not what I pictured from a man who works for the same network that brings me *Sesame Street* and *Nova*." His eyes were so blue up close. Like sapphires, sparkling in the overhead light. I prayed he wouldn't mind me using him to help me find the vase, though I decided to wait to ask him until after we had sex. (Just in case.)

"Not what I was thinking, but good point. Most of the guys I work with do look like they should be working at PBS, so I'll take your remark as a compliment."

"Please do. Here's another one." I leaned in again and laid another wet one on him, this time gently stroking and pinching his left nipple. I could feel the piercing beneath his shirt. The night, it seemed, was getting better with each passing minute.

"Get a room," Justin interrupted.

"Got one," Marvin replied, giving me a grin and a wink. Music to my ears. And speaking of which...

The DJ started playing Madonna's latest hit, so I grabbed Marvin's hand and thrust him onto the dance floor. I preferred to keep Marvin away from Justin until Ahmed was safely on the scene, as Justin was still a dangerous threat until he was securely in someone else's grasp. Fortunately, Justin still had his drink to finish and I, once again, was alone with Marvin.

"Nice move," Marvin said, grinding into my hip as he moved to the music.

"Keep that up and you'll see just how nice I can get."

"Promise?"

"Does a bear shit in the woods?"

"So they say on *National Geographic*. Must be true."

And then we just danced, safe in the knowledge that we'd be in love's warm embrace sometime later in the evening. There's something about a sure thing that puts me in a gloriously relaxed mood. Well, that and the drink. The sucker was wicked-strong.

And Marvin was a great dancer. Arms in the air, hips swiveling, feet gliding and hopping—and all to the music, which isn't always the case. Doesn't it suck when you pick up a guy at a club and he's cute and sexy and eager (and easy), then you go to dance, and he's clumsy and spastic and completely out of sync with the music? I never go home with a guy like that. Stands to reason, if he's got no rhythm on the dance floor, then he's probably got no rhythm in the sack. Why take the chance, right?

But not Marvin. He was smooth and self-assured. I could just picture him line-dancing on *Soul Train*. Too bad you never see people doing that anymore. It always looked like so much fun on TV.

Speaking of self-assured, a minute later, Justin and Ahmed joined us on the dance floor and interrupted my *Soul Train* revelry. Thankfully, they arrived with fresh drinks. Introductions were made all around, and the four of us danced happily en masse. Ahmed was still in his work outfit, which was highly distracting as he obviously had on no underwear. Needless to say, silk slacks hide very little. And Ahmed had very much. This was not lost on Justin, either. His eyes were riveted below Ahmed's belt. And Ahmed was all too happy to put on a show. Much to my delight, Marvin kept his eyes on me and me alone. Oh, happy day.

When we had worked up a sweat, the four of us left the dance floor and found an empty pink couch to sit on. We practically melted into the thing. Well, that and the second drink had really done a number on me. Between the lights and the music and the generous amount of alcohol, my head was spinning. But I was on cloud nine. No job, no income, and no vase were quickly fading from my mind and were being replaced by one man: Marvin. It just felt so... comfortable.

Of course, as most lives go, my life never stayed on a comfortable track for very long. And I suppose, as I've said before, that's what makes life so interesting in the first place. Why does there always have to be such turmoil?

The four of us were nicely paired on our cozy couch, snuggling up to our new beaus, chatting aimlessly, kissing frequently, and thoroughly enjoying ourselves, when—

"Em," Justin leaned over and said, "care to join me in the little boy's room?"

I did have to pee, since he had mentioned it, and politely accepted his offer, though I hated to leave Marvin even for a second.

"You'll be all right?" I asked Marvin, after I gave him a kiss on his bumpy nose.

"Right as rain," he replied, and blew me a kiss. Too bad the rain would soon be a torrential downpour. (Okay, enough foreshadowing. Here comes the bad shit.)

Justin and I peed, exchanged passing comments about each other's man, and hurried back to them. Halfway there, we noticed a commotion at approximately the same location as our comfy pink couch.

"Uh-oh," we both exclaimed, and ran over.

Once we had managed to push through the crush of onlookers, we were horrified to find both of our men punching and kicking—and yes, slapping—at each other. It was a nasty thing to behold. I ran for Marvin and Justin ran for Ahmed in the hope of pulling them apart. That's when we figured out what caused the fracas in the first place.

Ahmed, from what I could gather from Marvin's rantings, was Palestinian, and Marvin had relatives in Israel. I guess, even thousands of miles away, the relations between the two are still strained. Ahmed was yelling and screaming in some Arabic tongue, and I had no idea what he was saying. Though it sounded pretty bad judging from the tone. That and the amount of spittle that was hitting us from his side of the fight. And Marvin was shouting out every Arab-related insult he could think of. I was ashamed for the both of them. You'd think that being gay would've taught them to respect each other's differences or at least to tolerate them. No such luck. It took Justin and me several minutes to pry them apart.

I tried to calm Marvin down once I had managed to pull him to a quiet corner of the bar, but he was beyond my soothing influences. He kept cursing and raving and pacing around like a caged tiger. Needless to say, it was none too arousing for me. I kept thinking, Aren't there any nice, normal guys out there? (Funny thing, that. I guess anyone who hangs around with Justin and me long enough thinks the exact same thing.)

But nothing I could say or do would relax him, and he finally just stormed out of the disco and away from me. That was upsetting for two reasons. The obvious one, at that moment, was no nookie. I had my heart, and certain other body parts, set on a night of passion. Now the prospects looked dim. Second, and more important in the larger scheme of things, we were back to square one with the whole Mary thing. Marvin was our only hope for a quick solution. And yes, we had that picture of her from the show, but the thought of circulating that around Vegas seemed an awfully large and impossible task.

I was pondering the awfulness of it all when Justin came over and sat down with me. He too looked miserable.

"Where's Ahmed?" I asked.

"Gone. He left, gold lamé jammies flapping in the breeze. Men suck, dude."

"Though not on us. At least not tonight."

"Hey now, the night is young. Let's hear none of that."

"The night may be young, but I'm not. Let's just go back to our hotel and start fresh in the morning, okay?"

"Hmm, I suppose. I guess I'm getting kinda tired, anyway. How about one more drink in the casino and then we can go."

I only had to think about that for a split second. A drink sounded perfect right about then. The evening's upheaval had totally ruined my nice buzz. And some slot action seemed like a great way to help me forget my woes.

"Well, just one drink," I agreed, pulling myself up, dusting myself off, and starting all over again.

Actually, just being in the casino had a surprisingly calming effect on me. The hum of the slots was hypnotic. And the casino in the Aladdin was stunning. The Arabian Nights theme was played out in every nook and cranny, and the murals above the casino were breathtaking. My hands were pulling on the slot arms in mere moments. Yes, I still like to pull the arms even though you can just press the button if you want to spin the reels. Makes me feel more in tune with the machine. It's a Zen thing. Go figure.

A genie-clad waitress was upon us for our free drink orders within minutes, so all was balancing out in the universe once again. The tension in my shoulders was quickly abating, though the one in my pants was reluctantly staying put. And after a nice win of eighty quarters, the smile on my face had again returned. Who needs a man when you have a one-armed bandit to keep you company? (Don't answer that. I know it's pathetic. We all have our own ways of coping.)

Justin, hearing the win coming from my vicinity, came back over from the dollar slot section and took a stool next to mine.

"Feeling better?" he asked, sipping from his drink and grinning.

"Not worse," I answered, suspicious of his grin. (As well I should have been.)

"Want to feel even better?" he asked, setting his drink down.

"Do I?" I asked, preparing myself for what he had planned. "You tell me."

To which he replied, pointing somewhere in the distance, "Look over there."

I had had enough of that game back in the airport. "Just tell me, please."

"Okay, look straight ahead to the first Blackjack table and tell me what you see."

I had to squint to see that far, but it didn't take long to figure out what he was pointing at. "Holy shit," I squealed.

"Is that a good holy shit or a bad holy shit?" he asked.

"I suppose you knew he worked here, then."

"Duh, dude."

"And I suppose that we came to this hotel to dance so

that we'd run into him and you could have Marvin all to yourself?"

"Oh, please, now, does that sound like me?"

"It sounds exactly like you."

"Okay, then, yes, that's what I had planned. But look how well it worked out."

In case you hadn't figured it out yet, it was Chris, my studly Blackjack dealer from the farewell party, standing some twenty feet away and dealing cards. I had to admit, it was good to see him, even under such underhanded circumstances. It was hard to be mad at Justin, all things considered.

"Go talk to him," he said, shooing me over.

And that I did. I walked over and sat down at a vacant seat at his table. He didn't look up at me right away. And when he did, he didn't place me at first. But once he realized who I was, he allowed himself a bright though professional smile. I knew that the dealers had strict rules against fraternizing with the patrons, so I wasn't disappointed that he didn't run around the table to swoop me up in his muscular arms. I nodded at him, placed my bet, and accepted my cards. He took everyone's bets and then raised his arm in a "come here" motion. My fellow gamblers and I played out our hands and noticed another dealer that had come up from behind.

I lost, Chris was replaced with the new dealer, and we both walked off. I allowed him a short head start so as not to call attention to our meeting up, then noticed he was headed for the restroom. So that's where I went as well. I walked up the aisle of stalls and found him waiting for me in the last one. Naturally, I entered.

"I lost the hand," I whined.

"Can't cheat in Vegas, you know," he explained, wrapping his arms around me.

"Well, I think you'll have to make it up to me, then," I replied, firmly embracing him and rubbing my cheek on his neck.

"Guess I will," he moaned, moving his face so our lips could meet.

He tasted minty fresh. I forgot how great he felt to hold and to kiss. And I had to admit, making out in a casino bathroom felt just naughty enough to be highly erotic. It was all I could do to not strip him bare and have my way with him over the toilet. But he held me back, explaining that he only had a few minutes to take a bathroom break, and that he had to get back. By then, though, after the whole Marvin thing and now the not-so-chance encounter with Chris, I was hornier than a priest in an all-boy's school.

"I have to work for another three hours, but I'll give you a call tomorrow, okay?"

"Okay," I replied, sad that we had to separate so soon. I told him where Justin and I were staying and gave him our room number.

He whipped out his prick for me, for old time's sake, and gave it the familiar shake and slap. "Just to keep you interested," he said, then added, "Man, you guys must have been desperate for a room." He smirked, put his thickening dick away, and gave me a farewell kiss. "Say hello to Jacques for me," he said, leaving the stall. I guessed Vegas was just such a small town that all the queer boys knew each other. Then he waved and was off. I stayed there for a few minutes so as not to call attention to our little dalliance—or the raging boner in my pants.

Man, we'd only been in Vegas less than a day and I had already lost out on sex with two different men. I prayed the rest of our journey would run smoother. And, as if the good Lord had heard my prayer, there came a knock on the stall door.

"Yes?" I asked.

"Are you coming out anytime soon?" It was Justin.

"Maybe, maybe not." I said through the door. "Things haven't been going so great out there for me, you know.

Maybe I should just stay right here for the rest of our trip."

"Suit yourself," he said. "But I think you might want to take a peek out here. I have something to show you."

"Man, every time you say that, my life gets turned upside down."

"Just a peek, please."

So I unlatched the door and poked my head outside the stall. And there, standing before me, was Justin, and he had a receipt in his hand.

"I was only gone for ten minutes," I said in astonishment.

"Only takes one," he replied.

"How much?" I asked.

"Eight hundred and sixty-four dollars. Not bad for one night's work. Are we still having just that one drink?"

"Fuck, no, you're buying me a double," I ordered, and marched on out of the stall, grabbing a twenty he was holding in his hand for me.

"Good night for gambling," he said as we sat down in front of two machines.

"Better than for loving, that's for sure." I added.

"Isn't love always a gamble?" he quipped.

"Shut up and play, Justin. I've had enough talking for one evening."

All Hail, Caesar

THE NEXT MORNING, WE AWOKE BRIGHT AND EARLY TO THE fresh scent of chlorine and a somewhat loud knocking on our door.

"Come back in an hour, please," Justin shouted from his bed.

But again there was a knocking.

"In. An. Hour," he annunciated.

And there it was again. This time I jumped out of bed and poked my head out the door to see what the hubbub was about. I was shocked to find Marvin standing there, an enormous bouquet of roses in his hand, and a *please forgive me* look on his adorable face. He started talking before I could say anything.

"Look, I know I was an asshole last night. I swear that's not like me at all. I've had relatives killed in Israel and I get kind of touchy when I'm around Arabs."

"By touchy you mean punchy and kicky and slappy and yelly, right?"

"Something like that, yes. Please, please, please forgive

me. If you give me another chance I'll do anything you ask. *Anything*." He handed me the flowers, and then produced a mischievous grin that I assumed was to suggest that "anything" meant anything sexual. And I, of course, was all for that.

"Let him in," shouted Justin from his bed.

"Please, do come in," I said, and ushered him into our little fishbowl.

"Wow, what is that smell?" he asked, waving his hand in front of his face.

We both pointed out the window.

"Nice," he said, and plopped down on my bed. Damn, he looked good sitting there. I was still hornier than hell from the previous night's shenanigans, needless to say.

"We forgive you," Justin said, groggily.

"*We* do?" I asked, surprised that Justin was a.) answering for the both of us and b.) actually forgiving him. That was rare. Justin held grudges. Big ones. And the only reason he ever forgave anyone was—

"Yes, *we* do," he continued. "Under one circumstance. Actually, make that two. The first one being: never wake us up, and by us, I mean me, before ten o'clock."

"Can do," he agreed, nodding his head and stroking my hand. Hell, I had already forgiven him. You should've seen the flower arrangement.

"And number two," Justin said, "we need your help on a little sche— er, *project* we're working on." Ah, in all the excitement of a handsome gentleman caller at my door, I had completely forgotten about our need for Marvin's connections.

"Me? You need my help? But what can I do for you two?" he asked, looking to me for the answer.

"Well, oddly enough, and not to seem manipulative or calculating or anything, and you know I already like you and all—"

"Oh, for goodness sake, just ask him, damn it," Justin interrupted.

"Okay, fine, I saw this vase on *Antiques Roadshow*; it belonged to my dead grandmother; I want it back for my mother so she'll be happy; and the people at the show won't help me find the woman who has that vase in her possession—oh, and she might be here in Vegas; and you work for PBS; and—" I gulped for a breath and pointed to Marvin to indicate that he, in fact, was the "and."

"Ah, well, it is a small world, isn't it?" he said, nodding his head.

"Small and getting smaller," Justin offered. "So what'll it be? Do we forgive you or not?"

I sat there and waited, not wanting to pressure him, but still praying that he'd help so that I could get the vase back and have sex with him. (In no particular order.) And that's when the phone rang.

"Now what?" Justin sighed, irately.

"I'll get it," I said, and did. Guess who it was?

"Good morning, sexy." Yep, it was Chris. Damn, when it rains, it pours, don't it?

"Oh, hi, Chris."

"Did I wake you?"

"Um, no, we were just sitting here... Sitting here..." Marvin was staring at me, making me quite nervous.

"Yes, you woke us," Justin shouted from his bed.

"No, no, we were already awake. What's up?"

"Just wondering if you'd like to get together tomorrow night. I don't have to work and I thought we could *play*."

Man, that was a toughie. I had one man in my bed and another one on the phone. Should I say yes? Should I say no? They were both adorable. I knew what Justin would say. Actually, he'd probably invite the one on the phone to join the two in the bed. But I hated to use these seemingly nice men that way. (Did I mention that they were both adorable?)

"Sure, Chris, that sounds great. Why don't you come over here at, say, seven? Okay?"

I was trying not to sound too excited. Didn't want to make Marvin suspicious. Justin gazed over from his side of the bed, knowing what I had just agreed to, and gave me that *I've taught you well, Luke, now use the force wisely* look. The force, unfortunately, was weak in me. Justin was hogging it all. Still, now that Marvin was helping us, my stay in Vegas should've been dramatically cut short, so maybe I could get away with stringing two men along. Gay men have been doing that for eons. Genetically, I should have been amply prepared. Anyway, I figured, if one didn't work out, I could use the other for backup. A spare, so to speak.

"My cousin," I explained to Marvin when I hung up the phone. "He lives in Vegas. Haven't seen him in a while, and we're going to get together tomorrow night." That sounded good. Who could argue with that? Maybe this would work out after all.

"That's nice. Maybe we could all go out together, then," Marvin suggested. (Uh-oh.)

"No, I don't—"

"Hey, we still need that answer," Justin said, coming to the rescue. "Will you help us?"

Again with the pause. "I'll see what I can do. I do actually know a few people who work on that show; maybe they can help. No promises, but I'll try. Now am I forgiven?"

I looked at him, then at the flowers, then over to Justin. "Sure, why not?"

"Hallelujah," Justin shouted.

"Hallelujah," Marvin echoed. "Now I have to go to that convention. I'll come pick you up at six and then we can go do dinner, okay?"

Justin said, "How about seven? I prefer a late din-din."

"I think he meant just me and him," I pointed out, and

Marvin nodded a yes.

"Fine, your loss. Have fun. Don't worry about poor little old me. Alone in the big city, not knowing a soul. I'll be fine."

"Whatever, brave heart," I said, getting out of bed to walk Marvin to the door. I wrote down Mary's name and the details from the show, and handed them to our new friend.

"See you soon," Marvin said, leaning up to kiss me. Mmm, I got instant lumpage in my boxers. It didn't go unnoticed.

"Ooh, how will I ever make it through the day thinking about that?" he moaned, releasing the beast he now held in his hand. I had never stood in a hotel hallway with a boner before. And the maid down the hall had never seen one there either, apparently. She screamed, made the sign of the cross over her chest, and dropped her towels to the floor. I turned beet red, gave Marvin a peck on the lips, told him I'd see him at six, and hopped back into our room, slamming the door behind me.

Justin, rolling with laughter, peeked from under his covers and shouted, "Slut!"

"Takes one to know one."

"Touché. Now let's go eat breakfast. All this commotion so early in the morning has given me an appetite."

"Me too." But my appetite was for something completely different.

We opted for the breakfast buffet at our hotel. Now, just a quick piece of advice on the buffets in Vegas. Yes, indeed, you can eat all you want for a ridiculously low price at every single hotel in the city; however, I recommend you pay a couple of extra bucks and go to one of the nicer places along the Strip. Remember, you always get what you pay for. At the Atlantis, we got microwaved frozen waffles, powdered eggs, stale-tasting blintzes, mediocre danish, juice from concentrate, etc., etc. But hell, it was only seven dollars, all you could stand. Plus, we were lazy and hungry, and didn't want to deal with getting into yet another smelly cab just to go wait in line at one of the nicer places. Anyway, at home I would've paid the same price for a cup of coffee and a bagel, so, really, I wasn't complaining—any more than usual.

"I think my nose is permanently fucked from those chlorine fumes. This food has absolutely no flavor," Justin whined.

"Nope, your nose is fine. This food really does have no flavor, so eat up fast. I want to go exploring."

"By exploring do you mean gambling?"

"Gambling, exploring, whatever. When in Rome..."

"Ah, good idea. We eat and then go to Caesar's Palace."

"Not what I was implying, but sure, why not?"

With that agreed upon, we shoveled down our food and got ready to head on out to Caesar's, but not before a certain hotel manager descended upon us.

"Boys, boys, how on earth are you doing this morning?" asked Jacques. He was flushed with excitement at our presence. And who could blame him? Still, it was a bit early for such exuberance. Plus, he slid into our booth, landing achingly close to Justin.

"Just fine, Jacques, sweetie," Justin replied, hand on hand.

That sent him into overdrive. "Super, just super, boys. And, hey, if you're not doing anything later, come join me for the show tonight. We have an amazing tribute to the oldies of country music. You'll swear that Patsy Cline has risen from her grave, God rest her soul."

"Well, I don't—" Justin began to decline politely, but I beat him to the punch.

"What Justin is about to say is, I already have a dinner date, but he is as free as a bird." Speaking of punches, Justin

63

was slamming his fist into my thigh beneath the table and mercilessly kicking my feet.

"Oh, that is wonderful!" squealed Jacques in rapturous delight. "Meet me at the main bar at six. And everything is on me, Justin, honey. *Everything.*" And he was off before Justin could collect his thoughts and think of an excuse to get out of it.

"You suck," he said.

"I thought you liked him. What's the problem?" I asked innocently.

"If he let me tape his mouth shut, then yes, he'd be cute. But now I have to listen to that all night long. I'll get you for this, my pretty. And your little dog, too."

"Oh, please, take a pill, have a drink, and enjoy the show. You've done worse things to me a hundred times over. Who knows, maybe you'll find the love of your life."

"Not likely. And I hate Patsy Cline."

"Turn in your gay card now, sweetie. That's blasphemy."

"Fine, whatever, let's just get out of here before he comes back and offers us anything else. I hope we run into his brother again, Mr. Emphysema 2000, because I guarantee you'll be enjoying the presence of his company for the exact same show. Fucker."

"Sure, why not? I've never dated three guys simultaneously. What an adventure!" I shouted, exiting our booth.

"You want adventure? Join the navy, but please leave me out of it. Wait until you're dating five guys at once, then come and see me. I can say from experience, *that* is an adventure." He wasn't joking. And I wasn't even happy about seeing two. Still, it was a hell of a lot better than none. Besides, what could go wrong?

We decided to walk to Caesar's. The fumes from our room had not withdrawn from our heads yet, and we thought the fresh air would do us some good. In Vegas, however, fresh air is hot and dry. Our lungs, accustomed to cold and damp, were screaming up at us to hop into the shade and wait for a cab, but we persevered. Besides, it was only a mile or so to the casino.

After just five minutes of walking, however, the shirts had to come off. Now, mind you, I'm no prude, but I have this policy of removing my clothes only in the privacy of another man's bedroom or my own. There's never a need to walk through San Francisco shirtless. If anything, I constantly have to keep adding jackets over sweatshirts over T-shirts. Now I found myself walking down the street in nothing but a pair of shorts and sneakers. I felt naked. Naked and very, very pale. My skin hadn't seen the light of day since Luke had raped Laura on *General Hospital*.

"Um, how come you're so tan and I'm as white as a Donna Karan sheet?" I asked.

"You know that thing you do all day, what's it called?"

"Work?"

"Um, yeah. Well, while you're at work, I go to Dolores Park and lie out. Or, better yet, I try to use a natural tanning cream so I won't get skin cancer. And voilà—George Hamilton, eat your heart out."

"And I suppose while I'm working you're also getting those abs, pecs, biceps, and other assorted muscly things to look like that?"

"What? These old things? Just genetics, really. Oh, maybe I hit the gym a few times a week, but mostly I just sit in the sauna."

"My guess, you get more of a workout in the sauna anyway. Am I right?"

"Good guess."

Looking at Justin made me even more uptight about my body, so I slid my shirt back on and proceeded to broil in the midday heat. I live by the rule: It's better to look good than to feel good. And I certainly looked better with my clothes on; at least standing next to Justin I did. In my next lifetime, I plan on being friends with people less attractive than myself. It's so much better for your self-esteem that way.

"By the way," Justin added, "Did you happen to notice a black Mercedes pull out of our hotel parking lot at the same time we left?"

"Nope. Why do you ask?"

"Probably nothing, but the guy driving and his buddy ate breakfast at the same time we did this morning, and they were giving me the creeps."

"How so?" I asked, feeling uneasy.

"Just that every time I looked up, I could tell they were staring at us, but then they immediately looked back down."

"Sure they weren't cruising you? It's been known to happen." (Repeatedly and often.)

"No, these guys were straight. My gaydar reading was at zero. Anyway, it was probably nothing. Just some straight bigoted assholes taking a gander at two fabulous queens."

"So why did you ask me, then?"

"Because they just drove by, and I could've sworn that they slowed down a tad when they passed. Forget it—I'm sure it's this insane heat playing tricks on my already fragile mind."

Luckily we hit the Strip and Caesar's was only midway up, because I was getting the heebie-jeebies big time, and I needed a strong drink and a nice slot machine to calm me down.

Now, are you ready to continue our tour of Vegas hotels? Here we go...

Caesar's is a grand hotel and casino. It's not one of my favorites because of the onslaught of tourists who roam through, snapping pictures and bumping into you, but it is impressive. Outside, you can start walking from one end of it and many minutes later glance up and see that you still have a way to go before the end. And, of course, everywhere you look, inside and out, it's made to have that ancient Roman feel, with faux columns running from top to bottom. The statuary and fountains at the entrances are cool as well, if you're into that sort of thing. But it's the shows inside that are the true crowd-pleasers.

Like many of the casinos in Vegas, Caesar's also has a mall attached to theirs, which is always a big plus in my book. Set up to look like the Roman forum, there's even an overhead ceiling painted to resemble the sky. And the shops, which are all first class, are topped with faux buildings that look like the homes of ancient Rome, replete with statues and busts. (The face kind, not the bosom kind.) Throw in the phenomenal Coliseum theater, and you can see how Caesar's has created a small city unto itself.

The shows I mentioned take place at two of the three large fountains in the mall. At intervals throughout the day, the fountains magically come to life. Each of the statues becomes a living god. Well, at least that's what Caesar's wants you to believe. And honestly, for, like, the first five seconds, it's pretty nifty. But then you see how cheesy the animatronics really are. And the scripts that the shows follow are just way too insipid. No, the real show is watching the hordes of tourists running to witness these spectacles. Some of these people obviously haven't jogged in years; now they're heaving themselves back and forth between these two monstrosities, knocking people over, dropping their food, and pushing their bodies to dangerous limits. Well, I'm sorry, but that is the real show. Justin and I get there five minutes before they start just to see if anyone has a coronary. Is that cruel? Probably. In any case, let's move on.

These shows, though, are the fake shows. There's also a live show, just as cheesy and just as poorly scripted, but equally adored by the tourists: Caesar's court parading through the casino and the mall. Actually, most of the larger casinos have something similar to this, but at Caesar's, the masses really get involved. Photo ops are rampant. Anywhere you can go and see a six-foot-tall behemoth of a man dressed like a gladiator, you'll also see a line of people waiting to take a picture with him. I would love to know what these guys get paid. Did they go to college and get a degree, only to end up doing this for a living? Do their parents brag about their son, the gladiator? Did they have to slaughter a certain number of lions before they got hired? Or Christians? (Hey, maybe that would be fun.) Anyway, my point, and I'm sure I have one somewhere, is that ordinary people's ideas of entertainment are really fucked up. Well, that may or may not have been my point when I started this tirade, but it is now. So here comes the bitter irony.

When Caesar himself makes an appearance, all hell breaks loose. It's like, all of a sudden, these backwater hicks become the paparazzi. Disposable cameras, digital cameras, pocket Polaroids, every size, shape, and brand of video camera, they all appear as if by magic to capture the being of this sham Caesar. It's pathetic, it's demoralizing, it's…it's…

"Oh, my God, IT'S HIM!!!" shouted Justin.

"Um, you know that's not the real Caesar, right? He'd be over two thousand years old by now." I think that's about right. History was never my forte.

"I know, you big idiot. It's him!" Again with the shouting.

"Dude, tell me what you're talking about, please."

"That man dressed like Caesar is…is…is…oh, my God, it's *Bradley*." He fairly whispered the name and then dropped to his knees.

"Who the hell is Bradl—" I began, and then remembered who he was.

Bradley, from what I could recall, was the first guy Justin ever had sex with. Long story short: hot teen sex, followed by getting caught by parents, followed by never seeing or hearing from hot teen lover ever again, followed many years down the line by a twisted, emotionally unstable, relationship-retarded, adult Justin.

"Are you sure?" I asked.

I mean, he has had hundreds and hundreds of men since then. It would be a miracle if he could recognize the very first one. Actually, he has problems remembering the ones he's had sex with from a few weeks prior. Even a few days is difficult for him. My guess was that it was just wishful thinking. The man did look awfully stunning in his gladiator costume. And who wouldn't want to have sex with a guy who has a salad named after him?

Justin kneeled there for a few minutes, regaining his composure, then said, "I know it's been nearly fifteen years. I know that this man is fifty pounds heavier, and that his hair is different, and that his face is fuller, but you never forget your first. Never. *That* is definitely Bradley."

"Let's get a closer look, then, to make sure," I suggested.

In the ten years I'd known him, I had never seen Justin so nervous or tense. At least nothing like this. Well, there was that one time he found out that Estée Lauder bought out Aveda, and his hairdresser would no longer be carrying his hair gel; that really freaked him out. But then he found another hairdresser nearby who carried it, and all was fine. That couldn't hold a candle to this.

Justin looked practically catatonic at my suggestion. I had to nudge him to respond.

"Oh…okay. We could do that," he said, gulping. Yet he still didn't move.

"Dude, you're scaring me. This is not the Justin I know, love, and am terrified of. Snap out of it and go stand over there by the fountain so we can get a better look." He reluctantly obeyed. We sat down on the edge of a fabulous chariot-driven fountain and stared. And stared. And then stared some more.

"Um, dude, is it or isn't it him?"

"Again, I'm almost sure that it's him. Every hair on my body is standing on end, just like that first night fifteen years ago."

"That must itch like hell, seeing as every hair on your body is trimmed down to within a millimeter of its life."

"Fucker. This is no time for kidding. That man standing there might've been my one true love if it wasn't for my horrible parents interfering." He said it with so much conviction that I actually felt a pang in my heart. The thought that Justin could actually possess the capacity to love anyone other than himself was miraculous. The possibility that that person was standing before us was like winning the lottery and then getting hit by lightening, twice. (Okay, bad odds analogy, but you get the point.)

"So go talk to him," I told him.

"No. Why bother? Too much water under the bridge by now. Besides, I live in San Francisco and he lives in Vegas. I'm independently wealthy and he's a... well... Let's just say that Roman dictators were never much my thing. It just wouldn't work out. Why put myself through that heartache again?"

"Because life is all about taking risks. Because it's better to have loved and lost than never to have loved at all. Because regret is a nasty four-letter word. Because... Because..."

"Oh, please, regret is a six-letter word, just like shut up. Let's just drop it and get out of here. I need a drink or a pill or something. Okay?" He looked beaten.

"Shut up is two words," I corrected him, hoping to snap him out of it with some witty banter.

"So is fuck off, now let's go." So much for laughter being the best medicine.

"Fine, whatever," I conceded, getting up and walking away with him.

But first I had one last-ditch, sneaky trick up my sleeve. Just as we were walking past Caesar and his retinue, I pushed Justin. My friend went careening past the admiring throngs and right into the emperor himself, causing both to fall to the ground. It sounded like almighty Zeus himself had thrown a terrible thunderbolt to the earth, what with Caesar's heavy armor crashing to the marble floor and all.

The crowds ran over to see what the commotion was. I followed, not wanting to miss the grand reunion from up close.

"Oh, my goodness, I'm so sorry," Justin apologized, crimson in the face, as he rose precariously from where he had landed. "I must have tripped," he added, searching the crowd for yours truly. I ducked behind an obese elderly woman who had stopped to take a picture of the scene while she ate a monstrously huge cup of gelato.

"Oh—it's no problem," replied Caesar, struggling to get up. The breastplate alone must've weighed ten pounds. "These things hap—" he paused when he saw Justin, but quickly regained his composure "—pen."

Justin helped him to his feet, apologized again, and slunk back into the crowd. I intently watched Caesar's face to see if there was even a hint of recognition as Justin walked away, but the rest of Caesar's entourage had arrived and encircled him, and my view was obscured. Damn.

And, uh-oh, Justin had found me huddling behind the fat woman's enormous ass and was headed over. (Not a pretty picture, is it?)

"Oops," I said, in my defense, as he swooped in for the kill.

"Oops? Oops? Is that the best you can come up with?" he shouted at me.

If we hadn't been surrounded by tourists, I'm sure he

would have beaten me to a pulp. But instead, he walked on by and headed for one of the mall exits. Definitely not the Justin I knew. The Justin I knew would have walked on up to Caesar and planted a big wet one on his face. Crowds or no crowds. Still, what did I know? I never had a young love. Or an unrequited love. Maybe a young heart breaking is more fatal than when your heart breaks and you're tough enough to make it through the pain. I did know this, however: Justin seemed devastated. It was a hard thing to behold.

I caught up to him and apologized. "I'm sorry, dude. Just trying to help,"

"I know, Em, but please just let it go. I was hurt once already. I don't need or want that again. Okay?"

I didn't agree with him, but I said okay. Just then, a light-bulb flashed above my head. "Hey, I think I know a place that will cheer you up."

"Do they serve booze?" he asked.

"Don't think so." Strike one.

"Do they have cruisy bathrooms?" he asked.

"Doubtful." Strike two.

"Do they encourage recreational drug use?" he asked.

"Definitely not." Strike three.

"So how on earth would this place cheer me up?

"Outlandish clothes, enormous diamonds, and gaudy on top of gaudy everywhere." Home run! (I know, three strikes and you're out, but we were playing by my rules, and I was still up there swinging.)

Twenty minutes later, we were at the Liberace Museum: Nevada's gay mecca.

In actuality, the museum is in a run-down mall, miles from the Strip. Even calling it a museum is pushing it. And yet, despite the tragic surroundings, the place is utterly too, too fabulous.

Liberace, in my humble opinion, was a genius. How no

one pegged him as the big old queen he was, I have no idea. I guess it was just the times and all. But make no bones about it, Liberace was the granddaddy of all poofs. A megaqueen, if you will. And his remaining artifacts are testament to that fact.

Honestly, I had an entirely new admiration for the man by the time we had oohed and aahed our way through the place. Yes, he played a mean piano. Yes, he was a true showman. Yes, he could spend a wad of cash at the drop of a hat. But what got to us was how such a drab, unattractive mamma's boy could pull it all off, and so well at that. I felt that if he could do it, there was hope for me yet. And I think Justin was stunned that there was someone out there who was equally fabulous to himself. I say *equally* because Justin would never even consider someone being *more* fabulous. The biggest kicker of all was that this flaming queen was loved and adored by millions and millions of straight people worldwide. He was easily the Madonna of his day. How amazing is that?

We left there in high spirits and with renewed vigor.

"God bless the queen," I shouted as we walked back into the heat.

"Amen, sister," Justin replied.

"I'm sorry for pushing you into Caesar," I said as we boarded the bus back to the Strip, carefully avoiding the use of cabs now when at all possible. "Do you forgive me?"

"Hmm, we'll have to see about that," he replied, devilishly.

"Wh-what does that mean?" I stammered.

"Let's just say that I forgive you *for now*, but I reserve the right to get even with you at a later date."

"If it keeps you in this good mood, okay. But please remember that best friends let these things slide every now and again. You know, unretaliatory-like."

"Dude, what planet have you been living on? Does that

sound anything like me?"

"Nope, but I thought I'd give it a shot."

"Nice try. Now let's go back to our hotel. I need a nap before my big evening with Jacques."

"And a drink."

"Oh, that goes without saying."

Napping was not done easily. For one, I was nervous about my date with Marvin. And with Chris. For two, I was hornier than hell. Of course, Justin was out like a light. Sometimes I hated the bastard. But, then again, he had a date with Jacques and I landed Marvin, so, for a change, I had won. That put me in a better mood. Well, that and the gin and tonic I concocted from our minifridge. I was thinking about installing one of those when I got home. Talk about convenience.

Once Justin awoke, we primped and preened, downed our pre-date cocktails, and chatted benignly until six. Then, Justin left to go meet Jacques and I waited, nervously, for Marvin. Thank God he was prompt. Not a trait characteristic of most gay men, I find, especially yours truly.

Marvin looked yummy and tasted even better.

"Mmm," he said, after planting a deep, long wet one on my eager lips. "I missed you." Always nice to hear, especially from a handsome man.

"Likewise," I responded, nibbling his ear.

"I have some good news for you," he said, returning the favor on my ear.

"I know. I feel it thumping against my thigh."

"No, not that, though that's for you as well," he said with a slight smirk. "I semi-found Mary."

Yikes. Again I had forgotten about that little detail. I think I may have burned off one too many brain cells in the past few years. Pretty soon, I'll be running completely off my fat cells. Not a wonderful thought, but at least I have

74

plenty of those. Hearing Marvin's words pushed me out of horny mode and right into reconnaissance mode. Though both, at that moment, consisted of me being rather rigid, you know where.

I jumped up. I shouted a glorious "Yippee!" I did a minor dance routine around Marvin. And then I realized exactly what he had said.

"What do you mean, *semi-found*?" I asked, ceasing my little jig and staring blankly at him.

"Ah, well, it seems that Mary, at the time of the taping, was visiting her daughter, and left her daughter's address with the folks at *Antiques Roadshow*. My friend remembers her very well. The daughter is quite the head turner. Apparently, she resembles someone famous. Anyway, here," he said, handing me a slip of paper.

"You mean he actually gave you the daughter's address?" I asked, surprised.

"Hmm, no, not exactly. Look at the address."

I did as he said. "Marvin, this says the name of this hotel. What's going on?"

"She works here. Actually, she's the star of the show. A sort of Vegas celebrity. Almost single-handedly keeps the night club here afloat."

"Let me guess," I guessed. "She's the Patsy Cline impersonator, right?"

"Oh, so you've seen her already?"

"Nope, but I've heard of her talents. Mind if we catch the show after dinner?"

"Hell, no. I love Patsy Cline. What gay man doesn't?"

I giggled. "Well, I know of one."

"They should take his card away."

"That's what I say, but this guy's a charter member."

We decided on dinner at a nice little Italian restaurant away from the Strip and away from the throngs of vacationing straight couples and families. Not an easy task, but there are still places hidden away that attract mostly locals. We sat in a booth in the back of the restaurant. It was dark and quiet, and the air was ripe with desire. Well, maybe I'm exaggerating, but there was certainly some chemistry going on.

We ordered a nice bottle of red wine, some tasty appetizers, and wonderfully prepared pasta. Everything was lovely, especially the company. The conversation centered mostly on our backgrounds: upbringing, education, past loves, past travel. You know, the usual first date mumbo jumbo. And with each passing minute, I was growing more and more fond of him. He was nice and easygoing and just plain old normal—something I rarely encountered back in San Francisco. I pictured a life ahead of us, mowing lawns and visiting art galleries. Ah, average suburban bliss.

The mood was helped by the fact that he was sexier than hell, that he had a well-paying steady job, that he seemed to like me, and that his hand was gently stroking my inner thigh. (Mostly that last stuff.) When he leaned in to kiss me, my heart was racing, my lungs were expanding and contracting wildly, my foot was tapping, my bladder was pushing down relentlessly on my groin...

"Would you excuse me, Marvin? I need to use the restroom," I said, excusing myself. Sometimes your body can be your worst enemy. Or your best friend. When I returned, and shuffled my behind back into our booth, I peered down and saw that Marvin had undone his fly and a rather large, rather turgid penis was pointing up at me.

"Dessert," he informed, noticing my wide eyes.

"Ah, low in fat, high in protein," I commented, reaching my hand over to gently stroke it, his flesh now pulsing in my sweaty grasp.

"I think I'll have the same," he said, indicating that I should follow suit.

And I cautiously and carefully did. Which was hard to do without calling attention to myself, as my own member was equally stiff. Luckily, my pants had a fly and not buttons, and I deftly removed it without too much fanfare. So we sat there stroking each other's man-meat and continued our conversation. If the waiter noticed, he never let on. Not that we cared by that point, anyway. I mean, once you have your prick out in a restaurant, you're usually beyond worrying if you'll get caught.

But when he reached across for the butter, that's when I started to get nervous. It was one thing to have a boner beneath the table. It was quite another thing to have it lubed up with pats of Land O' Lakes. Not that it was an unpleasant feeling, mind you. Actually, it felt considerably smoother than my usual bottle of Wet. Maybe there was a whole new market for the butter people to conquer, I thought. The ads could read "Great on any kind of meat, even your own." Still, I would've preferred to be doing it lying in a nice king-sized bed, with the lights down low, and some nice romantic music on the radio, not with busboys removing our dinner plates and silverware. Call me old-fashioned.

When he reached over again and applied some to his own thickening stiffy, I knew we had a problem.

"Um, can't this wait?" I suggested.

"It could, but we could always have a repeat later," he replied, his breath quickened and raspy. The logic was sound, though it lacked a certain romanticism I was hoping for.

"Okay, then, I'm ready when you are," I whispered, mere seconds away from... From...

And then we both shot. At least we did it together. That's sort of romantic, isn't it? Now the nasty part. Cleaning up a lap full of butter and cum isn't easy with your standard dinner napkin. But we managed. Then we threw our napkins to the ground and cleaned up the remaining "mess" using our shoes. Not exactly the afterglow I had expected from our first time.

"That was hot," he whispered into my ear.

"That was *something*," I replied, not exactly sure how I felt about it. But at least I wasn't horny anymore. That *was* something.

We paid our bill and made a hasty retreat before our little secret was discovered on the floor. I was picturing the waiter picking up our napkins from beneath the table, and in my mind I was singing that classic Parkay commercial, "If you think it's butter, but it's not..."

"Well, I've never done that before," I said as we got into his rental car.

"I know it would have been nicer alone and in bed, but I'd been thinking about you all day and I couldn't wait any longer. Do you know what it's like to be hard an entire day?"

Sadly, the answer to that was a resounding yes. Fortunately, he wanted the same thing I did, so I was starting to feel better about what we had just done. And at least he wanted me just as desperately as I wanted him. That's always nice to hear.

"Want to do it again? I have some margarine in the glove compartment," he said.

"Well—"

"Just joking. Now let's go hear some Patsy!"

"Okay, but if there's any whipped cream on our daiquiris, stay away from my lap."

We arrived back at my hotel just a few minutes before the show started.

"What the hell are you two doing here?" Justin asked, as Marvin and I grabbed two chairs and joined them.

"I have a surprise for you," I said, shushing him, as the emcee walked on stage.

"What is it?" he whispered in my ear.

"Wait, you'll see in just a bit."

"Does it involve Mary?"

"Wait," I repeated, and held up a finger to indicate that he'd see in just a minute.

"Ladies and gentlemen, please welcome to the stage the legendary Miss Patsy Cline," said the emcee, after a short welcome to the show.

And lo and behold, you would have sworn that it was actually Patsy. She came out in full Western gear, complete with leather tassels around her long skirt and cuffs, and pristine white cowboy boots that matched her smile. I had goose bumps as she made her way around the stage, waving at the huge group of people who had come to our pissant hotel to see her. Jacques was beaming with pride at his star performer. Justin looked less than enthused, but I was beyond thrilled. And then she started to sing. It was as if heaven had opened up its gates and the voice of Patsy was coming through this woman's mouth. I was, needless to say, flushed with bliss.

Justin leaned in and whispered, "I'll tell you what's *crazy*. Spending fifty bucks to see this show, that's what's crazy. Now tell me what the surprise is."

"Damn, you're a pain," I whispered back to him.

"Tell me. Tell me. Tell me. Where is Mary?"

I pointed to Patsy, who couldn't have sounded lovelier, and said, "There you go."

"That is not Mary, you dumbass. I saw Mary. Mary is old, dude. How much have you had to drink tonight? And why do you smell like Country Crock and cum?"

Jacques was looking at us impatiently as we continued to chat through the first song, but once you get Justin going there's just no stopping him.

"Okay, fine, if I tell you, will you shut up?" I asked, also wanting to hear the rest of the show in peace.

He nodded and crossed his heart. Which never meant that much to me, as he had very little of one to swear on.

"That, my dear friend, is Mary's daughter and the key to my vase."

"No foolin'?" he asked, looking at me, then over to Jacques, then back at me. "Well, now, I don't think it's gonna be too hard to get a personal introduction, do you?"

"Nope. Now let's enjoy the show."

"Whatever you say." He reached over to hold Jacques's hand. That turned his frown upside down and got us one teensy step closer to Mary.

The rest of the show was wonderful, but the show-stopper was Patsy Cline, yet again, singing "Walkin' After Midnight" and "I Fall to Pieces." The woman sounded like an angel. By the time she was done, I was seriously thinking of taking up the slide guitar and learning how to yodel. Too bad I have no musical talent. (Well, any talent, really.)

"That was amazing," I said to Jacques, when the show was over and the house lights had gone up.

"Yes, Jacques, thank you so much for *that*," Justin added, forcing a smile on his face.

Judging from the way his fingers were digging into his right leg throughout the show, I believe he was miserable from beginning to end. But since the other leg had his date's hand firmly planted on it, I figured he would end the evening on a happy note, so I wasn't feeling too guilty about forcing him on the date to begin with. Besides, it was for a good cause.

"You're all very welcome. It was my pleasure. Would you like to meet the star?" he asked, pushing all of us to the end of our seats in anticipation.

"Yes, please," I responded eagerly.

"Then follow me," he said, and walked us over to a door on the side of the stage.

Our little trio gladly followed. And, if you must know,

I was tickled pink about going backstage. Not just because we were meeting Mary's daughter, but also because I'd never been backstage before, anywhere. I felt so cool. So hip. Like those people who wear black Armani suits and sunglasses indoors. (Okay, I'm tragic. But I think we knew that already.)

Jacques knocked on the dressing-room door, the one with the star on it, just like in the movies, and announced, "It's Jacques. May we come in?"

A few moments later, the door opened and Patsy was standing before us in a robe. Her makeup was mostly gone and her hair was pinned up where the wig had once been. The aura had sadly gone with it. She was no longer the Patsy of my dreams. Without the makeup and clothes, she barely resembled the legend. Sadly, the thrill of backstage life was ebbing fast.

"Yes?" she asked, staring at Jacques and then the three of us.

"My friends would love to meet you. Would you mind a little company?" he asked.

"No sweat, sugar. Ya'll come on in." Well, she might not have looked like Patsy anymore, but she sure as shootin' sounded like her. My spirits were once again lifted.

"You were amazing, Miss Cline. What an incredible voice. Thank you so much," I gushed. Thank goodness it wasn't a Barbra or a Bette impersonator; I might have fainted dead away.

"Please, darlin', call me Honey. Miss Cline's been gone and buried for years now. But I surely thank you for the compliment. Where you boys from?"

"San Francisco," the three of us answered.

"Ah, I see," she said knowingly.

Justin leaned in to Jacques and whispered something in his ear. Then he leaned in to me and whispered, "I told him I had a headache and asked if he'd walk me to our room

81

for an aspirin. Once we're gone, you better find Mary." I nodded my head in agreement.

Jacques said to her, "If you'll excuse us, Honey, Justin and I have something to attend to."

"Oh, I'm sure you do, sugar," she said with a smirk, then added, "You're awfully handsome, Justin. You an entertainer?"

"You could say that," he said, and left the room with Jacques in tow.

"You boys care for a drink?" she asked Marvin and me, once we were alone.

"You got any sarsaparilla?" I asked, completely drowning in the whole Southern ambiance.

"Naw, darlin'. Just some good old Kentucky Bourbon. Will that do ya?"

"Is a coon's ass fuzzy?" I responded.

"Now, I wouldn't rightly know about that, sugar, but I'll take that as a yes." And she poured us each a healthy shot. "Well, fellers, if there's nothing else I can do for ya—"

"Actually," I interrupted, "there is."

She looked bewildered at first, but then, after I explained the whole story to her, she sat there grinning and nodding. I hoped that was a good sign.

"My, my, my. Now, that is a mighty interestin' story. Yessiree, Bob. Ma was sure surprised when that appraiser told her what that vase was worth. Poor thing nearly had a heart attack, but knew that wouldn't look too good in front of the TV, so she stayed calm until that camera feller said Cut. Boy howdy, then she started a-screamin'."

"So she still has the vase, then?" I asked.

"Oh, hell, no. She sold that thing the very next day." (See, I told you they all do that.) "Didn't get nearly what that appraiser said she would, though. Still, for a few bucks' investment, she did pretty damn good. Excuse my French. I'm sure sorry for you, Em."

"Well, it's not your fault. Do you mind me asking what she got for it?" I asked, crestfallen that I had been so close to finding it.

"Let's see now. I believe it was something like fifteen thousand dollars. Ma's on the social security and all, so that money was a godsend. She bought a new rocker first thing. Just sits on her front porch a-rockin' and a-grinnin'. Bless her heart."

"Could you tell me who she sold it to?" I asked, praying that she at least knew that much.

"Sorry, sugar, sure can't. I wasn't with her at the time. But tell you what, I'm going to visit her tomorrow morning. She only just lives about an hour from here. You fellers are more than welcome to keep me company on the ride over there, and then me and Ma can take you to the place she sold it at. I'm sure she'd be happy to help. Probably fix you a good home-cooked meal to boot. How's that sound?"

"Well, ma'am, I'd say that sounds like a good plan. Mighty obliged to you for your help," I answered, still with a Southern twang of my own, which was highly persistent. Once I started using it, I couldn't stop.

"Not me, ma'am, thanks," Marvin said. "I still have work to do while I'm here."

That made me sad, as I was fast becoming attached to him, even with the butter incident and all. But, then again, I did have a date with Chris the next day; meaning a little distance might do me some good.

We said our goodbyes to Honey. I gave her our hotel room number and told her that Justin and I would be ready for her when she got there. And then Marvin and I exited, stage left. I'd always wanted to do that.

I have to say, I was disappointed that my vase was now in someone else's hands, but at least we were still hot on the trail. That was better than nothing. And a trip outside

Vegas sounded exciting, seeing as I'd never been anywhere else in Nevada before.

"Now what?" I asked Marvin as we stood in the hotel lobby.

"Now you come back to my hotel and we do it right," he answered.

"No butter, no waiter, no booth?"

"No, no, and no. Just me, my bed, and some good old-fashioned spit. How's that sound?"

"Less fattening, that's for sure."

"As if you had anything to worry about."

"You're fast becoming one of my favorite people, Marvin. Let's go. By the way, what hotel are you staying at?"

"The Bellagio."

"Make that my all-time favorite person."

I've Been Through the Desert on a Horse with No Name

THE NEXT MORNING I AWOKE FEELING OH SO RELAXED, and sped back to my hotel, wanting to make sure that I got there in plenty of time to hook up with Honey. I'd left a message with Justin the night before and told him of the forthcoming adventure in the Nevada wilderness, praying that he received it and that he'd be capable of getting up at such an early hour. Odds were against me, which is why I forced myself to leave Marvin's side even sooner than I had to. Not an enjoyable thing to do. I hadn't spooned like that in ages.

But I did have my priorities in order, for a change. And Marvin understood completely. Still, it was hard to leave him, his king-sized bed, the lack of malodorous fumes, and go back to our fishbowl. Oh, and don't worry, I'll fill you in on the Bellagio later. Talk about fabulous.

I arrived back at the Atlantis with a good half hour to spare. (So naturally I played the slots for ten minutes.) When

I arrived at our room, I knocked on the door and waited, just in case. I had no desire to catch Justin and Jacques *in flagrante delicto*. (Look it up.)

"Come in," came a strange voice from behind the door.

"Oh, my God," I managed, surprised at whom I found there.

"Oh, hi," said Justin, emerging from the bathroom, newly washed. "You remember Ahmed, right?"

"Yes, nice to see you again, Ahmed," I said, shaking his hand, and my head, in disbelief.

"Don't worry, Ahmed was just leaving and I'll be ready in ten minutes," he said, throwing me a sly wink.

"No sweat," I replied, plopping down on my bed and inhaling the familiar ghastly chlorine stench.

"Very stinky," Ahmed said to me, waving his hand in front of his face.

"Very," I agreed.

A few minutes later, he was kissing Justin goodbye and leaving—looking considerably less exotic without his silk slacks, but still yummy, nonetheless.

"Poor, poor, Jacques," I lamented, once we were alone.

"Poor Jacques, nothing. This was not my doing."

"Come on, who are you trying to kid?"

"No, really. Jacques and I did come back here last night after we left you, but when we got to the door Ahmed was waiting for me. I had told him what hotel we were staying at, and he knows someone who works here, and he got our room number. Needless to say, Jacques was not amused when we arrived and Ahmed threw his arms around me like we were long-lost lovers. He stormed off in a huff, and I was left with Ahmed."

"And, naturally, you didn't want to look a gift horse in the mouth."

"Naturally. And speaking of horses, you should have seen the size of his—"

"Never mind, Honey will be here in a second. Just get dressed."

A few minutes later, Honey came a-knockin'. She was dressed in Western-style jeans, a cowboy shirt, and a nifty pair of boots.

"Come on in, Honey," I said. "We're ready to go."

"Phewee," she sang, "What is that awful smell?" The ritual awful-smell-hand-wave soon followed.

We were getting used to the reaction, and did our pool-point, in unison.

"You should get some flowers in here or something, boys," she suggested. "That smell is plumb awful."

"You get used to it," Justin lamented, and, sadly, I nodded my agreement.

"Okeydokey, then. But you fellers are gonna have to change before we go. Those there ain't no ridin' clothes."

"Excuse me?" I said. "What do you mean, *ridin' clothes*?"

"You know, ridin' clothes. Those shorts and sneakers ain't gonna work on the horses," she explained, much to our city-boy chagrin. "Didn't I mention that yesterday? Ma lives out on her ranch in the desert. If we drive, it'll take something like three hours to get there, and most of the roads are dirt. The horses will get us there in a jiff. Besides, some of that clean desert air will do you boys some good." There went that hand wave again. Anyway, by that point, my lungs probably would've gone into shock if they came into contact with fresh air. A few more weeks in our room and I may have even grown a nifty pair of gills.

Justin looked less than happy at the thought of a horsey ride, and said, "Well, you know, Honey, we're in no rush. What's a few hours, right? The car is fine with us."

"Nonsense, the ride over there is beautiful, and I got two extra-gentle horses for you fellers. Ain't no way we're gonna drive. So get your long jeans on and some comfortable boots, and let's get a move on. Ma's a-waitin'."

How can you argue with that? So we obeyed and got appropriately dressed. I was beginning to wonder if the whole vase thing was worth it. I hadn't been on a horse since I was a child, and for all I knew, Justin had never been on one. My thighs were chafing in anticipation of the journey that lay ahead of us.

Minutes later, we were in Honey's pickup truck and on our way to a horse farm just outside the city. The look of dread on our boyish faces said it all. This was not how we expected to spend the day. And when we arrived at the farm, my stomach sank even further. I kept trying to tell myself that everything would be okay. Look, if a young Miss Elizabeth Taylor could ride that big Black Beauty, then I could certainly ride for an hour through the desert. I kept telling myself that, but it wasn't sinking in.

When we arrived, Honey parked the truck just outside the farm, as vehicles were not allowed in. Then we hopped a ditch and walked over to the stables. (And I thought our room stank. Damn, it was funky in there.) Then we met our horses. Mine was on the small side, thankfully, and was white with gray spotting. She was cute and nonthreatening-looking. My fears were, for the time being, allayed. Justin had a fine old stallion. He was big and brown and glorious-looking. Funny how our horses matched us to a tee. Honey assured us that both were fairly old and had very little fight left in them, so we had nothing to worry about. But, in my experience, it's always the quiet ones that you do indeed need to worry about.

Honey introduced me to my horse first. "Em, this here is No Name. They call her that because she doesn't answer to anything else. Kinda stubborn, she is. But gentle as can be. Hop on and let's see how you look up there."

Okay, that sounded easy enough. I put my foot in the stirrup, heaved myself up, and threw my leg on over. "Look at me," I shouted, "I'm Gene Autry!"

"More like Dale Evans," Justin said, mounting his horse, Lancelot.

"Now, boys, you be nice," admonished Honey. I felt all of eight years old again.

Honey spent a rather short few minutes giving us directions on how to ride. I nodded, but nothing was sinking in. From the ground, No Name was a beautiful, gentle mare. From eight feet up, she was a weapon of mass destruction. My mass, that is. But I held my tongue and, before I knew it, we were off. Honey, on a gorgeous white stud—oh, I should be so lucky—took the lead, and our horses followed. I held on to the reins for dear life and allowed myself to be carried away. Not much else I could do, really.

It wasn't long before the Vegas we had grown accustomed to receded in the distance and we were surrounded by mostly desert. It was more beautiful than I had expected: very serene, with patches of color here and there, and peacefully quiet, except for the sound of our horses clomping along the narrow trails. My earlier apprehensions had abated and I started to release the white-knuckle grip that I had on the reins. Justin too looked decidedly at ease—which I assumed meant that he popped a pretty blue pill sometime before we trotted off. Either way, it truly was relaxing getting back to nature. That is, however, until nature started getting back at us.

We were happily riding along, with Honey serenading us along the way, when No Name was stung by something. I can only assume that's what happened because, out of nowhere, she let out a horrible whinny and took off like lightning. Honey's crash course in riding hadn't prepared me for a crazy mare. All I could do was hold on for dear life as she hurtled past the shrubs, over small boulders, and around an occasional tree, all the while causing me to get whacked by passing branches and the intermittent limb. Ouch! All the hysterical pulling on the reins and all the shouting of

"Whoa, girl" was having no effect. It was like talking to a top who was hell-bent on ass, when all you wanted to do was lie there and cuddle. In other words, "Whoa, girl" was blatantly ignored and I was offered a painful pounding instead. That's when I noticed the cliff up ahead.

I know, I know. You think that stuff only happens in movies, but cliffs spring up in real life, too. This wasn't a major precipice hanging over a vast expanse of nothingness, mind you—it was more like a ledge over a big gully—but still, major bodily damage was fast approaching. And jumping off was out of the question. I certainly wasn't that brave. Instead, I prayed that No Name would notice *no ground* up ahead, and would stop of her own accord. Unfortunately, she showed no signs of slowing down as we rapidly approached the ravine. Twenty feet quickly became fifteen; fifteen became ten; ten became five. I shut my eyes, held on as tight as I could, and prepared myself for the inevitable. If I had had much of a life to flash before my eyes, I'm sure I would've seen it at that point.

Surprisingly, at the time I should've been hurtling over the edge, I was still galloping gaily forward. Out of curiosity, I peeked out of my left eye to see why I wasn't dead or dying. I was stunned to see my horse running parallel to the edge, instead of over it; and right next to us was Justin, acting as a barrier.

When he saw me open my eyes, he shouted, "Having fun yet?"

I shook my head a vigorous no and shouted back to him, "Stop the ride. I want to get off!"

He smiled and slowly veered Lancelot in front of No Name, causing her to eventually slow down and come to a stop, breathless and exhausted. (Her and me both.)

When I had recovered my senses, I slid off my horse and back onto the steady ground. Justin followed suit and sat next to me, draping his arm over my shoulder.

"Have you been taking stunt riding lessons behind my back?" I asked, head in hands, still shaking.

"Just one of the many perks of wealth, sweetie. Horse-back riding classes at age eight; first pony at age nine; first blue ribbon at age ten. Haven't you seen the trophies in my apartment?"

"I thought they were props. You know: there to impress."

"Nope. I can rope a bull too."

"Really?"

"Nope. See, *that* was an attempt to impress. Don't worry, you'll get it eventually."

But what I wanted to get, at that moment, was a drink and a good mile or two away from my horse. I'd had enough fresh air for the day. What I needed was some noxious fumes. I would have gladly given a good chunk of my money for one of those smelly cabs right about then. That, sadly, was not what Honey had in mind for me.

She came galloping up a short while later, looking worried as could be. I almost felt sorry for her, until I remembered that she was the one who put me on the damn thing in the first place. "You boys okay?" she asked, jumping off her horse and running over to us.

We both nodded a yes, though I had my doubts.

"That was some slick ridin' there, Justin. You plumb saved your friend's life, more than likely. Not to mention my horse's." She breathed a sigh of relief. I assumed that it was for me and not the horse. Least I hoped as much. "Well, now, just as soon as you're able to get on up there, Em, I think we should get a move on to Ma's. It's about to get purty darn hot out here."

"No, thanks," I responded. "I'll just wait here for the vultures. You two go on without me."

"Nonsense, you know what they say," she said.

"Those who turn and run away, live to fight another day?" I answered, defeatedly.

91

"Hell, no," She shouted, "When you fall off a horse, you need to get right back on."

"But I didn't fall off a horse," I tried to explain.

"It's an expression, Em," she explained back to me. "It just so happens we're actually dealin' with a horse in this case. It means you gotta pick yourself up, dust yourself off, and get your ass right back on that there horse, or you'll be a-scared for the rest of your life."

"Why should I stop being *a-scared* now?" I wondered aloud, as it certainly had gotten me this far. But Honey and Justin were already helping me back on my feet and into the stirrups.

This time Honey rode along to the right side of me, holding both our reins in her hand. My foray into horsemanship was over. If we hadn't been in the middle of nowhere and in near-hundred-degree heat, I probably would have taken my chances and walked. Justin, my unlikely hero, rode along to my left. Though still uneasy, I at least felt safer closed in like that. The passing scenery no longer interested me. I just wanted to get to the ranch and find out where my vase was.

Thankfully, there wasn't much of a ride left. We rode up to the ranch not twenty minutes later. Actually, calling it a ranch may have been pushing it. Hovel seemed a better term. Maybe even shack. If this is what social security was paying for these days, I planned on never getting old. The only redeeming qualities of the place were the surrounding landscape, which was breathtaking, and the satellite TV dish in the front yard. At least Ma wasn't living in the Stone Age. Actually, it looked more as if she was hiding out. Images of Butch Cassidy and his infamous Wild Bunch gang flashed though my head.

We rode up to a small barn in back and parked the horses. I was thrilled to be off No Name, and smacked her in the ass for good measure before I ran to the house (hut, cabin, lean-to—whatever, but it was no ranch). Maybe they had taxi service out there, I prayed, as I had absolutely no desire, or will power, to get back on that horse. I figured that if Ma had a TV and a well-stocked bar, I could just live out my days with her. I kept looking for one of those rugged handymen you always see in the movies to come around the corner. Then the scenario would've been perfect. However, I was not so fortunate. Mary herself came around the corner to greet us.

"Howdy, ya'll," she said, all smiling and waving. Funny, I felt like we were already old friends. She looked exactly as she had on television, except that she was dressed more countrified now.

"Ma, this here's them fellers I was telling you about. This is Justin and this is Em," Honey said, introducing us to my only hope of recovering the vase.

"My, my, that's a strange name your parents gave ya, but it's sure nice seeing you handsome fellers. Don't get much company around these parts, besides my daughter here."

I didn't have the energy to explain that it wasn't my real name, because people always want to know how I got the nickname, and we all know how long a story that must be, right? Instead, I shook her hand and gave her a howdy in return. Justin did the same, and then we were heartily welcomed into her home.

The inside was not as rugged in appearance as the outside. It was cozy and quaint and very warm and inviting. It was sort of like being in a gay Country-Western bar, minus the dancing queens. Mary offered us some homemade lemonade and cookies, which we gratefully accepted. Then she gave us a quick tour of the place, which was really quick seeing as the place was itty-bitty. And last, but not least, we were shown her brand-new television that came with that dish that we saw outside. That we could thank my grandma for. Seems it wasn't only a rocker Mary bought with the fifteen thousand dollars she received.

I was almost angry with her as we stood there admiring it, knowing how it would have upset my grandmother, but I just couldn't make myself feel that way. Mary looked so happy and motherly standing there stroking the damn thing as if it was a favorite pet (really, the woman was sweet as a bee's ass) that all I could do was congratulate her on her good fortune and munch on her fabulous homemade cookies.

"Well, Em, I guess I have you to thank for this. I'm terribly sorry about the circumstances surrounding it, though. I wish we could have found each other sooner," Mary said, turning away from the television and offering us a seat.

"Me too, ma'am, but it certainly wasn't your fault, and I'm glad my grandma's vase has afforded you so much happiness. It's not doing too much for me right now," I replied.

"You know, I was visiting my sister that weekend when we were at the garage sale and found your vase. Honestly, I had no idea it was so valuable. When you think about it, why would anyone sell a vase for a few dollars when it really costs tens of thousands, right?" (You'd have thunk so.) "The real reason I brought it in to the Antiques Roadshow was because you have to bring something with you to get in, and your vase was the only thing I had that looked like it could be worth something," she explained, apologetically, wiping away any lingering feelings of hatred I had for her. Looking around her home, I could see she was being honest. Besides the TV, there was nothing of any substantial value there.

"It's okay, Mary. Thanks for your honesty. At least we know where the vase is now, right?" I asked, attempting a smile.

She looked warily at Honey, and then back to me, before she answered. A large and terrifying UH-OH popped into my brain. "Er, yes, we sure do know that, Em, darlin'."

"Buuuut?" I butted, knowing there was one a-comin'.

"But, sugar, it seems like the whole town found out about

Ma and that vase just after she sold it." Honey paused, biting her lip.

"Aaaand?" I anded, afraid of what she had to add.

"And," she continued, "Ma told me last night over the phone that Mr. Hartwell, the man that bought the vase from her, also found out about how it was on the show and all."

"Uh-oh," I uh-ohed, figuring out where she was going with the story.

Justin said, warily, "I bet the vase is no longer worth fifteen thousand, right?"

"No, sir," said Mary.

"Not thirty, either. Am I correct?" asked Justin.

"Keep goin'," said Honey.

"I'm not liking this game anymore," I interjected.

"Sorry, sugar," Mary said, patting my hand. Then she told me the actual cost. "You see, your vase probably should be worth thirty thousand, just like that appraiser person said. But once somethin' is on *Antiques Roadshow*, the price usually goes up. Seems people have a hankerin' for items that appear on the show. Mr. Hartwell is now askin' forty-five thousand dollars for it. Has it proudly displayed in his store window with a sign that reads: 'As Seen on *Antiques Roadshow*.' Apparently it's been gettin' a lot of attention there."

"Apparently," I moaned, remembering my suitcase with the mere thirty thousand in it.

"Well, then, I guess that's that," I conceded.

"That's what?" Justin asked.

"That's someone else's vase now. Remember, I don't have forty-five thousand dollars," I reminded him.

"Nonsense," he said, slapping my arm. "All you need is another fifteen thousand. We are in Vegas, after all; and I, for one, am not ready to throw in the towel."

Man, he seemed so self-assured, so eager, so raring to go, that I had to sit there and reevaluate my next step. On the one hand, that was a lot of money to raise. But I had come into the thirty thousand pretty easily—what was another fifteen? Also, Marvin had two more days left at the convention, and I did want to stay at least that long. Oh, and let's not forget about Chris. And I would miss my slots if I left. So, the more I thought about it—

"Okay, we'll stay!" I shouted, jumping out of my chair. "What the hey. Not like I have a job to go back to."

"That's the spirit," Mary said. "Now let's at least go see Mr. Hartwell. Might as well let him know of your intentions."

"Might as well," I agreed.

Thank God Mary had a car hidden behind the barn. The thought of getting back on my old horse was more than I could bear. Mary drove a '76 Pinto: another old horse. Once we got in and were under way, I began to think that the horses might have been a better idea. The Pinto kicked and groaned and sputtered way more than No Name. My poor kidneys might never be the same again. (Shudder to think.) Between the road, what there was of it, and the car, what there was of it, and Mary's driving, also not so hot, it took nearly a half an hour to reach Mr. Hartwell's store—and we only had to go fifteen miles.

I was amazed to see that Mary had quite a few neighbors. It seemed that her cabin was on the edge of a quaint little town, littered with diminutive cabins, like Mary's, and a small number of businesses: a grocery store, a gas station/mechanic, a couple of restaurants run out of people's homes, and, lastly, an antique store. Namely Mr. Hartwell's: Old But Not Forgotten—which was an apt description of Mr. Hartwell himself.

First thing we saw, as we exited Mary's jalopy, was grandma's vase, staring achingly at us through the window of the store. My stomach twisted, my heart sank, my brain fizzled. Let's face it, I was a mess. I felt so helpless and depressed seeing it there, painfully out of reach and out of place in the ancient store window, that I wanted to cry. And then I wanted to turn and run back home. Actually, I wanted to hurl a brick through the window and run off with the damn thing, but, alas, there were no bricks in sight, just tiny pebbles and small rocks. Not enough to do much damage. So I gave in to my fate, and Justin and I followed Mary and Honey into the store. The four of us in there made us maximum capacity.

Mr. Hartwell came tottering out of his back office to greet us. Seeing as he looked a few years older than most of his relics, I'd say he was the original owner of most of them.

"Well, howdy there, folks. What can I do you for?" he asked, sounding a tad like Jed Clampett.

Mary and Honey took turns explaining the story to him. I no longer had the energy. And when they were done, he stood there and nodded.

Then he wheezed, "Well, now, you see, that there vase has been attracting quite a bit of attention. Word's been getting around about it, don't you know. So I'm afraid I couldn't let it go for less than the asking price of forty-five thousand dollars. Sorry, young feller, but I'm a businessman."

Judging from the merchandise and the piles of dust sitting upon it all, I'm not sure how good a businessman Mr. Hartwell actually was. My guess was that he lived off his social security more than his sales, and that he was eager to make a grand deal off my vase and then probably retire. The fifteen thousand he gave Mary was likely his life savings. Maybe he knew his business better than I thought; it looked like everyone was getting something from that vase but me.

"Tell you what I'll do," he continued. "As soon as anyone makes me an offer of forty-five thousand, I'll call you fellers and give you one last shot to come in and buy it from me. How's that sound?"

Sounded like crap. Sounded God-awful. Sounded like... Like... Well, it sounded like I had very little time to go raise fifteen thousand dollars. So I said, "Thank you, Mr. Hartwell. That's very kind of you."

I wrote my name, our hotel name, and our phone number on a piece of paper and handed it to him. At least there was still a chance, however slim. And with that, we left Mr. Hartwell, his raggedy store, and my dear, beloved vase behind. (How very, very sad.) Then we piled back into Mary's heap and crept on home.

"At least he was nice enough to do that for me," I said, glumly.

To which Mary replied, "Don't count on it, Em. That man ain't got a nice bone in his whole darn body. Oh, sure as shootin' he'll call you, but only to jack up the price. He just about owns the entire town. Don't you let that rickety old shop fool you, son. He's rich as Rockefeller and twice as sneaky."

Well, I sure was fooled. So much for his retiring off my vase. Now I was faced with having to finagle even more money than before, it seemed, to beat the next offer. I was royally screwed, without the usual sticky benefits. And, to add insult to injury, I still had the horse ride ahead of me to get back to our hotel. I must have really fucked up my karma in a past life to earn this kind of punishment in this one—something akin to drop-kicking kittens, I'd surmise.

After our car trip back to Mary's, we were offered sandwiches and iced tea, which we gladly accepted. Then we thanked Mary for all her help and jumped back on our vile horses. And to think, a week earlier I'd been happily straddling my comfortable chair at work. Now look at me. Just goes to show you, anything can happen and frequently will. Luckily, the horses were subdued for the return trek, and we could sit back and enjoy the scenery once again. I let my mind go blank (no hard stretch there), as I didn't want to contemplate how I was going to come up with all that money. I would utilize Justin's devious brain for that. Meantime, I whistled a happy tune and counted the cacti.

After our grueling hour-long ride back, we piled into Honey's truck and headed for our hotel. When we arrived we thanked her for all her help.

"No problem, fellers. Anything else I can do, just ask," she replied.

"We will, thanks," Justin said as we waved our good-byes and hobbled our way into the hotel.

But just before we made it inside, Justin tapped my shoulder and whispered, "Look over there."

"God damn it, you know how I hate that game. Just tell me what it is you want me to see," I whispered back to him, irritably.

"Don't look now, but that black Mercedes is in the parking lot again, and those same two guys are sitting inside," he said.

"First you say look, then you say don't look. Make up your mind," I replied, looking anyway.

And, sure enough, there really was a black Mercedes with two creepy-looking guys in it, sitting there, staring at us. I had chills from top to bottom.

"Holy cow," I whispered as we hurried into the hotel. "That is weird. Why would they be sitting out there like that?"

"Beats me. Anyway, I'm sure it's a coincidence. They're probably just waiting for someone to come out. Besides, we have enough to worry about now without letting our imaginations get the best of us," he rationalized.

"Fuck!" I rationalized back. "Why us, dear God, why?"

But we were both too exhausted to start pondering that, and decided to risk our health and take a long nap. It had been an exhausting day, and maybe a good rest would set our mind juices flowing so we could figure out how to raise all that cash. Of course, the thought of my date with Chris set other juices flowing, and kept my mind off the vase and the mysterious black car. Oh, well, judging from the lack of customers in Mr. Hartwell's shop, I assumed I had plenty of time to come up with the money; and the two men didn't look all that menacing, really. (I know. I didn't believe it either.)

We awoke to the pungent odor of chlorine and the racket of screaming children playing out by the pool, but at least we were refreshed after our long morning's journey. So, we decided to raid the minibar and watch some TV before my date with Chris. Our immediate problems could wait. Remember our motto: Why do something today when you can put it off until tomorrow? Words to live by.

I reached over and grabbed the remote and started flicking through the channels.

"Oh, A&E. Let's watch *Biography*," I said, watching scenes from Jane Fonda's life pass before us. *Barbarella* is too fabulous, especially that lovely angel man.

"Nope," replied Justin, "too political." I assumed he meant Jane, not the show.

"Oh, oh, MTV," I said as another repeat of the MTV Video Music Awards flashed on the screen. Whatever happened to music videos? I see they get awards, but I never catch them on MTV anymore. That's what you call i-ron-y.

"Too straight," Justin said, and I couldn't agree more, so I did some more channel surfing.

"Hey, Lifetime! *The Golden Gir*—"

"PASS!"

"That leaves the news, then," I said, pausing briefly to wait for a negative response.

Instead, when I turned to look over at Justin, he was gazing intently at the screen. Seeing as he never, ever watched the news, or anything remotely educational, I knew it must have been something dramatically earth-shattering, so I turned to watch as well.

"Holy shit!" I screamed, and jumped off the bed. "That's Mr. Hartwell's store!"

I turned up the volume and we raced to the foot of our beds to see what had happened: there was a huge, gaping hole in the storefront, and my vase was noticeably missing. My stomach sank to the ground. Then the newscaster came on and told us the story. It was horrifying and short. Mr. Hartwell had been shot and died on the way to the hospital. Apparently, all that had been stolen was an antique vase that had recently been on the PBS series *Antiques Roadshow*. No word yet on any suspects, but it seemed that it had been a robbery gone sour.

"Poor Mr. Hartwell," I said. I was near tears.

"Poor us. Now how are we going to find that vase?" said Justin, less overcome by Mr. Hartwell's death than myself. Though I hated to admit it, that was the thought going through my mind as well.

Just then, the phone rang. We both jumped.

"Em, have you seen the news yet?" It was Honey, and she sounded flustered.

"Yes, Honey, we're watching it now. Do you know anything else that they haven't mentioned?" I asked her.

"Not really. I just got off the phone with Ma. She said that no one saw anything. But that's not surprisin'. In the middle of the day, no one leaves their homes in them parts. Too hot. So the police have no suspects, and the only motive is your vase."

Hearing it said out loud like that did make me cry. Now I had no options. No way to find the vase. No way to get it back to my mother. Honey, hearing my whimper, assumed I was crying for Mr. Hartwell.

"Sugar, don't you cry none. That old man didn't have

too much longer on this planet anyway. He must've been nearly ninety. And I hope the good Lord doesn't strike me dead for sayin' this, but he was a cantankerous old coot. Didn't have nearly a friend in the world and no family to speak of. I suspect most of the town will be celebratin' his death more than mournin' it. The man owned practically everyone's homes and businesses, and he let you know it every second you were with him. So you just stop your cryin'. The police will find the man that did this, and then you'll have your vase back."

That did stop my crying and got my mind reeling. Now how long would we be in Vegas? Should we wait here for them to catch the thief or should we go back to San Francisco and wait? What if they did find the thief and my vase? Then what? Would I be able to get it back from the police? Should we be scared for our own lives, seeing as we were connected to the vase as well? Or was it a random act of violence? Or maybe it was one of the townsfolk? If everyone really hated Mr. Hartwell like Honey said, it could have been one of them. Certainly everyone there knew how valuable the vase was. My head was full of questions that I had no answers to.

"You there, Em?" Honey asked, concerned by the long pause.

"Oh, sorry, Honey, yes, I'm still here. Please let me know if you hear anything else, okay?"

"Okay, sugar. Don't you worry. The Las Vegas police are a good bunch. They'll have your vase back in no time, and that murderin' thief will be behind bars. And if I hear anything, anything at all, I'll give you boys a ring. Bye for now." Click.

My heart was racing and my hands were trembling. I even had a hard time holding on to the drink that Justin had prepared for me.

"Now what?" I asked.

"Now we wait. It's too soon to go home. Let's give it a week. If they find the person before then, we'll go down and claim the vase. Do you have pictures of it in your grandmother's house?" Justin asked.

"Yes, why?"

"Because then we can show it to the police to prove that it was yours. If Mr. Hartwell really did have no family, they'd probably give you the vase back. At least I would think so, anyway."

"Oh, okay. I'll call my brother and have him go through the family albums. I'm sure the vase is in there, somewhere."

"Then we wait it out. In a week, if no thief, we go home. Fair enough?"

"Why not? At least here I'm getting laid."

"There you go. That's the way to be, Em. Always look on the bright side."

And since the bright side was due to arrive in about half an hour, I had to hurry up to shower and get ready. Between the morning's expedition and the afternoon's robbery and murder, I surely needed my date with Chris to lighten my load, so to speak.

He arrived right on time, looking sexy as ever, with a single red rose in his hand. Not exactly the bouquet I received from Marvin, but just as sweet. (Well, maybe not *just* as.) Without delay, he placed a warm, tender kiss on my lips and gave me a great big bear hug. It felt wonderful. He felt wonderful. My cares were melting away. Aahhh.

"Get a room," said Justin, from his bed.

"Got one. Why don't you go get ready in the bathroom," I replied, not letting go of Chris for a second.

"Nah, I think I'll stay for the show," he replied.

Chris rescued the conversation. "Never mind. We were just leaving, anyway. I have dinner reservations for us, and we need to get a move on."

"You do?" I asked, glad to hear that I was being pampered for a change.

He nodded a yes, then added, "Man, what is that stink?"

Should have seen that one coming. We answered with the requisite pool-point and he nodded that he understood. Funny, we had gotten used to the smell already. But the sound of screaming children you never get used to. It's like a dagger plunged into your chest, repeatedly.

"What are you going to do tonight, dear one?" I asked Justin as we opened the door to leave.

"It's a surprise," he answered.

"A good surprise or a bad surprise?" I asked, pausing at the door, afraid of the answer. Experience had taught me well never to trust Justin's surprises.

"Oh, sweetie, they're all good." But before I could interject, he added, "Check at the front desk for a message from me before you come back up to the room, whenever that may be." I blushed, knowing what he was getting at. Odds were good that I'd be waking up at Chris's. Too bad you can't bet on things like that in Vegas. I might have actually won some money then.

We left for our date. In Chris's Honda, on the way, I filled him in on the details of the past couple of days, excluding the whole Marvin episode. Why spoil a good thing? Chris was extremely understanding and nurturing. He told me that everything would be okay. He rubbed my neck when I got tense at the recounting. He said that he'd be there for me when and if I needed him. Basically, he was saying all the right things. Did this make me feel good? Hmm, good question. Yes and no. I mean, it was nice to hear all those things, but I felt instantly guilty. Chris was wonderful, yet I was seeing Marvin behind his back. Plus, I felt guilty for Marvin as well, seeing Chris behind *his* back. Oh, what a tangled web we weave when we sleep with two dudes at once. That, coupled with the vase crap, made me feel decidedly on edge. What I needed was—

"Care for a drink before we head on out to dinner?" Chris asked. (Bingo!)

Luckily, there was a gay bar along the way to wherever it was he was taking me. On a side note, there aren't all that many gay bars in Vegas; most are small and a fair distance from the Strip. There's a gay disco or two, but if you're going to Vegas to revel in your homosexuality, don't bother. The bars and the scene, for the most part, are fairly unremarkable. Go to gamble and see the sights. If you want queer, go to San Francisco or New York or Atlanta or any other major city, not Vegas. Now, the bar we stopped in, Slots, was no exception to this rule. It was small, slightly run-down, and tired. It appeared to be filled with mostly locals, as you can always pick out a tourist in a crowd. I suggested we make it a quick drink, and Chris happily agreed.

We both ordered a gin and tonic. Always a good sign when your date orders the same drink as you. It was strong, which is just what I needed. My nerves were frazzled. But, at least in a gay bar, we could be openly affectionate. And between the drink and his nuzzling my neck, I was starting to feel much better.

(Are you waiting for another bomb to drop? Damn, you are perceptive. Here goes...)

"Shit, there's that asshole, Brad," Chris mumbled, looking down at his drink. "Don't look up."

Come on. Never say *don't look up* if you don't want someone to look up. Naturally, I looked.

The man I wasn't supposed to be staring at appeared vaguely familiar. Sort of like, like—

"Did you say Brad?" I asked. "As in Bradley?"

"Yeah, why? Do you know him?" he asked me.

"No, I semi-know *of* him, but I don't know him. Never met him before. He's Caesar, right?" I asked, my heart racing again for the umpteenth time that day.

"God, yes. Something he never lets you forget. Around the casinos, that's what you call a Prized Part. What a jerk. Damn, he's coming this way," Chris cursed, and set his drink down.

"Chrissy Chris, how good it is to see you," Bradley gushed, fake as a rhinestone. "It's simply been ages. Where have you been hiding?"

"You know, work and all. Keeps you busy. Not too much extra time for the *finer things* in life," Chris said, his hand motioning around the bar.

"Oh, this place, yes, rather dreary, I agree. But the spirits pack a punch and the men can sometimes be moderately passable. Ooh, and speaking of passable..." He turned to me and ogled. Cree-eepy. "Who is this divine creature?"

He reminded me of someone, but I couldn't yet put my finger on it.

"Brad, Em. Em, Brad," Chris introduced us.

He shook my hand in his mighty Roman emperor death grip and lingered too long for my liking, looking deep into my eyes the entire time. He obviously thought of himself as a smooth operator. But to me, he was slimy. It was easy to see why Chris wanted to avoid him. Mind you, he was devastatingly handsome, so I'm sure this act of his got him far in the bars around Vegas. I, however, could not be charmed. After all, I had spent my whole adult life with Justin. And compared to him, Bradley was... Bradley was... Then it became obvious who Bradley reminded me of. He was exactly like Justin! I could feel the heavens tearing apart at the thought that there were two Justins out there—and they were within five miles of each other. Talk about concentrated evil.

"Em, it's a pleasure to meet you," he oozed, then asked, "Have we met before? I would never forget such a pretty face."

106

I shuddered, then replied, "No, I don't think so. Though I did catch your act yesterday at Caesar's."

He paused when I said that, looked me over closely one more time, then shook his head no.

"Nope, I'd remember *you*."

I didn't exactly believe him. I had the feeling he did indeed recognize me. Something about the way he paused before he said *nope*. But I didn't want to push it. I knew Justin wanted me to drop it, so I dropped it. My life was in enough turmoil as it was.

"You obviously don't live around here, Em. I'd have noticed you for sure. Where are you staying?"

"The Atlanti—"

"Well, Brad, it was great seeing you," Chris interjected, downing his drink in one fell swoop, "but Em and I have dinner reservations and we have to get going."

"Oh, okay, then, it was a delight to see you, Chris. Don't be a stranger. And Em, always a rare pleasure to meet such a handsome man around these parts. Perhaps we will meet again."

"Perhaps," I echoed, and downed my drink as well. I was anxious to leave.

We practically ran out of there and away from Bradley.

"Wow, you must really hate him," I said as we got back into Chris's car.

"Hate? I detest that man. He is vile. He is loathsome. He is despicable and evil and boorish. He is... He is..."

"He's Justin," I finished.

He paused, pondered it for a second, then said, "I can see the resemblance, yes. But Justin is less, er, more, well, Justin is...Justin. He pulls it off better, I guess. But now that you mention it, there were times I couldn't stand him either."

"Ditto," I agreed, then told him how I knew Brad/Bradley.

"Whew," he whistled when I was done. "That is a whopper of a tale. Sort of sad, really. Maybe neither one of them ever got over their forced separation and that's why they are the way they are. Seems a likely explanation for their egomaniacal similarities."

"That, or their mothers were both impregnated by Satan," I said, only half joking. Justin is a Sagittarius, after all: half man, half beast.

We drove, giggling at that thought, for a good twenty miles, past the hotels and casinos, just beyond the outskirts of town and along several curved roads, before we pulled up to a stunning pink marble, unbelievably elegant, just short of enormous, mansion.

Chris got out of the car, ran around to open my door for me, and grandly proclaimed, "Welcome home!" I nearly fainted.

"Whose home?" I gasped.

"Well, technically it's my boss's boss's, but for the next week, it's mine. I'm house-sitting. And for tonight, at least, it's ours." Man, he looked so devilishly handsome standing there. I could only imagine the filthy thoughts running through his head. And, if I was lucky, I'd get to experience them firsthand.

"And that reservation you mentioned?" I asked.

"Ah, surprise number two," he said, glowing. He ushered me into the house. "Voilà!"

Mind you, I've been in my share of luxury homes before—San Francisco is full of them. But nothing compared to this. Whatever the word beyond elegant is, that's what this place was. Every stick of furniture, every piece of art, every knickknack looked original and one of a kind. And each was stunning in its own way. One look and you just knew that the interior decorator had to be gay. But what Chris was *voilà*ing to was the table set up in the middle of the entryway, which happened to be beneath one of the largest crystal chandeliers I'd ever seen, and on this, a meal fit for a king (or a queen or two).

I looked at him in astonishment, and he explained, "Our host said to help myself. So I did. He'll never notice. He eats most of his meals down at the hotel, anyway. Besides, you only live once."

"Yes, but that meal will cut at least one year off my life," I joked.

"Oh, don't worry, you'll be working it off soon enough," he said, seductively, causing a rumble in my pants. Naturally, I was not disappointed.

You know, I rarely go into the details of my sex life, but considering it was sex in a mansion, I'll make an exception. Bragging rights and all, I mean. Besides, it started, well, unusually enough.

After we ate, and I'd sufficiently stuffed myself, I asked where the bathroom was. As it turned out, there were six of them. Chris led me to the master bath, larger by far than my entire apartment.

"Is that a bidet?" I asked, never having seen one in person, so to speak, before.

Chris grinned. "Yep, wanna see how it works?"

Actually, I did. "Yep, I do. If you give me a demonstration." I winked lasciviously at him and stood back a few inches, offering him ample room.

Slowly, he unbuttoned his shirt, dropping it to the marble floor, where his sneakers quickly joined it. Then the button to his jeans was popped open and his zipper slid down. I watched, my eyes riveted to his slim waist, as he pulled the pants down and off. He was going commando, his cock dangling down, his balls swaying as he straddled the porcelain.

He looked up at me. "I'll let you do the honors, sir," he said, pointing with a flourish at the button to his side.

"My pleasure," I told him, reaching in for a press.

In an instant, a fountain sprang up beneath him, spraying his hair-lined crack and yummy hole. "Mmm," he groaned, his cock stirring, rising, arcing up and out. Instinctively, I bent down for a suck and a slurp, engulfing his fat rod in one fell swoop, as I reached a finger up and between, tickling his now wet hole.

"Dirty man," he sighed.

"Good thing we're in the bathroom, then," I replied, between licks and gulps, the finger sliding in, feeling the smooth muscled interior of him, before it was joined by another.

"Three's the charm," he offered, and I happily obliged, now stroking his prick as I mashed my mouth into his, swapping some heavy-duty spit. He came in a surprising instant, his eyes staring deep into mine, his moans and groans ricocheting across the tiled room as one load after the next erupted forth. "Sorry," he said with a chuckle, "I couldn't wait. The next time will last a lot longer, promise."

"The next time, huh?" I said, slipping out of my clothes.

"And the next and the next. We've got all night, Em."

And that we did, and then the morning. With a huge breakfast to boot. But all this did put me in an awful predicament. Now I had two men in my life who were just about perfect. I know, I know, I can't believe I'm complaining either, but my heart had a hard time dealing with that much simultaneous emotion. The obvious answer would have been to dump Chris and stick with Marvin, as at least Marvin lived in San Francisco; but whenever I was with Chris, I ached with desire. He was much more free-spirited, though equally sexy. So, I followed my own advice and put it off for another day. Why rock the boat? These things always have a way of working themselves out, I figured. Unfortunately for me, however, they usually didn't work out right, they just worked out. That's probably why I was going with the flow for the time being. It was, after all, better than nothing.

All good things must come to an end, and Chris eventually drove me back to the Atlantis and my chaotic life. My lips were still tingling from all the kissing we did the prior evening, and my stomach was still full from both meals, but I felt noticeably more relaxed and ready to deal with what the day had to offer. I prayed it wasn't much.

Remembering Justin's command from the previous day, I checked for a message at the front desk. There were two.

The first one was from Marvin. It read: *Dearest Em, would love to skip the dinner at the convention tonight and spend the night with you. Are you free? Please leave me a message at my hotel. Until then, hope the vase search is going well. Yours, Marvin.*

Ouch went my guilt pang. Where was this guy all these years while I was sitting alone in my apartment, gorging myself on Ben & Jerry's?

The second note was from you-know-who, and it read: *Fucked our way to a nicer suite. See you in room 511.* Justin doesn't amaze me anymore, so the note was no shocker. Though I was astounded when I arrived at our new accommodations. We were now in a two-room suite, complete with his-and-his bathrooms and a view of the mountains. Instead of chlorine, my nostrils were greeted to a lovely bouquet of jasmine and juniper. But that was not the biggest surprise. That came before I entered, when I knocked on the door and heard the familiar, "Come in." Again it was Ahmed. This time, in a lovely pair of shimmering purple satin undies and nothing else. (I have to stop shopping at Macy's. They don't have enough selections, evidently.)

"No more stinky," he said to me as I entered.

"Apparently," I replied, looking around for Justin.

"He's in shower," Ahmed notified me, thankfully getting dressed. Ripped, thin, hairless boys are not my cup of tea; but I am human, after all, and he *was* rather distracting.

"Thanks," I said, plopping down on my new king-sized bed.

"I get dressed and go now. You please tell Justin I say goodbye, okay?" he asked, in his melodic Middle Eastern accent. Looking and listening to him made you melt. It was all I could do not to gawk. (Well, I gawked a little, when he wasn't looking. I hadn't seen a waist that small since I was twelve.)

He was out the door in no time flat. I could hear the shower turning off in the bathroom just as he shut the door behind him. I was simply full of questions, and eagerly awaited Justin's entrance. I wasn't to wait for long.

"I'm done, my Arabic stallion. Are you ready for a second helping?" he proclaimed as he shot into the room, naked and hard. Not exactly the entrance I would've preferred.

"Do you really talk that way when I'm not around?" I asked, causing him to cover himself up. Or at least try to. Fortunately, I had seen it all before (been there, done that), and was not impressed by the show.

"Yes, and where is Ahmed?" he asked.

"Gone, but obviously not forgotten," I replied, pointing to his softening member. "Better question is," I continued, "where's Jacques?"

"Ah, that did require my various *talents* yesterday. You know, I simply could not tolerate that awful room for another moment, so I found our friend Jacques and asked if there was any way, *and I mean any way at all*, we could switch rooms. Well, the look on his face said it all; and when he invited me back to his suite to talk about it, I knew that it was a fait accompli. I merely applied my masculine wiles once we arrived there and, lookie, lookie, brand-new suite."

"Meaning, you *applied* your naked body to his," I said.

"Precisely, my dear Watson. My, you do catch on quick. Besides, it was for a good cause: my sanity. Those screaming children were driving me to drink."

"Like that was a far drive. I would think it was more like a hop, maybe even a short step. In any case, I, for one, applaud your intentions and am thrilled with the results. Here, here!" I exclaimed, raising an imagined drink up in the air, which he thankfully replaced with a real one a short moment later. "But where did he come up with the room?"

"Ah, that was easy. Another gay couple had reserved it last week. They're due to check in tonight, and Jacques will tell them that there were some plumbing problems. Then he'll offer them our old room. Seeing as there are no other rooms left in Vegas, I don't see they'll have much of a choice but to accept. Honestly, I'd love to see their faces when they see *the fishbowl* when they were expecting this," he said, indicating our large, luxurious suite. "I hope they brought earplugs."

"I'd like to say that I feel guilty over that," I said, "but I just can't. After yesterday's mess, I needed this bit of good news. Thank you, dear Justin. Thank you for being such a slut."

"My pleasure," he said, bowing his head, then added, "Or should I say, Jacques's."

"Now, one more question."

"Ah, would that be how I came to acquire the company of our lithe little friend Ahmed for another evening?" he guessed. I nodded in the affirmative as I sipped my martini. "Dear Ahmed arrived just as I was switching rooms. Thank goodness Jacques went back to work because that would've been a dreadful mess. He's painfully jealous, apparently. Luckily my stamina is so high. Twice in one night can be somewhat exhausting," he confessed, and then plopped down on his bed, martini in hand. I knew what he was talking about. Twice in two days was exhausting enough for me.

"Why wasn't Ahmed at work?" I asked.

"He said he was working days for now. But who cares?

The boy is a wonder in bed. The things he does to me would result in death and dismemberment back in his home country. Lord only knows where he learned all that stuff, but I, for one, am grateful. And that accent—oh, man."

I had heard the accent already, so I knew of what he spoke. It was sexy as all get-out, as was the man who spoke it. Something about Ahmed's appearances and disappearances made me a tad edgy, though. I chose to keep my opinions to myself, however, as Justin was obviously in heaven with the situation. That, and I knew once I told him about my encounter with Bradley, he'd go ballistic. I decided to wait for a good time. Five or six more drinks ought to have done the trick. Instead, I suggested we go do some gambling.

Another martini later, that's just what we did. I left a message with Marvin, telling him that I'd be delighted to have dinner with him. Chris had to work, and I was fast becoming accustomed to waking up in bed with a handsome man each morning—even if it wasn't the same man. Then we were off to play. Sadly, before we even made it out of the hotel, we were unexpectedly detained.

"Mr. Bill Miller?" asked the strange man Jacques was leading to us.

"That would be me," I replied, warily.

"Detective Lombard. I'm with the Las Vegas Police Department," he informed us.

"Yes, detective, how can I help you today?" I asked, nervously.

"I'm investigating the death of Mr. Hartwell, and your name and hotel were on a piece of paper found in the deceased's pants. Can you explain that?" he asked.

"Better the paper found in them than me," I joked, to relieve the tension. (Mine.)

He wasn't amused. "Please, Mr. Miller, a man is dead here. Can you just tell me your connection with Mr. Hartwell?"

So I did. And Detective Lombard wrote down everything I said. When I was done, he thanked me for my assistance and gave me his card, asking me to give him a call if I had any more information. I thanked him and told him I would. It was that simple. The whole interview couldn't have lasted more than ten minutes, but it gave me a pit in my stomach just the same. I'd never been part of a murder investigation before, however tangentially—and I wasn't thrilled to be part of one now, especially as my vase may have been the cause of it.

When he left, we heaved a sigh of relief. Jacques apologized for leading the detective to us, but I told him it was no biggie and he was just doing what he had to. Besides, my involvement should have been very minimal after that interview. (Should have been.) After that, we practically ran from the hotel.

"Where to?" Justin asked.

"Anywhere there is a bar/casino, dude. Like, duh," I replied, to which he responded with three fingers waved in the air, thereby officially whatevering me.

Once again, we proceeded to the Strip.

"Hey, let's go to the Bellagio," I suggested. "Maybe we'll run into Marvin. I could use a hug right about now."

"Sounds like a plan," Justin agreed, and we headed that way.

Which, of course, brings us back to your tour of Vegas. The Bellagio is near the center of the Strip, across from Paris. And the first thing you notice is the Fountains of Bellagio. Words cannot accurately express the grandeur and beauty of this enormous attraction. The display spans more than one thousand feet, with water soaring over two hundred in the air. The fountains are choreographed to music ranging from classical and operatic pieces to songs from Broadway to pop classics. All along the sidewalk out in front, people line up by the hundreds to watch the shows that run every half hour. I swear I get goose pimples every time I view them. Truly, they are just that magnificent.

And speaking of magnificent, the Bellagio has to rank right up there as one of the most spectacular hotel/casinos in the United States. From the lobby, with its two thousand individually blown glass pieces covering most of the ceiling, to the botanical garden, with its changing seasonal décor, you are seriously blown away at every turn. Not to mention the fact that they house Cirque du Soleil's "O," which is absolutely breathtaking. And as splendid as the hotel is, with first-class accommodations for all its guests, the casino has to be one of the most elegant on the Strip.

The best description of the Bellagio's casino would be: Classical Mediterranean. It's completely done in muted golds and deep reds and is snazzy everywhere you look. As are the patrons. You tend to see a lot fewer people in shorts and T-shirts at the Bellagio. So, with that said, and I realize that it sounds like I'm gushing, I have to say that I really don't like to do my gambling there. It's a lobster-and-caviar kind of casino, and I'm a meat-and-potatoes kind of guy: I prefer to hobnob with people of my own ilk, namely poor.

But gambling is gambling, and the chance to run into Marvin seemed to make the experience worth it. So I sat down at a lovely quarter slot machine and started pullin'. Justin sat directly behind me at one of his dollar machines, and the two of us gabbed away as we rapidly depleted our money. If it wasn't for the scene that was about to unfold, I might have sat there dumping quarter after quarter all the way up to my date with Marvin.

And speaking of Marvin, as I looked up in a desperate attempt to spot a cocktail waitress, whom should I spy across the casino floor, sitting at one of the many crowded bars, but the handsome man himself. If you detect any foreboding in my description, perhaps it's because he wasn't sitting alone. Not that that should have been reason for concern, mind you, except for the fact that he was sitting with none other than Bradley.

Talk about your gay dilemmas. Firstly, I wouldn't normally see anything amiss in two handsome men sitting and talking at a bar. Happens all the time. But having just recently met Bradley, I could only assume that he was forcing his charms on my poor defenseless man. (Granted, he wasn't *my man*, per se, but let's just forget that fact for a moment and continue.) Secondly, I would normally just walk over to the bar and find out the circumstances of their sitting together like that, so sickeningly close. I might even be discreet about it. That's just the kind of man I am. But, alas, there were no *normal* things to do when dealing with Justin. All bets were off. I couldn't go over and find out what was going on because Justin would then have to confront Bradley, something I simply wasn't up for just yet. Justin plus booze, plus crowded casino, plus tragic ex-love, didn't seem to add up to anything worth experiencing, at least not firsthand; so I choked down my agonizing curiosity and feigned a need for a break. I figured putting some distance between us and a possible scene was for the best.

Justin reluctantly agreed, downed his drink, and we both got up to leave. I heaved a sigh of relief as we made it out of the casino and back into the hotel. I was, unfortunately, premature in my assessment. Oh, we were so close, though. But close is only good in hand grenades and horseshoes. Apparently, as we left the casino, Bradley and Marvin were leaving the bar. We met up, almost simultaneously, right at the elevator that leads to Marvin's suite. They were together, obviously, as a, *groan*, couple. Too bad I didn't have one of those handy hand grenades then. I would've used it for sure to avoid the forthcoming confrontation.

Bradley started the volley. "Em, how wonderful it is to see you again."

Justin shot me an awful look. The "again" did not go unnoticed. As usual, I had been caught.

Marvin's look was equally bad, but for a different reason. He looked guilty as hell at being discovered. I didn't know whether to feel angry with Marvin or sorry for Justin. Instead, I went decidedly numb.

Seeing my consternation, Bradley started looking from me to Justin. From me to Justin. And then just to Justin.

"Um, don't I know you?" Bradley asked my troubled friend.

Long pause. I glanced over at Justin to see what he would say, but he just stood there, frozen and white as a ghost.

"Sort of. At least you did, once," Justin replied.

Again, long pause as the two of them stood there staring at each other. Marvin looked confused, but I wasn't about to fill him in on the details. Then a look of recognition came over Bradley's face and he lit up like a light.

"Holy shit," he shouted.

"Holy shit, indeed," Justin echoed.

"Holy shit, what?" Marvin asked.

"Holy shit, shut up," I told him.

Then Bradley did something I wasn't expecting. He lunged at Justin and wrapped his arms around him. Justin wasn't expecting this either and didn't know how to react. Basically, he stood there, stock still, and did nothing except let himself be hugged. When Bradley broke into tears, so did I. But Justin just stood there, motionless and emotionless. Marvin looked at me questioningly, but I just shot him a glare, and he hung his head in shame.

"I never thought I'd see you again, Justin," Bradley gushed. "I found out what your parents did to you after that day and I felt awful. For years I felt responsible for that. Now look at you. Standing in front of me like this. It's just amazing. You look incredible." My heart melted. But still, Justin just stood there.

Again the unexpected happened.

"Nice to see you again, Bradley. It has been a long time. You look great as well." Justin spoke robotically. Certainly not the reaction any of us expected, and it totally threw poor Bradley off.

"Oh," he said. "Yes, well, okay." He was flushed and didn't know how to continue with the surprise reunion. Justin put an end to it instead.

"Well, it looks like you were on your way somewhere, Bradley, so I won't keep you. It was nice seeing you again. Bye," he said, grabbing my arm and leading me to an exit door. I was stunned, but I still managed to shoot Marvin a wicked glower.

We were outside in a jiff. Justin never even turned around to see Bradley's reaction. We just kept walking until we were back on the sidewalk along the Strip. The silence was deafening.

"I'm sorry, Em," he eventually said, tears running down his cheeks. Something I'd never witnessed before.

"Don't be sorry, Justin. You were just taken by surprise, is all. I don't know how I would have reacted if the same thing happened to me."

"No, I'm sorry about you and Marvin."

"Oh, fuck that. Besides, it was just a fling," I lied. "But what about you and Bradley?"

"Me and Bradley ended being 'me and Bradley' a whole lifetime ago." Now *he* was lying. His tears gave him away.

"But it doesn't have to be that way. You're here. He's here. Certainly this can't be a mere coincidence," I tried, but I knew that once Justin had made up his mind, there was no changing it.

"Dude, that's all it is, a coincidence. I got over Bradley a long time ago. Let's just concentrate on the vase and then get out of here," he said, but I could hear the pain in his voice. It was so sad. Much sadder than the thought of Marvin cheating on me. (Well, maybe not *much*.)

"Okay, Justin, I'll drop it. Besides, that breastplate of his would be awfully cold in bed."

"And who wants to date a deposed dictator, anyway?" he added.

Despite his grandiose humor, I had a feeling *he* did.

As the last tear trickled down our faces, we made our way back to our hotel, neither saying a word about what had just happened. But I will tell you this: that was not the last we saw of Bradley. Naturally, I won't jump ahead of myself to tell you more; just be forewarned.

Murder & Martinis

WE ARRIVED BACK AT OUR HOTEL WORN OUT AND completely unprepared for what we were about to discover: there, in the parking lot of the Atlantis, were several cop cars, a fire truck, and two ambulances. Recent events led us to believe, quite accurately, that the scene playing out before our eyes had something to do with our little adventure. We prayed that it was a fire, or a bomb threat, or a roving band of gypsies that had kidnapped those screaming and hollering children who kept running around the pool. As usual, we were not so lucky.

"We have two choices," Justin said as we stood outside staring at the entrance to the hotel.

"Damn, only two?" I moaned.

"Well, two legitimate ones, anyway. The one where we sneak into the ambulance and steal the morphine probably wouldn't be in our best interest right now," he said.

"Ah, no, probably not. So what are the other two choices?"

"We can creep around the back, go to our rooms, get our

luggage, and leave, washing our hands of the whole mess. Maybe buy your mother a nice urn when we get home. But definitely we avoid whatever chaos this clearly is."

"Or choice number two?"

"Or two, we do the adult thing and march ourselves into that lobby and face the turmoil head on."

"You're joking, right?" I asked, seeing as we never, ever chose the *adult thing*.

"Just giving you the options here, Em."

But before we could even find the back entrance, two gurneys were wheeled out of the front one, and whoever was on each of them was most certainly dead, or had a problem with the sun. Otherwise, they don't usually wheel you out with the sheet over your face like that. We gulped as the two corpses went veering by. We gulped again when a nearly hysterical Jacques came out, saw Justin and me standing there, and then ran to us, arms flailing, as he screamed over and over and over again, "Thank God it wasn't you!" He landed at Justin's feet, sobbing uncontrollably. It was like a scene out of a bad movie. Too bad we all had starring roles.

"Um, Jacques, would you mind telling us what that cryptic statement means?" Justin asked, helping Jacques to his feet.

It took Jacques several moments before he could control himself enough to tell us. And once he did, I kept thinking how that gypsy scenario sounded so much better.

Actually, it was a short story, but it seemed to take years for Jacques to tell it. Each word came out in slow motion, one sentence after the next pulling us further and further down into a dark abyss. And once he was finished, all we could do was stand there and shake our heads in disbelief.

Here's how the story unfolded.

"Oh, my God! Oh, my God! Oh, my God!" he screamed, panic-stricken, repeatedly drawing the phrase out between sniffling sobs.

If it had really been a bad movie, I would've slapped him across the face to calm him down. Actually, the thought was rather appealing. His squealing was completely unnerving. I could tell that Justin was thinking the same thing, but Jacques caught his breath and saved himself from the embarrassment.

"Just tell us what happened, Jacques," Justin said in a smooth, reassuring, even voice.

"Oh, it was just awful," he began. "The maid found those two poor men that are being loaded into the ambulances."

"Found them how?" I asked.

"Found them dead," he answered. Justin shot me a *shut up so he can finish this* look, and I complied.

"Go on," Justin said, caressing Jacques's arm.

"She went into the room this morning to clean up and... and...and..." (More sobbing. My hand started to go up in slap mode. I was aching to let him have it.) "And they had been stabbed in their sleep. Oh, my God—the blood...the blood... It was everywhere. I almost fainted when I saw it all. It was horrible."

Again he started crying and wrapped his arms around Justin for support. I was sure that Justin was ruing the day he had sex with the man. It couldn't have been worth all this. And then, a strange thought passed through my mind. "Um, what exactly did you mean when you said, '*Thank God it wasn't you*'? I asked, terrified at his response.

He stopped bawling long enough to answer, pulled himself away from Justin's embrace, looked from one of us to the other, and then blurted out, "They were in your old room."

Uh-oh. Now it wasn't only Jacques who was hysterical.

"Our old room?" I screamed. "Our old room?" I screamed again, but louder. "The room we were in prior to the one we're in now?" I screamed, even louder, just in case

I was saying it wrong the first two times.

"YES!" Jacques shrieked back.

It took Justin all his reserves to calm the two of us down. By the time he did so, we were all quite hoarse. Then he asked Jacques a few more questions. Though I was reluctant to hear him out, I knew that it was definitely in our best interest to find out the whole story. And by our best interest, I meant our very lives.

"Who were those two men? Did you know anything about them?" Justin asked.

"They were a gay couple from Los Angeles. The only reason I knew about them at all is that a travel agent friend of mine called and asked if I could get them a room. Normally, I don't get involved with reservations, but I owed this guy a favor. Wait until I call him and tell him what happened. Oh, my God, it's my fault! It's my fault! It's my fault!"

Again Jacques resumed his caterwauling. We both comforted him as best we could until he stopped.

"Jacques, it's not your fault those men were murdered. It's the murderer's fault," Justin reassured him. "Now, tell me again what you saw when you got to the room."

He paused, caught his breath, and then answered, "As soon as the maid found them, she came running to find me. Then I called the police and waited for them to show up. I didn't think it was a good idea to go snooping around before they arrived. Luckily, it only took a few minutes for that whole menagerie outside to congregate, because word got around the hotel fast that there had been a murder. I'd never seen the casino so quiet before. It was dreadful.

"When the police walked in, I met them at the entrance and took them to the room. The men were both in one of the beds, sprawled out under the covers, which, by the time we got there, were entirely red from all the blood. It was the most horrible thing I've ever witnessed—besides Bush's election results, that is." (Well, at least he hadn't lost his gay sense of humor. Though I could see his point.)

"And what did the police tell you after they got there?" Justin asked.

"They didn't tell me anything. They pushed me to the side while they looked around, but I stayed in the hallway, so I heard most of everything they said."

"Which was?" I asked.

"Which was, that it didn't look like a robbery. Both of the guys' jewelry and wallets were left out, untouched. Oh, and the shades were still drawn and the lights were all off, so it must have been dark when it all happened—which they guessed to be several hours earlier, probably in the middle of the night. Nobody heard anything, so there couldn't have been much of a struggle. They were probably sound asleep when it happened."

"Anything else?" Justin asked.

"Nope. Well, they did ask if we supplied the rooms with corkscrews. I thought that was strange, told them yes, then asked why."

"Because that's what they thought the murder weapon was, right?" I guessed, and he nodded in the affirmative.

All three of us blanched. Talk about your gruesome murders, and right in our proverbial backyard. I would've felt guilty, except for the knowledge that if it hadn't been them, it certainly would've been us. Should I feel bad for admitting this? I suppose, but at a time like this, self-preservation is paramount.

Then the three of us stood there in a huddle and hugged. If there really was safety in numbers, I was hoping more of the hotel guests would come out and join us. My knees were knocking at the thought that it could have been us, or worse yet, it was supposed to have been us. Though why anyone would want to see us dead was beyond me. Let me rephrase that: why anyone would want to see *me* dead

125

was beyond me. Justin was an entirely different story.

Spotting us standing there like that—which wasn't hard, three hysterical queens being difficult to miss—our dear friend Detective Lombard came over to investigate. Now that we were connected to two murders in two days, our presence in Vegas had thrown suspicion our way. Go figure. Still, for our own safety, we explained to the detective our involvement up to that point. He looked at us dubiously, wrote everything down in his trusted notebook, and then informed us that we were involved in both murder cases and not to leave town. That was not what we wanted to hear. Vase or no vase, by that point we were sorely ready to head on back home.

Actually, I would think the police would be glad to get rid of us; people kept turning up dead whenever we were around. Not everyone was sad at that news, however. Jacques allowed himself a brief smile at the thought that he now had Justin at his disposal for an indefinite period of time. Shows you how much he knew.

Then, one by one, the emergency vehicles started pulling away, and we were left alone beneath the sweltering midday sun. I ached to be fog-enshrouded again. Nix that. I ached to be enveloped by fog again. For the time being, I thought it best to avoid words like *shroud*.

Needless to say, when Jacques invited us to the bar for free drinks, we thankfully accepted. And when we reciprocated with a cute little yellow pill for him, Jacques gratefully returned the thanks. Though nelly as all get-out, he certainly was a kindred spirit. I hoped being with us wouldn't cause him to become an *actual* spirit, though. We appeared to be having that effect on people. It didn't seem that Jacques was all that worried, however. Being around Justin seemed to calm him down—like a lost puppy following a new master. Funny, that. Justin was as calming to me as a double espresso.

Once safely inside, we sipped our very dry martinis and ruminated on our very awful predicament. "Okay, let's see what we know so far," I began. "We know that we're here to find my grandma's ill-fated vase."

"Who else knows that?" Justin asked, rhetorically.

"Let's see: the three of us here, Marvin, Ahmed, Mary, Honey, and Chris, and anyone that those people might have told. But if anyone was after the vase, for whatever reason, they wouldn't be coming after us. We don't have it. And everyone knows that too," I justified. Hearing Ahmed's name put an additional crease in Jacques's brow, but he kept his peace, in light of our current dilemma.

"True. Okay, then, who knew which room we were in, in case it was us the murderer was after?" Justin asked, sounding like a young Miss Nancy Drew.

"Again, the same people, though only Jacques knew we switched rooms, right?" I asked, and Jacques nodded that this was so. "But don't they all have alibis, pretty much?" I began to reel them off. "Mary's easy. She's too old to have murdered two grown men."

"But she also knew the value of the vase and knew where the vase was," Justin interjected. "Killing Mr. Hartwell should've been easy enough. Hell, a strong wind could've sent him to the great beyond. And it sure did sound like she wouldn't have minded him dead. Maybe she thought killing us would cover her tracks. And it's obvious from her living conditions that she needs the money and that she likes the finer things in life. For all we know, Honey may have been in on it with her. She looks strong as an ox. And killing two men in their sleep doesn't take a lot of strength. Plus, she may have access to the rooms, seeing as she works in the hotel. She also knew you have your thirty thousand with you. Thank goodness that's in the hotel safe. It just goes to prove what I always say," Justin said.

"Which is?" I asked.

"Never trust a Country-Western singer," he said.

"You've never said that," I retorted.

"Well, I'm saying it now!"

I hated to admit it, but what he said did make sense. Stranger things have happened. If a hillbilly can be elected president, then a hillbilly can be a murderer, even if it is a Patsy Cline impersonator, God rest her soul. Still, I found that scenario hard to swallow.

"Okay, you may have a point. But let's move on to the others," I said. "Now, we know for sure that it couldn't have been Chris, because he was with me the whole night. That much I do know for certain. So we can cross him off the list."

"Possibly, but he did know about the vase and your money, and he may have lured you away from the hotel so he could send a partner in to find one or the other or both. Money does strange things to people, you know. And what do we really know about Chris, anyway?" Justin asked, irritatingly.

"Fucker. What I know is that *you* set him up with me. So if he's involved in this mess, it's completely *your* fault," I pointed out.

"Oh, right. Let's cross Chris off the list, then. For now," Justin conceded.

The next person on the short list was Marvin, who, at that point, I would have almost liked to blame. Asshole. The whole Bradley thing was starting to work its way up to my brain again, and I was awfully pissed. Still, it seemed unlikely. Marvin did work for PBS, after all. If it were the U.S. Post Office, then okay, maybe, but I just couldn't see someone who worked at PBS being a triple murderer. Naïve, yes, but that was my opinion, and I said so. "Well, I doubt it was Marvin. Just doesn't seem the type."

"Maybe. Maybe not. Again, Marvin knows the whole scenario as well. And nobody but me and you and Jacques knows that your money is in the safe and not in our suite.

Plus, he may have found out about Chris and, in a jealous rage, broke into our old suite and murdered those two men thinking it was you and him. It was nighttime, after all, and it may have been too dark to tell. What do we really know about Marvin?"

What Justin said was true, but not what I really wanted to hear. Underneath my boiling hatred, I still cared for Marvin. Yes, I realize we had only known each other for a few short days, but so what. Sometimes that's all it takes.

"Okay, I'll take that under consideration," I allowed. "And that only leaves one person: Ahmed. And he was... with, er..." (Uh-oh, I was trampling on shaky ground here. Justin gave me a face that indicated I better shut up if I didn't want to be murder victim number four, but it was too late.)

"Ahmed was with who?" Jacques shouted, and rose to his feet.

Justin rose as well and held Jacques's hands. Probably so he wouldn't be bitch-slapped in the next few minutes. Then he said, "Um, okay, you're not going to like this, but he was with me."

"With you? With you? But I was with you!" Jacques declared, loud enough for most of the patrons at the bar to hear. Miss Thing was beyond caring by that point, though. Man, he was red in the face, but that may have been some preapplied makeup. It was awfully hard to tell.

"Yes, you were, sweetie. But then you left, and—"

"Oh, my God. You slut! And after all I've done for you two. You have one hour to pack your things and leave this hotel. I will not be treated this way!" he declared, and stormed off in a huff, sounding too much like a wounded Scarlett O'Hara. Thankfully, in his long history as a slut, Justin was used to such theatrics. And the rest of the bar seemed only too happy for the free show.

"I hate to say this," I said, "but let's not rule *her* out.

How much do we really know about Jacques, after all?"

"Idiot. He switched our rooms for us and knew that the money was in the safe. Why would he kill two innocent men like that?"

"Oh. True," I said. "There is one more suspect, an unlikely one," I added. "But you're not going to be too happy with me for telling you."

"Oh, God, now what?" he asked.

"Well, as you might have figured out by now, I ran into Bradley yesterday. Though he goes by Brad now. Can't say I blame him. Bradley sounds so formal. So stiff. So—"

"So continue, please! We only have an hour to find a place to stay now."

"Oh, okay. Anyway, I may have mentioned to Bradley where we were staying. It wouldn't have been too hard to find out our old room number. Maybe he did recognize you the other day at Caesar's, and when he saw you yesterday he went wild with desire to see you again, broke into the room, found two men sleeping there, thought it was you and another man, and in a moment of insanity killed the both of them," I suggested, rather animatedly.

"Are you through?" he asked, with a heavy sigh.

"Yes. Sorry," I mumbled.

"Good. Now let's go get our stuff and start looking for a new place to stay. And may I say one more thing? This vase adventure is turning out to be one big pain in the motherfucking ass. And I don't mean that in the good sense of the term."

"At least we got to see the desert," I tried.

"Shut up, already!"

" 'kay."

First thing we did was call our travel agent back home. When we told him of our predicament, he informed us of the obvious: there were still no rooms in Vegas, as COMDEX had another several days to go. (Do you think COMDEX was around two thousand years ago? Maybe that's why Mary and Joseph had such a hard time finding a room.) Then I called Chris at work. It took forever to get a hold of him, but once I did, he told me that he wished he could help, but that he didn't think it was a good idea to have guests at his boss's boss's home for an extended stay. And, to our greater dismay, he had rented his apartment out for the week to some conventioneers.

So, dispiritedly, we packed our belongings and left our lovely hovel away from home. No teary farewells. No long goodbyes. Just a speedy exit to…to… Well, we had no idea where we were headed, but we hopped inside a cab just the same.

"Where to?" asked the cabbie.

"Just drive around a bit and we'll let you know in a few minutes," I replied, and then looked over at Justin, beseechingly. I had a plan, but I knew he'd dislike it immensely.

"Uh-oh, I don't like that look, Lucy," he said to me in a thick Cuban accent. "What are you thinkin' of doin'?"

"Okay, Ricky, here are the facts. The authorities have forbidden us to leave Vegas." (The cab driver gave us a nervous look when he overheard that, so I decided to have some fun with him.) "Until we are cleared of the *three murder charges*, we need to set up a new base of operation, but there are no rooms at the inn. It's possible that someone is trying *to kill us*, so we need to find a place where nobody knows we're staying. We have no leads, nowhere to go, and virtually no friends to contact. Except…"

"Except whom?" he asked, sneering at me.

"Well, we do know one other person who could help. Someone who has hotel connections. Someone intimately connected to us. Someone *imperial*…"

"Nuh-uh, not him. I'm sure there's a nice YMCA we can stay at somewhere. Besides, I doubt he could help. And why make contact if he can't?" Justin said, but I sensed a lack of resolve.

"Look, we have no other choice here. Let's at least go try to find him and ask. What can it hurt?" I asked.

"It can hurt plenty, but, as much as I hate to admit it, you're right. Let's make it fast, okay. In and out. I don't want to prolong our meeting any longer than we have to."

I knew he'd cave. Justin is not one for YMCA life. Well, maybe the showers, but certainly not the sleeping accommodations.

"Driver, Caesar's Palace, please," I commanded.

"Yes, sir." He obeyed, sounding a tad scared at having two suspected felons in his backseat.

When we got to Caesar's, the cab driver said it was on him, hurried us out of the cab, and sped away. I made a mental note to remember that nifty little trick. I wonder what else you can get for free if people think you're a homicidal maniac. Did Son of Sam receive complimentary haircuts? Did Ted Bundy have his lawn mowed at no cost? Just a thought, but let's continue.

With luggage in hand, and yes, my moolah was with us as well—so much for tight security—we made it inside and parked ourselves, yet again, in the mall. When the gladiators started passing by, we knew our wait wouldn't be long. And not five minutes later, the emperor's court appeared, followed by Caesar himself. I let out a quiet "Yippee," and was painfully nudged in the ribs for doing so. Justin was not at all happy at our being there, but there was no way I was going to sleep on a cot anytime soon. It was bad enough that I was down one man and one hotel room, not to mention one vase and three corpses.

Happily, Caesar spotted us right away; not too surprising, as we were the only ones in the mall with more than several pieces of luggage. Well, that and the big sunbonnets we had on that we bought for a mere five dollars at one of the many discount stores along the Strip. Not wanting to make an even bigger spectacle of our appearance there, he nonchalantly strolled over to our area and started making small talk with us.

"Good day to you, fellow Romans," he said, Caesarly.

"Good day, your Highness," I said, and curtsied. Justin slapped my ass and told me to knock it off. I grimaced and whispered that he was jealous because he was just a mere queen and Bradley was an emperor. Bradley giggled, very unroyal-like.

"And what can I do for my loyal plebeians today?" he asked, enjoying his status, tenuous as it might have been.

"Funny you should ask," I remarked.

"Oh, really? Anything I can do for the working-class man, I'm here to help," he offered.

"Would *anything* involve finding us a hotel room? We have, rather suddenly, found ourselves without a place to stay and are in somewhat dire straits." I explained, without going into the gruesome details.

He nodded, smiled, and stood there rocking on his leather-clad feet. Justin rubbed his forehead and wrinkled his brow. He absolutely hated not being in control. I, on the other hand, had faith, and sat there smiling up at Bradley. My confidence didn't go unrewarded.

"You are in luck, my friends. Caesar has friends in high places." (Justin whispered to me, "I bet he made them in low places, though.") "Bring your belongings to the bell station and meet me for drinks at six in the main bar. Tell the bell captain I sent you. I'm not promising anything, but I'll do my best."

Justin and I nodded that we would indeed meet him at six. Then we shook his hand, thanked him profusely, and let him get on his royal way.

"See, not so bad," I said to Justin as we headed out of the mall.

"Like taking candy from a baby...alligator," he replied. "You know he'll want something in return."

"Please, dear heart, enough with the negative talk. We're here, we're queer, and we're out of harm's way, for the time being. So let's go enjoy the day, okay?"

"Fine, but when the time comes for the *I told you so*, you better not get pissed."

"Fine by me. Now let's get rid of our bags and out of this place."

Which we did. But first, Justin had a pit stop to make. "Um, we have to go to the Aladdin before we do anything else," he said.

"We do?"

"Mm-hm. Ahmed was supposed to come over tonight, and I want to tell him that we're not at the Atlantis anymore."

"Are you going to tell him where we are?"

"Maybe. I mean, we know it couldn't have been Ahmed. He was with me the whole night during the murders. Right?"

"I suppose so, but let's be careful about this. No more dead people, okay?"

"I'll try."

So we headed on over to the Aladdin, which was basically across the street from Caesar's. And since we are speaking of geography, sort of, maybe I should quickly tell you about the Strip in general.

It's about three miles long, but don't think it's not manageable. Almost all the newer and fancier casinos run along the last mile, where we had been the entire time. The two miles that are ahead of that are scattered with the remnants of the original Strip. Basically, everything before Treasure Island and the Venetian is old. Here you'll find the casinos your parents visited way back when: the Riviera, the Sahara, Circus Circus (WARNING: Stay away. Maximum child overload.), the Stratosphere, etc. The one exception to this is the Wynn, and this is just a smaller version of the Bellagio, and not much worth the walk past the Venetian. And if walking isn't your thing, and who can blame you, then there's the inter-hotel tram or the double-decker buses that run along the Strip, both for a small price.

So, unless you have unlimited time to spend in Vegas and you're not trying to escape death, like us, you don't really have to go to these places. They're tired and run-down and full, full, full of old people and cheap tourists. (Save for the Wynn.) There is one other exception, just off the Strip down that way, and that's the Hilton. It's fairly grand, has a nice casino, and best of all, houses Star Trek: the Experience. I can't recommend this highly enough if you're even remotely interested in *Star Trek*. Added bonus: there is a righteous Star Trek casino tacked on. Oh, and a cool Elvis statue, for photo ops.

Anyway, back to our adventure. We went directly to the disco at the Aladdin to find Ahmed, as he had told Justin that he was working days there now. The disco, not surprisingly, was dead, and there were only a few bartenders working, none of whom were Ahmed—though all of them looked sexy as hell in their little genie outfits.

"Can I help you?" asked the genie closest to us, who, as it turned out, did sort of resemble our lithe little Palestinian.

"Yes, thank you, we're looking for Ahmed. He's a friend of ours," Justin said.

Talk about your immediate reactions. His demeanor did a complete one-eighty. He went from friendly to fierce at the mention of Ahmed's name. He leaned across the bar to us and whispered, in a rabid Middle Eastern accent, "Ahmed no work here anymore. You know where he is? Tell me if you know."

"No, no, we don't know where he is. We're looking for him too," Justin said, stepping back a couple of inches, lest the bartender intended to reach over and grab him.

"If you see him, tell him Zahir is looking for him. You tell him, yes? Is very important," he told us.

His tone indicated that Ahmed was in trouble, and trouble was not what we were searching for—though it had a certain knack for finding us. So we backed away, nodding our heads to indicate that we'd tell Ahmed if and when we saw him. Zahir nodded a gruff thanks and went back to work. He scared the crap out of me, and I eagerly pulled Justin away and toward the exit of the disco. But, just before we were completely outside, we heard a "Psst."

Reluctant as I was to turn around, I did. Another genie was beckoning us over to another bar on the other side of the disco. This genie was blond and looked nothing like Ahmed. I took this as a good sign, and we crept over so as not to call attention to our return. Zahir seemed not to have noticed. I breathed a sigh of relief when we were out of his sight. Fortunately, the bright lights above the dance floor blocked the two bars well enough to keep our second genie conference a private one.

"Did I hear you asking about Ahmed?" asked the bartender, thankfully with no sounds of fury, rage, or wrath in his tone of voice.

"Yes, do you know where we can find him?" Justin asked. "I was supposed to meet with him later on tonight, and I need to change our plans."

"Actually, I'm not sure myself. He sort of, well, disappeared. Never said a word to anyone; just didn't show up for work. And I miss him, too. He's a great guy," he said.

"Do you think anything is wrong?" Justin asked, with real and unexpected concern creeping into his voice.

"Probably not. It happens all the time around here. Not to sound bigoted or anything, but a lot of the foreign workers in the hotels have problems. Sometimes with immigration, sometimes with money. Who knows? But I'm sure he's okay. Hey, if you like, you can leave me a message and I'll make sure to give it to him should he come back," he offered, nice as he could be. It was refreshing to see such a well-mannered genie for a change.

Justin wrote Ahmed a note on a napkin. It said to meet him in the food court at New York–New York at seven. That sounded like a good idea to me, as I was seriously jonesing for a Nathan's hot dog. Justin handed the note to the bartender, who promptly folded it and placed it in his pocket. We thanked him for his help and left. And if you find it strange that we were in a bar and didn't order a drink, well, hey, it was killing me too, but we didn't want to chance another run-in with the evil genie.

"I'm glad you didn't write down where we were actually staying, Justin. Good idea," I told him.

"Yeah, why take any chances. Besides, I have this sudden yen for a Nathan's hot dog." (I guess after spending so many years together, our minds were finally on the same wavelength. Too scary, huh? Well, I prayed that *he* was finally thinking like me and not vice versa.)

We made a hasty retreat from the Aladdin, and were on the sidewalk for less than a minute before we heard another "Psst." We both jumped at the sound. Recent events had made us both rather edgy, what with possibly being murdered and all. And when we turned around to see who was making the leaky tire sound at us, we were surprised to see Ahmed himself, in the glorious flesh.

"Ahmed!" we both shouted, causing our seemingly missing friend to wince.

He walked toward us very fast, with a nice-sized backpack slung over his shoulder and a worried look on his otherwise adorable face. It wasn't too hard to figure out that something was wrong. But did his problems have anything to do with ours? That was my greatest fear at that moment. We'd have to wait and find that out, though, as he was quickly pulling us away from the hotel and up the street, obviously not in the mood for chitchat. In any case, when Justin nudged me and indicated with his head that I should look over to our right, talk was the last thing on my mind. And Ahmed's too, because he noticed the now-familiar black car inching along beside us and promptly veered us onto the people mover that leads on into Bally's.

The car kept going as we turned, but my heart stopped for a few seconds and I let out an audible gulp. First off, Bally's is not on my top-ten list. Sure, the plaza out front is neat, what with the pulsating colored columns and nifty people mover and all, but the casino is average and has very little flair. But what really had me worried was the way our little friend Ahmed was hyperventilating and turning white, which wasn't easy considering his usually dark complexion.

"Are you okay, Ahmed?" I asked as we ever so slowly made our way along the people mover.

Fortunately, our movement was now motorized, because Ahmed didn't look as if he had the energy to be moving on his own. Rather than answer, he nodded a weak yes. We took that as a sign to continue, but neither of us said anything else. We were too worried for his health—or, more likely, for our own—to ask him any questions. And when we finally made it into the casino, he politely collapsed in a corner as we stood protectively over him.

"Now what?" I asked.

"Beats me."

"He's your boyfriend," I mentioned.

"Nice try. I'd say extended trick at this point, and I'm certainly not responsible for his well-being."

"Fine. What should we do, then? Leave him here like this?" I was tempted to do just that.

"Desperate times call for desperate measures," he replied, pulling out his wallet and his cell phone.

"Who are you calling at a time like this?"

He lifted his finger to indicate *wait*, and then dialed. He was looking at a business card I didn't recognize; from where I was standing, in front of our slouching friend, it was hard to see anything but the casino. Short of an angel, I couldn't begin to imagine who could help us.

Justin spoke into the phone. "Hello, Earl? This is Justin, do you remember me? ... (pause) ... Good, listen, we need your help. Could you pull up to Flamingo Road and meet us outside Bally's?... (pause again) ... Good. Thanks. See you soon, and please hurry."

He hung up and looked at me with a self-congratulatory grin.

"Who's Earl?" I asked.

He answered in a raspy, coughing, Harvey Fierstein-like voice, "How quickly you forget our friendly neighborhood cab driver."

"Ah, good idea," I said, helping him lift the near lifeless Ahmed up and over to the side exit of the casino.

"Well, it ain't no limo, but it's sure as hell better than a hearse," he said as we carried our downed acquaintance out to the street and over to the already waiting taxi.

Earl came running out to help us get Ahmed in. As the three of us worked on that, I started to think that I was getting too old for all of this. Is there an age limit for getting involved in life-threatening high jinks? Shouldn't I be settling down in the country somewhere with my partner and our Irish setter, maybe growing a nice little herb garden and taking pottery classes? Before I could dwell too much on the thought, however, my reverie was broken by the stink of the cab and the squeal of the tires as we sped away.

"I see you guys have been keeping yourself busy," Earl hacked, and looked at us though the rearview mirror. "Is that Ahmed you have back there?"

"How do you know Ahmed?" I asked curiously.

"Small town, few queers," he explained. "Nice kid, though. Is he all right?"

"Don't know. I think he's just exhausted, but it looks like he's in some kind of mess. Unfortunately, he sort of passed out before he could tell us anything," I explained.

"Well, then, where am I taking you this time? Jacques told me you were no longer staying at the Atlantis. I should've warned you that my brother is a bit, um, *dramatic* at times. Did you guys find an alternative?"

The answer to that, I realized sadly, was neither yes nor no. Our fate was still up in the air. And our latest unexpected pickle wasn't helping matters any. What do you do with a passed-out Palestinian? Taking him back with us to Caesar's seemed risky and difficult, seeing as we didn't even know if we had a room there yet. So, when we didn't answer his question, I think Earl sensed we were in trouble. Once again he came to our rescue.

"I'm getting off duty in a bit anyway, so Ahmed can come with me," Earl offered. "If he gets any worse, I'll take him to the hospital, but he looks like he's breathing back there, so maybe he's just sleeping it off. You guys can check in on him tomorrow, okay?" We wholeheartedly accepted and thanked him.

Granted, we didn't really know Earl all that well, but, for that matter, we really didn't know Ahmed either. And seeing as someone was either following or trying to kill one, two, or all three of us, it was probably the best thing to do. Besides, except for a little second-hand smoke inhalation, Earl seemed the safest bet right about then. Actually, as soon as Earl made the offer I breathed a sigh of relief. Justin and I were having enough trouble taking care of just the two of us.

We told Earl to take us to Caesar's, which was just up the block. He gave us his home number before he dropped us off, and we promised we'd call tomorrow to check up on the both of them. Then we jumped out of the taxi and screamed our thanks as he pulled away.

"What a day," I said as we headed into the Palace.

"Um, Em?" Justin said, looking over at me.

"Um, yes?" I said, looking back at him.

"Why are you carrying Ahmed's backpack?"

"Well, fuck me. Damn. I had it over my shoulder ever since he passed out. I forgot to leave it with him when Earl pulled away," I replied, smacking my head in disbelief.

"Oh, well," he said as we walked up to the bar where we were meeting Bradley. "No use crying over lost luggage. We'll just get it back to him tomorrow."

"What a day," I reiterated.

"And it ain't over yet," he quickly added, pointing toward the entrance, where Bradley had appeared, no longer in his royal attire.

Our newfound long-lost friend grabbed a seat as he ordered us a round of martinis. "Good news," he said.

"We could use some," I said. "Do we have a room?"

"Sure do!" he squealed. I guess the butch in him was only breastplate deep.

"That's great!" I shouted, happy for the first time that day.

Justin nodded his thanks, but it was plainly obvious that he was reluctant to be beholden to our regal rescuer. Still, we all knew the alternatives: none. And once we finished our martinis, and then another round for good measure, we were off to reclaim our belongings and see our latest digs. (Hey, I was willing to go for thirds, but Bradley had plans and needed to get going. I could only imagine that they were with Marvin, but was gracious enough not to ask.)

"Now, it's not much, but it's better than nothing," Bradley warned as we made our way down a long corridor. "The hotel almost never rents this room out."

I gulped as he unlocked the door and led us in. Once

more we were greeted with the now-familiar scent of chlorine. Again I could only imagine what we had done to fuck up our karma so badly, but as we threw our stuff on our beds, all I could say was thank you. The phrase "beggars can't be choosers" never before had so much meaning.

"Sorry, the treatment room for the pool is right next door, and the smell sort of wafts through the walls," Bradley explained.

"That's okay. Thanks for getting this for us. We were kinda desperate," I told him.

"Sure, not a problem, but I have to be running now, so if there isn't anything else I can do for you..." He lingered, looking over to Justin for a suggestion. Justin, however, simply nodded his thank-you and looked away. Poor Bradley, he really was making an effort, but Justin was having none of it. In any case, he was gone in a flash.

Now alone with Justin in our brand-new quarters, the best I could say was that no one knew where we were. So, for the time being, we were apparently safe and sound. (Well, safe, anyway.)

"Now what?" I asked.

"I don't know about you, but I'm still craving that hot dog. What say we walk down to New York–New York?" he suggested.

"Sounds like a plan," I said. "Let's go give our regards to Broadway."

"Show queen."

"Slut."

Isn't it amazing? Even under all that pressure, we still managed to show our love for each other.

We made our way up the Strip to New York–New York, incognito. Though one would have to wonder if giant white sun hats and rhinestone-studded sunglasses did much to make us any less conspicuous. Okay, granted, our lives may have been at risk, but dressing down simply wasn't our thing. Besides, it was nearing dinnertime and the streets were packed with people. We were awash in tacky tourists, many of whom were dressed similarly. (Scary, but true.) So, for the time being, we blended safely in.

Ten minutes later, we were nearing the end of the Strip and entering the casino. Now here's another one of those Las Vegas theme casinos that's simply not my cup of tea. I will admit that the enormity and scale of the whole complex is impressive, what with the tugboats blowing water beneath the Statue of Liberty, and the Brooklyn Bridge set out in front of the New York skyline, and the roller coaster winding its way around and through the buildings; but this hotel caters to families, as do many of the newer hotels, and I don't find it relaxing trying to sidestep children as I make my way to gamble and/or drink (more *and* than *or*). So here's a general rule for you: If a hotel has a game room for children somewhere on the premises, avoid that hotel. New York–New York just so happens to have a giant one.

Soon enough, we arrived at the food court, which is pure kitsch and the reason we like it. Well, we like it because it's so overdone and so fake-looking that we can't help but laugh at their attempt to recreate a Greenwich Village neighborhood with shop fronts and sidewalk dining. Of course, the leather shops, sex stores, and head shops are all sadly missing. In any case, none of this makes you feel like you're actually in New York—more like a Disneyfied version of it. And still, it's better than Excalibur in terms of the children quota and it's far cheaper than the food courts anywhere else, so we eagerly ordered our hot dogs, sat down at a tiny metal table, and made fun of the tourists who oohed and aahed their way before our eyes.

"Look at him," Justin whispered, his mouth full of beef by-products and sauerkraut, as he pointed to a slightly overweight, undertanned, prematurely graying man, surrounded by three screaming children and a whining, rotund wife. He was clearly checking out the shapely calves of the gentleman in front of him. Poor guy, he looked as though he must've been a cutie sometime in the mid-eighties.

"Closet case," we said, simultaneously.

"There but for the grace of God go I," Justin added.

"Oh, honey, please. Some people are born completely without closets. You, my dear friend, are one of them," I said.

"Thank the Lord," he said.

"Amen," we both said.

For the next half hour, we gorged ourselves on hot dogs. A giant cup of Coke later, I excused myself to go to the restroom. What with all the day's excitement, I had completely neglected my bladderly duties. Thankfully, the restrooms were ten feet away and were considerably cleaner than your average New York facility. Though it was a large food court, the bathroom was tiny, with two urinals and a toilet. (Makes you wonder what goes through an architect's head when they plan so poorly.)

Midway through my stream, I noticed, out of the corner of my eye, the guy next to me was checking me out. Years of bathroom cruising had made me ultrasensitive to that sort of thing. I quickly glanced up and found that it was the closet case from moments earlier. He smiled at me when I caught his eye. The poorly planning architect also failed to install urinal dividers in the too-tiny lavatory. I was beginning to appreciate his lack of forethought. Or maybe he was gay, and all of this was on purpose for just such an occasion. In any case, I wasn't complaining. I just adore an unobstructed view. And the view I was getting wasn't half bad.

Mr. Straighty backed up a few inches to give me a better look-see. Obviously, he'd done this before, and he wasn't shy. Oh, and he wasn't peeing either. So, I decided to play a little while I was in there.

"Nice family you got," I said, still staring over and down.

"Thanks," he mumbled, and moved back into his urinal.

"Nice family jewels, as well," I added, and got the reaction that I wanted.

"Thanks," he replied with more conviction.

This time he pulled half a foot away and two inches closer to me. He also dropped his shorts a few more inches to afford me a better view. My paunchy daddy was now sporting a rather hefty boner. Well, when in Rome, or make that New York, I always say, and I showed him my burgeoning member in return. He let out an appreciative moan. I decided to take the game to the next level and walked over to the stall. He followed and closed the door behind him.

Word of advice: a gay guy is always in control of a closet case. Basically, they are at your disposal, since they're usually so desperate for man-meat and all. I took advantage of this fact immediately.

"Drop 'em and bend over," I commanded, and he quickly obeyed.

The sound of my hand slapping his straight ass made a nice *ping* sound in the tiled room. And, judging from the rocking going on in front of me, my daddy liked his ass getting assaulted. I decided to make our encounter brief, however, seeing as he had a rather large family waiting for him outside and I had an impatient Justin waiting for me.

So I pulled down my pants, spat on my hand, and told him to get ready. A few strokes later, I shot a huge load all over his ass. Apparently he liked that because he started to shudder and moan almost immediately after I came on him. Then, seeing as we had no more business to attend to, I toilet-papered off, got redressed, and left my daddy in the stall. Just doing my share for gay–straight relations.

I felt considerably better upon leaving that restroom. Taking out my aggressions on a strange, straight ass was just what I needed—and I was ready to do some heavy bragging back at our table. Unfortunately, upon my return, Justin was nowhere in sight. His remaining hot dog was only half eaten and his hat and glasses were on the floor. My heart started to race. Where the fuck was he?

I searched the food court, and nothing. I ran through the casino, and nothing. I raced through the hotel lobby, and nothing. Needless to say, I was truly freaking out. I just knew that something was way wrong. Then I ran out to the street, and there was something. About twenty feet up the sidewalk, I could see the back of Justin's brunette head, and I could see a blond man right behind him. I walked faster to catch up and get a better view. When I was only a couple of feet away, I could tell that the stranger held something up to Justin's back and was pushing him forward with it. Now I have to tell you, I had watched enough television to know what that meant.

All of a sudden, my burgeoning maternal instincts kicked in, and I knew that I had to save my best friend. I stopped walking, took in some deep breaths to get my adrenaline flowing, then kicked my heels up and ran, with all my might, straight for them. (Oops, sorry, *forward* for them.) I leaped high into the air and landed on the blond man's back, sending him and Justin down with a crash. The rest was a blur. With all three of us on the ground, my hand instinctively went for the gun, which had been knocked out of the bad man's hand. Then, feeling oh so Angie Dickenson/Sgt. Pepper Anderson-like, I raised the gun up in the air and sent it smashing down on his blond head. Whatever movement there had been beneath me instantly subsided.

"That's for messing with my family, creep," I hollered, and then jumped up, grabbed Justin's arm, and helped him up. Then we both took off running through the small crowd that had quickly gathered to watch the spectacle. I slid the gun in my pants pocket for safekeeping.

We ran fast and hard until we made it back to our hotel, and headed right for our room and our minibar. The familiar scent of chlorine was actually comforting, or maybe it was the gin, but we both managed to catch our breaths and regain our composure before Justin told me what had happened.

"Thanks," he said. "That was too insane. When did you get so butch?"

"Dude, it's always been there, just packed deep, deep down for emergencies. Now, what the hell happened?" I asked.

"Well, I was sitting there waiting for you to come back from the bathroom when I felt something cold and metal on the back of my neck, and a man was telling me not to turn around. Then he grabbed my arm and lifted me up from my seat, and proceeded to push me out of the food court and then through the casino."

"Did he say anything to you during that time?" I asked.

"He told me to take him to the money or else. That's all he said, and he wouldn't answer any of my questions. So, my dear Em, I'd say, for sure now, we're in trouble."

"Damn, damn, damn. Did you recognize him?"

"Nope, never saw his face, but his voice sounded familiar. I guess we're being followed after all, huh?"

"Seems so. At least the money is in the safe, though, and no one knows where we are. I think we should keep it that way. Still, we have to figure out how someone found out about the money in the first place."

"I totally agree. Now go call our detective friend, tell him what happened, and then I think we should go check on Ahmed tomorrow and see if there's any connection there."

And that's what I did. Detective Lombard sounded overworked. He apparently took down everything I said, told me that he'd keep an eye out for us, but that since we couldn't identify the man, we'd just have to be extra careful. That's it. Very unhelpful.

Well, it looked like Justin and I had only ourselves now, but that was okay, as that's all we ever had, anyway. We hoped, at any rate, Ahmed could shed some light on all this.

The next morning we called Earl, who had taken the day off to tend to Ahmed. He invited us to come on over and see how our friend was doing. Kind of ironic to take a cab to a cabbie's home, but we were through with walking for now. Too dangerous. From now on, we would only catch rides from the back entrance of our hotel.

Earl didn't live too far from the Strip, but I suppose most of the people who work in Vegas live fairly close by. Besides Mary, I doubt that many people choose to live out in the desert. Earl was no exception. He lived in a small, one-bedroom house in a nice, clean neighborhood about ten minutes away. He greeted us at the door like long-lost relatives. I suppose he rarely had company—and judging from the fresh vacuum tracks on the carpet and the tidy appearance of his house, he had taken some time to make a good impression on us. Well, we thought it was for us, but we were soon to learn the real reason.

"Ah, welcome to my home," Earl said, and then gave us the grand, but short, tour.

His home was very basic, with just the necessities to live comfortably. The only overwhelming characteristic was the stench of cigarette smoke that permeated everything. Thankfully, he had the windows open or I don't know how long I would've lasted in there. The last stop on the tour was his bedroom. We stopped in front of the closed door to talk before he showed us in.

"How is he?" Justin asked.

"He's better now, just a little tired," Earl whispered.

"Did he tell you what's been going on? Why he fainted?

Who's following him?" I asked, also in a whisper. I guess we didn't want Ahmed to hear us talking about him. Not that it mattered. We were about to ask him the same questions to his face.

"Not too much, no. Whenever I bring it up, he goes sort of silent. He did tell me that he's having some immigration problems. That he lost his job for some reason, but wouldn't go into specifics. And that he's basically broke. I guess the reason he fainted was more out of starvation than anything else. The boy's been eating like a pig since he got here. He sure is a sweet kid."

Well, that didn't answer too many questions for us. Though, by the look on Earl's face, I'd say he was smitten with his new roomie. But who could blame him? Ahmed is adorable. It also explained why the house was newly cleaned. And then Earl opened the door to let us see Ahmed for ourselves. And yes, he most certainly was still adorable. He was propped up on the bed, wearing an overly large pair of jammies, and had a box of doughnuts sitting to his right and a bag of chips to his left. I wasn't sure if Earl was tending to him or fattening him up. In either case, Ahmed looked happy to be there.

"Hello, Justin. Hello, Em," he mumbled through his stuffed mouth.

"Hello, Ahmed. You're looking much better than the last time we saw you," Justin said.

"Oh, yes. Mr. Earl is taking much good care of me. I am very sorry for causing you worry," he said, looking like a remorseful child.

"Em and I are very happy to see you looking better. You had us very worried yesterday. Can you tell me why those men were following you?"

The smile on his face faded fast. He swallowed his food before answering. "What men were following Ahmed?" he asked.

"The men in the black car that made you so nervous," Justin replied.

"No men. I no remember any car. Just felt weak and ended up in casino," he explained, but there was hesitation in his voice, and his face was giving him away. He was definitely keeping something from us.

Justin backed off the topic and moved on. "Okay, then, Ahmed, can you tell me how you lost your job at the bar?"

"They fire me," he said.

"Yes, but why?"

"Oh... (pause)... immigration come around, asking questions. They not like that at the hotel, and they tell me to not come back. No job, no money. This is why I faint yesterday." He was looking more nervous by the second. I would've felt guilty had we not all been in such apparent danger.

"I'm sorry to hear that, Ahmed," Justin continued. "But why was immigration asking questions about you?"

"I don't know. My papers are in order. I have work visa. But when immigration comes looking for you, is a good idea to keep away from them. No way Ahmed is going back home. I like it here in U.S.A." Again I sensed we were only getting half-truths, but it seemed like a bad idea to argue: we didn't want to scare him off.

"Okay, Ahmed, I see your point. Can I ask you one more question?" Justin asked.

"Sure, okay," Ahmed told him, tentatively.

"Did you tell anyone that we had money with us or that we were looking for that vase I told you about?"

Now a bead of sweat trickled down from his brow. Whatever he was hiding, whatever danger he was in, I was sure it was somehow connected to us. But how? It didn't look like we were about to find out just yet, unfortunately, because Earl, seeing Ahmed's obvious distress, cut in and put our interview to a sudden end. "Okay guys, I think that's enough for the day. Ahmed here is weak and tired, and the stress is gonna make him sick. You can come back when he's a bit stronger. Right, Ahmed?" Earl said.

"Yes, please," Ahmed groaned. "I'm sorry I am no help, but I tell you everything I know. I swear. I know nothing about these things. I'm just trying to get by."

"Okay, Ahmed. We believe you. You just get your rest and we'll come back and see you when you're feeling better. All right?" Justin said, though I know he didn't believe him for one minute.

"Yes, Justin. That would be nice. Bye for now."

And that was the end of that. What else could we do? It was Earl's house, and we didn't want to piss him off, so we said our thanks to both of them and left. And really, it seemed pointless to argue, anyway. He was obviously not going to tell us what we needed to know. We'd just have to bide our time until he was ready to come clean. We prayed that we had the time to bide. Whoever was after us had left a trail of bodies, and if we had anything to say about it, we weren't going to be next. With or without Ahmed's help, as Gloria Gaynor used to sing, we would survive.

"Hey, Em," Justin said as we left Earl's. "You forgot Ahmed's backpack again."

"Damn it, I did. Funny how he didn't ask about it," I said.

"I think he was just relieved to see us go," he said.

"Well, next time remind me," I suggested.

"Yeah, that'll happen. With your two brain cells left, and my one, which is dangerously close to flickering out, I'd say we should just carry that damn backpack with us from now on if we're ever going to remember to bring it back to him."

"Never mind."

"Uh-huh, thought so."

And so we left, with a lot ventured and nothing gained. Par for the course, my friend. Par for the fucking course.

The Bitch Is Back

AFTER WE LEFT AHMED AND EARL, WE CAME UP WITH A plan of action. We were tired of sitting back and letting bad shit happen to us. It was time to do some shitting of our own. (Sorry for that one.) True, we could have or should have let the police handle it. That would've been the smart thing to do. But we also could have been killed while we were waiting. That would've sucked, obviously. And isn't it better to go out in a blaze of glory than let the flame eat you up alive? Okay, maybe I'm being a little overdramatic here. Point is, we were bored and scared and we knew we had to do something.

Basically, we had to get a handle on the whole mess; and we only had one real clue to go on. Once the shock of Justin's almost-kidnapping semi-wore off and our brains were back to working at their sick and twisted maximum capacity, we figured out who the blond with the bad disposition was. I know, it's, like, a total duh, right? Remember the blond bartender with a little napkin and our whereabouts written on it? Fine, so it took us a while to figure it out. But you try using deductive reasoning with a gun pointed to *your* back and then let's see what happens. Now the question was why.

"Well, we only have one resource now if we're going to find out anything from that guy," Justin proclaimed.

"Which is?" I wondered.

"My powers of sexual persuasion," he replied, very matter of factly.

"Oh, really? And what if your powers are useless on him? He looked straight to me," I said.

"Trust me. A boy knows. It wasn't just a gun he had pointed at my back, you know."

"Okay, fine. Not like we have any better alternatives."

"Way to go with the positive thinking, Em."

"Shut up and let's go strut your stuff. Oh, and besides, what makes you think you're his type, anyway? Maybe I'm the one who should be using his powers of sexual persuasion."

"Em, honey, I said positive thinking, not delusional thinking."

"Fucking dick."

"Exactly, now let's go."

We arrived back at the Aladdin nervous as hell, but equally determined. Again the disco was dead, due to the early hour; to our great relief, Zahir was not at his station. We did, however, spot the blond bastard at the same bar as before. He did a slight double take when he saw us enter, scrunched his face up a bit, and then was all smiles as before. That was enough to let us know that we had found the right man, though we played ignorant when we went up to speak with him. (Though really, there was nothing to play. We were ignorant.)

"Hi, remember us?" Justin asked.

"Oh, sure. How's it going? Um, I'm sorry, but Ahmed

hasn't been back. Guess he's gone," Blondie said.

"No, he's not gone. We found him," Justin said.

Boom!

"You did?! Where is he?!" He practically jumped over the bar, but then quickly regained his composure. Subtlety was not this guy's strong point. But we still didn't let on that we knew he was the culprit.

"Um, Em, don't you have to go meet your *friend* at the bar?" Justin turned to me to say, and gave me a *beat it* look with his eyes.

"Oh, er, sure, yep, my *friend*, right," I said, playing along. "Okay, bye, then. See you, um, later."

Not the smoothest, but I doubted our bartender knew we were on to him. He was, apparently, a natural blond. And then I left them alone, which was fine by me. The close proximity to our nemesis was making me quite uncomfortable. How fortunate for me that we were in a casino. Nothing more relaxing that sitting with a Malibu rum and a wad of cash at a lucky slot machine.

I say *lucky* because that's just what it was. Damn lucky. I sat down, a waitress materialized immediately to take my order, which never happens, and I slid my twenty-dollar bill in. I placed the maximum bet, pulled the arm, and up came genie...genie...genie. This was obviously a slot machine made specifically for the Aladdin, as I had never seen genies replacing the stereotypical joker or clown before.

I also had no idea what I had won, because no winnings slip was sliding down for my eagerly awaiting hands. How strange, I thought. But the light above the machine was lit, which indicated that a floor worker was being called over to give me something. Of course, had I just bothered to read the payout grid above the spinning wheels, I would've figured out what I had won, but I was too excited to bother with all that. Well, sure enough, some five minutes later a female genie appeared and handed me a receipt.

"What's this for?" I asked. Usually they pay out your winnings in cash right then and there if it's a really big win.

"You got three genies, sir," she said.

"Yes—and?"

"And three genies gets you a week's free stay at the Aladdin. See, it says so right here," she explained, pointing to the large letters on top of the machine that said just that.

"Oh, yes, I see," I said, nonchalantly. "Thanks."

I tipped her a few dollars and she was gone. I sat there grinning, playing it cool, so that the several grannies sitting around me wouldn't think I was a first-timer or anything— but inside I was ecstatic, brimming over with joy and delight. I was singing that golden ticket song from *Willie Wonka* in my head and thinking how I almost never, ever win anything big. And *this* was big. Huge, even. A week at the Aladdin had to cost nearly a thousand dollars. Our luck seemed to finally be changing. Or so I thought.

"What's with the big grin?" Justin asked, appearing to my right.

"Oh, hey, how did it go?" I asked.

"Not so well. The man's straight as an arrow and just as pointy-headed. I doubt he even knew I was flirting with him."

"So you got nothing from him? No indication as to why he's after us, our money, or Ahmed? No hint that he murdered three people?"

"No, no, no, and no. He acted like nothing was up. The entire meeting was nothing more than aggravating. And, while I was there, he made derogatory references to three women who passed by. Not only is he most likely a murderer and a thief, but he's also a sexist and a pig. Which gave me an idea."

"Oh, joy, another idea."

"Hey, if you want to wait around for the ax to drop on your head, that's fine by me. I'm just trying to be a little proactive here."

"Okay, fine, sorry. What's your idea?"

"I'll tell you, but first tell me what was with that silly-ass grin."

"Oh, right, look," I said, and handed him the receipt.

"Hey, perfect timing. It says we can use this anytime, and we're gonna need a room for her. How very fortuitous," he said.

"Um, who's *her*?" I asked.

"*Her* is our secret weapon," he answered.

"And just who is this secret weapon, pray tell?"

"Why, Em, the secret is Glenda."

"And since when is Glenda a secret?"

"Since she's going to find out why that bartender is after us, our money, our lives, etcetera."

"Ah, I see. And what makes you think she's going to help us and risk her own life in the process?"

"Dude," he said, and pointed to my bright, shiny receipt.

"Oh, so you're gonna get her here under false pretenses and then trick her into helping us?"

"Now you're thinking like a pro."

"No, now I'm thinking like you, and that scares me. But Glenda does sound like a good idea. Plus, I really miss her. You call her, though. Then I won't feel so guilty. Oh, and you have to tell her the real reason she needs to come here. You know, this whole mess is getting seriously dangerous, dude."

"Fine by me. Besides, now that we know who the bad guy is, and he doesn't know that we know, we're much safer. And we'll follow them everywhere and never let Glenda out of our sight. Okay?"

"Fine, sounds like it could work. Now, go call and let

me use the rest of these bills up. They're burning a hole in my pocket."

"Em, I think you have a problem."

"Oh, yes, *I* have a problem. *I* have a problem. How ironic is that?"

"Fucker."

"Dickhead."

"Here, use this roll of fifty-cent pieces too," he said, handing me the nice, thick stack.

"Ooh," I cooed. "Justin, I love you."

"Like, duh."

"Wait," I shouted as he got ready to leave, "I'll go with you, and then I'll spend your money. Not that I don't trust you, but—"

"But you don't trust me."

"No."

So I went with Justin while he made the call. It wasn't that I didn't trust him to tell the whole truth and nothing but, but, er, well, okay, I really didn't trust him. Years of hanging around with him had taught me otherwise. Besides, I wanted to say hello to Glenda and answer any questions she might have had related to our current predicament.

Fortunately, and to our great surprise and delight, she wholeheartedly agreed to our offer, even with the threat of doom looming over all our heads. Seems she was bored silly in San Francisco, with no job and no us to keep her company. Anyway, as she told me, she could take care of herself just fine. And years of hanging around with *her* had taught me just that. So we hung up the phone, she bought the plane tickets for the very next day, and I went and exchanged my receipt for a room for a week at the Aladdin. Even with COMDEX still in full force, they had the room available. I guessed that they saved rooms for high rollers and triple-genie winners, such as myself. And I was fairly certain that those rooms didn't stink like a pool.

Now all we had to do was make it through the night without getting followed, kidnapped, chased, or murdered. That should've been easy, but considering our recent luck, maybe not. To be on the safe side, we donned our overly large hats and studded glasses as we made our way back to Caesar's. And we looked over our shoulders every two minutes. Nothing was there to cause us concern. No black car. No blond bartender. No SWAT team. Just a few thousand tourists and us.

When we made it back to our room, there was a lovely red rose taped to the door, care of Caesar himself. And though he didn't say anything about it, I detected a slight grin on Justin's face. It seemed that my friend might finally have been softening. Apparently, getting kidnapped will do that to a person.

"So now what do we do?" I asked, after I plopped down on my bed.

"We move the dresser in front of the door and wait for Glenda to come to our rescue," he answered, and got up to do just that. I helped. Seemed like a good idea, all things considered. Besides, the housekeeper had already restocked the minifridge, meaning we were set for the night.

Glenda arrived the next morning, bright and early. We were so thrilled she was joining our little group again that we woke up way before our usual time and met her as she got off her plane.

"Wow, you guys must be desperate. It's only nine-thirty," she exclaimed, and promptly gave us both a hug.

"Why? Can't we just be happy to see an old, dear friend?" Justin asked.

"Not at nine-thirty, no," she responded.

"Yes, we're desperate," I admitted.

"Thought so," she said as we made our way through the airport.

We stopped at a coffee shop, loaded up on caffeine and danish, and filled Glenda in on all that had been going on with us. She shook her head in disbelief as the story unfolded. "So, you've barely been here a week, three people are dead, there's no vase, and someone is out to either kill you or steal the money that Brian gave you, right?" she summed it up. We nodded a yes in unison. "Well, that sounds like a typical week for you two," she said with a grin.

"Hardly," I said, and gave her another hug to indicate how happy I was that she was there.

"Hey now, cut out the mushy stuff. I'm here for the free room and board," she said, pushing me away.

"Who said anything about board?" Justin asked.

"Oh, there's board, all right. And none of that crappy off-the-Strip board, either. You guys are going to fatten this chick up but good. If I'm gonna risk my life for you two, it's gonna be on a full buffet stomach," she informed us, patting her tummy. We readily agreed to her demands. And then we were off to the Aladdin once again.

"What's the deal with the granny hats and glasses?" she asked as we got into a cab.

"Incognito," we answered, and handed hers to her. We came prepared.

Minutes later, we pulled up to the hotel and were in our new room, pronto. We decided that the less we were seen on the street, the better.

Now, to say that Glenda's room was bigger and better than ours at Caesar's would be a gross understatement. Her room was not only palatial in comparison, it also had this wonderful aroma of fresh-cut roses. Where we had two twin beds, separated by a tiny table lamp, Glenda had a fabulous king-sized one, complete with an expensive-looking comforter set and extra-fluffy pillows. Where we had our measly, poorly stocked minifridge, Glenda had a full kitchen and a welcome wine, fruit, and cheese basket fit for a queen.

And since we weren't the queens it was intended for, we were outrageously jealous. I was beginning to wonder if it had been a good idea to give Glenda that room instead of ours. She never would've been the wiser. (Alas, there's that nasty hindsight dilemma again.) But maybe, if we were lucky, she'd let us crash there. Oh, I prayed for that. My sinuses were not thrilled with the constant odor of pool.

"Nice room," she said, indifferently, and threw her luggage down on the plush bed.

"Nice? Is that all you can say?" Justin asked, indignant at the fact that he was sleeping in something one level up from a trailer and she was in this luxurious suite.

"Okay, nice—*and* would you like some champagne and orange juice?" she quickly added.

Justin didn't have to think too hard on that one. A minute later, we were downing our mimosas and talking strategy. Basically, the plan was simple. Glenda would go down to the disco, dressed to show some leg and some boob, she'd flirt shamelessly, and then agree to go out with our mystery bartender. Then she'd find out all she could about him. Okay, it smacked of danger, but it seemed that it could work, so we decided to stick with it for the time being. Actually, the three of us liked it because it was ridiculously easy to come up with and we didn't have the minds for any convoluted schemes so early in the morning. Well, okay, any time of day, really.

Once we were good and liquored up, we sent our genie lure into action. Glenda wasn't in Vegas for even an hour and she was already dressed like a common hooker: high heels, short skirt, and a low, low, low neckline. Oh, our little girl was growing up (and out). And then she was gone. I felt a twinge of guilt, but knew that it was this or Detective Lombard, and I doubted that the latter was hard at work for us. Just to be on the safe side, though, Glenda had brought us several pieces from her wardrobe for disguise.

We decided to put something on and go down to have a look-see for ourselves, just to make sure that everything was going okay.

With Justin in a blonde wig, a classy black mid-length dress, and two pairs of pantyhose to cover the leg hairs (he could go with a revealing neckline, as his chest, arms, and shoulders were always shaved, the big fag) and me in a brunette wig, a demure pair of slacks, and a cashmere pullover, we made our way down to the disco. Ah, to be in heels once again. It's amazing the sense of power you feel when you gain two inches and strap on a pair of fake boobs.

We got there just in time to discover Glenda already deep in conversation with our prey. He looked totally mesmerized by our gussied-up friend, and, from what we could see, Glenda was showing no restraint to reel him in. If she had placed her breasts any closer to him, she'd have been sitting right in his lap. To assuage my guilt I kept telling myself *King-sized bed and welcome basket. King-sized bed and welcome basket.* It was comforting that, at the very least, our bartender was on the cute side. I couldn't begin to imagine what we would've had to offer Glenda if he'd actually been ugly.

"Well, all appears to be going as planned," Justin said, a smile wide on his face.

"So far, so goo—"

"Can I get you lovely ladies something to drink?" interrupted Zahir.

Uh-oh.

"Yes, please," said Justin, in his barely feminine drag voice. "I'll have a double martini."

"And I'll have a double of what he's having," I added, demurely crossing my legs.

"Oh, I see you ladies have—how you say? A strong constitution."

"Yes, you could say that," I replied, and batted my

161

eyelashes at him. Why? I don't know. Something about being made up like that makes me act the hussy. In any case, Zahir winked at me and practically ran to get us our drinks.

"Slut," Justin said when we were alone again.

"Oh, you should talk. Just look at that outfit you have on. Could you be any more desperate-looking?"

"Jealous."

"Bitch."

We were rescued by Zahir and two very tall and very strong drinks.

"I am Zahir," he informed us after we took our first potent sips. "Are you ladies staying at the Aladdin?"

"Oh, no, we're just visiting a friend who's staying here," I informed him. "There she is over there." I pointed to Glenda, and Zahir made a nasty face.

"You should tell your friend to stay away from that man. He no good," he told us, and we nodded, already well aware of that fact.

Just then, Glenda stood up, shook the bartender's hand, giggled a bit, and then started to walk out of the bar. She did a double take as she passed our table, then turned back around to join us.

"*Girls*, how nice to see you," she said, suppressing laughter.

"Would your friend like a drink?" Zahir offered, and we accepted for her. Glenda's eagerness to help is only surpassed by the size of her liver. In other words, she could drink Justin under the table. A truly stupendous accomplishment, no doubt.

A minute later, we three ladies were sipping our smart cocktails and chatting aimlessly with Zahir, who seemed to have nothing better to do than stand there and flirt, primarily with me. *Gulp*. And when our drinks were done, Zahir made his move.

"I get off work at seven, pretty lady. Would you like to go have dinner with me?" he asked.

"Oh, Zahir, I'm flattered but—" I started to say.

"She'd love to," Justin finished my sentence. "Her name is Marilyn. She'll meet you here at seven."

"I will?" I asked, very confused.

"No," Glenda interrupted, "She'll meet you at the entrance to the hotel at seven."

"I will? I asked again, even more confused.

"Yes!" they both practically screamed.

Zahir looked equally confused, but took their yeses as my yes, and before I could even begin to think of a way out of it, he excused himself to get back to work. He told me he'd see me at seven and then left. I was too shocked to say anything but okay. Never in my wildest dreams, and let me tell you, they can get pretty wild, did I ever imagine that I'd go on a date with a straight man. And in drag, no less. What the fuck was going on?

"What the fuck is going on?" I asked them both.

Justin answered me. "Look, Zahir says that that bartender—"

"Bart," Glenda interrupted.

"Bart the bartender?" I asked, giggling.

Justin continued, "Fine, Zahir says that *Bart* is no good—"

"He did?" Glenda interrupted again.

Again Justin continued, perturbed by the continual interruptions, "Yes, he did. Which means that he may be able to shed some light on all this. And you, my dear *Marilyn*, are gonna pump him for that information."

"I hope that's all I'm gonna pump," I added.

"Whatever it takes," Justin said. That had me worried.

"But why did you make the date at the hotel entrance, Glenda?" I asked her.

"Because I'm meeting Bart here at seven and he, apparently, doesn't care for Zahir either," she explained.

"Ah," Justin and I aahed.

"And what will you be doing, my dear Tabitha, while the two of us are going out on our reconnaissance dates?" I asked Justin.

"I'm going to drop in on Earl and Ahmed and see what else I can find out," he/she told us.

"Wow, I feel like one of Charlie's Angels," I said, getting up to leave.

"I'm Jill!" we three shouted in unison.

We gave that one to Justin, as he was the blond.

"I'm Kelly," Glenda and I called.

We gave that one to Glenda, as she had the long brown hair.

And that left me as Sabrina, which was fine by me, as I always did have an affinity for Kate Jackson. (Well, I'd rather have been Farrah, truth be told, but who wouldn't?) And with that agreed upon, we headed back to Glenda's room to get out of our outfits.

"Okay, Angels, now that we have our individual assignments, let's get out of these heels and into the rest of that bottle of champagne. This isn't going to be easy and I think we need to be good and toasty if we're gonna get through it in one piece," Justin proclaimed as he swished through the lobby.

"Man," Glenda said as we boarded the elevator, "I missed you guys. San Francisco was so boring without you. This kind of stuff never happens to me when I'm by myself."

"And this is a bad thing?" I asked, scratching my head. (The wig was itchy.)

To which she replied, "Hmm. Good point."

Luckily, Glenda brought a lot of extra clothes, as I wanted to look just right for my first straight/drag date. Does that sound, er, creepy? Don't worry, it did to me as well—but since I was going *undercover*, I decided to go all out. We did have a lot to lose if one of us wasn't successful that night. And a cute, sexy Marilyn had a better chance of finding out some good dish than a homely, frumpy one. In the end, we decided on a long evening dress and a soft, feminine sweater-vest to cover up my otherwise manly physique. I even bit the bullet and shaved my arms and shoulders. (Yes, dear friends, I'm a big fag as well.)

When we were through, and my wig was combed out long and flowing, and Glenda applied enough makeup to cover up my stubble and add some lovely cheekbones, I looked, well, let's just say that I was no Bo Derek, but I was a far cry from Bo Jackson. Still, I planned on insisting on a dark restaurant with nice wide tables. No sense tempting fate by placing a horny Arab right next to my hairy knees. After all, I doubt he would have appreciated what I was hiding beneath my dress. (Impressive as it was.)

With the three of us dressed for our missions, we went into action. Justin left for Earl's, Glenda for the disco, and me for the lobby. Zahir was already there waiting for me when I arrived, with a lovely smile on his face and a pretty pink corsage in his hand. I nearly felt guilty for what I was about to do. I say nearly, because absolutely no one looks nice with a small spray of flowers pinned to their dress or adorning their wrist. And this was no prom we were going to. Still, when he offered it to me, I gracefully pulled it from his hand and quickly pinned it to my dress. There was no way I was going to let him touch the fake boobs. Actually, the tiny bouquet did a good job of hiding the fact that I had no nipples. (Big woman nipples, that is—I *have* nipples of my own, of course.)

"Ah, how beautiful you look tonight, Marilyn," he said, giving me the once-over. I hated to admit it, but he looked pretty swell too. Out of his genie outfit and in a nice pair of khaki slacks and a form-fitting button-down shirt, he looked downright handsome and devilishly sexy. Sort of like a grown-up-looking Ahmed.

If gay white guys who like Asian guys are called rice queens, what are gay guys who like Middle Eastern guys called? Mujadara queens? And how about gay guys dressed like straight women who like Middle Eastern guys? I have no answer for that one. Let me know if you find one. More than likely, I'm the only person on the planet with this fetish, so feel free to make something up. In any case, what I'm trying to say is that he was making me quite moist beneath my dress, figuratively speaking, naturally.

"Shall we go, then?" he asked.

"After you," I said, forgetting my new gender rules.

"No, ladies first."

"Oh, er, right. Thank you."

A moment later, we were in a cab and on our way to dinner.

And then, as luck would have it...

"Earl!" I shouted, noticing who our driver was.

"Do I know you, lady?" he asked, looking at me in his rearview mirror.

"Oh, um, oh, no, sorry. I just saw your name on your license up on the dash. Earl was my father's name. I guess I just get a little excited when I meet someone else with the same name. We were very close," I explained. Quick save.

"Apparently," said Earl. "Where to?"

"The Venetian, please," Zahir told Earl.

"Yes, sir." Earl looked up at me again through the mirror. "You know, you do look a bit familiar, ma'am. Maybe we have met before."

"Oh, no, I don't think so. I'm not from here. Never been here before this week. No, sorry." A mite too edgy, but, considering the circumstances, I think you can see why.

"Sure, calm down, lady," Earl said, his eyes returning to the road.

"Yes, Marilyn, calm down," Zahir said, reaching over to hold my hand. (Uh-oh.) "It's just that you are so beautiful. This man probably thought he see you in some fashion magazine."

"Oh, yeah, that's it," said Earl, snickering beneath his breath, but loud enough for me to hear. I let it go. No sense rocking the boat, or cab, as was the case.

"My, my, Marilyn, you sure have nice, strong, *large* hands," Zahir whispered in my ear, and gently lingered with his lips on my earlobe. (Did I say uh-oh already?)

Thankfully, the cab arrived at the Venetian not a moment too soon. It was getting awfully hot back there. And a nylon dress did little to protect against sudden bursts of, well, male turgidity. Especially since all I had on beneath the dress was a skimpy pair of Glenda's panties. I should've Saran-Wrapped myself down, but who knew that Zahir would turn out to be so brazenly sexy. And I was relieved as hell when Earl got out to open the door for me and I could release my hand from Zahir's grip. Between the smell of smoke and the smell of my date's cologne, not too mention his big, strong, hairy hands on mine, my poor little head was spinning.

He paid Earl and we walked into the stunningly beautiful lobby of the Venetian, and my heart started to flutter. Sick truth be told, I was semiexcited to be out with Zahir. Yes, it was under horrible circumstances, and yes, he thought I was a woman, but I was still flattered that he found me attractive. Okay, he found Marilyn attractive, but you have to assume that he must've seen my inner beauty as well, right? Well, whatever, *I* did, and that's all that matters.

Okay, before I tell you about our date, let me give you the quick rundown on the Venetian. Obviously, by the name, you can tell that the theme is Venice. Now, first thing, the Venetian is one of the few hotel/casinos in Vegas that from the outside is just as amazing-looking in the daylight as it is in the evening. At night, the Bellagio, Paris, Bally's, etc., are all stunningly beautiful, but during the day, they are somewhat drab and average-looking. This is not the case with the Venetian.

You walk up to the place on a ramp that has outdoor canals with authentic gondolas on either side. The water is a clear, cold blue, which goes so well with the off-white and muted tans of the entire building. To your far left is the clock tower of St. Mark's, complete with the standard big-screen casino ads. To your right is the beautiful Rialto Bridge, the Campanile, and Madame Tussaud's wax museum. (On a side note here, inside the wax museum you can take pictures with Bette, Barbra, Liza, Cher, and Judy. You go right on up and put your arms around them. Really. It's like, well, almost, sort of, like being there with them. Okay, if you're a big old screaming queen like me, this is something to get excited about.) The façade of the building is gloriously finished with intricate brick patterns, statuary, and Italian architectural features, which lets you know immediately that you're about to enter something grand. And trust me, you're not disappointed.

The main entrance to the building is the two-story Doge's Palace. The first floor takes you into the casino and the second into the Grand Canal Shoppes, which I'll get to in a bit. Either way you go in, or even if you enter through the side, which is the hotel entrance, you're greeted to spectacular ceiling murals and lots of gilt. (That's gilt, as in covered with gold, not guilt, which is what I was feeling for tricking poor Zahir.) The casino is lavish and large, and everything serves to make you believe that you're in Venice. From the murals to the rugs to the furniture, they don't spare a euro to bring you the real deal. But what really brings it on home is the Grand Canal Shoppes.

If you can't make it to Venice, this has got to be the next best thing. You enter into a space with a tranquil, cloud-covered blue ceiling overhead and beautiful marbled floors beneath. Between heaven and earth are faux houses, palaces, storefronts and, the pièce de résistance, a canal running down the center of the whole thing. And running up and down the canal are sleek gondolas manned by opera-singing gondoliers, and tacky tourists being serenaded by them. The ambience of the place, combined with the music and the sense that you're outdoors, really makes you feel relaxed and awed at the same time. When you reach the center of the mall, you are treated to a large open plaza surrounded by wonderful restaurants and fake two-story buildings. Honestly, it's magical, in an unreal sort of way.

And here is where my date, also somewhat magical, continues.

"The canals of Venice, they are beautiful, no?" Zahir asked, in his dreamy accent.

"No, um, I mean yes, they are," I answered, languishing in his sexy presence.

"Though not half as lovely as you," he added.

Just my luck to meet a straight man with charm *and* good looks. Why couldn't I meet gay guys with lines like that? I was falling for his magnetism when I should've been finding out what he knew about Bart. But then again, I figured, I had all night. Why not enjoy the moment?

"Oh, Zahir, you are such the sweet talker," I said, nearly blushing. Though through all the makeup, I'm sure it was impossible to tell.

"It helps when you are with someone as lovely as yourself."

Damn, he was good. With that little number, I allowed him to hold my hand again as he walked me to Lord knows where. Actually, that's about when I started wondering exactly where he was taking me. We'd walked almost to the very end of the mall when it dawned on me what he had planned. Needless to say, I was not thrilled at the prospect.

"Um, Zahir, you're not planning what I think you're planning, are you?" I nervously asked.

"Why not, my dear, is it not romantic?" he responded, surprised at my obvious apprehension.

"Oh, yes, it's romantic all right. It's just that I hardly know you," I justified.

"Well, then, this will give us a good chance to get—how you say?—*acquainted*," he countered. By then, arguing seemed moot, as we were already in line. He had made the requisite reservation beforehand, and I couldn't decline, politely or otherwise. So I agreed, and decided to make the best of things. Why not? It was just a little boat ride, right? A boat ride, trapped, on the water, in a mall, on a thin, tiny boat in drag and in front of hundreds of strangers. Oh, joy.

Moments later, we were climbing aboard our authentic white-and-gold gondola and introducing ourselves to our authentic white gondolier, Gino. And then we were off. I don't know about you, but traveling down a man-made canal, through a mall, and under a fake sky is not my idea of relaxing, even under the best of circumstances, which these clearly were not. But Zahir looked decidedly happy, so I sat wrapped in the crook of his arm as Gino started to serenade us with something operatic. Well, that's the way things were going, anyway, until…

"So, Zahir, I've seen Ahmed," I mentioned, casually, to start the ball rolling—forgetting, of course, that Marilyn had no way of knowing who Ahmed was. But the wig was tight, and I was confused. More confused than normal, that is.

Unfortunately, ball rolling led to boat rocking.

"Where he is?" Zahir shouted as he leaped up and looked anxiously down at me. That, of course, ended the evening's serenade. Especially when I jumped up to try and get Zahir to sit down. Now Gino had two distraught people danger-ously standing up and moving about.

"He's safe," I shouted, trying to push Zahir back into his intended seat.

"That is fine. Now tell me where he is." Again he was shouting, causing most of the tourists around us, on both sides, to come over to the wall to get a better look. I'm sure we were offering the best free show in town. Why pay a hundred bucks for a performance when you can watch a floating domestic dispute for nothing?

"Okay, okay," I shouted back to him, "I'll tell you, I'll tell you. Just please sit down. You're rocking the damn boat, Zahir!" But it was too late. Too late for our gondolier, that is. Our shenanigans weren't only rocking the boat, they were veering us off our intended course. And with Gino trying hard just to stay upright, he was no longer steering us forward. When we rammed into the wall to our right, he went flying into the water, shouting Italian obscenities at us the whole way. Poor guy. In Venice, his customers must've been better behaved.

"Okay," Zahir finally agreed. "I sit now. But you promise you tell me or we stay out here all night."

"I promise, I promise," I promised, and sat down. He followed suit.

But then we had a new problem. We now had two behaved, seated riders and no one to drive the boat. Or row the boat, as the case may be. Gino, fed up with the both of us, was sloshing through the two feet or so of water and was headed for the stairs on the other side of the canal, leaving us ever so stranded.

"Come back, Gino, come back," I shouted over to him, sounding like a bad Italian movie. (I felt like an overly done up, decidedly homelier Gina Lollobrigida.)

"Come back, Gino, come back," echoed Zahir. "We be good now."

"Come back, Gino, come back," the crowd yelled from above, thoroughly enjoying the spectacle. But it was too late. Gino was already up the stairs and on his way back to wherever it was authentic gondoliers go when they've had enough of inconsiderate Americans. (Of course, Zahir wasn't an American, but you get my point.)

I turned to look at Zahir and shrugged, but rather than appearing concerned, or even pissed, he was grinning and looking deep into my eyes. Then he did something completely unexpected. Actually, he did two things completely unexpected. First, he leaned in and planted a big wet one on my lipsticked lips. What did I do? I kissed him back. It seemed like the Italian thing to do. Next, he jumped up, grabbed the rowing thingamajig, and started us moving on our merry way again, with the by-then-enormous crowd cheering us on.

And when we reached the end of the canal, where the gondolas usually turned to go back up the way they came, and where the gondolier would briefly stop to serenade the audience, Zahir stopped, reached out to take my hand, and started to sing, at full voice and in his deep, rich accent, "I Got You, Babe." Caught up in the moment, I stood up and sang Cher to his Sonny. Western culture had apparently made its way to the Middle East.

The mob around us was applauding at full throttle and throwing change into the canal. What an enormous waste of slot quarters, I thought, but I bathed in the adulation, nonetheless. Far be it from me to lecture the masses.

Then, with our duet over and the crowds returning to wherever it was they were headed in the first place—oh, those fickle fans—Zahir rowed us back to our starting point. The other gondoliers gave us nasty looks as we passed by, but Zahir seemed not to notice. He was intent on staring at me and getting us both back safely at the same time. My hero. I was just glad that we hadn't followed Gino into the water. My disguise wouldn't have held up well. Still, it might have been funny to see the reaction from the spectators above.

My reverie was cut short, however, when we docked and were thrown back into reality. And the reality was this: Security at the Venetian was not overly happy with us. With a modicum of subtlety, they politely escorted us out of the shopping center and back to the street. That was fine by me. I was plenty over the Venetian by that point, anyway. There was one thing I forgot to do though, and it put me in a bit of a dilemma. Well, there were really two things I forgot. One, I didn't get a chance to find out Zahir's connection to Ahmed. And two—

"Um, I think I should've used the little girl's room first, Zahir. My teeth, like those gondolas back there, are floating," I said, rubbing my thighs together to indicate my need to pee.

"Ah, that is a problem, Marilyn. I don't think is a good idea to go back in this hotel anymore tonight. Do you want to try to make it across the street to Treasure Island? There is a restroom near the entrance, I believe," he offered, and I nodded a yes as I started to speed-walk across the street. But then something that could only happen in Vegas prevented us from achieving our intended goal.

"Goddamit!" I shouted, very unladylike, as we suddenly encountered the crowd that had gathered in the street and on the sidewalk to watch the nightly Siren spectacle that made Treasure Island famous. Now, normally, I'd have been thrilled to watch actors cavorting aboard ships and raising hell for the appreciative tourists, but I really had to go tinkle. Badly. And it would've taken forever to get through the crowd. Luckily, my hero came to the rescue yet again.

"I know where we can go. You follow me," he said, grabbing my hand and leading me around the crowd to the side of the hotel. When we arrived at a dark corner with nothing but bushes in front of us, my need to pee was replaced by my need to flee. Going to the bathroom in front of Zahir seemed not the best of ideas.

"Oh, well... Oh... You see, Zahir, er, I'm what you call—" I stammered.

"Pee shy?" He finished my train of thought.

"Yes, that's it," I said. "Pee shy."

"Nonsense, Marilyn. You go pee right here and I will not look," he said, pushing me into the bushes.

Well, he didn't have to tell me twice. My bladder was about to burst. Besides, I could just as easily squat as stand, and he'd never know the difference. So I ambled forward, found a nice spot between two bushes, crouched down, pulled my panties to the ground, and let go with a nice, powerful stream. Aaaahhh.

"Oooohhh!" I shouted, as Zahir joined me in my precarious position.

"I missed you, Marilyn," he whispered. We were face to face when he leaned in and gently pressed his lips to mine. And still I continued to pee. That is, until...

"Wh-what are you doing?" I asked, feeling Zahir's hands on my hips. He was gently raising my skirt. That shut my bladder right off. Nothing like the fear of getting beaten to a pulp to stop the flow of things, so to speak.

"I am touching your hips, Marilyn," he sighed, never taking his deep brown eyes off me.

"That's fine, just please keep them there," I said, sternly, so he'd get the point.

He didn't. "So I can't do *this*?" he asked, moving his hands to the bunched-up material around my thighs.

I grabbed his hands before he could make it to my honey pot, and again told him to cease and desist. He responded by swirling his tongue around my neck and earlobe. That felt too good to tell him to stop. Besides, it was way dark and there was no chance that he could see my rigidness, which was now standing straight out and was barely being covered by my dress anymore. Unfortunately, when my instincts kicked in and my hands let go to reach for his crotch, he again went for my G-spot. Though now, the "g" stood for gay.

"My, Marilyn, what a big dick you have," he said, giggling.

I nearly jumped out of my pantyhose, but instead fell backward into one of the bushes, panties around my ankles and dress flung up around my waist. My heart was racing, and I would've run for dear life had I not been in such disarray (and in the midst of a rather thick bush). I prayed that if he was about to pulverize me, he'd be so kind as to not disfigure my face. My body I could cover up.

But I was quick to discover that he had completely other intentions. My first clue was that he was rolling on the ground, howling with laughter. Not a sign that he was upset with my little charade.

When I had regained enough composure to speak to him, I asked, "And what are you laughing at?"

"Oh, Marilyn, I am sorry, but I am laughing at you," he said, relapsing into his laughing fit. I was not amused. Relieved, yes, but amused, no.

"So you knew all along?" I asked.

He stopped laughing long enough to say, "Oh, yes. You are not a very pretty woman, but you are a very cute man."

Okay, I wasn't so angry anymore. "So why did you let me go through all that?" I asked, and then scootched out of the bush and closer to him.

"Because I needed to find Ahmed. You were my only hope, dress or no dress," he replied, regaining his composure. "Ahmed is my brother and he's in trouble. And since you promised to tell me where he is, there was no longer a need for you to be a woman. I am sorry, Marilyn, but I very much love my brother and I have to find him."

The tenderness in his voice was melting my heart, but I had to wait just a bit longer before I could find out what kind of trouble Ahmed was in. Seems that even in the dark, Zahir's proficient hands had once again found their way beneath my dress, and he was gently stroking that sweet spot betwixt my thighs.

"Are you mad at me, Marilyn?"

"Not anymore, but don't stop, just in case."

Fortunately, the side of the building was dark and the bushes made it even darker. Even so, I could see him unzipping his fly and pulling out his hefty schlong. "There are hundreds of people all around," he said, leaning in for a deep, soulful kiss, "and none of these people are aware that two men are soon to cum together."

The thought made my cock pulse. "Better hurry, then, before they find out and want to get in on the action." I spit in my hand and began a slow even stroke on his hooded boner.

"They should be so lucky," he groaned, reaching out to match my rhythm.

It didn't take long, the riskiness of what we were doing getting my juices flowing even more than normal. "Close," I soon rasped into his mouth.

"Then shoot with me," he whispered.

And shoot we did, our heavy loads splattering in thick torrents against the ground beneath us, reflecting the white of the moon above.

"You stroke better than you row," I told him with a giggle, quickly getting my panties and dress back in order.

"And your dick is bigger than most women's I've been with," he replied, with a wink.

"Thanks, I think."

Hey, I figured, I'd take whatever compliments I could get, even strange ones such as that.

The next morning, our official one-week anniversary in Vegas, I awoke next to a six-foot-tall, amazingly hairy, totally sweet man. That old saying "the darker the fruit, the sweeter the juice" rang nicely true. And waking up enveloped in his big, meaty arms was like heaven. We had spent the night at Caesar's. I assumed that Justin was at Glenda's.

"Good morning, Marilyn," he said, licking the inside of my ear.

"You know that's not really my name, right?" I asked, rolling over so I could pet the thick matting on his chest.

"No?" he asked, innocently.

"No, it's Em," I told him.

"It's a Em?" he asked, a look of confusion spreading across his handsome face.

"No, it's Em, not a Em." I spelled it for him. By the time he figured out what I was saying, it didn't much matter anymore. We were happily in playback mode from the evening before, minus the bushes, the wig, the dress, and my itty-bitty panties. Glenda would surely be pissed when she saw the grass stains, but it was well worth it.

When we were done, he leaned in and said, "I definitely like you better as a man than a woman." He kissed me, long and perfect. "Now you take me to my brother, please."

"Okay, but first can we go find my friends and get me into some more appropriate clothes? I think I'm through with the Marilyn look for a while."

"Sure, but then we go see Ahmed, right?"

"I'll do my best, Zahir. I promise."

He smiled and nodded. I was glad that I could help him find his brother, but the question still remained...

"What kind of trouble is your brother in?" I asked, sitting up to look at him.

"Oh, that is good question. I wish I had good answer. Ahmed follow me to America maybe two years ago. I get him job. I get him place to live. I even get him boyfriend. But Ahmed is young and foolish. He takes to this country fast.

Drinking, drugs, gambling. Is hard to be gay in my country, so when you come here and have all this freedom, is easy to get out of control."

Hey, it's easy to get out of control when you're born here. Look at me. But I pressed on rather than having an open discussion about it. "And Ahmed got out of control?"

"Oh, yes. I try to be a good role model, but he is, as I say before, young. I am not quite sure why he not come to work lately, or why he leaves apartment and no returns, but I know he is in trouble. That is why I must see him soon."

He looked pained as he told his brief story. But at least I, for one, knew where Ahmed was. The problem now was to tell him about the murders and the possible connection to Bart, the bartender, without getting him even more upset.

"Um, any idea how Bart would play into all this?" I asked.

"Oh, Bart is nasty man. Why you ask?"

"We think that he's after your brother too, but we don't know why. At least not yet."

"Is true, Ahmed and Bart are friends. Oh, well, maybe not friends so much, but they do spend time together after work. I do not know what they do together, though. Bart is very, very straight. He loves the women. Ahmed is very, very gay. So Zahir have no idea what they do together. Ahmed tells me to mind my own business. I tell him, Ahmed is my business. Is very sad. But I think Bart not nasty enough to do anything bad to my brother."

When I told him the rest of it, about how we thought Bart tried to kidnap Justin and that he might have been involved in the three murders, that's when he shot out of bed and got the both of us dressed. Then we practically ran back over to the Aladdin. So much for not getting him upset.

We were back at Glenda's room in no time flat. The two of them were giving each other facials when we arrived. I was a tad peeved that they weren't concerned that I didn't make it back the night before, but, given the circumstances, I didn't broach the subject. "Ah, the wayward friend returns," said Justin as we entered the suite. His hair was wrapped up in a towel, his face was a shocking color of green mud, and he was warmly ensconced in one of the Aladdin's cozy bathrobes. I guess his pores were of a greater concern than my well-being.

"But where is Marilyn?" Glenda asked, looking like Justin's twin. Through the masses of goop on their faces they both shot me a knowing grin.

"Um, seems like Zahir saw through my little disguise and was hoping we could shed some light on his brother's whereabouts. Funny, huh?" I said, plopping down on the bed to join them. Zahir sat in a chair by the bed and faced our little ménage à mess. I quickly explained Zahir and Ahmed's story to them so they'd be in the know.

"That's all fine and dandy," Justin eventually said. "But there's a bit of a problem."

Zahir jumped up and shouted, "Where is my brother?"

The three of us let out little-girl squeals and practically fell off the bed. His sudden outburst had taken us by surprise. Poor guy. I reached out to hold his hand and bade Justin to continue.

"Well, that would be the problem. When I got to Earl's last night, Ahmed wasn't there," he explained, and Zahir's hand squeezed mine for dear life.

"Maybe he just didn't answer the door," I suggested.

"Good, Einstein. Yes, I thought that too. And after hanging around outside for an hour and seeing no movement within, I decided to do some investigating. I searched the sides and back of the house. There were no lights on, the shades were all open, and I could see that there was no one inside. And before you say that he could have been hiding under the bed, or some such genius notion, let me say that I too had that same idea and decided to find out for myself."

"Uh-oh," I moaned, which caused an even tighter vise grip on my hand.

"Uh-oh is right. Seems our friend Earl is not too diligent when it comes to locking up after he leaves. The window to his living room was noticeably unlocked."

"So you broke in?" Zahir practically shouted.

"Bingo," Justin answered, and touched his nose with his finger to indicate a right answer.

"Well, that's a lovely thing to do. What if you got caught?" I asked.

"Wait, he's getting to that," Glenda chimed in as she gingerly applied ruby-red polish to her toenails.

"Yeah, shut up and let me finish. Anyway, where was I? Oh, yes, breaking and entering. Maybe I missed my calling. It was oh so easy." (I was unaware that Justin had ever had a calling to anything besides happy hour, but I let him continue.) "First thing I did was to whisper Ahmed's name. But nothing. Not a peep. No sound of scampering little feet along the floorboards. So I went deeper into the bowels of the house."

"What deeper?" I interrupted again. "There's only the living room, bedroom, bathroom, and kitchen. You only had to walk a few feet to get to any one of them."

"Please let him finish, Em. I've already heard this story a bunch of times and I'm eager to be done with it," said Glenda, who was now applying the polish to Justin's toenails. I nodded for Justin to continue.

"Thank you, Glenda. Some people never learn. So, as I was saying, I decided to go exploring. And, as it's been so rudely pointed out, it didn't take me long to discover that the place was empty. Unfortunately, it was empty and somewhat ransacked. Perhaps it wasn't so smart to leave Ahmed there alone, I'm guessing." (I gave a little cough to remind Glenda and Justin that Ahmed and Zahir were brothers. I didn't want either one of them to say anything more about

Ahmed that might make Zahir even more upset.) "Anyway, when I realized that I was already in a home that had been burgled, I decided it was a good idea to leave. No sense getting myself into even more hot water. But, as they say, out of the frying pan—"

"And right smack into Earl," finished Glenda, and then added, "Sorry, it's just that I've already heard this part repeatedly before you both arrived." Justin shot her a nasty look for ruining his tale, but seeing as she had control over his feet, he allowed it and continued.

"And, yes, right into Earl. I was just leaving the bedroom and he was coming in the front door. Neither one of us was too happy to see the other. And when he noticed that (a) Ahmed was gone, and (2) his place had been robbed, guess who he blamed? He was just a few seconds away from calling the police when he noticed a note sitting on the nightstand. Luckily, Ahmed still had something of a conscience left, because he let Earl know that he had to leave fast and that he needed money. Apparently, Earl kept about a hundred dollars in one of his dresser drawers. Ahmed helped himself."

"I'm sorry for my brother," Zahir interjected, "but he must really be in trouble to do these things."

"Which leads us to the next question," I said. "What did Glenda learn from our friendly neighborhood murderer/kidnapper/bartender?"

"I learned that you guys are lucky this is a suite with a well-stocked bar. That guy's a total creep," she restated the obvious.

"And he's got a small weenie," Justin added.

"And we know this how?" I asked, my jaw dropping at the comment.

"Because he showed me," she answered.

"He showed you? *Where* did he show you?" I asked, now shocked.

"In his apartment," she answered, head held low.

"Oh, my God, how did you get there from here?" I couldn't begin to imagine.

"He tricked me," she answered.

"He tricked you to go to his house and he tricked you into looking at his prick?" I was beginning to sound like a deranged yet nelly Perry Mason.

"Uh-huh. But you guys wanted me to get you some information and I was just being...um...amenable." That shut me up. Guilt is nature's ultimate humbler. I sat back down, apologized for getting so upset, and asked Glenda nicely to continue. She shot me a nasty look and did just that. "Okay, I met him at the disco, as planned, and he was, like, ooh, look how sexy you are, and ooh, baby this, ooh, baby that; and I had to sit there and accept it. Every feminist muscle in my body was cringing, but I smiled and said thank you and forced my demure side to come out and play. Oh, did I mention the two bottles of Dom in the fridge that I charged to your credit card, Justin?" (We nodded that it was fine with us. Her self-respect was worth way more than that. Besides, he could afford it.) "Anyway, that's when he told me that we needed to go to his house so he could change. The alarm bells were going off, but what choice did I have? We couldn't go to dinner with him still dressed like a genie, so I said that was fine, smiled, and allowed his arm in my arm as he led me to his car."

The toenail treatment continued. Mine were next, and though red is not my color, I allowed her to paint me so that she had something to do with all that nervous energy— besides slapping us silly for talking her into our mess. Zahir removed his feet from our proximity for fear of being next. His Palestinian upbringing was coming through, and I felt bad for him, but I was glad he was now part of our team, for better or worse, because now we had a new challenge besides staying alive and finding that damn vase. Now we had to find Ahmed, too. I rubbed his thigh as Glenda went on so he'd feel like one of us. His smile brought a much-needed warm spot to my heart (and my loins).

She continued, "I knew, before we even reached the parking lot, that he drove a sports car. It totally fit with his personality. But when he pointed out the Corvette parked across two parking spaces, and I saw the gold paint job and the big silver pipes hanging out of the rear, I knew that I had severely underestimated his machismo quotient. And when we climbed in and I sank into the leopard-spotted bucket seats and he cranked up the heavy metal crap that he had in his CD player, and he started to make that head-banging motion with his arms and neck, I also knew that you guys would owe me big time. This guy was a Super Dick. He represented every repressed-little-boy, self-centered, egotistical stereotype that I loathe. He did everything but spit chewing tobacco out the window. Oh, and I had no doubt that he was thinking I found the whole routine irresistible. When, in reality, I was pressing my body as close to the door as I could so I could be as far away from him as I could get."

I jumped up on the bed and gave her a neck massage. Out of guilt? Hell, yeah. I was having super sex with Zahir while she was on the date from hell. Still, at least she was sleeping in a luxurious suite with absolutely no lingering scent of chlorine, so my pity level was not at its maximum. And the fact that she was sitting in front of me, safe and sound, lessened my remorse considerably. Plus, since we were all sitting there waiting for our nails to dry and not running from danger made for a nice peaceful feeling, which I, for one, truly needed by that point. But the specter of death still hung over us. One had only to look over at Zahir and see the worry on his face to know that this was just a breather from the very real and very dangerous journey we were on.

"And the tiny penis?" I asked, curious despite myself.

"You would obsess on that point," Justin said, checking out his new paint job.

"Well, just trying to get all the facts here," I replied.

"Uh-huh," he said. "What-ever, Mary."

"Play nice, ladies, or mamma won't finish her story." Glenda stepped into the foray and we both nodded that we'd try.

"Okay. Well, the penis thing went like this. When we got back to his place, which was covered in beer posters with scantily clad women and lots of particleboard furniture, he excused himself to go to the bedroom to get a change of clothes. I sat on the red vinyl sofa and counted backward from ten in the hope that a brief meditation session would calm my jangled nerves. When I reached one and opened my eyes, he was standing in front of me, yakking away, drinking a Miller, and changing his clothes. He obviously made good use of the bench press that he kept in the corner of the living room. I feigned appreciation for his pecs and abs, knowing that I was gaining points with each compliment. What he didn't know was that I was digging my nails deep into his nasty couch to keep from killing him. One nail went right through the material when he had the gall to get out of his genie slacks and into his tight jeans in front of me. No surprise: he didn't wear any underwear. And there you have it—one shrimpy peepee. My guess is that he hadn't seen many to compare it to, because he had no qualms about me seeing it. He even looked down at it appreciatively when he noticed me looking. Inside, I was laughing, but my face only showed admiration."

"You poor thing," I said, petting her back.

"No, not really. It gave me a sense of empowerment, knowing him intimately like that. Anyway, that's not the good part of the story," she said, now getting excited.

"There is a good part?" Zahir spoke, finally, from his chair. He was admiring our feet from afar. I think he was a bit jealous of our glamorous toes, but was too embarrassed to say anything. When I jiggled the nail polish bottle in front of his face, he nonchalantly shrugged, but didn't argue when I got on the floor, peeled off his socks, and initiated him into our little coven. (Is it weird that I popped a boner while I was polishing him up?)

"Well, there's a good part in terms of our little dilemma here," Glenda said. "When he excused himself to 'go take a crap,' as he so delicately put it, I knew that it might be my only chance to do some snooping. Once the door was safely closed behind him, I went into action. I ran through the house looking for anything that looked out of place. And that's when I found it."

"Found what? Found what?" shouted Zahir. He nearly knocked the bottle out of my hand with his newfound enthusiasm. And if you've ever spilled nail polish on a rug, you know how big of a bitch it is to get out, so I urged him to simmer down and bade Glenda to continue.

She smiled with a sense of well-deserved pride and finished her tale. "Oh, yes. Our man Bart is up to something. His garage is attached to his kitchen, which was right off the living room. I noticed that he parked his car on the street and not in the garage, so this was the first place I went looking. Lo and behold, spread out on every square inch of space, were dozens and dozens of televisions, stereos, VCRs, CD players, computers, and a whole bunch of other electronic equipment. He's either a thief or a fence, but no doubt, he's a bad guy."

"Unless he's collecting for charity," I chirped in, feeling very Zen as I worked over Zahir's hairy toes with my little brush. He was now tense as hell, more likely from Glenda's story than my paint job.

"Dude, this guy wouldn't have stopped to help his own mother if we'd passed her on the street and she was begging for spare change. He made sure to tell me, as we were driving home, that he was short on cash and that we'd have to go Dutch for the night. Meanwhile, he's got thousands and thousands of dollars worth of merchandise out in the garage. Please, charity is the last thing on this man's puny mind."

"Well, that's more knowledge than we had before," I allowed, "but how was the rest of the date?"

"Ah, that's the other good news. Having found what I was looking for already, I feigned cramps. Knowing that my condition meant no sex for him that night, he gladly drove me home. I shot out of the car before he could even try to kiss me good night. Mission accomplished. Bottles of champagne ordered."

"And how do you think Ahmed plays into all this, Zahir?" Justin asked, from the bed.

"I wish I knew. He did ask me for money before he disappeared, but I barely make enough to get by. I know Bart makes same as me. There is no way he could buy all the things you speak of. If Ahmed is involved in this, it can only mean no good," Zahir answered, shaking his head in shame for his brother. (Or he might have been looking down to see my progress. I could tell he liked his new look.)

"So now what?" I asked, putting away my tools and admiring my work.

"Now we go to Plan B," Justin answered.

"Plan B?" the rest of us asked.

"Oh, yes, Plan B. Or as I like to call it, Plan Bart."

"Which is?" I asked.

"I'll let you know. Still working it all out in my head, but I think it may solve all our problems," he answered.

If it were anyone else, I would've pressed for more. But I knew better than to disturb the master while he was at work. And I could practically see the gears moving in his twisted little brain as he sat there on the bed looking down at all our toes.

"I think Zahir wins," he proclaimed.

"Yes?" Zahir asked, looking down as well.

"Oh, yes," we all said, nodding our heads.

"Zahir thinks so too," he agreed, folding his arms in triumph. "When do we do our hands?"

"Ah," Justin aahed. "Now that would be the start of Plan B."

Plan B (Part One)

First thing we realized was that we'd have to infiltrate the enemy: the enemy being Bart, of course. And, since we knew of only one obvious weakness in our enemy, namely women, we figured that would be our primary line of offense. Glenda, who had her fill of Bart already, politely declined her services on that front. Actually, she said, "No fucking way." For which we couldn't rightly blame her. So Tabitha was enlisted. And since Justin rather enjoyed playing his alter ego, it wasn't a hard sell. The thought of spying on our adversary, undercover-like, made for a more interesting challenge, at least in Justin's devilish mind. And it was a hell of a lot better than sitting around doing nothing, though certainly a lot more dangerous.

Naturally, preparing for all this involved some heavy-duty girly shopping. Glenda's clothes were fine, on Glenda, but they weren't exactly Justin's taste, or size, for that matter. So on to the mall we went. Yes, believe it or not, Vegas has a Fashion Outlet only a short distance from the Strip. All we had to do was hop on a conveniently located shuttle and voilà—Donna Karan, Neiman Marcus, Versace, and dozens and dozens of other designer shops were right at our beautifully polished fingertips.

First, we had to kiss Zahir goodbye, as he had to go to work. Well, I had to kiss Zahir goodbye, anyway. My new, handsome, dark lover slipped me a note before he left so I'd keep him on my mind until we saw each other again. (As if I'd forget, right?) Then we were off to the shuttle, which was located at the MGM Grand. The sun was glaringly bright, so the three of us weren't overly conspicuous in our matching bonnets and glasses.

The MGM is about a half a mile up from the Aladdin; and, since you can just as easily walk through the casinos as alongside them on the sidewalk, we chose the former as our way of getting there. I justified that it would be harder to spot us and then follow us if we kept to that route. Naturally, I dropped a few dollars in the slots along the way. Why waste good gambling time? Funny thing, I was forty bucks ahead by the time we boarded the van. I figured I could at least buy one pretty frock for myself with my winnings, even though we were primarily going for Justin/Tabitha. (Why should he/she have all the fun?)

The van was luxuriously air-conditioned, which was wonderful because it was hotter than hell outside. We even managed to relax for a few minutes until...

"Um, Em?" whispered Justin, from the seat in front of me.

"Um, yes, my love?" answered I.

"I know you hate it when I say *Don't look now*, but—" he didn't say it, but pointed out the window instead.

"But there's that black Mercedes again, and it's riding right alongside us." I finished his sentence, then gulped. So much for relaxing.

"What black Mercedes?" Glenda asked from the seat next to mine.

I pointed it out to her and explained why this was a bad thing. She echoed my gulp.

For the rest of our journey, we rode in silence and watched our unknown neighbors ride alongside us. They never looked up, just watched the rode in front of them, and were never more than a few car lengths away. The only saving grace was that we pulled up to a carport when we arrived and could run out of the van and into the mall in no time flat. The black Mercedes was two cars behind us and still had to park, so we had at least a few minutes' head start. But head start to where?

Running through the mall, I shouted to Justin, "Now what?"

"Now this," he answered, and veered us into the Gap Outlet store to our immediate right.

The three of us hurried through the shop and into what quickly became a too-tight dressing room.

Glenda, thank goodness, took control of the situation. "Okay, you two stay here and I'll go get some disguises. Hopefully, they won't recognize me should they come looking. My guess, and I hope this is the case, is that they're only looking for you boys."

"Gee, so much for all for one and one for all," said Justin.

"Hey, I know you've lived enough for three people, but I'm not through yet," she snapped.

"And what about me?" I chimed in.

"Not-so-innocent bystander," she answered, and left our cubicle.

"Well, Lucy, here's another mess we've gotten ourselves into," I said, plopping my ass down on the small bench. I looked tired and worn-out in the mirror across from me. (Damn that fluorescent lighting.)

"Now, Ethel, we're not sunk yet. It's always darkest before the dawn," he quipped.

"Well, it's *dawned* on me that we're in some deep doo-doo," I quipped back.

"At least we have each other," he said, patting my head from his standing vantage point.

"Oh, joy," I replied, lackluster-like, and slumped down.

Our speedy friend appeared a short time later with three new outfits in hand. "Lucky I know your sizes," she said, handing us our duds and some matching pumps.

"You know how red makes my feet look fat," Justin complained as he tried to undress. Three was definitely a crowd in there, but at least we were well hidden.

"What's that saying, Justin? Oh, yeah, better red than dead," she said.

"Good point, but I think it's better dead than red," he replied, getting into his pullover.

"Will you two shut up?" I implored, tired of the chitchat. "We're running out of oxygen in here, already." Which was highly unlikely, as there was an open space just above the door. In any case, they took the hint and piped down for my sake.

Five minutes later, we were all in new clothes and shoes. Glenda thought it best that she have a disguise as well, to be on the safe side. I think she just wanted a new outfit for her troubles, but didn't say as much. See how mature I'd become? Still, standing there in my cashmere V-necked, short-sleeved cardigan and bun-hugging Gap jeans for women, I didn't think that mature was necessarily the right word. Maybe if we had run into Lord & Taylor, but not the Gap. Justin looked lovely in his knee-length khaki skirt and ribbon-adorned top. No surprise, Glenda went all out for herself with a rather fetching pair of leather pants and a matching leather top. I felt cheated. Which was sort of asinine considering the circumstances.

Glenda topped us all off with brand-new Gap caps and a layer of makeup for Justin and myself. Then she grabbed our wallets and put them in her purse. We'd have to leave our lovely granny hats and chic shades behind. I couldn't say that I'd miss them. It was not a good look for me. Then again, my ass didn't look too hot in my *new* look either. I had little time to inwardly bitch, however, because, as we emerged from the dressing room, we spotted our men in black on the other side of the mall, apparently looking for us in the Lane Bryant shop. As if our lithe bodies would be caught dead in there. (Oops, bad choice of words, huh?)

"Now what?" I asked, fairly trembling. Well, teetering was more like it. Glenda had picked a pair of pointy-heeled pumps for me. (Say *that* ten times fast.)

"Now we tuck our price tags into our outfits and stroll out of here. I guess the outlets in Nevada don't worry about those pesky security tags or are too cheap to bother. Let's just count our blessings they don't have them," Justin whispered, heading out of the Gap first. Glenda and I followed close behind. Thankfully for us, the store was busy and run by gawky, uncaring teenagers, because we made it out of there without even a sideways glance from anyone.

And when we strolled nonchalantly by our mysterious followers, they didn't even notice us. (Let me tell you, being gay certainly has its advantages sometimes. A straight man could never have convincingly pulled off those heels.) My heart nearly returned to normal once we were beyond their range of sight.

"And the plan now?" I asked as we hurried into a Starbucks for a much-needed pick-me-up.

"Now? Now we continue with our original plan of the day. Tabitha needs some new clothes, shoes, and accessories. And since these disguises seem to work to our advantage, I'd say that Marilyn needs some as well."

"Works for me," I replied. And it did. Shopping is the ultimate cure-all. Even shopping for Marilyn had an immediate relaxing effect on me. And Glenda could give Imelda

Marcos tips on shoe shopping. So the three of us, with our double lattes, went hog wild at the Las Vegas Fashion Outlet and completely forgot about those nasty men in black.

Almost.

We separated, to better maximize our energies. Justin went off for slacks, dresses, and tops; Glenda for her precious shoes; and me for accessories. I'm not ashamed to admit that a fabulous bracelet gives me a hard-on. A marvelous handbag can do the same. Hell, even a well-priced pair of earrings can make me break out in a sweat. (Okay, maybe I'm a little ashamed to admit it, but we all have our weaknesses, you know.)

I was admiring a darling little Gucci clutch, marked down twice, and I got so nervous that I dropped it. Oops. And while I regained my composure, I lost my balance and went toppling over, landing on said purse and tripping one of the men in black. Double oops. When I looked up and beheld what I had done, I nearly panicked. I say nearly, because it was obvious he didn't recognize me. And I looked right into his eyes before we both got up, so I would've been able to tell. Actually, he turned beet red when he saw that he had knocked down a woman (or the next best thing), and apologized profusely as he helped me back to my feet.

When he was satisfied that neither the purse nor I was damaged (I was much more concerned about the purse than myself. Did I mention that is was marked down twice?), he very politely left. No chase scene. No stabbing, shooting, beating. No nothing. And I, for one, was grateful. I had finally fooled *someone* into believing that I was a woman. The whole Zahir thing had given me my doubts.

And that's when I noticed it, sitting just beneath some stunning Versace scarves that were hanging down from a rack. I looked around to make sure he was out of sight and then I gingerly bent down to retrieve it. The man had dropped his wallet when we collided. Flipping it open, the first thing I saw was his badge and ID. It read: Detective Randall Shelling, F.B.I. I don't know whether it was from noticing that the scarves were half off or from it dawning on me that the F.B.I. was following us, but I started to hyperventilate. And I got weak in the knees. And then I plopped down on the floor and tried to catch my breath.

When I looked up to see if anyone had noticed my current state, I spotted the detective coming back down the escalator. From my position, I was sure he couldn't see me, so I crawled around the scarves, making sure to grab the prettiest one for myself, and hid my drag ass in the middle of a circular rack that was overflowing with marked-down furs. Now, normally, I'm opposed to the slaughter of animals for their fur, but in this case I made an exception. After all, now it was my own hide that was at stake. I sat huddled in the middle of all those soft jackets and waited. And waited. And waited some more. I didn't want to take any chances of getting caught.

"Marilyn, oh Marilyn, where is your nelly self?" It was Justin.

"I'm down here, you loud-assed queen," I replied, still hidden down below.

Justin bent down to find me among the furs, and asked, "Did we find a new way to shop for coats?"

"No, a new way to hide from the F.B.I."

Well, that got his attention. He too plopped down on the floor and slid in among the coats. It was, fortunately, a rather large rack, so we easily fit, even with the several bags of merchandise he now had on him.

"Excuse me?" he asked, feeling the plush merchandise around him.

"You heard me, F. fucking B. I." I flashed him the badge.

He took it from me and gaped in shock that it was now in my possession. "As if we weren't in enough trouble," he lamented, handing it back.

"Well, he did drop it. It's not like I took it or anything."

"No, but you didn't give it back to him either, did you?"

"Not exactly, no. But it all happened so fast, and I was shocked that he was who he was, so I hid here instead," I explained, but realized how damning it sounded as soon as I said it. Still, the less time spent with Detective Shelling, the better. We didn't know what he and his friend wanted with us, so I was playing devil's advocate and assuming the worst. Hence my foray into the world of fashionably expensive coats.

A few seconds later, we could hear Glenda sing-songing from somewhere close by, "Tabitha, oh Tabitha. Yoo-hoo, Marilyn."

"In here," we said, just above a whisper, and rocked the coat rack for good measure.

"Is this your version of the burning bush, only with fur?" she asked, standing a few inches away from our hiding place. She now had several boxes of shoes with her.

"Yes," Justin answered from within. "What's the password?"

"I have new shoes for both of you," she answered, correctly.

"Please, do come in," Justin said, parting the coats to make room for our companion. Now it *was* a tight squeeze, what with the third person and three boxes of shoes.

"Did you guys lose your room at Caesar's?" she asked as she tried to make herself comfortable.

"We'll tell you, but let's see the shoes first," demanded Justin.

"Take a look at these," she said, lifting the lids off her goods. There was one pair of stunning black-leather Ferragamos, one pair of sexy burgundy demi boots from Nine West, and an ultraglamorous pair of navy pumps from Jimmy Choo. All three were stunning. (And I've seen my share of ladies shoes to know. How very sad.)

"They're gorgeous," Justin exclaimed, grabbing for each one to get a closer look.

"And dirt cheap. Each for under a hundred bucks," she said, beaming. We sat there awed by her success.

"I know, this place is amazing," I said, showing them my purse and scarf, plus a few odds and ends I'd already purchased. They oohed and aahed at my bargains as if they were stolen treasures.

"And look at these," Justin said, adding to our fashion melee. He whipped out several slacks, skirts, and blouses. All were stunning and inexpensive.

Glenda and I whistled in amazement.

"Maybe we're living in the wrong town," she said. "These are the fiercest bargains I've ever seen."

"Um, Glenda, were any of the men who waited on you gay or at least reasonably cute?" Justin asked.

"Not that I noticed, no," she answered.

"Then we're not living in the wrong town," he retorted, and we nodded our agreement.

"By the way," she said, after putting the shoes back in their boxes, "why are we in this cavern of fur? You know my opinion on that."

"Unavoidable detour," I told her, and flashed her the badge. I was getting quite good at doing that. When I explained how it came into my possession, she just waggled her head and tsk-tsked me.

"Well, out of the frying pan and into...into... Well, at least it's something soft. Anyway, if it makes you feel any better, we can get out of this rack. I spotted the Feds leaving the store about five minutes ago," she informed us.

We gladly abandoned our new clubhouse for the spacious environs of the mall. On our way out I purchased my darling purse, scarf, and a few bracelets and clip-on earrings that I found on the way to the counter. Justin's outfits were lovely and the shoes were great, but it's all about the accessories, child. (Listen to your Auntie Marilyn.)

We three *ladies*, heavy with our shopping goodies, left through a side entrance and cabbed it back to the Aladdin. We agreed to leave all the clothes with Glenda, in case our room was being watched. That way, no one would know about our secret identities. Now we just had to keep Bart from finding out as well, and all would be grand. We hoped.

First thing I did when we got back to the Aladdin was to go visit Zahir. Justin and Glenda went up to the room for a nap. I was still high from our shopping spree and couldn't even think about lying down. Besides, I was horny for my desert lover.

"Oh, no," he said, seeing me approaching from the side of the bar, "Why is Em in girl clothes again?" I filled him in on the day's events. He was none too happy with the F.B.I. thing. That meant, more than likely, that Ahmed was in even bigger trouble than he thought. I hadn't even considered that, and felt truly awful for being the bearer of such bad news, so I decided to make up for it a little.

Sitting on the side of the bar, and with no one else near me, I ordered a frozen mai tai and flirted with Zahir. I noticed Bart on the other side of the same bar, but he was busy helping other customers, meaning Zahir and I were relatively alone. Well, as alone as you can get in the middle of a casino nightclub. Happily, it was still early and the place was only sparsely populated.

"Um, Mr. Genie, sir, I have a big problem," I whined, finishing my drink and lifting my skirt for him to see why panties were definitely not made for men.

"My, my, pretty lady, that is a *big* problem," he whistled, then added, "But I can definitely help you with it." He slid something atop the bar and winked at me. When I looked down, there was a lovely Aladdin key sitting on the counter.

"Wait ten minutes, then go to the end of the hallway to the left of the nightclub. There will be a door. Use the key, open the door, and wait for me, just like you are now, and I will help you with that problem of yours." He bowed.

I nodded my assent and shot him a wicked-ass grin just before I slid my skirt back down and hid my obvious stiffy with my purse. (Again, see how important those accessories are?) Actually, I got it down just in time. Our nemesis, Bart, approached from Zahir's left and peered down at me just as I hid myself. Talk about your close calls.

"Well, now, who is this pretty lady?" he asked, giving me the once-over. Normally, I'd be flattered, but seeing who the compliment was coming from, I was... I was... Okay, I'm vain, so I was flattered, but I barely gave him a smile in return.

"This is um, er, Marilyn, Bart. She is a new friend of mine," Zahir said, introducing me.

"Well, Marilyn, any friend of Zahir's is a friend of mine. And if you have any pretty girlfriends, send 'em my way. All are welcome," he said, repugnantly. I almost ignored the comment until I remembered Plan B.

"Actually, Bart, I think I know someone who would be just your type," I offered.

"You do?" Zahir asked, slightly taken aback.

"You do?" Bart asked, thrilled at the prospect.

"I do," I replied, proud of my quick thinking. "Her name is Tabitha, and she's free tonight if you boys want to double-date."

And before Zahir could think of a way to say no, Bart readily agreed to my offer. I gave Zahir a look to indicate that everything was all right and not to worry, but I could tell he was plenty worried. For good reason, I'm sure, but these were desperate times, and desperate times called for ridiculously impossible measures. I told the boys we'd meet them back at the nightclub at eight, politely excused myself, and went to search for my genie's private room.

That's when I got a tad confused. I mean, really, *you* drink an enormous mai tai and see if you can follow directions. Did Zahir say to go to the left or to the right? So I did what any half-drunk drag queen would do. I closed my eyes, spun around, and then pointed. I ended up going to the right. There was a door at the end of the hall, and I figured I picked the correct room. The key worked, so I let myself in and made myself comfortable. The room I was in appeared to be a breakroom for, I supposed, hotel employees pulling long shifts. I guessed that was why Zahir had a key.

Oh, by the way, did I say half-drunk? I realized, as my new quarters spun dizzily around me, that I was very nearly wholly drunk. But I did remember Zahir's command to appear as I had on the stool, so I lay down on the bed, hiked my skirt back up, and rested my head on the nice comfy pillow. I guess I must've dozed off, because I awoke to a very warm and wet mouth wrapped around my regained woody. Yes, perhaps I should've opened my eyes to see who it was, but I assumed it must've been Zahir. In other words, I sat back and enjoyed the attention. It wasn't until I moaned Zahir's name that I realized I had made a big mistake.

"Nope," came a voice from my crotch area.

Well, that shot me right up, drunk or not. That's when that fickle finger (and tongue) of fate appeared again, and they both belonged to none other than Chris. In all the excitement, and I certainly had plenty of that, I had almost completely forgotten about my hot dealer man.

"Chris!" I shouted.

"Who the fu— Wait, Em? Is that you?" he shouted back.

"Yes! What are you doing here?" I asked, scootching away from his slobbering mouth.

"I work at several casinos. Better question: What are you doing here, and why are you dressed like that? And who is Zahir?" Well, that was three questions and I wasn't prepared to answer any one of them. Shame really, I owed him that much, but before I could answer, the door flung open and Zahir walked on in.

"Did someone mention my name?" he asked, surprised to find me there with another man. Though not half as surprised as I was to be there with the two of them.

"What's going on?" they asked in unison, looking over at me.

I demurely shrugged.

"Do you know this man?" they both asked, still looking at me.

I nodded in the affirmative.

Well, that set Chris off. "Look, I don't know what game you're playing, but I'm not into drag queens. (Could have fooled me. He sure was going at my you-know-what pretty well.) And I'm not into threesomes or mind games, so maybe I should just leave."

Before I could object or even comment, Zahir interjected. "Well, maybe you should."

"Fine, I will," Chris said, bounding off the bed and out the door.

And another good man was out of my life. Listen, being gay has its distinct drawbacks. We, and by we I mean me, of course—though I'm not too sure about you—anyway, we walk a thin line between wholesome ethics and complete depravity. Some of us cross that line more than others, but it always seems to be there, nonetheless, waiting for us to make that leap. Lately, I'd been leaving that line far in the dust. In any case, at least there was one man still standing in my wake.

"I said to take a left, Marilyn, not a right," he said, when we were alone again. Since he was grinning, I took it that he still had his sense of humor.

"My bad," I oopsed. "Your mai tai got me all turned around."

"So this is my fault?" he asked, closing the door and hopping on the bed.

"Basically," I replied, again lifting my skirt. "But I forgive you. Now how about that problem of mine?"

"Your wish, my juicy Marilyn, is my command."

And again I crossed that line, but lines are made to be crossed, my friend. Aren't they?

Still in drag, and still a bit loopy from the booze but considerably more relaxed, I returned to Glenda's room to find my friends in bed watching *Absolutely Fabulous* on Comedy Central. The similarities between the lives of the television characters and our own were striking, right down to the champagne bottle on the bed, the cigarette smoldering in the ashtray, and the "Sweetie, darling" that greeted me upon my entrance. What was more shocking, I discovered, after I glanced at the screen, was that Edina had a purse quite similar to my own. Mere coincidence? Who knows, but I took it as a good omen and joined my friends on the bed.

"Let's see, now," Justin began, as soon as I was comfortable and a commercial was on. "Judging from that familiar pungent odor that's coming off of you and that silly-ass grin on your face, I take it that you did more than just have a drink at the bar. What were you doing all this time?"

"Getting you a date with Bart," I announced rather proudly. They both jumped up at the news.

"Nuh-uh," he said, and slapped me on the arm.

"Yuh-huh," I replied, and slapped him back.

"Oh, goody, another intellectual conversation," chimed in Glenda, who was cradling her champagne glass should we obnoxious boys knock it over.

"No, really," I said. "We're doubling tonight. You and Bart and me and Zahir."

His face scrunched up, but then he obviously saw the

genius in my plan. "Fine, just one question, Marilyn, darling."

"Which is?" I braced myself.

"Did you melt in his mouth or in his hands?"

"Oh, how droll. Now, if you don't mind, can we please go back to our own hotel and take a nap before our big date? All this undercover stuff is fairly exhausting," I said, stifling a yawn.

"Yes, leave, already. You two are depressing me," Glenda interrupted. "Here I am, a real, honest-to-goodness, attractive woman, and I have no one to go out with tonight. And there you two are, completely unattractive faux women, and you both have dates. And, even sadder, I'm bisexual, so my chances should be doubled." She took a swig of the champagne to drown her sorrows.

"Poor Glenda," said Justin as he rose from the bed to get ready to leave. "Would you like to trade? Bart can be all yours, sweetie."

"Nice try, just go," she said. "Besides, I've had no time to do any gambling. Oh, that reminds me, give me some money to go do some gambling."

"Sugar daddy to the rescue," I said, opening the door. Justin reluctantly forked over a few twenties.

"Thank you," she said, gladly pocketing the bills. "I'll make sure to pay you back should I win."

"Like that'll happen," he said, meeting me at the door.

We waved our goodbyes as Glenda added, "Now you boys behave yourselves, and remember, no getting killed."

Words to live by, literally. I made a mental note of it. Well, we were three against one, for the time being, so at least our odds were getting better.

Of course, we still had to make it back to our rooms. Sounded simple enough, right? Not so, my friends, not so. No sooner had we made it to the lobby of the Aladdin than we noticed an irate-looking Earl to our far left and the Feds to our far right. Caught between a rock and a hard place (and not the good kind of hard place), we strolled gaily forward and prayed that neither would recognize us in our drag disguises. We were not so lucky. As usual.

First, when we got to the front entrance, those damn COMDEX people were completely blocking the lobby with their equipment and preventing us non-nerds from exiting. We had little choice but to turn around and use the side exit. Unfortunately, we had to walk by Earl to get there. My guess was that he was waiting to see if Ahmed returned. Wouldn't that have been a fortuitous event? I would've loved to see Ahmed too, by that point. But it wasn't Ahmed he was looking for, as it turns out—it was Zahir. And guess who he recognized as we walked by? Yep, Zahir's date from the previous night.

"Excuse me, ma'am. Don't I know you?" he asked as we strolled by.

"No, I don't think so," Justin answered for me.

"Sorry, but your friend looks familiar. Weren't you in my cab the other night with a tall, dark fellow?"

I decided on honesty for a change. "Oh, yes, I think I was. You're name is Earl, right? Just like my father."

"That's right. Actually, I'm looking for your friend. I have a message for him from his brother," Earl said, holding up a folded-up note. "Could you tell me where I can find him? I know he bartends here at the nightclub, but he's not at work."

"Oh, um, sure. Actually, I'm seeing him tonight. Would you like me to give him the message?" I asked, praying that it would end our encounter before Earl could see through our thin disguises.

He looked out at his waiting cab, then back at me. Obviously, he was missing work by waiting for Zahir, so he reluctantly accepted my offer once I promised to give Zahir the message. I stashed the note in my lovely new purse, and he thanked me and sped away in his cab.

"Um, Earl has met Marilyn before?" Justin asked, surprised that Earl had recognized me. I guess I neglected to tell him about our chance encounter.

"Briefly, yes," I said, without explanation.

"I see," he said. "And what does that note say that he handed you?"

Good question. I popped open my purse and took out the note, but before I could read it, our two men in black approached. Only one of them flipped us his badge—I guess Detective Shelling couldn't get a replacement for his lost one that fast.

"Ladies, can we take a look at that note?" asked the detective I hadn't bumped into yet.

"Oh, sure, detective. Here you go," I said, handing him the note. What choice did I have? I gulped as he read it. Not a good thing to do when you're trying not to have your Adam's apple show, but neither man looked up or noticed. Thank goodness I had the forethought to use that wonderful scarf I had bought earlier to cover said body part. (Again, see how important it is to accessorize?)

Both men appeared embarrassed after reading it and promptly handed it back to me. They apologized for detaining us and excused themselves. We both found that very strange, but gladly accepted their apology and started out of the casino yet again. When the heat outside hit our faces, we breathed a sigh of relief and started to walk in the direction of our hotel.

I'm afraid we weren't out of the woods just yet.

"Ma'am, oh ma'am," came a voice from within the casino. We both turned around to look and spotted the detectives running our way.

"Uh-oh," said Justin under his breath.

"Yes, detective?" I asked, when they were standing in front of us again. "Is there something else you'd like?"

"Actually, I was wondering if we'd met before," Detective Shelling asked me.

"No, I don't think so," I said, starting to sweat—not so much from the Las Vegas heat as the thought of being locked up in a federal penitentiary for stealing an F.B.I. badge. Drag queens don't look good in horizontal stripes.

"Really? Because I never forget a face, and you look awfully familiar," he said, inching in for closer inspection. Too bad the circumstances were so lousy. He was damn cute.

I paused to think of something, anything, to say to get him to move away. My limited brain capacity was working feverishly for an answer. Why did I look familiar? Why did I look familiar? Why did I look—

"Randall? Randall Shelling?" I practically screamed at him, and with my limp lady wrist pushed him away like we were long-lost friends. (Sort of in that way Elaine does to Jerry, in case you watch *Seinfeld*.)

"Ye-es," he said, trying to retain his balance from my push and still attempting to place my face. "Do we know each other?"

His partner looked at him strangely, and Justin looked at me like I had finally cracked. (We both knew that would happen sooner or later. I think Justin preferred later and not in front of the F.B.I.)

"Why, Randall Shelling. Don't you recognize me? It's me. Marilyn. Marilyn...Siegfried," I practically shouted, mostly from shock at hearing my own voice spewing all that out. (Oh, and I was looking up at the Mirage sign when I said it, which is how I came up with the last name. Don't worry, I didn't introduce Justin as Tabitha Roy. That might just have given us away.)

And still Detective Randall looked at me quizzically.

"Oh, come on now. You know, from school," I continued, praying that I was going in the right direction.

"From Auburn?" he asked.

"Go War Eagle!" (Don't ask me where I got that one from. I guess my brain can pull out some practical bit of knowledge when it's facing a long jail sentence.) I raised my fist in the air and lifted my thigh up so he'd think I was a cheerleader. (A girl can dream, can't she?) The overall effect was, to say the least, bewildering.

"Marilyn? Marilyn Siegfried? Oh...um...yes, of course. I remember you now. How have you been?" Thank God he was too embarrassed at having not recognized me to admit that he really didn't recognize me.

"Oh, Randall, you old flirt. It's good to see you," I said, again slapping his brawny chest. Justin looked on in amazement. "You're still the same old Randall, aren't you?" Again he stared at me strangely. I looked over at his partner and asked, "Is he still flashing women in public with his, er, billy club? That's how we met. Isn't that right, Randy?" I stroked his lapel with my index finger and gave him a sly wink. That did it.

"Well, Marilyn, it was nice seeing you again. Sorry for inconveniencing you. Please, go back to doing whatever it was you were doing," he said, very nervously, then turned away, pulling his gaping-mouthed partner along with him.

When they were gone from earshot again, Justin, also gaping-mouthed, turned to me and said, "Em, good buddy, the student has just become the master." And he gave me a slight bow.

"Just don't expect a repeat performance," I said, locking arms with him and walking rapidly away from there, lest our new friends return. "That was my one great, shining, original moment. All remaining brain cells are now officially exhausted."

When we were halfway back to Caesar's, and the shock had worn off a bit, he turned to me and asked, "What exactly did that note say that would make two F.B.I. agents blush and run away? I doubt Ahmed is sleeping with his brother."

"Good question," I said, and pulled out the note. Once I read it I knew immediately what had happened. "No, but his brother is sleeping with me."

The note I had pulled out of my fabulous new purse (no, I never get tired of saying that) to show the detective was the note Zahir had evidently passed to me just before we parted the first time around. It read: *Marilyn, until we see each other again, please keep your bush out of the bushes. Cannot wait to fill your hole again.* Sweet, if not a tad raunchy. Just how I like it. I could see why the Feds turned red after reading it.

"What's that about?" asked Justin, strumming his fingers on his dimpled chin. "As if I couldn't guess."

"Whatever, Mary," I said, waving the three-fingered "whatever" sign at him. "Just be glad I didn't pull out Ahmed's note instead."

"Agreed," he agreed. "Now, what does *that* note say?"

"Ah, a good purse always has more than one inside pocket. Now let's see... Okay, here it is," I said, pulling out the other note and reading it aloud. "Zahir, I am in trouble. Need your help. Please meet me in the garden at Caesar's Palace at noon tomorrow. Your brother, Ahmed."

"Well, at least *Randy* didn't read that note. I guess that's a good thing. Now if we're done with the surprises, I'm ready to get out of these clothes and into a dry martini," Justin suggested, and I wholeheartedly agreed. I'd tell Zahir about the note sometime over dinner.

And if you thought the predinner show you just witnessed was a mess, wait until you see the main course.

We met the boys back at the nightclub promptly at eight. For Justin, *promptly* is a miracle akin to getting blood from a turnip. (Well, for Justin, let's make that tequila from a gin bottle.) Actually, I think he was a tad aroused at the prospect of going out with a straight man, albeit in drag, undercover, and, potentially, with a straight man who was also a murderer/kidnapper/thief.

The funny thing was, Bart was late. Very late. And Justin was fuming. Talk about putting the pump on the other foot. Inwardly, I was laughing at the circumstances. Time and time again, I've waited for Justin outside restaurants, bars, clubs, and theaters. Now it was his turn to wait. I hoped he learned a valuable life lesson from the experience, but I seriously doubted it.

Of course, Bart being late, I was able to give Zahir his brother's note without having to explain it. Though he was upset about the content, he was noticeably relieved to know that he would be seeing Ahmed the next day. And I was happy to see him happy. Though I couldn't get *too* happy, considering the tight skirt I had on. I guess women are lucky that all their privates are kept on the inside and not on the outside, like us guys. (Though I try not to dwell on that subject for too long.)

When Bart finally did arrive, Tabitha was there to greet him and was all smiles. If he was going to get any information out of him, he'd have to put on quite an act—and since Justin had been pulling the wool over men's eyes for years, that should be a snap. Fortunately, Bart obviously found Tabitha attractive, and he showed it. "Wow, Marilyn, you really do have sexy friends," he said to me, gawking at Tabitha's shapely legs. All those years of walking up and down steep San Francisco hills finally paid off, apparently.

"Thank you, Bart," Tabitha giggled, batting her big, fake eyelashes at him.

Zahir, clearly nervous, hurried us out of the hotel and into a taxi. And then we were off on our lovely drag double date. (Which, even in San Francisco, I doubt is a regular occurrence.)

"Where to?" asked our cabby. No, it wasn't Earl, but the stench was the same.

"The Lobster Tail," Bart answered, and I, for one, was okay with the suggestion. As a man, I never got to order lobster—too expensive; but as a lady, I was sure to get treated. Drag does have its advantages, I suppose.

"No, no Lobster Tail," protested Zahir, and my dreams of melting butter started to evaporate.

"Why not?" Bart asked, then said to the driver, without waiting for an answer, "Ignore him and head for the Lobster Tail."

"No, no Lobster Tail," Zahir reiterated. Only, this time, he was staring hard at Bart and shaking his head. For some reason, Bart backed down and changed his choice of restaurants to Soup and Salad. Now I was mad. I may have been dressed like a lady, but I had a man-sized appetite, and soup and salad wasn't going to cut it.

"The Lobster Tail has shitty food, anyway," Bart added, with little enthusiasm. Then he sat back in the seat and pouted.

"Yes, bad food. And I cannot eat shellfish. Very allergic," Zahir said to me, apologetically. I nodded that I was okay with it, but my stomach was protesting the sudden turn of events.

Thankfully, Soup and Salad also had potatoes and pasta, plus a nice dessert bar, so my stomach was made a little bit happier. Too bad the rest of me was miserable, stuffed in a booth between Zahir and Bart. The two bickered endlessly over my meal. (No, not about my meal, literally *over* it.) As two people who claimed not to like each other, they sure were proving it, but it was weird that they seemed to have a certain rapport with each other. Sort of a standing relationship. I chalked it up to the fact that they worked together every day.

Besides, we had way more to worry about. When he

wasn't arguing with Zahir, Bart was shamelessly flirting with Tabitha. I noticed, on more than one occasion, that he had his fingers clamped around my friend's knee. Naturally, Tabitha let him keep it there, though I wasn't quite sure if it was in keeping with *The Plan*, or if he was just being his usual slutty self. Zahir also looked worried about it, which may have been the reason for his edginess over dinner.

This wasn't helped in any way when Bart suddenly made the announcement, "Yo, Zahir, I always thought you were a fruit loop. Nice to see you with a pretty *woman* for a change."

I could feel Zahir's leg bouncing up and down as he fought to gain control of his rage, but he knew that lashing out wouldn't have done us any good. Especially for Ahmed's sake. So he waited a few seconds before answering, and then calmly said, "I guess Zahir has seen, as you say, the light, Bart." He reached out to hold my hand to push the point home. Bart smiled and did the same with my poor friend Tabitha. And I smiled, knowing that we had just passed a vital part of The Plan with flying colors. If Bart couldn't see through my disguise, Tabitha had a good shot at finding out what was going on.

Thank goodness Zahir had some self-control. Well, he did until midway through our meal, anyway. That's when the evening ended rather abruptly.

"So, Zahir," Bart began, "where's your brother, Ahmed, been lately?" Wouldn't we all like to know that one? I thought.

"Why you ask about my brother?" Zahir practically shouted, but quickly regained his composure.

"Oh, no reason, just curious, is all," he answered, not looking up from his plate.

I was hoping for a more straightforward reply, as this was the whole reason we were there: to find out Bart's connection with Ahmed, and to my vase, and to all the other shit going on.

"I no like a man who doesn't know how to mind his own business," Zahir said, staring over at Bart. Bart looked up from his plate and over at a seething Zahir. I no longer wished to be in the middle of these two men, but had little choice but to sit there and listen.

"Fine, you don't like me and I don't like you either," Bart said, pushing his plate away and standing up. He grabbed Tabitha's hand and yanked her up, too.

"Fine," Zahir said.

"Fine," Bart echoed, and pushed Tabitha out of the booth. "We're leaving, then."

Justin instantly looked panicked, and my stomach once again sank to the floor. (It was beginning to feel at home down there.) Zahir didn't seem to like that idea too much either.

"No. No, wait," he tried, with a trace of alarm in his voice.

"Yes. Yes, please wait," I echoed. "Why ruin a lovely evening over such a minor disagreement?"

But Bart didn't agree with my oh-so-ridiculous plea. Our evening had been anything but lovely. He took one last look at our beseeching faces, shot us a scowl, and then dragged Tabitha's ass out of the restaurant. She turned her head to give us a *please help me* look, but it was too late. We couldn't think of anything more to say, and Bart was too fast in hurrying them out of there. Before we knew it, Zahir and I were sitting alone with our non-lobster dinners.

"Dessert?" I asked, trying to lighten the mood. But Zahir was obviously not to be lightened. He sat there, head in hand, and fretted. It was nice that he was so worried about my friend, but I had the distinct advantage of knowing that he/she could take care of itself. I tried to explain that to Zahir, but he remained agitated. Which was too bad because, for

211

some reason, ever since our experience in the bushes, whenever I put on a dress I became instantly horny. Granted, the same held true when I put on a pair of jeans, shorts, slacks, etc., but now I was especially horny. And seeing the butter on the table, and knowing how good a lube it made, wasn't helping my furiously overstimulated imagination.

Unfortunately, I risked making a sexual overture to Zahir just then. As soon as I placed my hand on his leg, he cried, "How can you think of such a thing when your friend is with…is with…that man?"

Sure, when you look at it that way, maybe I did come off a bit, um, selfish, but had the Ferragamo been on the other nylon-clad foot, my so-called friend would already have been beneath the table doing Lord knows what. And when I tried to explain just that fact, I came off looking even worse: desperate. And nobody likes a desperately horny drag queen. But at least I wasn't drunk. That would've been worse yet. Still, it was no reason for him to storm out the way he did, leaving me alone—with the bill!

And guess what? My fabulously stunning purse contained everything but money. And I doubted they'd accept a rhinestone-covered bracelet in lieu of cash. I also doubted that offering sexual favors would work either, as I had a drag face not even my own mother could've loved. So, once again, Glenda was called to the rescue. And since I had to wait for her to get there, wasn't it fortuitous that I was at an all-you-can-eat salad/soup/pasta/potato/drink/dessert restaurant?

By the time she arrived, I was nearly popping out of my dress, and in all the wrong places.

"My, my, my, ain't you the pretty one," she said, looking down at me as I finished off my second helping of soft-serve chocolate and vanilla swirl ice cream.

"Pretty and poor," I responded, my mouth full and ice cream dripping down my chin.

"Well, then, you're in luck," she said, pulling out a wad

of bills that could've choked Linda Lovelace.

"I thought Justin gave you sixty bucks," I said, moving the remainder of my ice cream to the top of my double-chocolate brownie with walnuts.

"Oh, yes, he did. And then I did something I've always wanted to do," she said, sitting down at my table and helping me with my remaining dessert. "I took the sixty, cashed it in for three twenty dollar chips, and then bet it all on red. Same color as these fabulous shoes I bought."

"But look at the stack of dough you have. How many times did you bet red?" I asked.

"Seven times. My lucky number. And when I stopped betting, the very next number was black. You should have seen the crowd I had amassed by the time I cashed in," she said, finishing my brownie and getting up to fetch some more. Since she was now paying, who could argue?

"So, let me get this, for lack of a better word, straight," I said, once she had returned with two more servings of everything. "I've been in Vegas for about a week now and am approximately two dollars ahead, which by Vegas standards is good, and you've been here for less than two full days and have been gambling for—"

"Roughly fifteen minutes," she interrupted.

"Fifteen minutes. And you have all *that*?" She nodded an affirmative. "I officially hate you now," I added, starting in on a new piece of lemon chiffon cake.

"Fine," she said, chowing down on her pecan pie. "I'll just leave you here with your bill and your cake."

"Fine, I don't hate you that much," I replied, switching plates with her. I like my desserts (and my men) more *meaty*.

"Thought so," she said, adding a bowl of chocolate pudding with whipped cream on top.

"Trade you this bowl of ice cream for two hundred dollars," I said, sliding the bowl near her.

"I'm already paying the bill, dipshit, so legally that ice cream belongs to me," she replied, grabbing the bowl. "But that purse is another matter altogether."

"Fuck that," I said. "And pass me that banana pudding."

Some things you just can't put a price on. (But don't quote me on that.)

We got back to Glenda's room and waited for Justin to return. And we waited. And we waited. And no Justin. We were too worried to even bother to go out and gamble and get drunk, so we played Keno from the bed and drank from the minibar. When six in the morning rolled around, and we still hadn't seen hide or trimmed hair of him, I was tempted to call the police and notify them of a missing drag queen. Luckily, I didn't have to. He walked right in the door just as I was lifting the receiver. (Well, actually I was lifting my mimosa, but I was gonna lift the receiver just after that.)

"Where the fuck have you been?" I shouted as he closed the door behind him.

"And why didn't you call?" Glenda shouted as he approached the bed.

He didn't answer right away. First he walked over, sat down on the bed, reached for Glenda's purse, and pulled out a bottle of pills. Then he popped a pretty blue one in his mouth and waited a minute with his eyes closed before he answered. (Not coincidentally, our friends always come prepared when they're spending a lengthy amount of time with us.)

"Okay, I'm sorry. I knew you guys were worrying about me, but there was nothing I could do. Honest," he said, getting out of his Tabitha outfit and into a comfy Aladdin bathrobe. Then he rejoined us on the bed and poured himself a mimosa.

"Well, okay. At least you're here and all in one piece. That's the important thing," I said, mostly meaning it.

Glenda nodded her agreement and tacked on, "Now, where the fuck have you been?"

"Yes, pray tell," I said, refilling my glass in preparation.

He paused, sighed, and began his harrowing tale. "Well, naturally, I was terrified when Bart practically flung me out of that restaurant and into a nearby taxi, which took us to his disgusting butchmobile back at the hotel. The thing practically dripped testosterone," he began, and Glenda bobbed her head, remembering her own experience with Bart's car.

He continued, "Right away I knew I had to lull him into a false sense of security. So when he started in with 'Fucking Zahir, always telling me what to do. He thinks he's such a fucking big shot. Fucking fag ain't got nothing on old Barty,' I readily agreed. 'I know what you mean,' I told him. 'I, for one, was all up for the Lobster Tail. Who is he to dictate where we eat? And that last bit about Ahmed. You were just being concerned for your friend, right? Who does that guy think he is, anyway?' "

"Nice one," I chimed in.

"Yeah, he fell for it, too. He totally mellowed after I agreed with him, and he quickly forgot about Zahir. Unfortunately, he didn't forget about my short dress or the knee poking out from underneath. Thank God I had the smarts to start asking him about his precious car. That temporarily took his mind off sex. I had the impression that our dull-witted foe could only concentrate on one topic at a time. So for the rest of our journey, I made sure to discuss as many things about Bart as I could think to ask. And my knee was safe. At least until we pulled up to that rat's nest of his."

"Uh-oh," I moaned.

"Uh-oh is right," Justin agreed. "I certainly wasn't prepared to be going to his house so soon. I had little to no time to prepare. But that's when his being a pig turned out to be a good thing."

"Ooh, how so?" Glenda asked, wrapping her feet below her thighs as if she was at a campfire about to hear a good ghost story.

Justin, who liked an appreciative audience, gladly continued. "First thing he did was to give me a quick tour of his macho pig palace. And I kept thinking, *Thank God I'm gay and have a sense of style*. It was like being in a fraternity house. Cheap furniture, hot babe posters, and lots of beer. My gay nerves were totally cringing, but I made sure to tell him how cool and manly his place was and how much I liked it. Naturally, he saved the bedroom for last, but I managed to delay the inevitable by steering my drag ass to the bathroom. And that's where I discovered my salvation."

"Figures you'd finally find salvation and it would be in a man's bathroom," I interjected.

To which he replied, "They say the Lord is everywhere."

"Amen," we all agreed.

He continued, "Anyway, you know me, when I'm in a stranger's house and I use their *facilities*, I like to—"

"Snoop through their medicine cabinet," I interrupted.

"Exactly," he said. "Which is just what I did. And wouldn't you know it, right there next to the Preparation H and Stay Hard cream was the little prescription bottle that saved the day."

"Thank the Lord for quality prescription drugs." Glenda's turn for interrupting.

"Amen," we all amened again.

"But what was in the bottle?" I inquired.

"Ah, just what one might expect to find in a pig's medicine cabinet: Rufinols."

"Which are?" asked Glenda.

"Rohypnol. More commonly known as the 'date rape drug,' " Justin explained. "My guess is that dear Bart has a hard time getting his dates back to his house any other way."

"Unless they're slutty drag queens in search of pig prick," I interjected.

"So true. Thank the Lord for slutty drag queens," he said, and we all gave a big amen to that.

"And how did you manage to slip him one?" Glenda asked.

"Oh, that was easy. I pocketed the Rufie, plus a few for me for later trial inspection, and then I switched the labels on the Preparation H and the Stay Hard cream, which should make for an interesting experiment that I'm glad I won't be around to see. Then I went straight for the kitchen to get us some beers. I knew he'd be waiting in the bedroom and that he wouldn't mind a lady who likes her booze before her nookie. When he shouted at me to see what I was up to, I yelled back that I was getting a beer. He took the bait and said to bring him one too."

"Bingo," I said.

"B-I-N-G-O and idiot is his name-o," he sang. "Yes, it was that easy. I dropped the pill in, swished the bottle around, and prayed it had little flavor mixed up in there. When I walked the beers into the bedroom, I wasn't overly surprised to find Bart lying on his bed, shirtless and watching football. My guess, foreplay for Barty Boy."

"And of course," I said, "the television is in the bedroom, not the living room."

"Right," he said. "The living room is reserved for his workout equipment. So he invited me to join him on the bed, with the beers, of course, to watch some football. Just what every red-blooded American girl loves to do. So I sat down and handed him his beer. I was thrilled when he downed half of it in one fell swoop and let out an 'Ah' and a big burp to boot, with no signs that he tasted the Rufie. I was also thrilled that he was temporarily sidetracked with the game and was fairly ignoring me on the edge of the bed. Too bad for commercials. That's when he refocused his attention back to Tabitha."

We all cringed, and Justin became even more animated. (No, not nelly; he really was animated this time around.) "He looked over at me, rubbing his fingers down his body, and said, 'You like what you see, baby?' And I did. If he wasn't so repugnant as a person, he'd actually be a hottie. And knowing that he'd be unconscious in just a few minutes made it possible for me to have some fun."

"Uh-oh," I said again.

"Uh-oh," Glenda reiterated. "Will this be PG, R, or triple-X?"

"Come on, I think you know me better than that," he replied.

We did indeed. Both of us refilled our glasses to the brim.

"Anyway, where was I?" he continued. "Oh, yes, my shirtless, drugged, straight man. I asked him if he'd put his hands over his head so I could admire his big, strong upper body. He had no problem with that. And I had no problem touching and squeezing his sinewy muscles. He seemed to be enjoying it enough, too, because when the commercials stopped, he was still paying attention to me. He closed his eyes when I started tweaking his nipples, which was definitely a good thing because I was developing quite a woody in my too-tight, too-short dress. And then he started to slur, 'That's it baby, yeah, that's it.' I knew it wouldn't be long before he'd be out and I'd be home free. Sure enough, a few more moments of me running my Lee Press-On Nails down his stomach, and he was out like a light. Now, normally, I'd never take advantage of such an unusual situation."

"No, never," I intoned, sarcastically. Glenda let out an appreciative snort.

But Justin carried on, ignoring my snide comment. "No,

never. But I knew I had plenty of time. Those Rufies stay in your system for a long while, or so I've been told. And I wanted to see if Bart was as *small* as Glenda said."

"And was he?" I asked. (Inquiring minds wanted to know.)

"Boo, yeah. Itty-bitty micro-peepee. Maybe that's why he's such a schmuck. I've heard that Hitler and Napoleon had small ones, too. Such a thing must fuck you up in the head. Maybe that's why *I'm* so grounded and normal." (We snickered, but let him continue.) "Anyway, while I was down there, I decided to have some fun. I went into the bathroom, found his electric razor, and shaved his bush right down to the skin. Naturally, that was kind of hot, and I figured there was no use wasting the boner I had, so—"

"You didn't," Glenda squealed with a gleeful gasp.

"Oh, I most certainly did. Spooged all over his tight belly. And then, like the good spy that I am, I got down to business. First thing, I went to get my phone to call you guys and say that I was okay—but I had forgotten my cell, and his was dead. The fucker apparently hadn't bothered to charge it up. Remind me next time to put it in my purse, okay? Now, since I knew that I was relatively safe, I figured you two could wait to see me when I got back here. Sorry." (We grimaced, but we understood.) "And then I went right for the garage and the aforementioned merchandise. Glenda was right on target: there was every kind of appliance you can imagine piled up in there. But what Glenda didn't have time to discover was the fact that it all came from the hotels, casinos, and nearby restaurants. Most of the items had the names of their rightful owners still on them, the rest had been scratched out. Obviously, I figured, my drugged-out date is a member of some ring of thieves that operates throughout Vegas. And, most likely, Ahmed is working for him and/ or has threatened to turn him in. That would explain his disappearance and Bart's desperate attempts to locate him.

Where your vase fits into all this is anyone's guess."

"Bravo. You're a regular Sherlock John Holmes," I said. "But why are you coming back to us so late? Or make that early. Damn, the sun is coming up already." I got up to draw the curtains.

"Ah, I figured it was in our best interest to play the date out to the bitter end. No sense making Bart suspicious. So I turned on the TV and watched Turner Classic Movies until the moron woke up. At least he had cable; otherwise, I'd have been bored silly. And when he appeared to be regaining consciousness, I flicked it off and pretended to be getting dressed. When he saw me standing there, he groggily asked, 'What's going on, baby?' I told him that it was getting late and I needed to get home. I thanked him for the amazing sex, and he just looked at me in bewilderment. So I went on and on about how *skilled* he was, and that's when he started to smile. And when he noticed the dried cum on his tummy, not to mention the new manscaping on his bush, that's when I knew I was home free. Then I said goodbye, walked about a mile—in these heels, mind you—found a pay phone, and called a cab. And, end of story, here I am."

"Well," I said, shaking my head in disbelief, "you're lucky to be alive."

"Hell, luck had nothing to do with it. Just thank the Lord he invented stupid straight men."

We all let out a resounding, final "Amen" as we clicked our mimosa glasses together for a well-deserved toast.

Plan B (Part Deux)

BEFORE WE LEFT GLENDA'S ROOM TO GO BACK TO OUR own, I called Zahir to see where and when we'd all hook up before meeting with Ahmed. I was shocked to find that Zahir had no interest in having us attend the reunion. I calmly reminded him how much we all had at stake, such as, at most, our very lives, and, at least, my vase. But he refused to let us join him, saying that it was his brother and he needed to handle the situation alone. No amount of arguing with him would've worked, so I dropped it. That is to say, I dropped the argument with Zahir, but I intended to be there nonetheless. Now I had to convince a few other people to go along with me.

"So when do we meet up with Zahir?" asked Justin, as we prepared to go back to Caesar's.

"That depends," I answered cryptically.

"On what?"

"Well, that depends on whose plan you're going with," I answered.

"Uh-oh," Glenda chimed in. "I feel a headache coming

on. Sounds about as much fun as picking out insurance plans."

"In a way, we are." I said. "We're insuring that we stay alive. So are you with me?"

"We haven't heard the options yet," Justin said, folding his arms as he gave me a stern look. I had hoped to worry them enough that they'd just go along with whatever I said. I should've known better. They were evil and twisted, not dumb.

"Okay, fine. Zahir's plan is to go to his brother, find out what's wrong, see if he can help him, and then report back to us. He would prefer it if we didn't accompany him," I put it mildly.

"Let me remind you, my dear Em, before you continue, that we're already working on one Plan B. Do you intend to offer us yet another one?" Justin asked.

"No, smart-ass, I don't," I answered, also crossing my arms for effect. "But Plan *Two* goes something like this. (They both groaned.) Seeing as the meeting is at Caesar's and seeing as we're friends with Caesar himself, I say we find a way to attend that little tête-à-tête without them knowing it."

"Genius, but let me remind you that, (a) we are not *friends* with Caesar and (2), to use your ordering system, how on earth do you suppose we'll be able to be there at the meeting and not have them know it?" he asked, shaking his head at me in disbelief.

"Ah, wait and see, wait and see," I said, opening the door and ushering my friends out. Though really, I had no idea myself. (Surprised?)

Caesar was easy to find. Now all we had to do was convince him to help. And we only had a couple of hours until the appointed hour of the brothers' get-together, so time was of the essence.

"My subjects, so good to see you again," Bradley announced, giving us his royal salute and patting our shoulders. We made a quick introduction to Glenda and then got on with the plan.

"Good to see you as well, *Caesar*," I said, keeping with the theme of things. "You have been most generous in your accommodations for us."

"Ah, that was my pleasure. Anything I can do to help my old friend and new friends, I'll be happy to do," he said, still smiling his big, fake Caesar smile.

"Anything?" Justin asked.

Caesar looked to the three of us, saw our grim visages, and cut the act. "What's up?" he asked, arms akimbo.

So we filled him in, from start to finish, and when we were through he stood there staring at us, shaking his head. "Man, you guys are in some bad shit. That guy Bart is big trouble. Don't know all the details, but I've heard through the grapevine that he's a lunatic and that he works for some dangerous people. I'm not quite sure that I can help this time. Or even want to," he told us, the smile now gone from his face.

I couldn't really blame him. We were asking him to get involved, albeit tangentially, in a plan that could prove dangerous. And it wasn't as if we, and by we I mean Justin, were going out of our way to be friendly to him. Actually, Justin had been downright cold up to that point. But when the chips were down in the past, Justin almost always stepped up to the plate and at least gave it a try; and that's just what he did now.

"Look, Bradley," he began, "I know it's been a long time, and I know I haven't exactly welcomed you back into my life with open arms, but our lives may very well be at risk right now and we need your help. Isn't there anything you can think of?" Damn, even pleading, Justin was sexy as hell. I knew before Bradley answered that there was no way he could say no to those big, soulful eyes. Thankfully, I was right.

"Weeeeell, maybe there's one thing," he said, the smile reappearing, "but it's gonna cost you."

"How much?" Justin asked, getting his wallet out.

"It's not going to be that easy, pal. It's going to cost you one date with me."

"Oh." Justin paused. I nudged him in the ribs. "Fine. One date."

"Hey, don't look too overjoyed," Bradley said, backing away.

"No, no, he's thrilled," I interjected, grabbing him back into our little circle. "He just has a hard time showing his emotions. Isn't that right, Justin?" I squinted my eyes at him to let him know that he'd better play along, or else.

"Yes, yes, sorry, I was just taken aback, is all. I'd be delighted to go out on a date with you, Bradley," he said, all sugar and spice and everything, er—well, he's never been nice, so let's just say *not mean*.

"Great, then here's the plan. There's plenty of extra gladiator uniforms for the fellows and a lovely Roman ensemble for the lady. The helmets will cover up Em and Justin, and I think we can find a scarf to cover up Glenda's pretty face. At noon, we'll parade in and get close enough to eavesdrop. I doubt they'll be able to recognize you, and if they do—"

"We're in some deep doo-doo," I interrupted.

"Probably, but let's think happy thoughts. And just to be on the safe side, maybe we should have a few drinks first," he said.

"Um, how would that help? And aren't you working?" Justin asked.

"Um, it couldn't hurt, and yes, I am. So what? This shit's making me nervous, and if I'm going to appear *Caesarly*, it's going to take several gin and tonics. And you're buying," he said to Justin. Surprisingly, he already sounded like one of us. (Ain't that scary?)

"Yes, Caesar," Justin said, grinning, and then he left to get us our drinks.

"Damn, that's a nice ass," Bradley noted, watching my friend swish his way to the bar. "You should have seen it when he was fifteen."

"Gross, for one, and probably illegal, for two, but sweet of you to notice, I guess," I said, trying to block the image from forming in my already addled brain.

Justin returned with the drinks before Bradley could make any more observations. Thank goodness. And once we had downed them, we were off to get changed into our new outfits. And these were some outfits, too. Caesar's didn't scrimp when it came to authenticity. The sandals were real leather, the skirt was thick cotton, the breastplate was some kind of ridiculously weighty metal, and the helmet was hot, hard, and heavy. I had a whole new respect for Bradley. Being Roman was much harder than I expected. Worse than drag. And he had to do it forty-some hours a week. Though the updraft was rather nice, I must admit.

After we finished dressing and admiring our new selves in the mirror, we hooked back up with Bradley, who had a fresh round of drinks stashed behind a slot machine, waiting to be drunk. We fulfilled their destinies and drank them, gladly. My helmet was quickly producing a headache and the leather straps on my sandals were digging into my feet. Not to mention, the chest thing weighed a ton and my back was starting to bitch. It was going to take a hell of a lot more than two drinks to get me through the next hour or so. Of course, when you have friends like Justin, these things are taken care of.

"Here you go, my weak little friend. These will help," he said, handing me some lovely pink tablets. I took them, swallowed, and said, "Fuck you, clone."

"Nice legs. Are we going for the funky chicken look?" he retorted.

"Least mine aren't shaved down to nothing," I volleyed back. "Friggin' queen."

"That's 'cause if you shaved yours, you'd lose half the thickness you have now, bitch."

Then the pill kicked in and I let it go. Plus, our fourth member had arrived. And Glenda couldn't have looked lovelier, or less encumbered. Apparently, the women of ancient Rome weren't made to wear heavy armament. It was a shame she had to cover up her gloriously painted face with a scarf, but that's certainly what she had to do.

"Nice outfits," she said. "Maybe you should try the Stairmaster once in a while, Em."

Such nice friends I have, right? "Dyke," I said to her under my breath.

"Fag," she retorted.

"Um, when you first-graders are ready, I think we should start heading for the garden. It'll take a while to get by all the tourists and their cameras," Bradley said, breaking up our friendly banter.

Just as he had warned, almost immediately tourists eager for photo-ops began assaulting Bradley. And waiting around as one overweight, straight hausfrau after another crowded in to get her picture taken with the mighty Caesar was definitely not what we had in mind. So we continued on to the garden without him. Unfortunately, since Caesar was obviously busy, and we were the next best things, we too were stopped and asked to pose. Though, as usual, Justin, who most certainly filled his gladiator costume better than I, got most of the attention. And when Glenda was accosted by a herd of Japanese conventioneers, each with his own camera, I was on my own. No matter, I thought, we still had some time to get to our destination, and I was fine roaming the hotel and nodding pleasantly to the plebeians. Too bad the costume had no pockets. It was painful to walk by all those glorious slots with no money to drop in them.

Eventually, even I got some attention as I made my way along. Two teenage girls stopped me and asked if I minded taking a picture. Unfortunately, they meant of them, not me. I grimaced, but obliged. And then, with only a few minutes to spare, I made it to the garden. Justin quickly approached from my left, and Glenda and Bradley came up from behind—and then it was show time at Caesar's.

The long-elusive Ahmed was standing in a corner nervously smoking away. I was glad to see him still alive and looking well, even though he was obviously a bad seed and had caused us so much grief. The four of us Romans huddled unobtrusively to the side and waited for Zahir to arrive. Fortunately, that didn't take too long. He showed up and walked right to Ahmed and hugged him first, but then immediately started lecturing him. Regrettably, at our distance we couldn't make heads or tails of the conversation.

Seeing as this wasn't getting us anywhere, we decided to try for a closer inspection, to see if we could pick up the gist of the mostly one-sided discussion. Justin and I inched our way nearer to the pair, with our helmets over our faces so as not be recognized. Luckily for us, a French couple stopped us for some photos, so we had good reason to be standing so close to our prey. While the tourists snapped away, we eavesdropped on Zahir and Ahmed.

Too bad what we overheard was mostly in Arabic. It seemed, from what we could gather, that Zahir wanted Ahmed out of town, indefinitely. He had brought with him a surprisingly large wad of cash to get him on his way. At first, Ahmed seemed to be turning him down, but since he eventually pocketed the money, we assumed he finally relented. Justin and I agreed that Ahmed was probably in enough trouble to warrant a speedy and extended departure, but still found Zahir's behavior, well, slightly odd. We knew he had good reason to be angry with Ahmed, but the whole confrontation was bitterly cold and nervously quick. Knowing how bad Justin's relationship was with his own family, we didn't give this much thought at the time. Not all families get along, even under the best of circumstances, which clearly these weren't.

"That was fast," Glenda said as we returned from our first gladiatorial mission.

"Yup. Short but not too sweet," I replied, and told our friends what we had learned.

"Zahir sure seemed eager to get rid of poor Ahmed," Justin added.

"Wouldn't you be?" I replied.

"Probably, but he seemed so interested in finding him. Even obsessed, I'd say. And then he finds him, only to get rid of him. I just think that's strange," Justin said.

"This coming from the king of strange," I said.

"Whatever, Mary. It was just an opinion. Besides, don't we have more important things to worry about? I mean, with Ahmed possibly leaving, aren't we going to maybe miss the chance to find out where your vase is or learn more about Bart? We still don't exactly know Ahmed's connection to all this, and with him gone, we probably never will."

"True, but what can we do now?" Glenda asked.

"Hold on, let me see if I can do something," Justin said, and ran out of the courtyard, causing his skirt to rise suddenly. Apparently, not many people were wearing underwear that day.

"What's he gonna do?" asked Bradley.

"Who knows? With Justin it's better not to ask. Besides, it's not like we can get in any deeper than we already are," I replied, though I had a nagging feeling that we weren't quite into it all the way, just yet.

Five minutes later, he returned with a new round of drinks for all of us.

"The prodigal slut returns," I said, grabbing for my drink.

"So where did you go?" asked Bradley, draping an arm over Justin's shoulder. A surprise move, but even more surprising, Justin let him keep it there.

Justin downed half his drink. "To chase down Ahmed," he answered.

"You did what?" I shouted, and spit out nearly half of my own.

"You heard me. I found him just outside the hotel. I told him that we knew he was in trouble. I told him that we knew about Bart. And I asked him if he'd help us find out the rest of the story."

"And what did he say?" Glenda asked.

"He said, 'Since when you working at Caesar's?' Which was kind of funny, actually. And then he thought about what I had asked him and agreed to help. He said he didn't want to be running forever, and that Bart was just the tip of the iceberg. He said that whoever Bart worked for was the real brains behind all this; if we could find out who that was, he could probably go to the authorities and trade the information for clemency. I agreed with that. So now, I say that Tabitha should go on one more date with Bart to try to find out who his boss is. If that doesn't work, we go to the police with what we have so far and hope for the best. Then we go home. Vase or no vase. This game is getting boring and I need a good fuck."

Bradley seemed to like the latter suggestion and proceeded to glide his hand under the back of Justin's skirt. Again he let him. Glenda and I stood there and thought over the plan. One more date seemed okay to me. So far, Bart hadn't caught on. And I too was ready to go home, even though I had had several good fucks already. So we agreed.

One more date. Then the police. Then home.

"But where's Ahmed?" I asked.

"Still waiting outside. Shall we go get him?"

"We'd better," I said. "Ahmed has a way of disappearing on us. And I don't want to spend another day looking for him." We hurried out of the garden and back into the hotel.

Thankfully, he was still outside waiting for us, though he looked nervous at seeing a team of gladiators running his way; he came with us just the same. After we got out of our costumes, we went back to our room upstairs. Bradley came along to help us keep an eye on Ahmed, as Justin and I had other plans.

"Oh, no," Ahmed said as the five of us piled into our room. "You have stinky room again."

"Stinky room is better than stinky street," Justin said as he started to get back into Tabitha gear. I did likewise. We were a duo, after all. Ahmed looked confused, but decided it was better not to ask questions. Which was probably a good thing considering that I, and my alter ego Marilyn, were both dating his brother.

Soon after, Tabitha and Marilyn were off with Glenda back to the Aladdin. We thanked Bradley for his help as we shut the door. He yelled after us as we were leaving, "Oh, Justin will be making this up to me."

"Justin's got a boyfriend, Justin's got a boyfriend," Glenda and I sang as we made our way down the corridor and then out of the hotel.

"Guess that would make me the queen of Rome," he said.

"Oh, man," I retorted, "I'd say you were queen of the whole fucking universe."

"Bitch."

"Whore."

Glenda interrupted. "Please, can we go one day without a catfight? You she-males are driving me crazy."

We agreed to a temporary truce as we arrived at the Aladdin. Then we went to the disco and hunted for our men. Glenda tagged along just in case she too could find a man, or at least get a drink. Judging from the luck we were having with men lately, I'd say the drink was a hell of a lot less trouble. She stayed clear of the bar and a repeat encounter with Bart.

Zahir must've raced back to work after meeting with Ahmed because he was already behind the counter, busily pouring drinks alongside Bart. He grimaced when he saw me in drag yet again, but fixed us all tall, frosty drinks just the same. Maybe when I got back to San Francisco, I figured, I'd find me a nice bartender to date. The fringe benefits seemed to be amazing. Then again, maybe I should worry about getting a job first. Better still, staying alive should really be priority number one.

And then Bart noticed Tabitha, and his repugnant face lit up.

"Oh, joy," Tabitha said, between her lipstick-smudged teeth, "the fucker's glad to see me."

We girls waved a yoo-hoo to our working men. Both came over to join us while there was an apparent lull at the bar.

"You're looking foxy as ever, Tabitha," Bart said as he went to plant a wet one on my friend's lips. She's a fast one, though, and managed to turn her head just in time to catch it on the cheek. I, however, let Zahir give me a big one on my ruby lips. Then I started in on my drink. (See, I do have my priorities in order, after all.)

"So, baby, whatcha doin' later?" Bart propositioned Tabitha.

"Going out with you, Bart?" she asked, batting her lashes and then attacking her drink.

"You betcha," he said, grinning inanely at her. I doubted he got very many second dates.

"And me?" I asked, looking up at Zahir.

"Anything for my Marilyn," he replied. Too bad when I batted my fake lashes one fell off. Luckily, Bart was too enraptured to notice.

Justin dragged us out of there quick, but not before we agreed to meet the fellows back at the disco at eight for our—hopefully—final dates. Though I'd be sad to say goodbye to Zahir, the chilly environs of San Francisco were calling me back home. And since the clang, clang, clang of the slots was calling as well, we decided to kill, for lack of a better word, time, before said dates. Yes, hours go by like minutes when you're gambling away what little money you have, meaning we had just enough time to change into something pretty before we had to meet back up with the boys. Of course, I hoped to be out of my outfit soon after my date began.

We arrived back at the disco just as Zahir and Bart were getting off work. They greeted us at the entrance and promptly escorted us out. Zahir steered me to the left. Bart took Tabitha to the right. We waved at each other over our shoulders. I hoped that our separation would be a brief one; we had, after all, tempted fate enough over the last several days, and I think it was getting pissed at us.

"Zahir needs to get Marilyn out of that dress," he said to me when we were outside.

"Ooh, Marilyn would like that," I replied, but then realized that going back to my hotel room was a big no-no. I didn't think Zahir would be too happy finding his brother back there. So I added, "But I think Tabitha plans on going back to our hotel with Bart. Maybe we should go to your house instead."

Pause. He had to think about that for quite some time before he answered. I was almost deeply offended while he hemmed and hawed and then finally said yes. I couldn't begin to imagine what the big deal was.

We arrived at his home, a lovely two-bedroom, nice-sized

ranch house just outside the city, and I let out a big "Wow." Then added, "I didn't know bartending paid so much."

To which he gruffly replied, "Family money."

It was even lovelier on the inside. All leather furniture, warm high-napped rugs, candles, and crystal knickknacks throughout. Either Zahir had missed his calling as an interior decorator or he had enough of that family money to hire one. Either way, I was impressed and said so. Zahir seemed less than enthused at my gushing. As a matter of fact, he quickly ushered me in and, without so much as a brief tour, showed me to the bedroom. Well, I thought, at least he wanted me badly enough that he was willing to show me his rude side to get me naked and in bed.

He mellowed out as soon as we were behind the bedroom door and I started to undress. "Oh, Em, you are much more sexy without that dress on," he said as I slithered out of my Marilyn gear. He too looked sexy, splayed out on the bed, his big, hairy calves poking out from beneath his pant cuffs. I put the dress and purse down on an overstuffed side chair and got into the bed with him. He held me in his big, dark, hairy arms for some time, then he said, "Please excuse me, Em, I need to make quick phone call. Can I get drink or something for you?"

"Sure, whatever you're having is fine by me," I replied as he got up and left me alone in the room. He closed the door behind him. I guessed that it was a private phone call because there was a phone right by the bed that he could've used.

Not being one to be able to just sit there and do nothing, I got up to look around. His bedroom was just as nice as the rest of the house and extremely well furnished. Next to the television were pictures of him and Ahmed from their teen years. They looked a lot happier together than when I had seen them last, at Caesar's.

And that's when I noticed it out of the corner of my eye:

a little white metallic sticker in the left rear corner of the television. I'd seen them before and knew what they were for. I leaned down to get a closer look, and sure enough, *Property of the Venetian* was printed across the label. My heart started to pound. Then I went over to the VCR and flipped it around. This time, *Property of the Mirage* was on the sticker. Uh-oh. Not good. I told myself that he'd probably just bought it all hot. Zahir was a good genie, not an evil one like Bart. And I almost believed that until—

"Here you go, sexy man. Champagne and shrimp cocktail. Nothing is too good for my Em," he said, plopping back down on the bed with a tray that held two champagne glasses, a bottle of Dom Pérignon—which I knew for certain was way out of a bartender's price range—and a plate full of some very large and yummy-looking shrimp, plus a small bowl of cocktail sauce. Now, normally, a plate of seafood would have put a smile on my face and a growl in my tummy, but not this time. My brain hearkened back to our night in the cab when my beloved Zahir had insisted we not to go the Lobster Tail because of his allergy to shellfish. Guess what? The delicious-looking shrimp lying before us was shellfish, as I'm sure you already knew. Something didn't add up.

And then I remembered all those murders and got scared.

"Um, Zahir, I need to use your restroom," I said, and got up off the bed as nonchalantly as possible. I knew better than to tip him off to my newfound knowledge. Though I still didn't really *know* anything.

I headed for the bathroom, picking up my purse on the way. "Medication," I said by way of explanation. He nodded an okay and started in on the shrimp. My heart skipped, and not the good kind of tra-la-la skipping.

As soon as I was in the bathroom and had shut the door behind me, my knees started to buckle and I broke out in a cold sweat. We never should've attempted all this by ourselves. We should've let the police handle it all along. We should've told the Feds everything we knew. I should never, ever have listened to Justin. I sat on the toilet, shaking my head.

Then, as luck would have it, I noticed my purse. It wasn't mine. I must've switched mine with Justin's.

And you know what that meant.

Those fabulous Rufies were in this one, along with some nice blue Xanax for yours truly. Needing all the help I could get, I downed one, lickety-split. Now I just had to slip Zahir the Mickey to get out of there alive.

"Come back to bed, baby. Zahir misses his Em," he yelled from the bed, where he was now laying naked and hard. (Just my luck—champagne, shrimp, and a hard, naked man, and all I could think of was how on earth do I get the hell out of there.)

"Okay, sweetie," I said, slipping back into bed with him. But that's when my usual clumsiness worked to my distinct advantage. Em, plus bed, plus cocktail sauce, equals one big mess. The bowl spilled almost as soon as I got comfortable. Zahir jumped up to get a towel, and I slipped him the Rufie. Didn't even have to use my brains to figure that one out, which was a good thing, as it was my brains that got me into the mess in the first place.

I stirred the pill into the champagne and watched as it dissolved. Zahir returned, towel in hand, just as the foaming action abated. If he detected any chicanery, he didn't let on. Besides, he was way too concerned for his satin sheets to have noticed.

"I'm so sorry, Zahir. Please let me make it up to you," I said, displaying my body in a most provocative manner. Well, that did catch his attention. He threw the towel in the closet, gingerly placed the tray on the nightstand, and hopped back into bed with me. That woody of his returned remarkably fast, which wasn't a good thing for me.

"How about a toast, Zahir?" I said, quickly grabbing for the champagne glass as he went diving for my neck.

Looking a bit peeved at the interruption, he grabbed his glass, clinked it to mine, and downed his drink in one fell swoop. Aaah... My body relaxed a bit. (Though that may have been the Xanax kicking in.)

"Now," he said, "where were we?"

Okay, so I had sex with him. What choice did I have? Anyway, I knew he'd be out cold in a few minutes. Though Zahir's a pretty large fellow (everywhere), and a few minutes was more like an hour. I was actually getting quite nervous again, despite my own medication, until he let out a big yawn and said, "Hmm, I'm getting kind of tired. Mind if I take nap?"

Needless to say, I didn't mind at all. A minute later, he was out like a Palestinian light and I was, once again, temporarily safe. So I got up and had myself a good look-around. Sure enough, every appliance in the house had originally come from a hotel. And both bathrooms were full of hotel linens. But that was nothing compared to his garage. Judging from what Glenda and Justin had said about Bart's, Zahir must've hit the mother lode. I even found several pieces of dinnerware from the Lobster Tail, which may have been the real reason Zahir didn't want to go there that night. And that's when my rattled brain put it all together. Ahmed said that the real coup would be to find Bart's boss. I think I had just found him. It sure went a long way to explaining Zahir's obvious control over Bart, and Bart's willingness, albeit reluctant, to go along with Zahir's wishes. It also explained how two men could get by tending bar during the day in a disco. That was probably where they worked out of. It certainly provided a good cover.

And I could only assume that Ahmed was working for Bart, but he didn't know about Zahir, and vice versa.

Which was probably why Zahir was so eager to get rid of Ahmed. Ahmed probably told Zahir exactly what kind of mess he was in, and Zahir freaked out when he realized that Ahmed could get them all in a load of trouble. But why the murders? Well, that I could wait to find out later, and, hopefully, not firsthand. I thought it best to get out of there fast before Zahir woke up, found me with his stash, and then made me the fourth victim.

I slid on my dress and ran out the door as fast as my little pumps could carry me. But now what? Where was I? I could barely see the lights of Vegas. Then, to make matters worse, guess whose favorite Feds pulled up? Do those guys have some sixth sense or what? Now, I know I should've waved them down with Justin's purse and gotten the whole mess over with right then and there, but I wanted my friends all together and safe first. And I wanted to make sure that Ahmed got into as little trouble as possible—though, for all I knew, he was somehow involved with all the murdering going on. Plus, I really didn't want to be in some holding cell in drag. (What an awful mug shot that would've made.)

Instead, I hid in a bush and waited for them to leave, which they did—twenty-five minutes later! My poor dress was a shambles. And it was starting to get chilly out there in the desert at night. Too bad there was nothing in that purse to help me forget about the cold. What I needed was a hot coffee with some Kahlúa. What I found, instead, was Justin's cell phone, which he had remembered this time. Once again, it was Glenda to the rescue. Seriously, I just know she's keeping track.

Soon after, the cab pulled up, with Glenda in the backseat. "You're a mess," she said as I got in.

"Nice to see you, too. Now let's go find Justin and go get the police. I know who Bart's boss is, and he'll be awake and probably very angry in a few short hours."

Oh, to be so lucky.

On the way back to Caesar's to get a change of clothes, I filled Glenda in on the events of the few past hours. She was less than happy.

"So let me see if I understand this correctly," she said, counting off on her fingers. "You're dating the bad guy, who may or may not be a murderer as well. Justin's on a date with the bad guy's assistant, who may also be a murderer. And I'm stuck in a cab with a guy in a ripped dress and a purse full of Rufies. Why did I leave San Francisco again?"

"Because you were bored and you missed us?" I answered.

"Next time, stop me," she moaned, glaring out the window.

"Let's hope there is a next time," I lamented.

"Good point. Maybe we should go find Justin after you get back to being a man, fashionably speaking, I mean."

I nodded in agreement. "Can you remember where Bart lives?"

"Yeah, I think I can find the place," Glenda said, unsurely. "Maybe. I mean, I remember the landmarks, but not the streets, exactly." Not the answer I had hoped for. And we didn't have Bart's phone number to call to see if my best friend was okay. I suppose we could've waited for him back at the hotel, but what if he was in trouble? I'd never forgive myself if something bad happened to him. And Glenda felt the same way.

After we got back to the hotel and I changed, and then called Bradley back at the Aladdin to tell him the bad news, I had an idea. "Well," I said to Glenda, "there may be one person who can help us find Bart's place, but he may be disinclined to help."

She looked at me quizzically as I dialed the number on the card.

"Hello, Earl?" I said.

"Yeah, who's this?"

No, he wasn't tickled to hear from me, but he was glad that Ahmed was safe and sound, for the time being. And he was willing, albeit reluctantly, to help us out one more time. When he picked us up fifteen minutes later in front of Caesar's, I truly hoped that this would be the last time we would need his help. I'd forgotten how awful his vehicle reeked. Much worse than our hotel rooms.

Glenda told Earl what she remembered about where Bart lived. Earl immediately knew the vicinity, as he had been driving around it for many, many years. My heart pounded as we sped to the area. "Oh, please, Lord, let my friend be all right," I prayed, over and over again. "I promise to be a good... I promise to be a decent... I promise to be...to be... Oh, just let my friend be okay, please."

We spotted Bart's car a few minutes later. "That's it!" Glenda shouted, pointing at Bart's pig palace. I gulped, audibly, and told Earl to pull over.

"Now what?" Glenda asked.

"Good question," I said, my face in my hands as I sat there and rocked backward and forward.

"I could go up and ask if anybody called for a cab," Earl suggested.

"Well, at least you might be able to see if he's okay," I said. "But I really don't want you to get involved, Earl. Bad things have been happening to innocent people."

"Too late," he said, getting out of the cab. "I'm already involved and I ain't so innocent. Now you two duck down while I go take a look-see." We obeyed. Luckily, we could see what was going on from the rearview mirror. What we saw was Earl walking up to the door. He rang the bell. Bart answered. The two talked briefly, and Earl returned to the cab. The whole encounter took less than a few minutes.

"Well?" we shouted from the floor of his cab, which, by the way, smelled even fouler than the seating area. If we ever got out of this alive, I was going to buy Earl a lifetime supply of air fresheners and carpet deodorizers.

"He's fine," Earl said, starting the motor and driving away.

"What?" we asked, getting back into our seats.

"He's fine," he repeated. "I saw him sitting on the sofa, drinking a glass of wine."

"Did he see you?" I asked.

"Yeah. He looked shocked when he saw me at the door and then he waved at me three times. I pretended not to notice him so Bart wouldn't get suspicious, and then I left."

"Stop the cab!" I shouted.

"What's wrong?" Glenda asked. Earl pulled over and turned around to look at me.

"He's in trouble," I said to them both.

"But I just told you that everything looked okay," Earl said.

"Three waves is Justin's secret code to come rescue him," I said.

"What?" Glenda asked, looking nervous.

"When we're at a bar, and I see Justin wave to me three times, it means that I should come over and rescue him from an unwanted suitor. Can't get more unwanted than Bart," I explained.

"Uh-oh," Glenda said.

"Uh-oh," Earl echoed.

"Uh-oh," I agreed. "And again, now what?"

"Now we go rescue your friend, like we're supposed to," Earl said.

"But how?" I asked.

"With this," he said, pulling a big, black gun from under his seat. "I brought it just in case." Again he got out of the cab and walked up to Bart's door. He rang the bell, and Bart opened the door. But here's where stinky old Earl shocked us all. When Bart asked him what he wanted, Earl raised his gun, pointed it at Bart's face, and motioned to Justin to follow him out.

The rest was sort of a blur. We could hear the shouting all the way from the cab, but we didn't know what was being said. What we did know was that Justin was running out of the house as fast as his shaven legs could carry him, and we were screaming at him to get in the cab. When Earl saw that we were all safely inside, he backed away from Bart's front door, but he kept his gun pointed at Bart until he too had made it back to the cab. Bart just stood there, shocked and mildly terrified. That is, until we pulled away—then terror gave way to anger. I could see it in his face as we drove by. We had not seen the last of him, I knew. Not by a long shot.

The Inevitable
Chase Scene

"WHAT TOOK YOU SO LONG?" MY SO-CALLED FRIEND asked me, once we were a few hundred feet away. He was his usual calm self, which meant that he too had some pills on him. (Oh, the joys of self-medication.)

I sat there staring at him, stunned at his flippancy. Then he grinned and reached out to hug the two of us.

"Fucker," Glenda said to him first.

"Prick," I added.

"Ah, friends," Justin said, hugging us harder.

When we pulled away, I asked, "So, were you really in trouble back there? I recognized the wave signal."

"Boo, yeah, sweetie. Big time. Bart-o ain't as dumb as he looks. Well, maybe close. Of course, it doesn't take a rocket scientist to figure that something's up when you witness it firsthand," he said.

"Don't tell me *you* got caught," I broke in.

"Well, let's just say that I didn't account for Bart's vanity and the few extra mirrors he has up around his house. He spotted me, from the mirror in the bathroom, which reflected the mirror in the bedroom, which was angled just enough to see me in the living room, trying to slip him a Mickey yet again. Luckily I had some sleeping pills in my change purse because I accidentally took your purse when I threw it in there." (Which I already knew, of course.) "Earl, here, showed up just in time. I doubt that me being a woman, or at least Bart *thinking* I was a woman, would've saved me from his wrath." Justin settled back between Glenda and myself in the backseat of the cab. "Thanks, Earl," he quickly added.

"Don't thank me yet," he cautioned. "We're being followed."

"What?" we shouted in unison. But even as I said it, I could see Bart's psycho-car in the rearview mirror. That's when we felt the first bump.

"God damn it," Earl shouted. "That fucker's ramming us."

"Speed up!" Glenda yelled the obvious.

"Brilliant idea," Justin muttered.

"Do you have a better one?" Glenda gave him a well-deserved punch in the arm.

"Yeah, I'm taking all suggestions under consideration," Earl said, speeding up a bit. I had serious doubts that his beat-up jalopy could outrace Bart's souped-up sports car for very long.

Justin leaned forward. "Earl, do you know where the stables are? The ones just outside of town? I think they're at a ranch called the Lucky Slots."

Earl nodded that he knew of them. "Hold on," he shouted, taking a firm hold on the steering wheel and yanking it all the way to the left. The cab's backside did a spin and, in the blink of an eye, we were facing in the opposite direction. Bart's car kept speeding forward and just slightly clipped us as he sped past. "You boys better have won some money while you were in Vegas. That's gonna cost you," Earl notified us as he slammed his foot on the gas, sending his three passengers tumbling around the backseat.

"Not to worry," Justin responded, once he'd regained his seating. "Just get us to the stables before Bart."

"Okeydokey," Earl said. "But I hope you know what you're doing. This baby can't keep ahead of that schmuck forever."

"Yeah, Justin, you better know what you're doing," I echoed, searching his purse for whatever was keeping him so calm. Glenda's hands soon delved in as well.

"What's this white one?" I shouted. The cab's engine was causing quite a ruckus. I doubted it ever got above fifty in the city. Now it was pushing eighty and, apparently, not too happy about it.

"Just take it, please," Justin responded.

Glenda had already grabbed one and downed it. I followed suit. "What was it?" I shouted again.

"A breath mint. You stink!" he hollered back, waving his hands in front of his face. We both punched him. And before we could go digging through his purse again, we heard the roar of Bart's car gaining on us fast.

"How soon until we reach the stables?" Glenda yelled to Earl. "He's almost right on our asses again."

"About a mile," Earl answered, just as Bart rammed us a second time. "That's another two hundred and fifty dollars for you," he said, and then yanked the steering wheel to the left again, sending us tumbling one more time. He repeated this several times as we approached wherever it was we were headed. I still had no idea what Justin had up his sleeve, and I prayed that, whatever it was, it would get us out of this horrible race. Thankfully, the constant turning up and down streets was working. Earl was maintaining a good fifty-foot distance from the lunatic behind us.

"Almost there, Justin. Now what?" Earl yelled back. Bart was once again gaining on us.

"Now drive straight up to the entrance of the stables as fast as you can," Justin yelled back.

"Okay," Earl shouted, "but isn't there a—" Just as he got within a few feet of the entrance, Earl once again whipped the steering wheel as far to the left as it would go and slammed on the gas. Our car veered around a bit and sped down a dirt road. That's when we heard the crash.

"Isn't there a what?" Glenda shouted hysterically. Had she turned around, as Justin and I had, she would have seen the *what*.

"A ditch," Earl finished his previous sentence.

"Oh, by the way, Earl," Justin said as we slowed down and stopped the car, "watch out for the ditch."

"Thanks, Justin. Good idea," Earl responded, turning around to take his turn punching Justin in the arm.

Apparently, my friend's usually rattled brain somehow remembered that ditch from our earlier journey through the desert with Honey. I hadn't remembered seeing it until I turned around and saw Bart's car flipped over on its end and steaming in the distance. The ranch didn't allow cars on the property. I guess their means of accomplishing this worked. And it worked well. Bart's car was totaled. Unfortunately, we couldn't say the same thing for Bart. From his precarious situation, which was upside down, he managed to get the door open and was shimmying out of his vehicle and onto the ground. He appeared unharmed, but, judging from the kicking and screaming, he was way pissed at the loss of his prized automobile.

"Mission accomplished, children," Earl said, slowly driving away from the scene.

"Temporarily, yes," Justin lamented, "But he's still alive, which means he'll be back for us just as soon as he can."

"Well, at least he doesn't know where we're staying," I added, but Justin didn't say anything. He just shook his head.

"What is it?" Glenda asked, concerned with Justin's current expression of dread.

"Um, when Bart caught me with the pills, he grabbed my purse and saw the Caesar's room key. I'm sure even he can put two and two together.

"Well, then, I say we go to the police right now in case he tries again to get the two and two of us," Glenda suggested, the anxiousness in her voice unmistakable.

"I'm for that," Earl offered.

"Normally, I'd agree with you, but I think they'd have an easier time believing our story if I weren't still dressed like Tabitha," Justin said. We reluctantly agreed with him.

"Okay, then," I offered, "how about we go back to Caesar's, call Bradley, and tell him to gather up Ahmed and meet us at the police station. Then we call Detective Lombard and have him wait for us there as well, and then we get changed and hightail it over there ourselves? I'm ready to be through with all this *stuff*."

"Amen," Justin amened. "I'm through with being Tabitha for a good long time."

"I meant the murders and the chase *stuff*," I said.

"Oh, that too," he concurred.

We arrived back at Caesar's several moments later. We told Glenda and Earl to wait in the cab, and Justin and I ran in to set the wheels of justice in motion. When we got back to our room we found a note from Bradley saying he'd taken Ahmed to a safer place, namely his house. Safer, obviously, being a relative word. So Justin called Bradley and he agreed to get Ahmed to go down to the station. Then I called our old friend Detective Lombard. He wasn't in, but I left a message for him with another officer, telling him briefly what had happened and that we'd be down there in ten minutes. I was quickly getting undressed when I looked up and noticed him Justin out the window. I asked him what was up.

"Dude, we're in some shit now," he groaned, looking worried for a change. (Justin rarely if ever appeared worried. He was too concerned with frown lines and crow's-feet to let that happen.)

"Wh-what's the matter now?" I stammered.

"Bart," he said, still staring out the window.

"We left Bart at the ranch with his totaled car," I said, moving over to join him at the window.

"True, but there he is, limping out of that cab." Justin pointed down to the parking lot. It didn't take long for me to spot him. He was a wreck. His clothes were dirty and he was walking with a heavy limp. My blood turned to ice at the sight of him.

"Fuck," I said, slumping down on the bed.

"Ditto," Justin said, his body sliding down the wall until his fine ass landed on the rug.

"What now? Do we sit here? He probably couldn't find us. But what if Glenda and Earl come looking for us—then what? What if he spots them and hurts them, or makes them lead him here? And what if we leave and he spots *us*? Are we dead meat?" I asked, trembling.

Justin sat there thinking about what I'd said. He didn't say a word for several moments. His silence was driving me up the wall. And then, just as I was about to shout several profanities at him, he snapped his fingers and pointed to the tiny armoire across the room.

"What?" I asked, looking over.

"I guess Tabitha and Marilyn ain't through just yet," he said. And then it dawned on me what he had in mind.

"You don't think he'll recognize us if he spots us?" I asked, getting up off the bed and walking over to the armoire.

"Doubtful, and I don't think we have an alternative, anyway," he said, joining me as I opened the door. Our shiny showgirl outfits sparkled from within. Thank good-

247

ness we had brought them. Though, at the time, we thought we'd be wearing them for fun. *This* was no fun.

"Ready?" he asked.

"As I'll ever be," I answered, pulling out my dress. Justin retrieved his and we started to put them on. We certainly weren't enjoying ourselves like last time, but last time we weren't trying to escape from a homicidal maniac. Still, once we had donned our showgirl headdresses—I don't know, it's hard to explain, but with our towering messes of wire and sequins and feathers on top of our heads, we felt, I guess, invincible. Okay, fine, there was that, and Bart's gun. We still had it from when I tackled him during the kidnapping. It fit snugly now just behind the feathered front of my headdress.

"Well, how do I look?" I asked, teetering on my stilettos in front of the bathroom mirror.

"Fabulous," Justin answered, now sharing the mirror with me. And we did, really, once we'd put on a few coats of shimmering red lipstick, plus several coats of base, rouge, eye shadow, and, of course, the inch-long fake eyelashes. (Yes, my friends, it does indeed pay to come prepared.)

"Okay, then, it's now or never," Justin said, turning the lights off and heading for the door.

"How about a third choice. Like, *maybe sometime later*," I offered, following close behind.

"Nah, this'll be easy. All we have to do is walk down the hallway, go down the elevator, walk across the casino, and back out to Earl's cab. A snap," he said to me as we turned sideways so our headdresses could make it out of the room. I said a silent prayer that he was correct.

The hallway was easy, especially since it was lined with mirrors and we could practice our showgirl walks. Without girlie hips, the saunter was quite difficult, and we tried to make it look not so forced. The elevator was a piece of cake as well. It too was all mirrors. The lights above made our outfits shine like two long, moving disco balls. The effect was dazzling. And the casino was nothing; just a few snapshots with the tourists, and we were off. We sashayed our way between the machines and the gamblers, smiling down from our staggering heights, and slowly, without causing too much attention to ourselves, despite the fact that we were now seven feet of swaying, shimmering, drag fugitives, made our way to the casino exit and to freedom.

We could actually see the light from outside, the cement driveway, and just a hint of the front of Earl's cab when the inevitable happened.

There was Bart roaming near the exit. He looked up when he saw us approaching, but I didn't think he recognized us. Still, we thought it in our best interest to turn around and go the other way. Why tempt fate yet again? So we made our way back through the casino and toward the exit on the other side. It was only a five-minute walk or so. At least, that's what it should've been.

Halfway through the place, we were stopped by an irate-looking man who was screaming at us in some kind of strange, guttural brogue. About all we could make out were the words *late* and *move it*. We were too much in shock from recent events to argue, and besides, he was already aggressively pushing us away from our desired location and toward a stage area within the casino. I shrugged at Justin as we were forcefully shoved backstage. At least there was no Bart. There was, however, a new problem to contend with.

Our pushy friend had deposited us in a tiny backstage area—and we weren't alone. There were a dozen other showgirls, each with outfits remarkably similar to our own, though in various different colors. They paid us little heed as we roamed among them. Actually, they were running around fixing their headdresses, their makeup, their shoes, and their nails. And they were yapping up a storm. Picture, if you will, a flock of flamingos careening past each other, and you might get the imagery I'm trying to convey. It was terrifying to behold. And nothing in my gay past could prepare me for this. So we stood in a corner and tried to look inconspicuous. (I know, good luck, right?)

When we heard "Five minutes, girls," we looked at each other in abject terror.

"Now what?" I asked. It seemed to be the question of the week.

"Got me. Let's just stand here and hope they don't notice us," he answered.

Five minutes went by like five seconds. And though we stood in the back and to the side, it *was* a small, cramped space and we had little choice but to line up with the other *girls*. And sneaking out was not to be. We tried, but the nasty little man who herded us in was standing just outside the door. I suggested that we use the gun, shoot the guy, and run for it, though we doubted we'd get very far in our current disguises. So we surrendered to the inevitable and took our places in line. Thank heavens we had our limited stage experience or I think I might have dropped dead right on the spot when the curtain opened and, one by one, we glided out onto, *gulp*, a fully lit stage.

As I said, we were in a theater within the casino. This was one of those freebie shows they put on for the beleaguered gamblers. Luckily, it was still rather early and the crowd was sparse. Besides, as we soon found out, the routine was easy. (At first.) All we had to do was glide and stop, glide and stop, glide and stop. All the while, one line of girls bisected another. And finally, we were lined up, smiling from ear to ear and showing off our glorious outfits, the lights making us glow like fireflies.

That's when I noticed two things. Or people, I should say. The first was Bart. He was, quite to our dismay, watching the show. He was probably still in shock from his recent misfortune and didn't realize that he was a big old mess. (Or just didn't care.) Plus, old habits die hard. He saw a bunch of scantily dressed women and he stopped to ogle. Stupid hetero! The other person I spotted was last week's catch, Chris. Chris, apparently, worked at a bunch of casinos, Caesar's being one of them. And while Bart may not have realized who was on stage, Chris spotted us in a jiff. I could tell because he looked shocked and followed our every move on stage with his eyes.

Noticing him, however, made me neglect my performance. Each girl, one after the next, was leaping up in the air and landing in a split. I heard the strange *splat* noises to my right, but was too rattled by Chris and Bart's presence to realize what was happening. It didn't dawn on me until Justin took off for his leap and tried his best to manage a split. Of course, Justin being Justin, it wasn't out of his field of expertise. He could maneuver his legs in just about any position he wanted. He was no ballerina, but he was, at least, on the floor with the other showgirls, who were rather quickly noticing that one of their own was left standing. Guess who?

There was no way that Em in a showgirl outfit was about to even attempt a jump followed by a split. Em in shorts and a T-shirt wouldn't even take a shot at such a thing. So I just stood there, with my hands flung up in the air, in a *Ta-da!* kind of stance, and smiled radiantly. There was a hush over the crowd as they stood and watched the renegade showgirl. Even the other showgirls were looking up at me. And that's when Bart-o snapped his fingers and pointed to the stage.

"Uh-oh," I mumbled.

"Uh-oh is right," Justin whispered back. "I'm stuck."

"Fuck, here he comes," I said, louder. And now Bart was pointing a gun right at the stage—which, of course, had the expected results. First, our sister showgirls started to notice and began to scamper away. It wasn't very glamorous, getting up from their splits and all, but it was a reasonable reaction. Justin, in the meantime, was indeed stuck in his split and I was frozen on the spot, what with the gun pointed at me and everything. The next thing to happen was that the audience responded with that whole *crowd mentality, shriek in panic, and rush far away* thing. What was left was two immobilized drag queens and one homicidal maniac with a gun. Not a winning combination in anybody's book.

That's when I heard Justin's little voice coming from the stage. "Get *your* gun."

"What?" I used the corner of my mouth to whisper.

Bart was rapidly approaching and was repeating over and over again, "You bitches wrecked my car."

"The gun," Justin repeated, from his odd position.

"What gu— Oh, the gun," I said, remembering Bart's other gun. The one neatly tucked into my headdress.

"Don't move," Bart said, inching closer. He looked really pissed and completely crazed, so I did as he said. The weird thing was that he kept alternating between pointing the gun at us and scratching his crotch with it. Not exactly a smart thing to do, I thought. In fact, it made me cringe every time he did it.

The good thing—and yes, believe it or not there was a good thing—was that between concentrating on us and scratching his crotch, Bart didn't realize that Chris was also inching closer and was nearly right behind him. It was hell waiting for Bart to shoot us (and I was hoping that at least he'd shoot Justin first), or for Chris to reach him before he could shoot either of us. I decided on a diversion just in case.

"You know, Zahir told us that you shot Mr. Hartwell and stabbed to death those two guys at the Atlantis, and that he was going to tell the cops if he ever got caught," I said quickly, grasping at straws. It worked. Bart stopped dead in his tracks.

"That fucking liar," he shouted, clawing at his groin again with the gun. "The first one was an accident and the other two I thought were some other guys with a load of cash." Little did he know that the other *guys* were the two of us girls.

Not what I wanted to hear, but really, what was I expecting, anyway? So it was Bart who had killed everyone. But why? Better question, were we next? Luckily, however, the question slowed him down enough for Chris to get right behind him. Unluckily, just as Chris went to slug him in the back of the head, Bart bent down again to work on his crotch. Chris swung and just barely caught Bart's hair. Well, naturally, Bart turned to face his new opponent. And though we felt awfully bad, at the moment, that Chris had come to our aid only to be whaled on by Bart, it at least allowed us some time to react.

I hunched over and the gun fell to the ground near Justin, who scooped it up and pointed it at our enemy. Bart, however, was now entwined with Chris; firing the gun was out of the question. Oh, woe was me, what was a showgirl to do in such a situation? For a change, I had come prepared.

"Freeze!" I shouted. "F.B.I." I pulled Detective Shelling's badge from my padded bosom and raised it in the air. Bart, upon hearing my declaration, did indeed freeze, especially when he saw Justin, still in his split, with a gun pointing at him. Though he was still scratching himself down below, for some odd reason.

Moments later, and entirely too late if you ask me, Caesar's security team arrived, promptly grabbed Bart, and held him in place. He was less than happy. And once we were no longer in mortal danger, I was able to reach down and help my friend out of his precarious position, which made *him* happy. And then we joined Chris and the rest of the gang, who were looking on in bewilderment.

"Um, excuse me," I said to the nearest security guard, "I

think if you called Detective Lombard down at the police station, he would be more than delighted to come pick this scumbag up." The guard got on his walkie-talkie and did just that.

"You fucking bitches," Bart howled as he struggled with the security guards. He was still desperately trying to scratch himself.

"What's up with that?" I asked Justin as we moved in closer—like dazzlingly dressed moths to a flame.

When we were within inches of our former foe, Justin said, "Ah, must be from when I shaved him the other night. Been there, done that, and *itchy*." We felt safe now that three large guards were holding him until the real authorities arrived.

"I'll kill you bitches when I get out of this," Bart shouted at us, even louder.

"Um, sirs, are you holding him really, really tight?" Justin asked the guards.

They nodded that they were. That was our clue.

"One," Justin said.

"Two," I followed.

"Three," we shouted together with glee, yanking off our headdresses. "Surprise!"

Well, that did it. It took Bart a few moments to figure it out, but when he finally did, yikes, he went off like a rocket. Screaming and hollering and wriggling around, in a state of complete and utter rage, he pulled his arms and legs out of the grip of those three men and, with an Incredible Hulk roar, broke free and dived for his gun, which was still on the floor where he had dropped it.

"YOU FUCKING FAGGOTS!" he shouted, pointing his gun at us with a trembling hand. The guards moved to grab him again, but Bart cocked the gun and threatened to shoot unless they moved back. I held my breath as they took several steps away.

"Now look, Bart," I began, my voice breaking in fear, "you wouldn't want to shoot an F.B.I. agent, would you?"

He thought about it and aimed his gun at Justin. Not a good reaction. As always, my friend surprised the hell out of me by not even flinching. He just stood there, as always, cool, calm, and collected. (Well, and medicated. Let's not forget that.)

"Now, now, Bart. I thought we had something special," he said, taunting him. I nudged Justin in the ribs so he'd stop. It seemed a completely inappropriate comment, even for him.

"You...you...tricked me. Fucking faggot," Bart stammered, probably trying to wipe out of his messed-up head the thought that he'd slept with a man. He was still pointing the gun right at Justin. I gulped at the inevitable.

"Oh, come now. Didn't you notice this?" Justin asked, fingering his Adam's apple. A couple of the people who had gathered to watch the spectacle started to snicker. Enraged, Bart shouted that everyone should back up and shut up or he'd shoot the two of us, and anyone else who pissed him off. Well, Las Vegas isn't known for attracting the smartest people. After all, smart people rarely gamble their money away. So, while they did shut up, no one seemed to back up. I, on the other hand, was ready to run for it. I mean, really, it was better than standing there like a dead duck. Or, more appropriately, dead peacock. Of course, even I wasn't about to leave my partner standing there like that. Probably.

"You better put the gun down," Justin said, taking a step closer to Bart.

"What the fu—" I started to say, but Justin waved from behind his back that I shouldn't interfere.

"No, *you* better stay put," Bart responded, inching in even closer until they were a foot apart and the gun was right in Justin's face.

"Okay, then," Justin said, "I warned you." Then he did

something that threw us all off. Way off. In the blink of an eye, he shot his arm straight out and grabbed hold of Bart's nuts. Naturally, Bart had two reactions to this. One, he pulled the trigger, and two, he sank to his knees in pain.

"Bang," Justin said, adding, "Oops, did I forget to mention that I emptied your gun the other night, right after I shot my load all over your chest?"

The small crowd around us started to applaud, and then the guards moved back in to take control. Moments later, the police, led by Detective Lombard and the F.B.I.'s Detective Shelling, rushed in to gather up Bart. We stood there and, like the pros we were, took our bows. Job well done. Sort of. Not counting the three dead people and all.

Bart was led away, the crowd was dispersed, and Justin, Chris, and I were left with our law enforcement friends.

"Care to explain all of this, Officer Jennings?" my old F.B.I. friend, Randall, asked.

We looked around to see whom he was addressing. Yes, we were stunned when Chris spoke up. "Um, this *gentleman* here, er, apprehended the suspect in...in—"

"In his crotch," Justin interrupted. (Isn't he just full of surprises?)

"Well, I'm not sure how you did it," Detective Lombard said. "Though I'm afraid I'm gonna have to find out, eventually. But if you, um, *fellows* have any information on the guy we just escorted out of here, I'm sure the City of Las Vegas would be very happy to hear it. He's been under surveillance for several weeks now, and we had what we thought was enough evidence to obtain a search warrant. Then all of this went down."

"If you'll let us get out of these costumes, I'm sure my friend and I would be delighted to come down to the station and help you all out," Justin suggested. I nodded, and they agreed, leaving us alone now with Chris. And that's how Glenda and Earl found us when they came rushing up.

256

"What's going on now?" Glenda asked, huffing and puffing. "You guys look like ten pounds of potatoes in a five-pound sack."

"Good question. Why don't we ask our friend, *Officer Jennings*, over here," I said, still stunned at Chris's revelation. And a bit peeved at Glenda's reaction to our fabulous ensembles.

"That may take a while. Why don't we go back up to your room so you can get changed, and then I'll try to explain," Chris said.

I, for one, was glad to oblige. My potatoes were starting to feel rather lumpy, after all. And my Tater Tots were throbbing inside my ever-so-high heels.

Back in our chlorine-drenched room, we promptly undressed and waited for Chris's explanation. Oh, but first we fixed ourselves a drink. Our nerves, after that brouhaha, were completely fried. (And since we were drinking Courvoisier, for a change, I'd say that we were *French*-fried. Sorry, enough of the potato humor.) Anyway, once we had drinks firmly in hand and were situated comfortably on our beds, Chris let us in on his involvement.

"Okay, I suppose you guys were wondering why I keep showing up in all these casinos, right?" he began.

"It did cross our minds," I answered.

"Well, I've been working undercover for years all along the Strip. The F.B.I. likes to have its eyes and ears around, and the casinos don't mind so long as we're discreet. This time we were investigating a ring of thieves that was operating in and around the hotels. We're involved because it seems to be run mostly by illegal aliens, as well as aliens with green cards. Your friend Ahmed was under the most scrutiny."

"Ah," I broke in. "That explains why you guys were following him and then us."

"Well, trying to following you, anyway. Ahmed turned up missing and you guys kept appearing and disappearing. Now that I've seen your *disguises*, I'm not surprised." He giggled. My fondness for Chris was quickly returning.

"Oh, speaking of Ahmed, he's probably down at the police station right now. But he's willing to cooperate and he has helped us as much as he could," Justin interjected.

"Not to worry. I'm sure that'll all be worked out down at headquarters. Besides, it appears that he's the low man on the totem pole, anyway. It wasn't too difficult to tie in your friend Bart to all of this. Ahmed was pretty easy to follow, at first. And all roads were leading back to Bart. Still, with no evidence of his connection to the ring or to any of the robberies, there wasn't much we could do in terms of moving in on him. And we knew, judging from his background, that he wasn't bright enough to be the head guy. That has proven to be tough, finding out who his boss is."

"Oh, not really. That's an easy one," I said. "Zahir is the boss."

"Zahir, the guy he works with?" Chris asked.

"Yep. They probably do all their scheming at the disco. So, unless you guys had that place wired, I'd say you'd never have been able to tie them together. They seem to have little fondness for each other and spend no time together outside of the Aladdin."

Chris said, "Well, we tried to wire the place, but it was too loud in there. Pretty smart move on their part."

"Oh, that was probably Zahir's idea. You were right, Bart's a complete idiot," I said. "But he did confess to killing those three people. The two at the Atlantis he thought were Justin and I, and I don't know why he killed the old man at the antique shop. Most likely, it was somehow related to my grandma's vase. But let's not go into all that right now."

"Okay, that's fine. Why don't we go down to the police station so I can put out an APB on Zahir, and then we can talk to Ahmed and see what he can do for us," Chris suggested. We all agreed. I, for one, was eager to see that asshole put behind bars.

A few hours later, here's what we found out. Well, first, police stations have really uncomfortable seating and horrendous overhead lighting. They desperately need a gay man's touch. And speaking of gay men touching, Bradley and Justin were getting quite, hmm, what's the word I'm looking for? Let's say *grabby*. But that's probably not what you were interested in, right? (Hey, you know, it's not all about *you*.) Okay, anyway, when Chris finally emerged from his intensely long interview with Ahmed, he had a lot to say.

"That was interesting," Chris began, serving us all some rather awful but much needed coffee. "Too bad we didn't have Ahmed several weeks ago. Three people would still be alive now if we had, not to mention many thousands of dollars' worth of merchandise secured."

"Wait until you see what Bart and Zahir have in their garages," I informed him.

"Oh, don't worry. We're getting search warrants right now, and we'll be confiscating everything we can get our hands on. Let's just hope Zahir has been good enough to hang around; then we might have some closure on all this."

"Amen," we all amened.

"And how's Ahmed?" Justin asked. I think his feelings for Ahmed ran a little deeper than he was willing to admit, especially now that he seemed to have found Bradley again.

"A little shaken up, but he appears to be doing fine. He'll turn state's evidence against Bart and Zahir in return for clemency. He's pretty much guilty of just some minor thefts anyway. The information he's supplying us right now is significantly more valuable to us than having him in jail.

259

And from what we can gather, he doesn't seem to be directly involved in any of the unfortunate deaths."

"Not *directly*? I asked.

"Mmm, not exactly. That vase of yours sort of started the whole thing," Chris said, sitting down with us. He looked worn out (and awfully cute). That's when it dawned on me that I had had sex with an F.B.I. agent. How fabulous is that?

"Mm—my vase?" I stuttered. I made a silent vow to steer clear of PBS from then on out.

"Yep, your vase. Seems that just before you guys stumbled into Ahmed's life, he'd stolen some merchandise from Bart and tried to skedaddle out of Vegas. Bart caught him and, even though what he stole was only worth a few thousand dollars, threatened to turn him over to his boss if Ahmed didn't give him thirty thousand dollars. Ahmed was terrified. Though he'd never met Bart's boss before, he'd heard rumors that the guy was a wacko."

"But he hadn't a clue that it was his own brother?" Glenda asked from the sidelines.

"Ironic, but no, he didn't," Chris answered.

I added, "And Ahmed had little chance of coming up with the thirty grand until—"

"Until *we* showed up with the story of our thirty-thousand-dollar vase," Justin finished my train of thought.

"Exactly," Chris said. "An easy and perfect little way to solve his problem. Unfortunately, he let Bart know about his plans to get him his money, namely your vase."

"Bart beat him to it?" I asked.

"Nope. Ahmed did indeed go to steal the vase. Unfortunately, Bart picked the same day to steal it, arriving a few minutes after Ahmed had already left with it. Ahmed saw Bart's car pulling up just as he was leaving. He assumed, from what he saw on the news the next day, that Bart broke into Mr. Hartwell's store, was interrupted by the old man, and then shot him to death. After Bart killed Mr. Hartwell, he must've fled the scene in a panic and completely forgotten about your vase, apparently never even noticing that it had already been stolen."

"And the other two murders?" I asked, hesitantly.

"Unfortunately, Ahmed also told Bart about the suitcase of money you guys brought with you. Ahmed told us that the next day, after Bart killed Mr. Hartwell, he was a total lunatic and threatened Ahmed until he told him what room you guys were in. Seems he wanted that money come hell or high water. Ahmed had a feeling that Bart may have been stealing from his boss, who we now assume is Zahir. This would go a long way to explaining his desire to steal the vase and then try for your suitcase. But he didn't think that Bart was stupid enough to kill two more people, or he would never have given him your room number."

"Guess he didn't know that Bart is stupid enough to do anything. The guy's a total psycho," I said. "And I guess we're lucky that we switched rooms when we did, or we wouldn't be here right now talking about it." I knew how lucky we really were, but I felt such a huge pang of guilt for those poor guys who had lost their lives over a mere thirty thousand dollars.

"Exactly. And Ahmed said that Bart went berserk when he couldn't find your suitcase. That's when our friend Ahmed disappeared. He figured that his luck couldn't hold out too much longer, and he didn't want you guys in any more danger than you were already in, so he left. Probably a good idea, all things considered."

"Thank goodness someone had the bright idea to leave," Justin grimaced.

"Well, if it makes you feel any better, you guys just helped solve a big case for us, and you saved Vegas a few million dollars a year. Now, are you guys ready for the good news?" Chris asked, a sly grin appearing on his adorable face.

"There's good news?" I asked.

"For you two, yes," he answered, handing us a piece of paper.

"Holy shit," I screamed, jumping up off the incredibly uncomfortable bench we had been sitting on.

"What? What is it?" Glenda asked, wondering why Justin and I were doing a little jig around the otherwise somber police station.

"We're rich!" we shouted, thrusting the paper into her hands.

"Huh?" she said, reading the arrest warrant. It was for dear old Bart, whose real name was Dwayne Burns. Dwayne was wanted in connection with two other murders, several robberies, and a whole list of misdemeanors that went back over the last ten years. There was a fifty-thousand-dollar reward for information leading to his arrest. Since Ahmed was an accomplice, the money would go to us.

"Fuckin-A," was all Glenda could say, but it seemed enough.

When we left the police station, it was completely dark out and very late. We were starving, exhausted, and completely worn out—and we wanted one thing and one thing only: to get back to San Francisco.

"Now what?" I asked, though finally that question wasn't out of desperation.

"Let me answer that one," Glenda offered as we all got back into Earl's cab—we hoped for the last time. "Now we go back to our rooms, pack, and go home. I'm over Vegas in a big way."

"Amen to that," I said.

"Do you mind if I don't drive you guys to the airport?" Earl asked. "I don't think my cab can take anymore." No, we didn't mind. I was ready for our crazy California taxi drivers and their smoke-free cabs. Besides, with our newfound wealth, we could afford a limo. Though Lord only knew how long it would take the authorities to fork over the dough.

Fifteen minutes later, Earl dropped Glenda off at the Aladdin and then Justin, Bradley, and me off at Caesar's.

"Well, Earl, I can't say it's been fun, but thanks. Thanks for everything," I said as we all shook his hand.

"Hey, that's what sisters are for," he said as he started to drive away. I'm not sure we agreed with him, but we were grateful nonetheless, even after we gave him our address in San Francisco so he could send us his cab repair bill.

"Damn," Bradley said, "hasn't that man heard of car deodorizers before?"

We giggled, and I said, "Why, did it smell in there?"

Bradley looked at us funny, and then we all broke out in a much-needed and deserved laugh.

"Well, old and new friends, looks like here's where we part. I've been missing from work all day, and I think I should go and make up some cockamamie story before they fire me," Bradley said, a frown appearing on his face.

"Hey, Bradley," I said, putting my hand on his beefy shoulder, "the truth is stranger than fiction."

"Fuck that. No one would believe me if I told them that story," he said. "Besides, I'm Caesar. They can kiss my royal ass." We both smiled at his arrogance.

"Um, I'm sorry we have to leave so suddenly," Justin said, his hand on Bradley's other shoulder.

"Hey, no sweat. I understand. But you still owe me that date," he said, leaning in for a group hug.

"Can't wait for that," Justin replied, pecking him on the cheek. I backed away so they could have a moment alone. It was nice to see my best friend thinking about someone other than himself for a change. And it seemed as if Bradley was more than a match for Justin, which is saying an awful lot. Maybe there are happy endings after all. (Maybe, maybe not. Remember, I am telling this story from a drafty old church closet, you might recall.)

"Nice guy," I said as Justin and I bid our adieus to Bradley and headed for the elevator.

"But am I ready for the responsibilities of palace life?" he asked, jokingly.

"Honey, you are *the* queen, hands down. The question, my love, is, are they ready for you?"

"Good point. Now let's get the hell out of here. This desert heat is ruining my lovely complexion."

I agreed and we headed for our pool-stinking room one last time. We packed lickety-split and called the airlines to make a reservation for Glenda, Justin, and myself on the very next plane. Then we called Glenda and told her to meet us at the airport as soon as possible. She was only too happy to oblige.

"Well, Em, case closed. Did we forget anything or anyone?" Justin asked, looking around the room.

"No, I don't think—wait, what's that under the bed?" I asked, spying a blue strap.

"Hmm, let's see." He walked over, bent down, and retrieved Ahmed's long forgotten backpack.

My heart started to flutter. "Are you thinking what I'm thinking?" I asked, sitting down on the bed as Justin started to unzip the pack.

"Yuh-huh. Now, let's see," he said, poking his hand in the bag. "Um, would this be your—"

"Grandma's vase!" I shouted. "Goddammotherfuck, it's been sitting under the bed this whole time."

"Looks that way," Justin laughed, shaking his head in disbelief. "Not a very pretty thing, is it?"

"Fucker."

"What? I'm just saying—"

"Never mind. Let's just get the hell out of here, okay?" I said, repacking the vase and heading for the door.

"Fine by me," he said, flicking off the lights. "Besides, all's well that ends well."

Not quite.

Out of the Closet

SAN FRANCISCO WAS LUXURIOUSLY CHILLY UPON OUR return. No broiling sun. No blinding lights. And no over-weight straight people in tank tops and short shorts. Just fog, followed by crisp, blue skies. Noticeably missing also were murderers (at least people trying to murder us), show-girls (we packed the outfits way in the back of the closet), and slot machines (the one drawback to our homecoming). In short (or is this medium-long now?), we were glad to be home. Though returning to our "normal" lives was a bit difficult at first. Your heart grows accustomed to all that pounding and has a hard time reverting to the humdrum of a merely average existence. (I'm sure Justin would take offense at that, of course.) Not to mention that we still had unfinished business back in Vegas, so it was tough sinking completely back into our old routines.

Chris had seen us off at the airport in Las Vegas, and informed us that we'd need to return in a couple weeks to make our official statements and to testify against Bart and, with luck, Zahir. We also needed to give evidence supporting

Ahmed's story. Not fun, but it was something we had to do, and we were resigned to doing it. Besides, Chris's farewell kiss left me wanting more, and I could tell that Justin wasn't nearly finished with Bradley just yet.

After two weeks of lounging around San Francisco—no car chases, no gunfights, no muggings, kidnappings, or any other assorted bits of foul play—we headed back to Sin City. And no, we didn't stay at the Atlantis, the Aladdin, or Caesar's. We opted, instead, for a hotel farther down the Strip. One that wouldn't bring back any of those nasty memories. One that didn't reek of chlorine. (At least not in our own room.) And one with no showgirls. We checked into the stunning Mandalay Bay.

Are you ready for one last bit of Vegas trivia? A sort of final tour of the area, if you will? Okay, well, Mandalay Bay is at the end of the row of hotels along the Strip. Past the last cluster of casinos: New York–New York, the MGM, Excalibur (warning again: massive family alert!), the Tropicana (yuck-o), and the Luxor. The Luxor, by the way, is way cool. That whole Egyptian theme makes for an interesting gambling experience.

But none of these is even remotely as stunning as Mandalay Bay. Which is, naturally, why we chose it. Of course, we were anticipating the fifty grand; otherwise we couldn't have afforded it. (Well, Justin could have, but not me.) The entire hotel and casino has a completely opulent-tropical feel to it. It's exotic, lush, and very, er, wet. There's water flowing practically everywhere: in the casino, through the eleven-acre tropical sand beach, up the lazy river ride, into the three gorgeous pools, and all the way to the incredible shark reef, with almost two million gallons of seawater. There's also an events center not to be rivaled in all of Las Vegas. Justin and I would be in heaven if we lived there, as they manage to book every eighties band that's still around. There's even a House of Blues and some of the best and most unusual restaurants you'll find anywhere along the Strip. All in all, we were delighted to make this our final hotel stay at the end of our grand adventure.

At least, while enduring the discomfort and dread of reliving our misadventures with the police, we'd be able to relax in a lovely, peaceful setting. Least that's what we thought, nay, prayed. First thing we did, upon arriving, was to go down to police headquarters to meet with Detective Lombard and Chris, who would be representing the F.B.I. in the investigation. That part was, thankfully, easy. We simply told them everything we knew. No sweat. Chris told us that basically we were corroborating Ahmed's story, thereby making their case against Bart and Zahir an easy one.

The difficulty came at the end of our little tête-à-tête.

"Well, that was simple," I said to Chris, once he was alone with Justin and myself.

"Um, *ish*," he replied, mumbling just a bit.

"*Ish*?" I asked, unsure of what couldn't have been easy about it.

"Simple-ish," he restated. "We're not exactly where we want to be with the case."

"Huh?" I huhed. "You've got the merchandise, the evidence, and several witnesses. What could be missing?" Justin stood beside me nodding his head up and down in agreement.

"No Zahir. And, apparently, Zahir's got the names of the entire ring of thieves. Your old friend Bart is willing to testify against Zahir if we don't press for the death penalty for his involvement with the murders, but he says that only Zahir knows all the members of the ring. And we need that to close the case," Chris explained. Justin's nod shifted from up and down to side to side.

"But how could you have lost Zahir? He didn't even know you were on to him, and last I saw him, he was passed out," I said in disbelief.

"Bart called him from his cell phone before he went looking for you guys in the casino. Seems Zahir was groggy but lucid. He got out of his place in no time flat, taking with him any paper trail or little black book or whatever we would need to convict him of being the ringleader. And with only Bart's testimony to say otherwise, we have no hard evidence that Zahir is the high man on the totem pole."

"And Bart's testimony isn't exactly ideal in front of a jury. What with him being a murderer, a thief, and a kidnapper, right?" I interjected.

"Exactly," Chris replied. "But don't get too upset. At least we've stopped the ring, for now. And we did catch one of the bad guys. And I'm sure we'll find Zahir soon enough." But we could tell that he wasn't exactly thrilled at having lost him.

"And what if Zahir finds us first?" Justin asked the obvious, sending those familiar chills down my spine.

"Don't worry. We have agents following you wherever you go. If Zahir comes within fifty feet of you, we'll catch him." I hoped, for our sakes, he was right.

"Well, make it a hundred and we have a deal," I said, only half joking.

"Hey, enough of the worrying. Let's go get a drink and celebrate. There's one less murderer on the streets now, anyway," Chris said, conveniently changing the subject. And far be it from me to argue against a celebratory drink. Besides, I was glad to be back in his company. I'd missed him the last couple of weeks, especially since he told me that he'd been ordered by his superiors to stop our affair while the investigation was on. This occurred just after our last time together. Seems it's not a good idea to sleep with the man you suddenly find yourself investigating. Catching me with Zahir was a perfect excuse for him to walk away. He apologized for being so underhanded, but I told him that I understood. He also said that fate had been smiling down on him regarding this whole mess (though probably not on us and certainly not on the dead guys), because he was in town the week of our going-away party and ran into Justin. Seeing as everyone thought he was a blackjack dealer, he didn't want to blow his cover, so he agreed to work the party. Talk about freakish timing. Without that encounter, none of *this* would've happened.

We drank and celebrated and, for a change, relaxed. Vegas, after all, had not been a stress-free environment for us. And when Chris told us that we'd have to testify against Bart the next day, we were so happy to be among friends, with tall margaritas and a stack of chips for each of us, that we didn't even flinch. We said we'd be there and we left it at that. Though, in the back of my wee little brain, I was secretly dreading the event. It was fine by me if I never saw that creep again. But in a few days I knew it would all be over, so I pushed my fears deep, deep down, I put on a happy face, and I rolled merrily along.

"Well, boys, I've got some F.B.I.-ing to do. You'll be okay without me until tomorrow?" Chris asked, getting up to leave.

"Do we have a choice?" I asked.

"Mm, no," he said, "Now give me a kiss goodbye." .

"Yes, please."

And then Justin and I were alone again, though we knew there were friendly eyes following us somewhere nearby—that was somewhat comforting. And we only had a day until we had to testify. We knew it would go by fast. And there were worse things than a day of drinking and gambling in Vegas, right? Imagine if we'd witnessed all we'd witnessed in, say, Detroit.

"So what'll it be? A drink, some gambling, a show?" Justin asked.

"Yes, yes, and yes," I responded. "But I don't think you'll appreciate my choice of venue."

"God, no, please."

"Aw, come on. I'll never ask you again," I pleaded.

"Dude, I seriously doubt that I'm ever gonna follow you to Vegas again, so you'll never get the chance."

"So this will be the last time, then. A perfect reason to go," I tried.

"That doesn't make a lick of sense, but I'm too tired and too much in need of a drink, or six, to argue. Besides, I have to go out with Bradley tonight and it's probably best if I'm not alone with him."

"That's a surprise, but I'm not going to argue."

I suppose Justin knew he'd have to go back to San Francisco and Bradley would have to stay in Vegas, so why should he open his heart up to the possibility of him and Bradley? Sad, but true. And it would be no fun seeing Honey again all alone. Plus, I wanted to fill her in on all the recent events.

After a couple of rounds of drinks, Bradley arrived for his promised date and we were off again to the Atlantis. If he was upset at the third wheel thing, he didn't let on. I guess he knew, as well, that the distance problem would never work itself out. And Justin was smiling, so I was happy to have him along.

"Are you ready to witness the rebirth of Miss Patsy Cline?" I asked Bradley as the cab approached the hotel.

"Huh? Is that what we're going to see. Jeez, the chick's dead. Let her and that yodel of hers rest in peace," he replied. I shot Justin a look that said he'd better keep quiet, and I kept my mouth shut at Bradley's awful remark. Something was obviously amiss in their gay gene makeup, a faulty chromosome or something.

Moments later, we arrived and I gleefully skipped into our old hotel. Jacques, thank goodness, was nowhere in sight. I was hopeful we'd be able to watch the performance, fill in Honey about my vase, and get out of there with no confrontations. There was a show starting in about half an hour, so we settled into our seats, right up front, ordered several strong drinks, and patiently waited for the festivities to begin.

"Ladies and gentleman, please welcome to the stage, the star of the show, the lovely Miss Patsy Cline." The show had started. Yippee! And Honey looked and sounded as wonderful as the last time we saw her. Justin and Bradley grimaced but otherwise remained well behaved. I, on the other hand, was tickled pink.

She stepped onto the stage in a fabulous, all-white leather ensemble, complete with white fringe tassels on her jacket and pants. And I swear, as soon as she opened her mouth to sing, my heart leaped to my throat. Even though I had heard her before, I was still amazed at her ability to imitate the legendary country singer. The moment was pure magic, for me anyway; my cohorts were less than enthused, though they were quite happy with their hurricane glasses full of Malibu rum and pineapple juice.

I focused on her face as she made her way around the small stage. Her smile was dazzling and radiant as she scanned the crowd. That is, until she spotted our little gaggle. Was she shocked? Was she thrilled to see us? Was she rattled by our presence? Who knows? All I know is that when she saw us sitting there, with me beaming up at her from the front row, well, she just sort of had a momentary pause. Kind of like a midsong hiccup. And the smile on her face disappeared for just an instant and was replaced by—as best I can put it, by nothing. She just sort of went blank. Ever the professional, however, the moment passed in just an instant. It didn't go unnoticed by the three of us, though.

"What was that?" Justin asked in a whisper.

"Dunno. Guess she was surprised to see us," I answered.

"But was that a good surprise or a bad surprise?" Bradley asked.

"Well, she didn't fall off the stage or anything, so I'd say it was a good one. Guess we'll have to wait and see once the show's over," I said, but was still unsure. A good surprise would've been a smile and a wave. But she was performing, so what could she really do, right?

After that, the show went off without a hitch. She was lovely and charming and richly talented. I was in Patsy heaven. My friends were happy playing with each other beneath the table and getting good and liquored up, which was fine by me. At least they remained quiet. An hour and several drinks later, the show was over and we hurried backstage.

I knocked on the door and we waited patiently for the star to great us. It took several minutes, but she finally answered.

"Well, boy howdy, what a pleasant surprise to see you fellers back again," she said, ensconced in an all-white terry-cloth bathrobe and smiling brilliantly at us. "What brings you back to Las Vegas?"

We told her the whole story, briefly, from when we last saw her to our upcoming testimony, including a quick introduction to our new friend Bradley. She nodded politely throughout, but seemed somewhat distant. I just chalked it up to postshow exhaustion. Toward the end, she received a call on her cell phone and asked us to wait a moment. Justin leaned in and whispered to me, "How did she know we'd left Vegas?"

My brain started to hum. True, yes, we had never called to say goodbye or anything. And the press wasn't involved yet. But I assumed she just figured, after such a long time between visits, that we had left Vegas and then returned. Made sense, right? Least that's what I whispered back to Justin. He nodded an okay and we waited for Honey to get off the phone. It was a brief call consisting mostly of *mm-hmms* and *uh-huhs*, and it ended with a "Right now."

"Sorry about that, fellers. Business call," she explained, setting the phone down. "Well, that was some story, all right. Glad to see you all are okay now, though. What an awful time you must've had."

"Pretty bad, yes," Justin replied, and then added, "But it seems to be almost at an end. Anyway, thanks for everything you've done. We better get going now."

"No," she said, a little too loudly, and then jumped up and moved to her minirefrigerator. "I mean, no, not yet. We need to have a farewell drink before you all skedaddle off. In celebration of finding the vase and everything." She quickly regained her composure and poured four glasses of champagne. I looked at Justin for some direction.

"Well, okay, one drink, thanks, but then we have to meet our friends for dinner," he said to her, and Bradley and I nodded in agreement.

"Sure, boys, just the one." She said, raising her glass to us. "To justice!"

"To justice!" we echoed. Seemed an appropriate toast.

"Okay, then, Honey, thanks for the champagne and everything. Until next time," Justin said, moving for the door. Bradley and I were right behind him, eager to get out of her cramped dressing room.

"Sorry, boys, there ain't gonna be a next time," she said behind us, and we heard a "click." (And you thought you only heard lines like that in bad spaghetti Westerns.)

The three of us turned to look at her. "Wh—what's that for, Honey?" I stuttered, now staring down the barrel of a small handgun.

"Well, now, that's a funny thing," she said, indicating with the gun that we should move away from the door and have a seat.

"Funny ha-ha or funny strange?" I asked, trembling just a bit as I took my seat again.

274

"Ha-ha for me, strange for you," she replied. "You see, boys, you've done stuck your noses in a bad pile of horse dung, and now I'm afraid you're gonna be buried in it."

Gulp. I liked the chlorine odor problem much better. Now we had *crap* to contend with.

It was time for Justin's brand of calm under pressure. "Okay, I see you're *upset*, Honey, but you can't kill all three of us, at least not here and with that gun. Best you could do is injure one of us, and then the other two would rush you and hold you down until the police arrive. Now, what say you put the gun down and we talk about this like civilized adults. I'm sure there's something we can work out."

Hey, I was all for that. Too bad she wasn't.

"Oh, I'm not gonna kill you fellers," she said, smiling, just as the door to her dressing room opened. "But he is."

And in walked, you guessed it, Zahir. And he didn't look happy to see us. Needless to say, the feeling was mutual. "You fuckers are very dead," he said as he quickly shut the door behind him, brandishing a larger version of Honey's shotgun. (Man, I really have an uncanny ability to pick men, don't I?)

I guess I should've realized that Zahir wasn't smart enough or cunning enough to be the leader of the gang. Honey's hick routine must've been just that, a routine. She certainly fooled all of us. And her surprise at seeing us there was starting to make sense, too. Without our testimony, and with only Ahmed and Bart to back it up, the case against Zahir wasn't nearly as strong and the tie-in to Honey would be doubtful. Now here we were, right in her lap. She must've been fucking thrilled to see us there in the front row. Talk about your sitting ducks.

"Okay, then, fellers, celebratin's over. Time for us to leave," she informed us, indicating with the gun that we should move to the door. And with her gun in my back and Zahir's gun in Justin's, the three of us were led out of the dressing room, through the casino, and out to the parking lot, where there was one more surprise waiting for us.

"Fuck," I said in disbelief.

"Now, now, is that a way to talk in front of a lady?" Honey asked, then shoved us all in the backseat of Earl's still banged-up cab. There was that familiar stench I had so hoped I'd never have to smell again. But no Earl. Well, no Earl that I could see, but as soon as we were all in, I could hear him kicking and screaming in the trunk. (And I swear I could smell him, too.)

Zahir let out a sinister chuckle as he started the cab and drove us out of the parking lot to Lord knows where.

"What's so funny?" Honey asked him.

"It looks like we are one big, happy family again," he said, laughing now. (Talk about dysfunctional.)

"Just drive, Zahir, and no more jokes, please," she ordered. She was, evidently, very much in charge. Zahir obeyed, but I could see, in the rearview mirror, a sneer on his face. Knowing Zahir as I did, which was not well enough, apparently, I was sure he didn't like taking orders from a woman.

"So, Honey, what exactly is your involvement in all of this?" Justin asked. I too wanted to know, but wasn't ballsy enough to inquire.

"You'll be dead soon, why bother?" she said. (What a bitch, right?)

"True, but humor me," he replied.

"Let's just say that celebrity impersonation doesn't exactly pay the bills," she said. (Neither does female impersonation, by the way.) "And my boys do a good job keeping the money rolling in."

"But not good enough, huh, Zahir?" Justin added, causing a low grumble from the driver's seat.

Honey spoke for Zahir. "Everything was fine until you horse's patoots started nosing around, causing trouble."

The conversation was starting to sound like a bad *Scooby-Doo* episode.

"If we said we were sorry, would you let us go?" I tried.

"You're gonna have to ask the boss that," she said. "Lucky for us you all showed up, or we was gonna have to close up shop. Now it looks like we're back in business."

Justin whispered in my ear, "I pick the entertainment next time."

To which I replied, glumly, "What next time?"

"It's always darkest before the dawn," Bradley chimed in. We looked at him as if he was crazy, but at least one of us wasn't giving up hope.

A long while later I noticed something familiar. We were driving in the direction our horses had traveled several weeks earlier.

"Where we headed?" I asked. Though I thought I already knew the answer.

"We're not headed anywhere. We're here already," she said as we pulled up to Mary's house. "Ready to meet the boss, fellers?"

Hell, no was what I was thinking. Oh, I was also thinking about how badly I had judged people of late. If you had asked me a few weeks earlier what I thought about these individuals who now held our very lives in their hands, I would've said that they were the salt of the earth. Now they wanted to bury us in it.

Zahir and Honey led us, at gunpoint, back into Mary's home. It didn't seem quite so homey this time around. Mary was there, watching her television and rocking back and forth. She barely flinched when we walked in. I guess Maury Povich was more interesting to her than we were. Only when the commercial broke in did Mary decide to talk to us.

"About time you caught these jackasses," she said to Zahir and Honey. "Wasn't looking forward to packing up and leaving again."

Again? How often did they do this?

Mary stood up to face us. "If I had known how much trouble that darn vase was going to cause me, I'd have tossed it out the window a long time ago. What a mess it nearly made."

"I wish you'd have tossed it too, Mary," I said. It made her laugh. The jocularity was not going to last for very long. I added, "Then three people wouldn't have had to die, not including the three of us."

"Well, those last two fellers had nothing to do with us, and we still don't know who killed Mr. Hartwell. That really put a crimp in our plans, though. That dang old goat was our primary means of selling the hotel stuff off. (Which went a long way to explaining his reported wealth but lack of significant inventory.)

"Oh, we know who killed Mr. Hartwell, don't we, Zahir?" Justin said, knowingly. Zahir squirmed as Mary and Honey turned to face him.

"What's he talking about, Zahir?" Mary asked.

"Who knows? He is just desperate to stir up big trouble," Zahir answered, but the look on his face was giving him away. It was not the look of an innocent man.

"Not true," I said. "Ahmed told us that Zahir was stealing money from his boss"—Honey—"and needed the vase to get the money to pay her back. Mr. Hartwell found him in his shop and Zahir killed him. Then he went to steal our money and mistakenly killed those other two guys." Now, this wasn't exactly true, since Bart was really responsible for all those unfortunate deaths, but I had a feeling the lie would work in our favor.

That's when all hell broke loose. Honey's gun went from pointing at us to pointing at Zahir; Zahir's gun turned to Honey; and Mary, very unladylike, started hollerin' and cussin' up a storm. This had a very desirable effect: the three of them were no longer paying attention to the three of us.

Justin was nodding furiously toward the television, so Bradley and I inched our way over to it. Justin did the same and then whispered that on the count of three we should lift it up.

"One..." Zahir was vehemently denying that he killed anybody.

"Two..." Mary was yelling at Honey that they should never have trusted a foreigner.

"Three..." Honey looked confused at who she wanted to shoot more, Zahir or her mother.

She didn't have much time to give it a second thought. Up went the television over our heads and, a split second later, down it came crashing on Zahir's foot. He dropped his gun and Bradley picked it up. Zahir, now in audibly severe pain, went teetering forward, knocking Honey over onto the floor. And Mary went rushing over to her precious television. So much for maternal instincts.

Realizing that this was our only chance, the three of us leaped over the mess of bodies and ran back out into the hot desert air. We rushed to the cab and got in. Now what? No keys. Uh-oh. We shouted to Earl, still in the trunk. He didn't have any spares on him. Not that it would matter; he was in the trunk. Uh-oh. We got out of the cab.

"Fuck, now what!" I shouted, as we ran around the cab, not knowing where to go or what to do.

"Run!" shouted Justin as Zahir came limping out of the house, Honey's gun in hand.

So I ran—and ran—and ran. I had no idea where Justin and Bradley ran to. And I couldn't hear anyone behind me or see anyone to the side of me. I just ran until I couldn't run anymore. Literally. I was, all of a sudden, stuck. The end of Mary's property was protected by barbed wire. Mercifully, the wire fence was only about four feet high or I might've done some heavy-duty damage to my face. This way, I only did damage to my clothes. They were, sadly, enmeshed in the wire. And pulling and yanking on it was having a delete-rious effect. My shirt and jeans were tearing and the barbed wire was sinking into my flesh. Major ouch. I felt like a giant fly caught in a metal spider web.

So you see, I had no choice. I slid my arms down through the short sleeves, which were pinned up on the fence, and pulled free. Then I gingerly removed myself from my shirt. My sneakers and pants went practically the same way. I only wish I had had enough time to remove them from the fence. Once I was liberated, I turned my head—only to see Zahir and Honey in the distance, running my way. What choice did I have? Again I ran. Unfortunately, I had only two options: left and right. Straight ahead was very much out of the question now.

"Eeny, meeny, miney—" The ho-mo went left. I was running away from Mary's house, and that seemed like the smart way to go. It felt like forever until I came to a large rock by the fence. I was able to stand on it and leap over the darn thing. We were out in the desert, so I landed on soft, yet oh-so-hot sand. Still, I was off Mary's property and on my way to...to...Fuck. I WAS OUT IN THE DESERT! No phone, no lights, no motor cars, not a single luxury.

That's when I spotted it, about a football field away. A church. Talk about your signs from God. My legs were getting awfully sore by that point, but I ran as fast as I possibly could until I made it inside.

"Hello. Anybody home?" I shouted, but only got my echo in return. I guess God was on a break. A moment later, I heard another, more ominous echo. It was a gunshot.

And that's how I ended up in this closet, alone, in my underwear, with nothing to protect me but a bunch of Bibles. And since you don't have a gun (do you?), I'd say I was up shit creek. (Though I'm sure as heck praying a lot for any and all alternatives.)

* * *

Ten minutes later, I hear scampering noises outside the door. My heart is racing.

Bang! Bang! Two gunshots somewhere within the church.

And then, more footsteps. The sound is getting louder as whoever is outside approaches my hiding space. I have to pee, badly, or shout, loudly, but I'm thinking that neither is a good idea.

The footsteps stop and a hand turns the knob of the closet door. I've spent a lifetime coming out of the closet, only to be killed in one. Is this bitter irony, or what? When the door opens, a shaft of light pours into my hiding space and temporarily blinds me. All I can see is the figure of a man standing outside the door and a...a...a gun. Pointed right at me.

"Ahhhhhhhhhhhh."

You know how they say your whole life flashes before you when you have a near-death experience? Well, I may or may not have seen that. I sort of, um, passed out. The last thing I remember seeing was that gun pointing at me. (Hey, at least I didn't pee my undies.) And, thank goodness, when I regained consciousness, it was Detective Shelling standing over me and not one of the baddies. This is what happened...

"You okay?" he asked me.

"Sure Randy, how 'bout yourself?" I was still in a daze. He grinned and said he was fine.

I snapped out of it. "Where's Justin and Bradley? They're in trouble—"

"Calm down. Calm down. I'm sure they're fine. We have the property surrounded. Don't you worry, everything will be all right," he said, trying to soothe my rattled nerves. Naturally, I felt guilty. What with...

"Um, Detective Shelling, I have something that belongs to you."

He looked puzzled. I handed him back his badge. (Yes, I'd been carrying it around the whole time in my undies—it made me feel safe, for some strange reason.) He turned several shades of red and gladly accepted it.

"Don't worry. I won't mention it to anyone."

He nodded his approval and helped me to my feet. I was anxious to find my friends and make sure that they were okay. First thing, I had to wrap a choir robe around myself before we left the church. I wasn't about to go prancing through the desert in my skivvies.

When we went outside, we saw Zahir lying on the ground, his hands handcuffed behind his back, with blood seeping from a wound in his calf. He looked fairly miserable. I, of course, was thrilled.

"Don't worry, an ambulance is on the way for him," Detective Shelling said.

"Oh, I'm not worried. Let him fry out here for a while," I said, blowing a kiss to my ex-whatever it was he was. "By the way," I said, "how did you find us?"

"We spotted you leaving the Atlantis and followed you here. The police sent for backup almost immediately. We were about to rush the house when you three came tearing out. I ran after you and Zahir. And I'm sure someone rescued your friends."

I felt much better after we walked back to the house and I spotted them sitting on the front porch, none the worse for wear, apparently.

"Hark, an angel approaches," Justin hollered. He and Bradley stood up to greet us.

"Funny. You wouldn't know an angel if he ran up and bit you in the ass," I quipped, and hugged them both.

"Are you making passes again?" Justin joked back.

"Shut up and hug me," I said, tears streaming down my

face. The past several hours had finally caught up with me.

"Stop your bawling. All the bad people have been caught and are on their way to jail. The three of us are safe and sound. And, after we testify tomorrow, we'll be fifty thousand dollars richer. All in all, I'd say that we've had a pretty good month. Minus the death and stuff," Justin reasoned. I smiled, not the least bit astonished at his attitude. It was par for the course.

"Told you so," Bradley interjected.

"Told us what?" I asked.

"That it's always darkest before the dawn," he said.

"Guess we never should have doubted Caesar, huh, Justin?" I asked.

"All hail, Caesar," he responded.

"All hail me," Bradley said, and the three of us walked away from the house and into the sunset.

Epilogue

WELL, WE DIDN'T ACTUALLY WALK INTO THE SUNSET. Actually, we walked back over to Earl's cab. In all the confusion, no one had thought to rescue poor Earl. And we didn't have the keys. They were still on Zahir. Luckily, for Earl anyway, the police were able to pry the trunk open and rescue him. He was a little shaken, very parched, and a bit irritable, what with no cigarettes the whole time and all, but he was glad that we were all still alive. (Amen to that, right?)

So here's what's happened in the month since we made it out of that mess...

Justin, Earl, Bradley, and I all testified the next day, as did Ahmed. The police and the F.B.I. are still gathering up the evidence, which there was a lot of. Mary kept good records, the dear. They'll be tried and sentenced sometime soon. Chris keeps us informed, and he said that Bart will certainly get life without parole, and Zahir, Honey, and Mary will all get a minimum of fifty years to life without parole for more than a dozen felonies, including attempted murder and kidnapping.

Ahmed is already free, but has to report to a probation officer once a month. He's living with Earl. Chris says they make a cute couple. I have a hard time picturing that, but wish them well. Earl has quit his cabbing and his smoking and gone to work with his brother. Recent experiences have made him appreciate life and family more, or so I hear. Good for him, right?

Glenda got a job at the new Edges, the one that's in our old location. She's hard at work making sure that the gay and lesbian section is still in place and thriving. And, as she likes to say, keeping her friends close and her enemies closer. Personally, I say it's her new butch boss, Helen, but I don't say it to Glenda's face. One near-death encounter is enough for me, thank you very much.

And Bradley? Well, the jury's still out on that one. I wish I could say that he packed his toga and moved to San Francisco, but I can't. As Bradley (or Mel Brooks) would say, "It's good to be the king." But he and Justin do talk regularly. And Justin has been back to Vegas once and Bradley's been here once. For Justin, that's a long-term relationship. I'm amazed, but keeping quiet. Telling Justin one thing amounts to him doing the opposite. Still, it's nice to see him happy and occupied, for a change.

And as for little old me? Well, we're still waiting on our reward. Chris says it could take a while. The federal government is never too eager to part with its money. But we will get it, he assures us. I'm not holding my breath. I've never been one to count chickens, hatched or otherwise. Anyway, I still have, more or less, my thirty thousand from the sale of the bookstore to live off until I can find a real job. All my years with Justin have taught me nothing if not how to live off a sizable nest egg.

Actually, I'm seriously thinking about taking the money and getting my own cab. Smoke free, of course. After all, you know what they say: if you can't beat 'em, join 'em. Oh, and Chris says that the F.B.I. is always looking for a few good men. You know what I told him? "Who isn't?" In any case, I'm young, mostly, and who knows what'll happen. I've learned one very important lesson from all this, though, and that's to live life day by day and to enjoy it while I can. And that's what I intend to do.

Now—what about that pesky vase?

We didn't leave Las Vegas and go directly home. That was planned from the get-go. The vase was still with us, though now it was protected in a wooden crate and not an old backpack. Instead, we flew to Kansas to surprise my mom. We arrived at midday. She was home, cleaning and watching TV, when we pulled up in our rental car. (We were still kind of shaky around taxis.)

"Well, my goodness, what on earth are you boys doing here?" she asked, dragging us inside.

Once we had explained that everything was all right, and she had eagerly fixed us a snack, we sat down in the living room and told her we had something for her. We placed the crate in front of her and watched as she opened it. I almost started to hyperventilate as she gently pried the thing open, one side at a time. The look on her face went from bewilderment to surprise to shock. Justin and I felt as if we were at the racetrack watching our fifty-to-one horse cross the finish line way out ahead of the pack.

Finally she held the vase in her hands for the first time in many years.

"Well?" I shouted.

"Well... I don't know what to say," she said.

"Well, say something."

"Well, I hope you boys didn't go to too much trouble," she said, looking up at us with tears in her eyes.

Justin and I looked at each other and grinned.

"No, ma'am, not too much trouble," we said.

The vase immediately went back in the corner of the living room.

No one's allowed to touch it.

Trust me, no one wants to.

About the Author

ROB ROSEN LOVES HÄAGEN-DAZS CHOCOLATE CHOCOLATE Chip ice cream, but feels guilty about eating it; he opts instead for Ben & Jerry's Cherry Garcia Low Fat Frozen Yogurt. (See what you learn by reading this far!) When not calorie-counting (and watching his carb intake), he thinks of new and innovative ways to grow his facial hair. Seriously. In his spare time, what little is left, he's busy writing. *Divas Las Vegas* is his second novel. Sandwiched between these (on whole grain bread, of course), he's written for well over fifty anthologies. Rob lives with his strikingly handsome husband, Kenny, in San Francisco. You can visit him at www.therobrosen.com or contact him at robrosen@therobrosen.com.